Richard Brinsley Sheridan

The dramatic works of the Right Honourable Richard Brinsley Sheridan

Richard Brinsley Sheridan

The dramatic works of the Right Honourable Richard Brinsley Sheridan

ISBN/EAN: 9783742854247

Manufactured in Europe, USA, Canada, Australia, Japa

Cover: Foto ©Raphael Reischuk / pixelio.de

Manufactured and distributed by brebook publishing software
(www.brebook.com)

Richard Brinsley Sheridan

The dramatic works of the Right Honourable Richard Brinsley Sheridan

THE DRAMATIC WORKS

OF THE

RIGHT HONOURABLE

RICHARD BRINSLEY SHERIDAN.

THE RIVALS — ST. PATRICK'S DAY — THE DUENNA ·
THE SCHOOL FOR SCANDAL — THE CRITIC — TRIP TO SCARBOR
PIZARRO — VERSES TO THE MEMORY OF GARRICK.

LEIPZIG

BERNHARD TAUCHNITZ

1869.

THE RIVALS.

A COMEDY.

PREFACE.

A PREFACE to a play seems generally to be considered as a kind of closet-prologue, in which — if his piece has been successful — the author solicits that indulgence from the reader which he had before experienced from the audience: but as the scope and immediate object of a play is to please a mixed assembly in *representation* (whose judgment in the theatre at least is decisive), its degree of reputation is usually as determined as public, before it can be prepared for the cooler tribunal of the study. Thus any farther solicitude on the part of the writer becomes unnecessary at least, if not an intrusion: and if the piece has been condemned in the performance, I fear an address to the closet, like an appeal to posterity, is constantly regarded as the procrastination of a suit, from a consciousness of the weakness of the cause. From these considerations, the following comedy would certainly have been submitted to the reader, without any farther introduction than what it had in the representation, but that its success has probably been founded on a circumstance which the author is informed has not before attended a theatrical trial, and which consequently ought not to pass unnoticed.

I need scarcely add, that the circumstance alluded to was the withdrawing of the piece, to remove those imperfections in the first representation which were too obvious to escape reprehension, and too numerous to admit of a hasty correction. There are few writers, I believe, who, even in the fullest consciousness of error, do not wish to palliate the faults which they acknowledge; and, however trifling the performance, to second their confession of its deficiencies, by whatever plea seems least disgraceful to their ability. In the present instance, it cannot be said to amount either to candour or modesty in me, to acknowledge an extreme inexperience and want of judgment on matters, in which, without guidance from practice, or spur from success, a young man should scarcely boast of being an adept. If it be said, that under such disadvantages no one should attempt to write a play, I must beg leave to dissent from the position, while the first point of experience that I have gained on the subject is, a knowledge of the candour and judgment with which an impartial public distinguishes between the errors of inexperience and incapacity, and the indulgence which it shows even to a disposition to remedy the defects of either.

It were unnecessary to enter into any farther extenuation of what was thought exceptionable in this play, but that it has been said, that the managers should have prevented some of the defects before its appearance to the public — and in particular the uncommon length of the piece as represented the first night. It were an ill return for the most liberal and gentlemanly conduct on their side, to suffer any censure to rest where none was deserved. Hurry in writing has long been exploded as an excuse for an author; — however, in the dramatic line, it may happen, that both an author and a manager may wish to fill a chasm in the entertainment of the public with a hastiness not altogether culpable. The season was advanced when I first put the play into Mr. Harris's hands: it was at that time at least double the length of any acting comedy. I profited by his judgment and experience in the curtailing of it — till, I believe, his feeling for the vanity of a young author got the better of his desire for correctness, and he left many excrescences remaining, because he had assisted in pruning so many more. Hence, though I was not uninformed that the acts were still too long, I flattered myself that, after the first trial, I might with safer judgment proceed to remove what should appear to have been most dissatisfactory. Many other errors there were, which might in part have arisen from my being by no means conversant with plays in general, either in reading or at the theatre. Yet I own that, in one respect, I did not regret my ignorance: for as my first wish in attempting a play was to avoid every appearance of plagiary, I thought I should stand a better chance of effecting this from being in a walk which I had not frequented, and where, consequently, the progress of invention was less likely to be interrupted by starts of recollection: for on subjects on which the mind has been much informed, invention is slow of exerting itself. Faded ideas float in the fancy like half-forgotten dreams; and the imagination in its fullest enjoyments becomes suspicious of its offspring, and doubts whether it has created or adopted.

With regard to some particular passages which on the first night's representation seemed generally disliked, I confess, that if I felt any emotion of surprise at the disapprobation, it was not that they were disapproved of, but that I had not before perceived that they deserved it. As some part of the attack on the piece was begun too early to pass for the sentence of *judgment*, which is ever tardy in condemning, it has been suggested to me, that much of the disapprobation must have arisen from virulence of malice, rather than severity of criticism: but 'as I was more apprehensive of there being just grounds to excite the latter than conscious of having deserved the former, I continue not to believe that probable, which I am sure must have been unprovoked. However, if it was so, and I could even mark the quarter from whence it came, it would be ungenerous to retort: for no passion suffers more than malice from disappointment. For my own part, I see no reason why the author of a play should not regard a first night's audience as a candid and judicious friend attending, in behalf of the public, at his last rehearsal. If he can dispense with flattery, he is sure at least of sincerity, and even though the annotation be rude, he may reply upon the justness of the comment. Considered in this light, that audience, whose *fiat* is essential to the poet's claim, whether his object be fame or profit, has surely a right to expect some deference to its opinion, from principles of politeness at least, if not from gratitude.

As for the little puny critics, who scatter their peevish strictures in private circles, and scribble at every author who has the eminence of being unconnected with them, as they are usually spleen-swoln from a vain idea of increasing their consequence, there will always be found a petulance and illiberality in their remarks, which should place them as far beneath the notice of a gentleman, as their original dulness had sunk them from the level of the most unsuccessful author.

It is not without pleasure that I catch at an opportunity of justifying myself from the charge of intending any national reflection in the character of Sir Lucius O'Trigger. If any gentleman opposed the piece from that idea, I thank them sincerely for their opposition; and if the condemnation of this comedy (however misconceived the provocation) could have added one spark to the decaying flame of national attachment to the country supposed to be reflected on, I should have been happy in its fate; and might with truth have boasted, that it had done more real service in its failure, than the successful morality of a thousand stage-novels will ever effect.

It is usual, I believe, to thank the performers in a new play, for the exertion of their several abilities. But where (as in this instance) their merit has been so striking and uncontroverted, as to call for the warmest and truest applause from a number of judicious audiences, the poet's after-praise comes like the feeble acclamation of a child to close the shouts of a multitude. The conduct, however, of the principals in a theatre cannot be so apparent to the public. I think it therefore but justice to declare, that from this theatre (the only one I can speak of from experience) those writers who wish to try the dramatic line will meet with that candour and liberal attention, which are generally allowed to be better calculated to lead genius into excellence, than either the precepts of judgment, or the guidance of experience.
THE AUTHOR.

DRAMATIS PERSONÆ.

AS ORIGINALLY ACTED AT COVENT-GARDEN THEATRE IN 1775.

SIR ANTHONY ABSOLUTE	*Mr. Shuter.*	DAVID	*Mr. Dunstal.*
		THOMAS	*Mr. Fearon.*
CAPTAIN ABSOLUTE.	*Mr. Woodward.*	MRS. MALAPROP	*Mrs. Green.*
FAULKLAND	*Mr. Lewis.*	LYDIA LANGUISH	*Miss Barsanti.*
ACRES	*Mr. Quick.*	JULIA	*Mrs. Bulkley.*
SIR LUCIUS O'TRIG-GER.	*Mr. Lee.*	LUCY	*Mrs. Lessingham.*
FAG	*Mr. Lee Lewes.*	Maid, Boy, Servants, &c.	

SCENE — BATH.

Time of Action — Five Hours.

PROLOGUE.

BY THE AUTHOR.

SPOKEN BY MR. WOODWARD AND MR. QUICK.

Enter SERJEANT-AT-LAW, *and* ATTORNEY *following, and giving a paper.*

Serj. WHAT'S here! — a vile cramp hand! I cannot see
Without my spectacles.

Att. He means his fee.
Nay, Mr. Serjeant, good sir, try again. [*Gives money.*

Serj. The scrawl improves! [*more*] O come, 'tis pretty plain
Hey! how's this? Dibble! — sure it cannot be!
A poet's brief! a poet and a fee!

Att. Yes, sir! though you without reward, I know,
Would gladly plead the Muse's cause.

Serj. So! — so!

Att. And if the fee offends, your wrath should fall
On me.

Serj. Dear Dibble, no offence at all.

Att. Some sons of Phœbus in the courts we meet,

Serj. And fifty sons of Phœbus in the Fleet!

Att. Nor pleads he worse, who with a decent sprig
Of bays adorns his legal waste of wig.

Serj. Full-bottom'd heroes thus, on signs, unfurl
A leaf of laurel in a grove of curl!
Yet tell your client, that, in adverse days,
This wig is warmer than a bush of bays.

Att. Do you, then, sir, my client's place supply,
Profuse of robe, and prodigal of tie —
Do you, with all those blushing powers of face,
And wonted bashful hesitating grace,
Rise in the court, and flourish on the case. [*Exit.*

Serj. For practice then suppose — this brief will show it, —
Me, Serjeant Woodward, — counsel for the poet.
Used to the ground, I know 'tis hard to deal
With this dread court, from whence there's no appeal;
No tricking here, to blunt the edge of law,
Or, damn'd in equity, escape by flaw:
But judgment given, your sentence must remain;
No writ of error lies — to Drury-lane!
Yet when so kind you seem, 'tis past dispute
We gain some favour, if not costs of suit.
No spleen is here! I see no hoarded fury; —
I think I never faced a milder jury!
Sad else our plight! where frowns are transportation,
A hiss the gallows, and a groan damnation!
But such the public candour, without fear
My client waves all right of challenge here.

No newsman from our session is dismiss'd,
Nor wit nor critic we scratch off the list;
His faults can never hurt another's ease,
His crime, at worst, a bad attempt to please:
Thus, all respecting, he appeals to all,
And by the general voice will stand or fall.

PROLOGUE.
BY THE AUTHOR.
SPOKEN ON THE TENTH NIGHT, BY MRS. BULKLEY.

GRANTED our cause, our suit and trial o'er,
The worthy serjeant need appear no more:
In pleasing I a different client choose,
He served the Poet — I would serve the Muse.
Like him, I'll try to merit your applause,
A female counsel in a female's cause.
    Look on this form*, — where humour, quaint and sly,
Dimples the cheek, and points the beaming eye;
Where gay invention seems to boast its wiles
In amorous hint, and half-triumphant smiles;
While her light mask or covers satire's strokes,
Or hides the conscious blush her wit provokes.
Look on her well — does she seem form'd to teach?
Should you expect to hear this lady preach?
Is grey experience suited to her youth?
Do solemn sentiments become that mouth?
Bid her be grave, those lips should rebel prove
To every theme that slanders mirth or love.
    Yet, thus adorn'd with every graceful art
To charm the fancy and yet reach the heart —
Must we displace her? And instead advance
The goddess of the woful countenance —
The sentimental Muse! — Her emblems view,
The Pilgrim's Progress, and a sprig of rue!
View her — too chaste to look like flesh and blood —
Primly portray'd on emblematic wood!
There, fix'd in usurpation, should she stand,
She'll snatch the dagger from her sister's hand:
And having made her votaries weep a flood,
Good heaven! she'll end her comedies in blood —
Bid Harry Woodward break poor Dunstal's crown!
Imprison Quick, and knock Ned Shuter down;

* Pointing to the figure of Comedy.

While sad Barsanti, weeping o'er the scene,
Shall stab herself — or poison Mrs. Green.
  Such dire encroachments to prevent in time,
Demands the critic's voice — the poet's rhyme.
Can our light scenes add strength to holy laws!
Such puny patronage but hurts the cause:
Fair virtue scorns our feeble aid to ask;
And moral truth disdains the trickster's mask
For here their favourite stands*, whose brow severe
And sad, claims youth's respect, and pity's tear;
Who, when oppress'd by foes her worth creates,
Can point a poniard at the guilt she hates.

ACT I.

SCENE I. — *A Street.*

Enter THOMAS; *he crosses the Stage;* FAG *follows, looking after him.*

Fag. What! Thomas! sure 'tis he? — What! Thomas! Thomas!

Thos. Hey! — Odd's life! Mr. Fag! — give us your hand, my old fellow-servant.

Fag. Excuse my glove, Thomas: — I'm devilish glad to see you, my lad. Why, my prince of charioteers, you look as hearty! — but who the deuce thought of seeing you in Bath?

Thos. Sure, master, Madam Julia, Harry, Mrs. Kate, and the postillion, be all come.

Fag. Indeed!

Thos. Ay, master thought another fit of the gout was coming to make him a visit; — so he'd a mind to gi't the slip, and whip! we were all off at an hour's warning.

Fag. Ay, ay, hasty in every thing, or it would not be Sir Anthony Absolute!

Thos. But tell us, Mr. Fag, how does young master? Odd! Sir Anthony will stare to see the Captain here!

Fag. I do not serve Captain Absolute now.

Thos. Why sure!

* Pointing to Tragedy.

Fag. At present I am employed by Ensign Beverley.

Thos. I doubt, Mr. Fag, you ha'n't changed for the better.

Fag. I have not changed, Thomas.

Thos. No! Why didn't you say you had left young master?

Fag. No. — Well, honest Thomas. I must puzzle you no farther: — briefly then — Captain Absolute and Ensign Beverley are one and the same person.

Thos. The devil they are!

Fag. So it is indeed, Thomas; and the ensign half of my master being on guard at present — the captain has nothing to do with me.

Thos. So, so! — What, this is some freak, I warrant! — Do tell us, Mr. Fag, the meaning o't — you know I ha' trusted you.

Fag. You'll be secret, Thomas?

Thos. As a coach-horse.

Fag. Why then the cause of all this is — Love, — Love, Thomas, who (as you may get read to you) has been a masquerader ever since the days of Jupiter.

Thos. Ay, ay; — I guessed there was a lady in the case: — but pray, why does your master pass only for ensign? — Now if he had shammed general indeed ——

Fag. Ah! Thomas, there lies the mystery o' the matter. Hark'ee, Thomas, my master is in love with a lady of a very singular taste: a lady who likes him better as a half pay ensign than if she knew he was son and heir to Sir Anthony Absolute, a baronet of three thousand a year.

Thos. That is an odd taste indeed! — But has she got the stuff, Mr. Fag? Is she rich, hey?

Fag. Rich! — Why, I believe she owns half the stocks! Zounds! Thomas, she could pay the national debt as easily as I could my washerwoman! She has a lapdog that eats out of gold, — she feeds her parrot with small pearls, — and all her thread-papers are made of bank-notes!

Thos. Bravo, faith! — Odd! I warrant she has a set of thousands at least: — but does she draw kindly with the captain?

Fag. As fond as pigeons.

Thos. May one hear her name?

Fag. Miss Lydia Languish. — But there is an old tough aunt in the way; though, by the by, she has never seen my master — for we got acquainted with miss while on a visit in Gloucestershire.

Thos. Well — I wish they were once harnessed together in matrimony. — But pray, Mr. Fag, what kind of a place is this Bath? — I ha' heard a deal of it — here's a mort o' merry-making, hey?

Fag. Pretty well, Thomas, pretty well—'tis a good lounge; in the morning we go to the pump-room (though neither my master nor I drink the waters); after breakfast we saunter on the parades, or play a game at billiards; at night we dance; but damn the place, I'm tired of it: their regular hours stupify me — not a fiddle nor a card after eleven! — However, Mr. Faulkland's gentleman and I keep it up a little in private parties;—I'll introduce you there, Thomas—you'll like him much.

Thos. Sure I know Mr. Du-Peigne — you know his master is to marry Madam Julia.

Fag. I had forgot. — But, Thomas, you must polish a little — indeed you must. — Here now — this wig! — What the devil do you do with a wig, Thomas? — None of the London whips of any degree of *ton* wear wigs now.

Thos. More's the pity! more's the pity! I say. — Odd's life! when I heard how the lawyers and doctors had took to their own hair, I thought how 'twould go next: — odd rabbit it! when the fashion had got foot on the bar, I guessed 'twould mount to the box! — but 'tis all out of character, believe me, Mr. Fag: and look'ee, I'll never gi' up mine — the lawyers and doctors may do as they will.

Fag. Well, Thomas, we'll not quarrel about that.

Thos. Why, bless you, the gentlemen of the professions ben't all of a mind — for in our village now, thoff Jack Gauge, the exciseman, has ta'en to his carrots, there's little Dick the farrier swears he'll never forsake his bob, though all the college should appear with their own heads!

Fag. Indeed! well said, Dick! — But hold — mark! mark! Thomas.

Thos. Zooks! 'tis the captain. — Is that the lady with him?

Fag. No, no, that is Madam Lucy, my master's mistress's maid. They lodge at that house — but I must after him to tell him the news.

Thos. Odd! he's giving her money! — Well, Mr. Fag——

Fag. Good-bye, Thomas. I have an appointment in Gyde's Porch this evening at eight; meet me there, and we'll make a little party. [*Exeunt severally.*

SCENE II. — *A Dressing-room in* Mrs. Malaprop's *Lodgings.*

Lydia *sitting on a sofa, with a book in her hand.* Lucy, *as just returned from a message.*

Lucy. Indeed, ma'am, I traversed half the town in search of it: I don't believe there's a circulating library in Bath I ha'n't been at.

Lyd. And could not you get *The Reward of Constancy?*

Lucy. No, indeed, ma'am.

Lyd. Nor *The Fatal Connexion?*

Lucy. No, indeed, ma'am.

Lyd. Nor *The Mistakes of the Heart?*

Lucy. Ma'am, as ill luck would have it, Mr. Bull said Miss Sukey Saunter had just fetched it away.

Lyd. Heigh-ho! — Did you inquire for *The Delicate Distress?*

Lucy. Or, *The Memoirs of Lady Woodford?* Yes, indeed, ma'am. I asked every where for it; and I might have brought it from Mr. Frederick's, but Lady Slattern Lounger, who had just sent it home, had so soiled and dog's-eared it, it wa'n't fit for a Christian to read.

Lyd. Heigh-ho! — Yes, I always know when Lady Slattern has been before me. She has a most observing thumb; and, I believe, cherishes her nails for the convenience of making marginal notes. — Well, child, what have you brought me?

Lucy. Oh! here, ma'am. — [*Taking books from under her*

cloak, and from her pockets.] This is *The Gordian Knot,* — and this *Peregrine Pickle.* Here are *The Tears of Sensibility,* and *Humphrey Clinker.* This is *The Memoirs of a Lady of Quality, written by herself,* and here the second volume of *The Sentimental Journey.*

Lyd. Heigh-ho! — What are those books by the glass?

Lucy. The great one is only *The Whole Duty of Man,* where I press a few blonds, ma'am.

Lyd. Very well — give me the sal volatile.

Lucy. Is it in a blue cover, ma'am?

Lyd. My smelling-bottle, you simpleton!

Lucy. Oh, the drops! — here, ma'am.

Lyd. Hold! — here's some one coming — quick, see who it is. — [*Exit* Lucy.] Surely I heard my cousin Julia's voice.

Re-enter Lucy.

Lucy. Lud! ma'am, here is Miss Melville.

Lyd. Is it possible! —   [*Exit* Lucy.

Enter Julia.

Lyd. My dearest Julia, how delighted am I! — [*Embrace.*] How unexpected was this happiness!

Jul. True, Lydia — and our pleasure is the greater. — But what has been the matter? — you were denied to me at first!

Lyd. Ah, Julia, I have a thousand things to tell you! — But first inform me what has conjured you to Bath? — Is Sir Anthony here?

Jul. He is — we are arrived within this hour — and I suppose he will be here to wait on Mrs. Malaprop as soon as he is dressed.

Lyd. Then before we are interrupted, let me impart to you some of my distress! — I know your gentle nature will sympathize with me, though your prudence may condemn me! My letters have informed you of my whole connection with Beverley; but I have lost him, Julia! My aunt has discovered our intercourse by a note she intercepted, and has confined me ever since! Yet, would you believe it? she has absolutely

fallen in love with a tall Irish baronet she met one night since
we have been here, at Lady Macshuffle's rout.

Jul. You jest, Lydia!

Lyd. No, upon my word. — She really carries on a kind of
correspondence with him, under a feigned name though, till
she chooses to be known to him; — but it is a Delia or a Celia,
I assure you.

Jul. Then, surely, she is now more indulgent to her niece.

Lyd. Quite the contrary. Since she has discovered her
own frailty, she is become more suspicious of mine. Then I
must inform you of another plague! — That odius Acres is to
be in Bath to-day; so that I protest I shall be teased out of
all spirits!

Jul. Come, come, Lydia, hope for the best — Sir Anthony
shall use his interest with Mrs. Malaprop.

Lyd. But you have not heard the worst. Unfortunately
I had quarrelled with my poor Beverley, just before my aunt
made the discovery, and I have not seen him since, to make
it up.

Jul. What was his offence?

Lyd. Nothing at all! — But, I don't know how it was, as
often as we had been together, we had never had a quarrel,
and, somehow, I was afraid he would never give me an opportunity. So, last Thursday, I wrote a letter to myself, to
inform myself that Beverley was at that time paying his
addresses to another woman. I signed it *your friend unknown*,
showed it to Beverley, charged him with his falsehood, put
myself in a violent passion, and vowed I'd never see him more.

Jul. And you let him depart so, and have not seen him
since?

Lyd. 'Twas the next day my aunt found the matter out.
I intended only to have teased him three days and a half, and
now I 've lost him for ever.

Jul. If he is as deserving and sincere as you have represented him to me, he will never give you up so. Yet consider, Lydia, you tell me he is but an ensign, and you have
thirty thousand pounds.

Lyd. But you know I lose most of my fortune if I marry
without my aunt's consent, till of age; and that is what I
have determined to do, ever since I knew the penalty. Nor
could I love the man, who would wish to wait a day for the
alternative.

Jul. Nay, this is caprice!

Lyd. What, does Julia tax me with caprice? — I thought
her lover Faulkland had inured her to it.

Jul. I do not love even his faults.

Lyd. But apropos — you have sent to him, I suppose?

Jul. Not yet, upon my word — nor has he the least idea of
my being in Bath. Sir Anthony's resolution was so sudden.
I could not inform him of it.

Lyd. Well, Julia, you are your own mistress, (though under
the protection of Sir Anthony,) yet have you, for this long
year, been a slave to the caprice, the whim, the jealousy of
this ungrateful Faulkland, who will ever delay assuming the
right of a husband, while you suffer him to be equally impe-
rious as a lover.

Jul. Nay, you are wrong entirely. We were contracted
before my father's death. That, and some consequent em-
barrassments, have delayed what I know to be my Faulkland's
most ardent wish. He is too generous to trifle on such a
point: — and for his character, you wrong him there too. No,
Lydia, he is too proud, too noble to be jealous; if he is
captious, 'tis without dissembling; if fretful, without rudeness. Unused to the fopperies of love, he is negligent of the
little duties expected from a lover — but being unhackneyed
in the passion, his affection is ardent and sincere; and as it
engrosses his whole soul, he expects every thought and emotion of his mistress to move in unison with his. Yet, though
his pride calls for this full return, his humility makes him
undervalue those qualities in him which would entitle him to
it; and not feeling why he should be loved to the degree he
wishes, he still suspects that he is not loved enough. This
temper, I must own, has cost me many unhappy hours; but

I have learned to think myself his debtor, for those imperfections which arise from the ardour of his attachment.

Lyd. Well, I cannot blame you for defending him. But tell me candidly, Julia, had he never saved your life, do you think you should have been attached to him as you are? — Believe me, the rude blast that overset your boat was a prosperous gale of love to him.

Jul. Gratitude may have strengthened my attachment to Mr. Faulkland, but I loved him before he had preserved me; yet surely that alone were an obligation sufficient.

Lyd. Obligation! why a water spaniel would have done as much! — Well, I should never think of giving my heart to a man because he could swim.

Jul. Come, Lydia, you are too inconsiderate.

Lyd. Nay, I do but jest. — What's here?

Re-enter Lucy *in a hurry.*

Lucy. O ma'am, here is Sir Anthony Absolute just come home with your aunt.

Lyd. They'll not come here. — Lucy, do you watch.
                                        [*Exit* Lucy.

Jul. Yet I must go. Sir Anthony does not know I am here, and if we meet, he'll detain me, to show me the town. I'll take another opportunity of paying my respects to Mrs. Malaprop, when she shall treat me, as long as she chooses, with her select words so ingeniously misapplied, without being mispronounced.

Re-enter Lucy.

Lucy. O Lud! ma'am, they are both coming up stairs.

Lyd. Well, I'll not detain you, coz. — Adieu, my dear Julia, I'm sure you are in haste to send to Faulkland. — There — through my room you'll find another staircase.

Jul. Adieu!   [*Embraces* Lydia, *and exit.*

Lyd. Here, my dear Lucy, hide these books. Quick, quick. — *Fling Peregrine Pickle* under the toilet — throw *Roderick Random* into the closet — put *The Innocent Adultery* into *The Whole Duty of Man* — thrust *Lord Aimworth* under the sofa — cram *Ovid* behind the bolster — there — put *The Man of Feeling* into your pocket — so, so — now lay *Mrs. Chapone* in sight, and leave *Fordyce's Sermons* open on the table.

Lucy. O burn it, ma'am! the hair-dresser has torn away as far as *Proper Pride*.

Lyd. Never mind — open at *Sobriety.* — Fling me *Lord Chesterfield's Letters.* — Now for 'em.   [*Exit* LUCY.

Enter Mrs. MALAPROP, *and* Sir ANTHONY ABSOLUTE.

Mrs. Mal. There, Sir Anthony, there sits the deliberate simpleton who wants to disgrace her family, and lavish herself on a fellow not worth a shilling.

Lyd. Madam, I thought you once ——

Mrs. Mal. You thought, miss! I don't know any business you have to think at all — thought does not become a young woman. But the point we would request of you is, that you will promise to forget this fellow — to illiterate him, I say, quite from your memory.

Lyd. Ah, madam! our memories are independent of our wills. It is not so easy to forget.

Mrs. Mal. But I say it is, miss; there is nothing on earth so easy as to forget, if a person chooses to set about it. I'm sure I have as much forgot your poor dear uncle as if he had never existed — and I thought it my duty so to do; and let me tell you, Lydia, these violent memories don't become a young woman.

Sir Anth. Why sure she won't pretend to remember what she's ordered not! — ay, this comes of her reading!

Lyd. What crime, madam, have I committed, to be treated thus?

Mrs. Mal. Now don't attempt to extirpate yourself from the matter; you know I have proof controvertible of it. — But tell me, will you promise to do as you're bid? Will you take a husband of your friends' choosing?

Lyd. Madam, I must tell you plainly, that had I no preference for any one else, the choice you have made would be my aversion.

Mrs. Mal. What business have you, miss, with preference and aversion? They don't become a young woman; and you ought to know, that as both always wear off, 'tis safest in matrimony to begin with a little aversion. I am sure I hated your poor dear uncle before marriage as if he'd been a blackamoor — and yet, miss, you are sensible what a wife I made! — and when it pleased Heaven to release me from him, 'tis unknown what tears I shed! — But suppose we were going to give you another choice, will you promise us to give up this Beverley?

Lyd. Could I belie my thoughts so far as to give that promise, my actions would certainly as far belie my words.

Mrs. Mal. Take yourself to your room. — You are fit company for nothing but your own ill-humours.

Lyd. Willingly, ma'am — I cannot change for the worse.
                                                    [*Exit.*

Mrs. Mal. There's a little intricate hussy for you!

Sir Anth. It is not to be wondered at, ma'am, — all this is the natural consequence of teaching girls to read. Had I a thousand daughters, by Heaven! I'd as soon have them taught the black art as their alphabet!

Mrs. Mal. Nay, nay, Sir Anthony, you are an absolute misanthropy.

Sir Anth. In my way hither, Mrs. Malaprop, I observed your niece's maid coming forth from a circulating library! — She had a book in each hand — they were half-bound volumes, with marble covers! — From that moment I guessed how full of duty I should see her mistress!

Mrs. Mal. Those are vile places, indeed!

Sir Anth. Madam, a circulating library in a town is as an evergreen tree of diabolical knowledge! It blossoms through the year! — And depend on it, Mrs. Malaprop, that they who are so fond of handling the leaves, will long for the fruit at last.

Mrs. Mal. Fy, fy, Sir Anthony! you surely speak laconically.

Sir Anth. Why, Mrs. Malaprop, in moderation now, what would you have a woman know?

2*

Mrs. Mal. Observe me, Sir Anthony. I would by no means wish a daughter of mine to be a progeny of learning; I don't think so much learning becomes a young woman; for instance, I would never let her meddle with Greek, or Hebrew, or algebra, or simony, or fluxions, or paradoxes, or such inflammatory branches of learning—neither would it be necessary for her to handle any of your mathematical, astronomical, diabolical instruments.—But, Sir Anthony, I would send her, at nine years old, to a boarding-school, in order to learn a little ingenuity and artifice. Then, sir, she should have a supercilious knowledge in accounts;—and as she grew up, I would have her instructed in geometry, that she might know something of the contagious countries;—but above all, Sir Anthony, she should be mistress of orthodoxy, that she might not mis-spell, and mis-pronounce words so shamefully as girls usually do; and likewise that she might reprehend the true meaning of what she is saying. This, Sir Anthony, is what I would have a woman know;—and I don't think there is a superstitious article in it.

Sir Anth. Well, well, Mrs. Malaprop, I will dispute the point no further with you; though I must confess, that you are a truly moderate and polite arguer, for almost every third word you say is on my side of the question. But, Mrs. Malaprop, to the more important point in debate — you say you have no objection to my proposal?

Mrs. Mal. None, I assure you. I am under no positive engagement with Mr. Acres, and as Lydia is so obstinate against him, perhaps your son may have better success.

Sir Anth. Well, madam, I will write for the boy directly. He knows not a syllable of this yet, though I have for some time had the proposal in my head. He is at present with his regiment.

Mrs. Mal. We have never seen your son, Sir Anthony; but I hope no objection on his side.

Sir Anth. Objection!—let him object if he dare!—No, no, Mrs. Malaprop, Jack knows that the least demur puts me in a frenzy directly. My process was always very simple — in

their younger days, 'twas "Jack, do this;"—if he demurred,
I knocked him down — and if he grumbled at that, I always
sent him out of the room.

Mrs. Mal. Ay, and the properest way, o' my conscience!
— nothing is so conciliating to young people as severity. —
Well, Sir Anthony, I shall give Mr. Acres his discharge, and
prepare Lydia to receive your son's invocations;—and I hope
you will represent her to the captain as an object not altogether illegible.

Sir Anth. Madam, I will handle the subject prudently. —
Well, I must leave you; and let me beg you, Mrs. Malaprop,
to enforce this matter roundly to the girl. — Take my advice
— keep a tight hand: if she rejects this proposal, clap her
under lock and key; and if you were just to let the servants
forget to bring her dinner for three or four days, you can't
conceive how she'd come about.   [*Exit.*

Mrs. Mal. Well, at any rate I shall be glad to get her from
under my intuition. She has somehow discovered my partiality for Sir Lucius O'Trigger — sure, Lucy can't have betrayed me! — No, the girl is such a simpleton, I should have
made her confess it. — Lucy! — Lucy! — [*Calls.*] Had she
been one of your artificial ones, I should never have trusted
her.

Re-enter LUCY.

Lucy. Did you call, ma'am?

Mrs. Mal. Yes, girl. — Did you see Sir Lucius while you
was out?

Lucy. No, indeed, ma'am, not a glimpse of him.

Mrs. Mal. You are sure, Lucy, that you never mentioned——

Lucy. Oh gemini! I'd sooner cut my tongue out.

Mrs. Mal. Well, don't let your simplicity be imposed on.

Lucy. No, ma'am.

Mrs. Mal. So, come to me presently, and I'll give you
another letter to Sir Lucius; but mind, Lucy — if ever you
betray what you are entrusted with (unless it be other people's
secrets to me), you forfeit my malevolence for ever; and your
being a simpleton shall be no excuse for your locality. [*Exit.*

Lucy. Ha! ha! ha! — So, my dear Simplicity, let me give you a little respite. — [*Altering her manner.*] Let girls in my station be as fond as they please of appearing expert, and knowing in their trusts; commend me to a mask of silliness, and a pair of sharp eyes for my own interest under it! — Let me see to what account have I turned my simplicity lately. — [*Looks at a paper.*] For *abetting Miss Lydia Languish in a design of running away with an ensign!* — *in money, sundry times, twelve pound twelve; gowns, five; hats, ruffles, caps, &c. &c., numberless!* — *From the said ensign, within this last month, six guineas and a half.* — About a quarter's pay! — Item, *from Mrs. Malaprop, for betraying the young people to her* — when I found matters were likely to be discovered — *two guineas, and a black paduasoy.* — Item, *from Mr. Acres, for carrying divers letters*—which I never delivered—*two guineas, and a pair of buckles.* — Item, *from Sir Lucius O'Trigger, three crowns, two gold pocket-pieces, and a silver snuff-box!* — Well done, Simplicity! — Yet I was forced to make my Hibernian believe, that he was corresponding, not with the aunt, but with the niece: for though not over rich, I found he had too much pride and delicacy to sacrifice the feelings of a gentleman to the necessities of his fortune.   [*Exit.*

ACT II.

Scene I. — Captain Absolute's *Lodgings.*

Captain Absolute *and* Fag.

Fag. Sir, while I was there Sir Anthony came in: I told him, you had sent me to inquire after his health, and to know if he was at leisure to see you.

Abs. And what did he say, on hearing I was at Bath?

Fag. Sir, in my life I never saw an elderly gentleman more astonished! He started back two or three paces, rapped out a dozen interjectural oaths, and asked, what the devil had brought you here.

Abs. Well, sir, and what did you say?

Fag. Oh, I lied, sir—I forget the precise lie; but you may depend on't, he got no truth from me. Yet, with submission, for fear of blunders in future, I should be glad to fix what has brought us to Bath; in order that we may lie a little consistently. Sir Anthony's servants were curious, sir, very curious indeed.

Abs. You have said nothing to them?

Fag. Oh, not a word, sir, — not a word! Mr. Thomas, indeed, the coachman (whom I take to be the discreetest of whips) ——

Abs. 'Sdeath! — you rascal! you have not trusted him!

Fag. Oh, no, sir — no — no — not a syllable, upon my veracity! — He was, indeed, a little inquisitive; but I was sly, sir — devilish sly! My master (said I), honest Thomas, (you know, sir, one says honest to one's inferiors,) is come to Bath to recruit — Yes, sir, I said to recruit — and whether for men, money, or constitution, you know, sir, is nothing to him, nor any one else.

Abs. Well, recruit will do — let it be so.

Fag. Oh, sir, recruit will do surprisingly — indeed, to give the thing an air, I told Thomas, that your honour had already enlisted five disbanded chairmen, seven minority waiters, and thirteen billiard-markers.

Abs. You blockhead, never say more than is necessary.

Fag. I beg pardon, sir — I beg pardon — but, with submission, a lie is nothing unless one supports it. Sir, whenever I draw on my invention for a good current lie, I always forge indorsements as well as the bill.

Abs. Well, take care you don't hurt your credit, by offering too much security. — Is Mr. Faulkland returned?

Fag. He is above, sir, changing his dress.

Abs. Can you tell whether he has been informed of Sir Anthony and Miss Melville's arrival?

Fag. I fancy not, sir; he has seen no one since he came in but his gentleman, who was with him at Bristol. — I think, sir, I hear Mr. Faulkland coming down ——

Abs. Go, tell him I am here.

Fag. Yes, sir. — [*Going.*] I beg pardon, sir, but should Sir

Anthony call, you will do me the favour to remember that we are recruiting, if you please.

Abs. Well, well.

Fag. And, in tenderness to my character, if your honour could bring in the chairmen and waiters, I should esteem it as an obligation; for though I never scruple a lie to serve my master, yet it hurts one's conscience to be found out.

[*Exit.*

Abs. Now for my whimsical friend — if he does not know that his mistress is here, I'll tease him a little before I tell him —

Enter FAULKLAND.

Faulkland, you're welcome to Bath again; you are punctual in your return.

Faulk. Yes; I had nothing to detain me, when I had finished the business I went on. Well, what news since I left you? how stand matters between you and Lydia?

Abs. Faith, much as they were; I have not seen her since our quarrel; however, I expect to be recalled every hour.

Faulk. Why don't you persuade her to go off with you at once?

Abs. What, and lose two-thirds of her fortune? you forget that, my friend. — No, no, I could have brought her to that long ago.

Faulk. Nay then, you trifle too long — if you are sure of her, propose to the aunt in your own character, and write to Sir Anthony for his consent.

Abs. Softly, softly; for though I am convinced my little Lydia would elope with me as Ensign Beverley, yet am I by no means certain that she would take me with the impediment of our friends' consent, a regular humdrum wedding, and the reversion of a good fortune on my side: no, no; I must prepare her gradually for the discovery, and make myself necessary to her, before I risk it. — Well, but Faulkland, you'll dine with us to-day at the hotel?

Faulk. Indeed I cannot; I am not in spirits to be of such a party.

Abs. By heavens! I shall forswear your company. You are the most teasing, captious, incorrigible lover! — Do love like a man.

Faulk. I own I am unfit for company.

Abs. Am not I a lover; ay, and a romantic one too? Yet do I carry every where with me such a confounded farrago of doubts, fears, hopes, wishes, and all the flimsy furniture of a country miss's brain!

Faulk. Ah! Jack, your heart and soul are not, like mine, fixed immutably on one only object. You throw for a large stake, but losing, you could stake and throw again: — but I have set my sum of happiness on this cast, and not to succeed, were to be stripped of all.

Abs. But, for Heaven's sake! what grounds for apprehension can your whimsical brain conjure up at present?

Faulk. What grounds for apprehension, did you say? Heavens! are there not a thousand! I fear for her spirits — her health — her life. — My absence may fret her; her anxiety for my return, her fears for me may oppress 'her gentle temper: and for her health, does not every hour bring me cause to be alarmed? If it rains, some shower may even then have chilled her delicate frame! If the wind be keen, some rude blast may have affected her! The heat of noon, the dews of the evening, may endanger the life of her, for whom only I value mine. O Jack! when delicate and feeling souls are separated, there is not a feature in the sky, not a movement of the elements, not an aspiration of the breeze, but hints some cause for a lover's apprehension!

Abs. Ay, but we may choose whether we will take the hint or not. — So, then, Faulkland, if you were convinced that Julia were well and in spirits, you would be entirely content?

Faulk. I should be happy beyond measure — I am anxious only for that.

Abs. Then to cure your anxiety at once — Miss Melville is in perfect health, and is at this moment in Bath.

Faulk. Nay, Jack — don't trifle with me.

Abs. She is arrived here with my father within this hour.

Faulk. Can you be serious?

Abs. I thought you knew Sir Anthony better than to be surprised at a sudden whim of this kind. — Seriously, then, it is as I tell you — upon my honour.

Faulk. My dear friend! — Hollo, Du Peigne! my hat. — My dear Jack — now nothing on earth can give me a moment's uneasiness.

Re-enter FAG.

Fag. Sir, Mr. Acres, just arrived, is below.

Abs. Stay, Faulkland, this Acres lives within a mile of Sir Anthony, and he shall tell you how your mistress has been ever since you left her. — Fag, show the gentleman up.

[*Exit* FAG.

Faulk. What, is he much acquainted in the family?

Abs. Oh, very intimate: I insist on your not going: besides, his character will divert you.

Faulk. Well, I should like to ask him a few questions.

Abs. He is likewise a rival of mine — that is, of my other self's, for he does not think his friend Captain Absolute ever saw the lady in question; and it is ridiculous enough to hear him complain to me of one Beverley, a concealed skulking rival, who ——

Faulk. Hush! — he's here.

Enter ACRES.

Acres. Ha! my dear friend, noble captain, and honest Jack, how do'st thou? just arrived, faith, as you see. — Sir, your humble servant. — Warm work on the roads, Jack! — Odds whips and wheels! I've travelled like a comet, with a tail of dust all the way as long as the Mall.

Abs. Ah! Bob, you are indeed an eccentric planet, but we know your attraction hither. — Give me leave to introduce Mr. Faulkland to you; Mr. Faulkland, Mr. Acres.

Acres. Sir, I am most heartily glad to see you: sir, I solicit your connections. — Hey, Jack — what, this is Mr. Faulkland, who ——

Abs. Ay, Bob, Miss Melville's Mr. Faulkland.

Acres. Odso! she and your father can be but just arrived before me: — I suppose you have seen them. Ah! Mr. Faulkland, you are indeed a happy man.

Faulk. I have not seen Miss Melville, yet, sir; — I hope she enjoyed full health and spirits in Devonshire?

Acres. Never knew her better in my life, sir, — never better. Odds blushes and blooms! she has been as healthy as the German Spa.

Faulk. Indeed! — I did hear that she had been a little indisposed.

Acres. False, false, sir — only said to vex you: quite the reverse, I assure you.

Faulk. There, Jack, you see she has the advantage of me; I had almost fretted myself ill.

Abs. Now are you angry with your mistress for not having been sick?

Faulk. No, no, you misunderstand me: yet surely a little trifling indisposition is not an unnatural consequence of absence from those we love. — Now confess — isn't there something unkind in this violent, robust, unfeeling health?

Abs. Oh, it was very unkind of her to be well in your absence, to be sure!

Acres. Good apartments, Jack.

Faulk. Well, sir, but you was saying that Miss Melville has been so exceedingly well — what then she has been merry and gay, I suppose? — Always in spirits — hey?

Acres. Merry, odds crickets! she has been the belle and spirit of the company wherever she has been — so lively and entertaining! so full of wit and humour!

Faulk. There, Jack, there. — Oh, by my soul! there is an innate levity in woman, that nothing can overcome. — What! happy, and I away!

Abs. Have done. — How foolish this is! just now you were only apprehensive for your mistress' spirits.

Faulk. Why, Jack, have I been the joy and spirit of the company?

Abs. No indeed, you have not.

Faulk. Have I been lively and entertaining?

Abs. Oh, upon my word, I acquit you.

Faulk. Have I been full of wit and humour?

Abs. No, faith, to do you justice, you have been confound-edly stupid indeed.

Acres. What's the matter with the gentleman?

Abs. He is only expressing his great satisfaction at hear-ing that Julia has been so well and happy — that's all — hey, Faulkland?

Faulk. Oh! I am rejoiced to hear it — yes, yes, she has a happy disposition!

Acres. That she has indeed — then she is so accomplished — so sweet a voice — so expert at her harpsichord — such a mistress of flat and sharp, squallante, rumblante, and quive-rante! — There was this time month — odds minims and crotchets! how she did chirrup at Mrs. Piano's concert!

Faulk. There again, what say you to this? you see she has been all mirth and song — not a thought of me!

Abs. Pho! man, is not music the food of love?

Faulk. Well, well, it may be so. — Pray, Mr. —, what's his damned name? — Do you remember what songs Miss Mel-ville sung?

Acres. Not I indeed.

Abs. Stay, now, they were some pretty melancholy purl-ing-stream airs, I warrant; perhaps you may recollect; — did she sing, *When absent from my soul's delight?*

Acres. No, that wa'n't it.

Abs. Or, *Go, gentle gales!*   [*Sings.*

Acres. Oh, no! nothing like it. Odds! now I recollect one of them — *My heart's my own, my will is free.*   [*Sings.*

Faulk. Fool! fool that I am! to fix all my happiness on such a trifler! 'Sdeath! to make herself the pipe and ballad-monger of a circle! to soothe her light heart with catches and glees! — What can you say to this, sir?

Abs. Why, that I should be glad to hear my mistress had been so merry, sir.

Faulk. Nay, nay, nay — I'm not sorry that she has been happy — no, no, I am glad of that — I would not have had her sad or sick — yet surely a sympathetic heart would have shown itself even in the choice of a song — she might have been temperately healthy, and somehow, plaintively gay; — but she has been dancing too, I doubt not!

Acres. What does the gentleman say about dancing?

Abs. He says the lady we speak of dances as well as she sings.

Acres. Ay, truly, does she — there was at our last race ball ——

Faulk. Hell and the devil! There! — there — I told you so! I told you so! Oh! she thrives in my absence! — Dancing! but her whole feelings have been in opposition with mine; — I have been anxious, silent, pensive, sedentary — my days have been hours of care, my nights of watchfulness. — She has been all health! spirit! laugh! song! dance! — Oh! damned, damned levity!

Abs. For Heaven's sake, Faulkland, don't expose yourself so! — Suppose she has danced, what then? — does not the ceremony of society often oblige ——

Faulk. Well, well, I'll contain myself — perhaps as you say — for form sake. — What, Mr. Acres, you were praising Miss Melville's manner of dancing a minuet — hey?

Acres. Oh, I dare insure her for that — but what I was going to speak of was her country-dancing. Odds swimmings! she has such an air with her!

Faulk. Now disappointment on her! — Defend this, Absolute; why don't you defend this? — Country-dances! jigs and reels! am I to blame now? A minuet I could have forgiven — I should not have minded that — I say I should not have regarded a minuet — but country-dances! — Zounds! had she made one in a cotillion — I believe I could have forgiven even that — but to be monkey-led for a night! — to run the gauntlet through a string of amorous palming puppies! — to show paces like a managed filly! — Oh, Jack, there never can be but one man in the world whom a truly modest and delicate woman ought to pair with in a country-dance; and, even then, the rest of the couples should be her great-uncles and aunts!

Abs. Ay, to be sure! — grandfathers and grandmothers!

Faulk. If there be but one vicious mind in the set, 'twill spread like a contagion — the action of their pulse beats to the lascivious movement of the jig — their quivering, warm-breathed sighs impregnate the very air — the atmosphere becomes electrical to love, and each amorous spark darts through every link of the chain! — I must leave you — I own I am somewhat flurried — and that confounded looby has perceived it.   [*Going.*

Abs. Nay, but stay, Faulkland, and thank Mr. Acres for his good news.

Faulk. Damn his news!   [*Exit.*

Abs. Ha! ha! ha! poor Faulkland five minutes since — "nothing on earth could give him a moment's uneasiness!"

Acres. The gentleman wa'n't angry at my praising his mistress, was he?

Abs. A little jealous, I believe, Bob.

Acres. You don't say so? Ha! ha! jealous of me — that's a good joke.

Abs. There's nothing strange in that, Bob; let me tell you, that sprightly grace and insinuating manner of yours will do some mischief among the girls here.

Acres. Ah! you joke — ha! ha! mischief — ha! ha! but you know I am not my own property, my dear Lydia has forestalled me. She could never abide me in the country, because I used to dress so badly — but odds frogs and tambours! I shan't take matters so here, now ancient madam has no voice in it: I'll make my old clothes know who's master. I shall straightway cashier the hunting-frock, and render my leather breeches incapable. My hair has been in training some time.

Abs. Indeed!

Acres. Ay — and tho'ff the side curls are a little restive, my hind-part takes it very kindly.

Abs. Oh, you'll polish, I doubt not.

Acres. Absolutely I propose so — then if I can find out this

Ensign Beverley, odds triggers and flints! I'll make him know the difference o't.

Abs. Spoke like a man! But pray, Bob, I observe you have got an odd kind of a new method of swearing ——

Acres. Ha! ha! you've taken notice of it — 'tis genteel, isn't it! — I didn't invent it myself though; but a commander in our militia, a great scholar, I assure you, says that there is no meaning in the common oaths, and that nothing but their antiquity makes them respectable;—because, he says, the ancients would never stick to an oath or two, but would say, by Jove! or by Bacchus! or by Mars! or by Venus! or by Pallas, according to the sentiment: so that to swear with propriety, says my little major, the oath should be an echo to the sense; and this we call the *oath referential or sentimental swearing* — ha! ha! 'tis genteel, isn't it?

Abs. Very genteel, and very new, indeed! — and I dare say will supplant all other figures of imprecation.

Acres. Ay, ay, the best terms will grow obsolete.—Damns have had their day.

Re-enter FAG.

Fag. Sir, there is a gentleman below desires to see you. — Shall I show him into the parlour?

Abs. Ay — you may.

Acres. Well, I must be gone ——

Abs. Stay; who is it, Fag?

Fag. Your father, sir.

Abs. You puppy, why didn't you show him up directly?
[*Exit* FAG.

Acres. You have business with Sir Anthony. — I expect a message from Mrs. Malaprop at my lodgings. I have sent also to my dear friend Sir Lucius O'Trigger. Adieu, Jack! we must meet at night, when you shall give me a dozen bumpers to little Lydia.

Abs. That I will with all my heart. — [*Exit* ACRES.] Now for a parental lecture — I hope he has heard nothing of the business that has brought me here—I wish the gout had held him fast in Devonshire, with all my soul!

Enter Sir Anthony Absolute.

Sir, I am delighted to see you here; looking so well! your sudden arrival at Bath made me apprehensive for your health.

Sir Anth. Very apprehensive, I dare say, Jack. — What, you are recruiting here, hey?

Abs. Yes, sir, I am on duty.

Sir Anth. Well, Jack, I am glad to see you, though I did not expect it, for I was going to write to you on a little matter of business. — Jack, I have been considering that I grow old and infirm, and shall probably not trouble you long.

Abs. Pardon me, sir, I never saw you look more strong and hearty; and I pray frequently that you may continue so.

Sir Anth. I hope your prayers may be heard, with all my heart. Well then, Jack, I have been considering that I am so strong and hearty I may continue to plague you a long time. Now, Jack, I am sensible that the income of your commission, and what I have hitherto allowed you, is but a small pittance for a lad of your spirit.

Abs. Sir, you are very good.

Sir Anth. And it is my wish, while yet I live, to have my boy make some figure in the world. I have resolved, therefore, to fix you at once in a noble independence.

Abs. Sir, your kindness overpowers me — such generosity makes the gratitude of reason more lively than the sensations even of filial affection.

Sir Anth. I am glad you are so sensible of my attention — and you shall be master of a large estate in a few weeks.

Abs. Let my future life, sir, speak my gratitude; I cannot express the sense I have of your munificence. — Yet, sir, I presume you would not wish me to quit the army?

Sir Anth. Oh, that shall be as your wife chooses.

Abs. My wife, sir!

Sir Anth. Ay, ay, settle that between you—settle that between you.

Abs. A wife, sir, did you say?

Sir Anth. Ay, a wife — why, did not I mention her before?

Abs. Not a word of her, sir.

Sir Anth. Odd so! — I mustn't forget her though. — Yes, Jack, the independence I was talking of is by a marriage — the fortune is saddled with a wife — but I suppose that makes no difference.

Abs. Sir! sir! — you amaze me!

Sir Anth. Why, what the devil's the matter with the fool? Just now you were all gratitude and duty.

Abs. I was, sir, — you talked to me of independence and a fortune, but not a word of a wife.

Sir Anth. Why — what difference does that make? Odds life, sir! if you have the estate, you must take it with the live stock on it, as it stands.

Abs. If my happiness is to be the price, I must beg leave to decline the purchase. — Pray, sir, who is the lady?

Sir Anth. What's that to you, sir? — Come, give me your promise to love, and to marry her directly.

Abs. Sure, sir, this is not very reasonable, to summon my affections for a lady I know nothing of!

Sir Anth. I am sure, sir, 'tis more unreasonable in you to object to a lady you know nothing of.

Abs. Then, sir, I must tell you plainly that my inclinations are fixed on another — my heart is engaged to an angel.

Sir Anth. Then pray let it send an excuse. It is very sorry — but business prevents its waiting on her.

Abs. But my vows are pledged to her.

Sir Anth. Let her foreclose, Jack; let her foreclose; they are not worth redeeming; besides, you have the angel's vows in exchange, I suppose; so there can be no loss there.

Abs. You must excuse me, sir, if I tell you, once for all, that in this point I cannot obey you.

Sir Anth. Hark'ee, Jack; — I have heard you for some time with patience — I have been cool — quite cool; but take care — you know I am compliance itself — when I am not thwarted; — no one more easily led — when I have my own way; — but don't put me in a frenzy.

Abs. Sir, I must repeat it — in this I cannot obey you.

Sir Anth. Now damn me! if ever I call you Jack again while I live!

Abs. Nay, sir, but hear me.

Sir. Anth. Sir, I won't hear a word — not a word! not one word! so give me your promise by a nod — and I'll tell you what, Jack — I mean, you dog — if you don't, by ——

Abs. What, sir, promise to link myself to some mass of ugliness! to ——

Sir Anth. Zounds! sirrah! the lady shall be as ugly as I choose: she shall have a hump on each shoulder; she shall be as crooked as the crescent; her one eye shall roll like the bull's in Cox's Museum; she shall have a skin like a mummy, and the beard of a Jew — she shall be all this, sirrah! — yet I will make you ogle her all day, and sit up all night to write sonnets on her beauty.

Abs. This is reason and moderation indeed!

Sir Anth. None of your sneering, puppy! no grinning, jackanapes!

Abs. Indeed, sir, I never was in a worse humour for mirth in my life.

Sir Anth. 'Tis false, sir, I know you are laughing in your sleeve; I know you'll grin when I am gone, sirrah!

Abs. Sir; I hope I know my duty better.

Sir Anth. None of your passion, sir! none of your violence, if you please! — It won't do with me, I promise you.

Abs. Indeed, sir, I never was cooler in my life.

Sir Anth. 'Tis a confounded lie! — I know you are in a passion in your heart; I know you are, you hypocritical young dog! but it won't do.

Abs. Nay, sir, upon my word ——

Sir Anth. So you will fly out! can't you be cool like me? What the devil good can passion do? — Passion is of no service, you impudent, insolent, overbearing reprobate! — There, you sneer again! don't provoke me! — but you rely upon the mildness of my temper — you do, you dog! you play upon the meekness of my disposition! — Yet take care — the patience of a saint may be overcome at last! — but mark! I

give you six hours and a half to consider of this: if you then
agree, without any condition, to do every thing on earth that
I choose, why — confound you! I may in time forgive you.
— If not, zounds! don't enter the same hemisphere with me!
don't dare to breathe the same air, or use the same light with
me; but get an atmosphere and a sun of your own! I'll strip
you of your commission; I'll lodge a five-and-threepence in
the hands of trustees, and you shall live on the interest. — I'll
disown you, I'll disinherit you, I'll unget you! and damn me!
if ever I call you Jack again!   [*Exit.*

Abs. Mild, gentle, considerate father — I kiss your hands!
— What a tender method of giving his opinion in these matters Sir Anthony has! I dare not trust him with the truth.
— I wonder what old wealthy hag it is that he wants to
bestow on me! — Yet he married himself for love! and was in
his youth a bold intriguer, and a gay companion!

Re-enter FAG.

Fag. Assuredly, sir, your father is wrath to a degree; he
comes down stairs eight or ten steps at a time — muttering,
growling, and thumping the banisters all the way: I and the
cook's dog stand bowing at the door — rap! he gives me a
stroke on the head with his cane; bids me carry that to my
master; then kicking the poor turnspit into the area, damns
us all, for a puppy triumvirate! — Upon my credit, sir, were
I in your place, and found my father such very bad company,
I should certainly drop his acquaintance.

Abs. Cease your impertinence, sir, at present. — Did you
come in for nothing more? — Stand out of the way!
                            [*Pushes him aside, and exit.*

Fag. So! Sir Anthony trims my master: he is afraid to
reply to his father — then vents his spleen on poor Fag! —
When one is vexed by one person, to revenge one's self on
another, who happens to come in the way, is the vilest in-
justice! Ah! it shows the worst temper — the basest ——

Enter BOY.

Boy. Mr. Fag! Mr. Fag! your master calls you.
3*

Fag. Well, you little dirty puppy, you need not bawl so!
— The meanest disposition! the ——

Boy. Quick, quick, Mr. Fag!

Fag. Quick! quick! you impudent jackanapes! am I to
be commanded by you too? you little impertinent. insolent,
kitchen-bred ——   [*Exit kicking and beating him.*

Scene II. — *The North Parade.*

Enter Lucy.

Lucy. So—I shall have another rival to add to my mistress's
list — Captain Absolute. However, I shall not enter his name
till my purse has received notice in form. Poor Acres is dis-
missed! — Well, I have done him a last friendly office, in
letting him know that Beverley was here before him. — Sir
Lucius is generally more punctual, when he expects to hear
from his *dear Dalia*, as he calls her: I wonder he's not here!
—I have a little scruple of conscience from this deceit; though
I should not be paid so well, if my hero knew that Delia was
near fifty, and her own mistress.

Enter Sir Lucius O'Trigger.

Sir Luc. Ha! my little ambassadress — upon my conscience, I have been looking for you; I have been on the
South Parade this half hour.

Lucy. [*Speaking simply.*] O gemini! and I have been waiting for your worship here on the North.

Sir Luc. Faith! — may be that was the reason we did not
meet; and it is very comical too, how you could go out and I
not see you — for I was only taking a nap at the Parade
Coffee-house, and I chose the window on purpose that I might
not miss you.

Lucy. My stars! Now I'd wager a sixpence I went by
while you were asleep.

Sir Luc. Sure enough it must have been so — and I never
dreamt it was so late, till I waked. Well, but my little girl,
have you got nothing for me?

Lucy. Yes, but I have — I've got a letter for you in my
pocket.

Sir Luc. O faith! I guessed you weren't come empty-handed. — Well — let me see what the dear creature says.

Lucy. There, Sir Lucius. [*Gives him a letter.*

Sir Luc. [Reads.] *Sir—there is often a sudden incentive impulse in love, that has a greater induction than years of domestic combination: such was the commotion I felt at the first superfluous view of Sir Lucius O'Trigger.* — Very pretty, upon my word. — *Female punctuation forbids me to say more; yet let me add, that it will give me joy infallible to find Sir Lucius worthy the last criterion of my affections.* DELIA.
Upon my conscience! Lucy, your lady is a great mistress of language Faith, she's quite the queen of the dictionary! — for the devil a word dare refuse coming at her call — though one would think it was quite out of hearing.

Lucy. Ay, sir, a lady of her experience——

Sir Luc. Experience! what, at seventeen?

Lucy. O true, sir—but then she reads so—my stars! how she will read off hand!

Sir Luc. Faith, she must be very deep read to write this way — though she is rather an arbitrary writer too — for here are a great many poor words pressed into the service of this note, that would get their *habeas corpus* from any court in Christendom.

Lucy. Ah! Sir Lucius, if you were to hear how she talks of you!

Sir Luc. Oh, tell her I'll make her the best husband in the world, and Lady O'Trigger into the bargain! — But we must get the old gentlewoman's consent—and do every thing fairly.

Lucy. Nay, Sir Lucius, I thought you wa'n't rich enough to be so nice!

Sir Luc. Upon my word, young woman, you have hit it:— I am so poor, that I can't afford to do a dirty action. — If I did not want money, I'd steal your mistress and her fortune with a great deal of pleasure. — However, my pretty girl, [*Gives her money,*] here's a little something to buy you a ribbon; and meet me in the evening, and I'll give you an an-

swer to this. So, hussy, take a kiss beforehand to put you
in mind.   [*Kisses her*.

Lucy. O Lud! Sir Lucius — I never seed such a gemuuan!
My lady won't like you if you're so impudent.

Sir Luc. Faith she will, Lucy!—That same—pho! what's
the name of it? — modesty — is a quality in a lover more
praised by the women than liked; so, if your mistress asks
you whether Sir Lucius ever gave you a kiss, tell her fifty —
my dear.

Lucy. What, would you have me tell her a lie?

Sir Luc. Ah, then, you baggage! I'll make it a truth
presently.

Lucy. For shame now! here is some one coming.

Sir. Luc. Oh, faith, I'll quiet your conscience!
                          [*Exit, humming a tune.*

Enter FAG.

Fag. So, so, ma'am! I humbly beg pardon.

Lucy. O Lud! now, Mr. Fag — you flurry one so.

Fag. Come, come, Lucy, here's no one by—so a little less
simplicity, with a grain or two more sincerity, if you please.
— You play false with us, madam. — I saw you give the baronet a letter. — My master shall know this — and if he don't
call him out, I will.

Lucy. Ha! ha! ha! you gentlemen's gentlemen are so
hasty. — That letter was from Mrs. Malaprop, simpleton. —
She is taken with Sir Lucius's address.

Fag. How! what tastes some people have! — Why, I suppose I have walked by her window a hundred times. — But
what says our young lady? any message to my master?

Lucy. Sad news, Mr. Fag. — A worse rival than Acres!
Sir Anthony Absolute has proposed his son.

Fag. What, Captain Absolute?

Lucy. Even so — I overheard it all.

Fag. Ha! ha! ha! very good, faith. Good bye, Lucy, I
must away with this news.

Lucy. Well you may laugh — but it is true, I assure you.

— [*Going.*] But, Mr. Fag, tell your master not to be cast down by this.

Fag. Oh, he'll be so disconsolate!

Lucy. And charge him not to think of quarrelling with young Absolute.

Fag. Never fear! never fear!

Lucy. Be sure — bid him keep up his spirits.

Fag. We will — we will.   [*Exeunt severally.*

ACT III.

Scene I. — *The North Parade.*

Enter Captain Absolute.

Abs. 'Tis just as Fag told me, indeed. Whimsical enough, faith! My father wants to force me to marry the very girl I am plotting to run away with! He must not know of my connection with her yet awhile. He has too summary a method of proceeding in these matters. However, I'll read my recantation instantly. My conversion is something sudden, indeed — but I can assure him it is very sincere. So, so — here he comes. He looks plaguy gruff.   [*Steps aside.*

Enter Sir Anthony Absolute.

Sir Anth. No — I'll die sooner than forgive him. Die, did I say? I'll live these fifty years to plague him. At our last meeting, his impudence had almost put me out of temper. An obstinate, passionate, self-willed boy! Who can he take after? This is my return for getting him before all his brothers and sisters! — for putting him, at twelve years old, into a marching regiment, and allowing him fifty pounds a year, besides his pay, ever since! But I have done with him; he's anybody's son for me. I never will see him more, never — never — never.

Abs. [*Aside, coming forward.*] Now for a penitential face.

Sir Anth. Fellow, get out of my way!

Abs. Sir, you see a penitent before you.

Sir Anth. I see an impudent scoundrel before me.

Abs. A sincere penitent. I am come, sir, to acknowledge my error, and to submit entirely to your will.

Sir Anth. What's that?

Abs. I have been revolving, and reflecting, and considering, on your past goodness, and kindness, and condescension to me.

Sir Anth. Well, sir?

Abs. I have been likewise weighing and balancing what you were pleased to mention concerning duty, and obedience, and authority.

Sir Anth. Well, puppy?

Abs. Why then, sir, the result of my reflections is — a resolution to sacrifice every inclination of my own to your satisfaction.

Sir Anth. Why now you talk sense — absolute sense — I never heard any thing more sensible in my life. Confound you! you shall be Jack again.

Abs. I am happy in the appellation.

Sir Anth. Why then, Jack, my dear Jack, I will now inform you who the lady really is. Nothing but your passion and violence, you silly fellow, prevented my telling you at first. Prepare, Jack, for wonder and rapture — prepare. What think you of Miss Lydia Languish?

Abs. Languish! What, the Languishes of Worcestershire?

Sir Anth. Worcestershire! no. Did you never meet Mrs. Malaprop and her niece, Miss Languish, who came into our country just before you were last ordered to your regiment?

Abs. Malaprop! Languish! I don't remember ever to have heard the names before. Yet, stay — I think I do recollect something. Languish! Languish! She squints, don't she? A little red-haired girl?

Sir Anth. Squints! A red-haired girl! Zounds! no.

Abs. Then I must have forgot; it can't be the same person.

Sir Anth. Jack! Jack! what think you of blooming, love-breathing seventeen?

Abs. As to that, sir, I am quite indifferent. If I can please you in the matter, 'tis all I desire.

Sir Anth. Nay, but Jack, such eyes! such eyes! so inno-

cently wild! so bashfully irresolute! not a glance but speaks
and kindles some thought of love! Then, Jack, her cheeks!
her cheeks, Jack! so deeply blushing at the insinuations of
her tell-tale eyes! Then, Jack, her lips! O Jack, lips smiling
at their own discretion; and if not smiling, more sweetly
pouting; more lovely in sullenness!

Abs. That's she indeed. Well done, old gentleman. [*Aside.*

Sir Anth. Then, Jack, her neck! O Jack! Jack!

Abs. And which is to be mine, sir, the niece, or the aunt?

Sir Anth. Why, you unfeeling, insensible puppy, I despise
you! When I was of your age, such a description would have
made me fly like a rocket! The aunt indeed! Odds life!
when I ran away with your mother, I would not have touched
any thing old or ugly to gain an empire.

Abs. Not to please your father, sir?

Sir Anth. To please my father! zounds! not to please —
Oh, my father—odd so!—yes — yes; if my father indeed had
desired—that's quite another matter. Though he wa'n't the
indulgent father that I am, Jack.

Abs. I dare say not, sir.

Sir Anth. But, Jack, you are not sorry to find your mistress is so beautiful?

Abs. Sir, I repeat it — if I please you in this affair, 'tis
all I desire. Not that I think a woman the worse for being
handsome; but, sir, if you please to recollect, you before
hinted something about a hump or two, one eye, and a few
more graces of that kind — now, without being very nice, I
own I should rather choose a wife of mine to have the usual
number of limbs, and a limited quantity of back: and though
one eye may be very agreeable, yet as the prejudice has always run in favour of two, I would not wish to affect a sin-
gularity in that article.

Sir Anth. What a phlegmatic sot it is! Why, sirrah,
you're an anchorite! — a vile, insensible stock. You a soldier! — you're a walking block, fit only to dust the company's regimentals on! Odds life! I have a great mind to
marry the girl myself.

Abs. I am entirely at your disposal, sir: if you should think of addressing Miss Languish yourself, I suppose you would have me marry the aunt; or if you should change your mind, and take the old lady — 'tis the same to me — I'll marry the niece.

Sir Anth. Upon my word, Jack, thou'rt either a very great hypocrite, or — but, come, I know your indifference on such a subject must be all a lie — I'm sure it must — come, now — damn your demure face! — come, confess Jack — you have been lying — ha'n't you? You have been playing the hypocrite, hey! — I'll never forgive you, if you ha'n't been lying and playing the hypocrite.

Abs. I'm sorry, sir, that the respect and duty which I bear to you should be so mistaken.

Sir Anth. Hang your respect and duty! But come along with me, I'll write a note to Mrs. Malaprop, and you shall visit the lady directly. Her eyes shall be the Promethean torch to you — come along, I'll never forgive you, if you don't come back stark mad with rapture and impatience — if you don't, egad, I will marry the girl myself! [*Exeunt.*

Scene II. — Julia's *Dressing-room.*

Faulkland *discovered alone.*

Faulk. They told me Julia would return directly; I wonder she is not yet come! How mean does this captious, unsatisfied temper of mine appear to my cooler judgment! Yet I know not that I indulge it in any other point: but on this one subject, and to this one subject, whom I think I love beyond my life, I am ever ungenerously fretful and madly capricious! I am conscious of it — yet I cannot correct myself! What tender honest joy sparkled in her eyes when we met! how delicate was the warmth of her expressions! I was ashamed to appear less happy — though I had come resolved to wear a face of coolness and upbraiding. Sir Anthony's presence prevented my proposed expostulations: yet I must be satisfied that she has not been so very happy in my

absence. She is coming! Yes!—I know the nimbleness of
her tread, when she thinks her impatient Faulkland counts
the moments of her stay.

Enter JULIA.

Jul. I had not hoped to see you again so soon.

Faulk. Could I, Julia, be contented with my first welcome — restrained as we were by the presence of a third
person?

Jul. O Faulkland, when your kindness can make me thus
happy, let me not think that I discovered something of coldness in your first salutation.

Faulk. 'Twas but your fancy, Julia. I was rejoiced to
see you — to see you in such health. Sure I had no cause
for coldness?

Jul. Nay then, I see you have taken something ill. You
must not conceal from me what it is.

Faulk. Well, then — shall I own to you that my joy at
hearing of your health and arrival here, by your neighbour
Acres, was somewhat damped by his dwelling much on the
high spirits you had enjoyed in Devonshire — on your mirth —
your singing — dancing, and I know not what! For such is
my temper, Julia, that I should regard every mirthful
moment in your absence as a treason to constancy. The
mutual tear that steals down the cheek of parting lovers is a
compact, that no smile shall live there till they meet again.

Jul. Must I never cease to tax my Faulkland with this
teasing minute caprice? Can the idle reports of a silly boor
weigh in your breast against my tried affection?

Faulk. They have no weight with me, Julia: No, no — I
am happy if you have been so — yet only say, that you did
not sing with mirth — say that you thought of Faulkland in
the dance.

Jul. I never can be happy in your absence. If I wear a
countenance of content, it is to show that my mind holds no
doubt of my Faulkland's truth. If I seemed sad, it were to
make malice triumph; and say, that I had fixed my heart

on one, who left me to lament his roving, and my own cre-
dulity. Believe me, Faulkland, I mean not to upbraid you,
when I say, that I have often dressed sorrow in smiles, lest
my friends should guess whose unkindness had caused my
tears.

Faulk. You were ever all goodness to me. Oh, I am a
brute, when I but admit a doubt of your true constancy!

Jul. If ever without such cause from you, as I will not
suppose possible, you find my affections veering but a point,
may I become a proverbial scoff for levity and base ingratitude.

Faulk. Ah! Julia, that last word is grating to me. I
would I had no title to your gratitude! Search your heart,
Julia; perhaps what you have mistaken for love, is but the
warm effusion of a too thankful heart.

Jul. For what quality must I love you?

Faulk. For no quality! To regard me for any quality
of mind or understanding, were only to esteem me. And
for person—I have often wished myself deformed, to be convinced that I owed no obligation there for any part of your
affection.

Jul. Where nature has bestowed a show of nice attention
in the features of a man, he should laugh at it as misplaced. I
have seen men, who in this vain article, perhaps, might rank
above you; but my heart has never asked my eyes if it were
so or not.

Faulk. Now this is not well from you, Julia — I despise
person in a man — yet if you loved me as I wish, though I
were an Æthiop, you'd think none so fair.

Jul. I see you are determined to be unkind! The con-
tract which my poor father bound us in gives you more than
a lover's privilege.

Faulk. Again, Julia, you raise ideas that feed and justify
my doubts. I would not have been more free — no — I am
proud of my restraint. Yet — yet — perhaps your high respect alone for this solemn compact has fettered your inclinations, which else had made a worthier choice. How shall I

be sure, had you remained unbound in thought and promise,
that I should still have been the object of your persevering
love?

Jul. Then try me now. Let us be free as strangers as to
what is past: my heart will not feel more liberty!

Faulk. There now! so hasty, Julia! so anxious to be free!
If your love for me were fixed and ardent, you would not lose
your hold, even though I wished it!

Jul. Oh! you torture me to the heart! I cannot bear it.

Faulk. I do not mean to distress you. If I loved you less
I should never give you an uneasy moment. But hear me.
All my fretful doubts arise from this. Women are not used
to weigh and separate the motives of their affections: the
cold dictates of prudence, gratitude, or filial duty, may sometimes be mistaken for the pleadings of the heart. I would
not boast — yet let me say, that I have neither age, person,
nor character, to found dislike on; my fortune such as few
ladies could be charged with indiscretion in the match. O
Julia! when love receives such countenance from prudence,
nice minds will be suspicious of its birth.

Jul. I know not whither your insinuations would tend:—
but as they seem pressing to insult me, I will spare you the
regret of having done so. — I have given you no cause for
this!   •   [*Exit in tears.*

Faulk. In tears! Stay, Julia: stay but for a moment.—
The door is fastened!—Julia!—my soul—but for one moment!
— I hear her sobbing! — 'Sdeath! what a brute am I to use
her thus! Yet stay. — Ay — she is coming now: — how little
resolution there is in woman! — how a few soft words can
turn them! — No, faith! — she is not coming either. — Why,
Julia — my love — say but that you forgive me — come but
to tell me that — now this is being too resentful. Stay! she
is coming too — I thought she would — no steadiness in any
thing: her going away must have been a mere trick then —
she sha'n't see that I was hurt by it. — I'll affect indifference
[*Hums a tune: then listens.*] No — zounds! she's not coming!
— nor don't intend it, I suppose. — This is not steadiness,

but obstinacy! Yet I deserve it. — What, after so long an
absence to quarrel with her tenderness! — 'twas barbarous
and unmanly! — I should be ashamed to see her now. — I'll
wait till her just resentment is abated — and when I distress
her so again, may I lose her for ever! and be linked instead
to some antique virago, whose gnawing passions, and long
hoarded spleen, shall make me curse my folly half the day
and all the night.   [*Exit.*

SCENE III. — MRS. MALAPROP'S *Lodgings.*

MRS. MALAPROP, *with a letter in her hand*, *and* CAPTAIN
ABSOLUTE.

Mrs. Mal. Your being Sir Anthony's son, captain, would
itself be a sufficient accommodation; but from the ingenuity
of your appearance, I am convinced you deserve the character
here given of you.

Abs. Permit me to say, madam, that as I never yet have
had the pleasure of seeing Miss Languish, my principal inducement in this affair at present is the honour of being allied
to Mrs. Malaprop; of whose intellectual accomplishments,
elegant manners, and unaffected learning, no tongue is silent.

Mrs. Mal. Sir, you do me infinite honour! I beg, captain,
you'll be seated. — [*They sit.*] Ah! few gentlemen, now-a-
days, know how to value the ineffectual qualities in a woman!
few think how a little knowledge becomes a gentlewoman! —
Men have no sense now but for the worthless flower of
beauty!

Abs. It is but too true, indeed, ma'am; — yet I fear our
ladies should share the blame — they think our admiration of
beauty so great, that knowledge in them would be superfluous.
Thus, like garden-trees, they seldom show fruit, till time has
robbed them of the more specious blossom. — Few, like Mrs.
Malaprop and the orange-tree, are rich in both at once!

Mrs. Mal. Sir, you overpower me with good-breeding. —
He is the very pine-apple of politeness! — You are not ignorant, captain, that this giddy girl has somehow contrived to

fix her affections on a beggarly, strolling, caves-dropping ensign, whom none of us have seen, and nobody knows anything of.

Abs. Oh, I have heard the silly affair before. — I'm not at all prejudiced against her on that account.

Mrs. Mal. You are very good and very considerate, captain. I am sure I have done every thing in my power since I exploded the affair; long ago I laid my positive conjunctions on her, never to think on the fellow again; — I have since laid Sir Anthony's preposition before her; but, I am sorry to say, she seems resolved to decline every particle that I enjoin her.

Abs. It must be very distressing, indeed, ma'am.

Mrs. Mal. Oh! it gives me the hydrostatics to such a degree. — I thought she had persisted from corresponding with him; but, behold, this very day, I have interceded another letter from the fellow; I believe I have it in my pocket.

Abs. Oh, the devil! my last note.   [*Aside.*

Mrs. Mal. Ay, here it is.

Abs. Ay, my note indeed! O the little traitress Lucy.   [*Aside.*

Mrs. Mal. There, perhaps you may know the writing.   [*Gives him the letter.*

Abs. I think I have seen the hand before — yes, I certainly must have seen this hand before —

Mrs. Mal. Nay, but read it, captain.

Abs. [Reads.] *My soul's idol, my adored Lydia!* — Very tender indeed!

Mrs. Mal. Tender! ay, and profane too, o' my conscience.

Abs. [Reads.] *I am excessively alarmed at the intelligence you send me, the more so as my new rival* ——

Mrs. Mal. That's you, sir.

Abs. [Reads.] *Has universally the character of being an accomplished gentleman and a man of honour.* — Well, that's handsome enough.

Mrs. Mal. Oh, the fellow has some design in writing so.

Abs. That he had, I'll answer for him, ma'am.

Mrs. Mal. But go on, sir — you'll see presently.

Abs. [Reads.] *As for the old weather-beaten she-dragon who guards you* — Who can he mean by that?

Mrs. Mal. Me, sir! — me! — he means me! — There — what do you think now? — but go on a little further.

Abs. Impudent scoundrel! — [Reads.] *it shall go hard but I will elude her vigilance, as I am told that the same ridiculous vanity, which makes her dress up her coarse features, and deck her dull chat with hard words which she don't understand* ——

Mrs. Mal. There, sir, an attack upon my language! what do you think of that? — an aspersion upon my parts of speech! was ever such a brute! Sure, if I reprehend any thing in this world, it is the use of my oracular tongue, and a nice derangement of epitaphs!

Abs. He deserves to be hanged and quartered! let me see — [Reads.] *same ridiculous vanity* ——

Mrs. Mal. You need not read it again, sir.

Abs. I beg pardon, ma'am. — [Reads.] *does also lay her open to the grossest deceptions from flattery and pretended admiration* — an impudent coxcomb! — *so that I have a scheme to see you shortly with the old harridan's consent, and even to make her a go-between in our interview.* — Was ever such assurance!

Mrs. Mal. Did you ever hear any thing like it? — he'll elude my vigilance, will he — yes, yes! ha! ha! he's very likely to enter these doors; — we'll try who can plot best!

Abs. So we will, ma'am — so we will! Ha! ha! ha! a conceited puppy, ha! ha! ha! — Well, but Mrs. Malaprop, as the girl seems so infatuated by this fellow, suppose you were to wink at her corresponding with him for a little time — let her even plot an elopement with him — then do you connive at her escape — while I, just in the nick, will have the fellow laid by the heels, and fairly contrive to carry her off in his stead.

Mrs. Mal. I am delighted with the scheme; never was anything better perpetrated!

Abs. But, pray, could not I see the lady for a few minutes now? — I should like to try her temper a little

Mrs. Mal. Why, I don't know — I doubt she is not prepared for a visit of this kind.   There is a decorum in these
matters.

Abs. O Lord! she won't mind me — only tell her Beverley ——

Mrs. Mal. Sir!

Abs. Gently, good tongue.   [*Aside.*

Mrs. Mal. What did you say of Beverley?

Abs. Oh, I was going to propose that you should tell her,
by way of jest, that it was Beverley who was below; she'd
come down fast enough then — ha! ha! ha!

Mrs. Mal. 'Twould be a trick she well deserves; besides,
you know the fellow tells her he'll get my consent to see
her — ha! ha! Let him if he can, I say again.   Lydia, come
down here! — [*Calling.*]   He'll make me a go-between in
their interviews! — ha! ha! ha!   Come down, I say, Lydia!
I don't wonder at your laughing, ha! ha! ha! his impudence
is truly ridiculous.

Abs. 'Tis very ridiculous, upon my soul, ma'am, ha!
ha! ha!

Mrs. Mal. The little hussy won't hear.   Well, I'll go and
tell her at once who it is — she shall know that Captain Absolute is come to wait on her.   And I'll make her behave as
becomes a young woman.

Abs. As you please, ma'am.

Mrs. Mal. For the present, captain, your servant.   Ah!
you've not done laughing yet, I see — elude my vigilance;
yes, yes; ha! ha! ha!   [*Exit.*

Abs. Ha! ha! ha! one would think now that I might throw
off all disguise at once, and seize my prize with security; but
such is Lydia's caprice, that to undeceive were probably to
lose her.   I'll see whether she knows me.

        [*Walks aside, and seems engaged in looking at the pic-
        tures.*

                    Enter LYDIA.

Lyd. What a scene am I now to go through! surely nothing can be more dreadful than to be obliged to listen to the

loathsome addresses of a stranger to one's heart. I have heard of girls persecuted as I am, who have appealed in behalf of their favoured lover to the generosity of his rival, suppose I were to try it — there stands the hated rival — an officer too! — but oh, how unlike my Beverley! I wonder he don't begin — truly he seems a very negligent wooer! — quite at his ease, upon my word! — I'll speak first — Mr. Absolute.

Abs. Ma'am.   [*Turns round.*

Lyd. O heavens! Beverley!

Abs. Hush! — hush, my life! softly! be not surprised!

Lyd. I am so astonished! and so terrified! and so over-joyed! — for Heaven's sake! how came you here?

Abs. Briefly, I have deceived your aunt— I was informed that my new rival was to visit here this evening, and con-triving to have him kept away, have passed myself on her for Captain Absolute.

Lyd. O charming! And she really takes you for young Absolute?

Abs. Oh, she's convinced of it.

Lyd. Ha! ha! ha! I can't forbear laughing to think how her sagacity is overreached!

Abs. But we trifle with our precious moments — such an-other opportunity may not occur; then let me now conjure my kind, my condescending angel, to fix the time when I may rescue her from undeserving persecution, and with a licensed warmth plead for my reward.

Lyd. Will you then, Beverley, consent to forfeit that portion of my paltry wealth? — that burden on the wings of love?

Abs. Oh, come to me — rich only thus — in loveliness! Bring no portion to me but thy love — 'twill be generous in you, Lydia — for well you know, it is the only dower your poor Beverley can repay.

Lyd. How persuasive are his words! — how charming will poverty be with him!   [*Aside.*

Abs. Ah! my soul, what a life will we then live! Love shall be our idol and support! we will worship him with a

monastic strictness; abjuring all worldly toys, to centre every
thought and action there. Proud of calamity, we will enjoy
the wreck of wealth; while the surrounding gloom of ad-
versity shall make the flame of our pure love show doubly
bright. By Heavens! I would fling all goods of fortune from
me with a prodigal hand, to enjoy the scene where I might
clasp my Lydia to my bosom, and say, the world affords no
smile to me but here — [*Embracing her.*]   If she holds out
now, the devil is in it!   [*Aside.*

Lyd. Now could I fly with him to the antipodes! but my
persecution is not yet come to a crisis.   [*Aside.*

        Re-enter MRS. MALAPROP, *listening.*

Mrs. Mal. I am impatient to know how the little hussy
deports herself.   [*Aside.*
Abs. So pensive, Lydia! — is then your warmth abated?
Mrs. Mal. Warmth abated! — so! — she has been in a
passion, I suppose.   [*Aside.*
Lyd. No — nor ever can while I have life.
Mrs. Mal. An ill tempered little devil! She'll be in a pas-
sion all her life — will she?   [*Aside.*
Lyd. Think not the idle threats of my ridiculous aunt can
ever have any weight with me.
Mrs. Mal. Very dutiful, upon my word!   [*Aside.*
Lyd. Let her choice be Captain Absolute, but Beverley
is mine.
Mrs. Mal. I am astonished at her assurance! — to his
face — this is to his face!   [*Aside.*
Abs. Thus then let me enforce my suit.   [*Kneeling.*
Mrs. Mal. [*Aside.*] Ay, poor young man! — down on his
knees entreating for pity! — I can contain no longer. —
[*Coming forward.*] Why, thou vixen!—I have overheard you.
Abs. Oh, confound her vigilance!   [*Aside.*
Mrs. Mal. Captain Absolute, I know not how to apolo-
gize for her shocking rudeness.
Abs. [*Aside.*] So all's safe, I find. — [*Aloud.*] I have hopes,
madam, that time will bring the young lady ——
                                                    4*

Mrs. Mal. Oh, there's nothing to be hoped for from her! she's as headstrong as an allegory on the banks of Nile.

Lyd. Nay, madam, what do you charge me with now?

Mrs. Mal. Why, thou unblushing rebel — didn't you tell this gentleman to his face that you loved another better? — didn't you say you never would be his?

Lyd. No, madam — I did not.

Mrs. Mal. Good Heavens! what assurance! — Lydia, Lydia, you ought to know that lying don't become a young woman! — Didn't you boast that Beverley, that stroller Beverley, possessed your heart? — Tell me that, I say.

Lyd. 'Tis true, ma'am, and none but Beverley ——

Mrs. Mal. Hold! — hold, Assurance! — you shall not be so rude.

Abs. Nay, pray, Mrs. Malaprop, don't stop the young lady's speech: she's very welcome to talk thus — it does not hurt me in the least, I assure you.

Mrs. Mal. You are too good, captain — too amiably patient — but come with me, miss. — Let us see you again soon, captain — remember what we have fixed.

Abs. I shall ma'am.

Mrs. Mal. Come, take a graceful leave of the gentleman.

Lyd. May every blessing wait on my Beverley, my loved Bev ——

Mrs. Mal. Hussy! I'll choke the word in your throat! — come along — come along.

    [*Exeunt severally;* CAPTAIN ABSOLUTE *kissing his hand to*
       LYDIA — Mrs. MALAPROP *stopping her from speaking.*

SCENE IV. — ACRES' *Lodgings.*

ACRES, *as just dressed, and* DAVID.

Acres. Indeed, David — do you think I become it so?

Dav. You are quite another creature, believe me, master, by the mass! an' we've any luck we shall see the Devon monkerony in all the print-shops in Bath!

Acres. Dress does make a difference, David.

Dav. 'Tis all in all, I think. — Difference! why, an' you were to go now to Clod-hall, I am certain the old lady wouldn't know you: master Butler wouldn't believe his own eyes, and Mrs. Pickle would cry, Lard presarve me! our dairy-maid would come giggling to the door, and I warrant Dolly Tester, your honour's favourite, would blush like my waistcoat. — Oons! I'll hold a gallon, there an't a dog in the house but would bark, and I question whether Phillis would wag a hair of her tail!

Acres. Ay, David, there's nothing like polishing.

Dav. So I says of your honour's boots; but the boy never heeds me!

Acres. But, David, has Mr. De-la-grace been here? I must rub up my balancing, and chasing, and boring.

Dav. I'll call again, sir.

Acres. Do — and see if there are any letters for me at the post-office.

Dav. I will. — By the mass, I can't help looking at your head! — if I hadn't been by at the cooking, I wish I may die if I should have known the dish again myself! [*Exit.*

Acres. [*Practising a dancing-step.*] Sink, slide — coupee. — Confound the first inventors of cotillons! say I — they are as bad as algebra to us country gentlemen — I can walk a minuet easy enough when I am forced! — and I have been accounted a good stick in a country-dance. — Odds jigs and tabors! I never valued your cross-over to couple — figure in — right and left — and I'd foot it with e'er a captain in the county! — but these outlandish heathen allemandes and cotillons are quite beyond me! — I shall never prosper at 'em, that's sure — mine are true-born English legs — they don't understand their curst French lingo! — their *pas* this, and *pas* that, and *pas* t'other! — damn me! my feet don't like to be called paws! no, 'tis certain I have most Antigallican toes!

Enter SERVANT.

Serv. Here is Sir Lucius O'Trigger to wait on you, sir.

Acres. Show him in. [*Exit* SERVANT.

Enter Sir Lucius O"Trigger.

Sir Luc. Mr. Acres, I am delighted to embrace you.

Acres. My dear Sir Lucius, I kiss your hands.

Sir Luc. Pray, my friend, what has brought you so suddenly to Bath?

Acres. Faith! I have followed Cupid's Jack-a-lantern, and find myself in a quagmire at last. — In short, I have been very ill used, Sir Lucius. — I don't choose to mention names, but look on me as on a very ill-used gentleman.

Sir Luc. Pray what is the case? — I ask no names.

Acres. Mark me, Sir Lucius, I fall as deep as need be in love with a young lady — her friends take my part — I follow her to Bath — send word of my arrival; and receive answer, that the lady is to be otherwise disposed of. — This, Sir Lucius, I call being ill used.

Sir Luc. Very ill, upon my conscience. — Pray, can you divine the cause of it?

Acres. Why, there's the matter; she has another lover, one Beverley, who, I am told, is now in Bath. — Odds slanders and lies! he must be at the bottom of it.

Sir Luc. A rival in the case, is there? — and you think he has supplanted you unfairly?

Acres. Unfairly! to be sure he has. He never could have done it fairly.

Sir Luc. Then sure you know what is to be done!

Acres. Not I, upon my soul!

Sir Luc. We wear no swords here, but you understand me.

Acres. What! fight him!

Sir Luc. Ay, to be sure: what can I mean else?

Acres. But he has given me no provocation.

Sir Luc. Now, I think he has given you the greatest provocation in the world. Can a man commit a more heinous offence against another than to fall in love with the same woman? Oh, by my soul! it is the most unpardonable breach of friendship.

Acres. Breach of friendship! ay, ay; but I have no acquaintance with this man. I never saw him in my life.

Sir Luc. That's no argument at all—he has the less right then to take such a liberty.

Acres. Gad, that's true—I grow full of anger, Sir Lucius! —I fire apace! Odds hilts and blades! I find a man may have a deal of valour in him, and not know it! But couldn't I contrive to have a little right of my side?

Sir Luc. What the devil signifies right, when your honour is concerned? Do you think Achilles, or my little Alexander the Great, ever inquired where the right lay? No, by my soul, they drew their broad-swords, and left the lazy sons of peace to settle the justice of it.

Acres. Your words are a grenadier's march to my heart! I believe courage must be catching! I certainly do feel a kind of valour rising as it were — a kind of courage, as I may say. — Odds flints, pans, and triggers! I'll challenge him directly.

Sir Luc. Ah, my little friend, if I had Blunderbuss Hall here, I could show you a range of ancestry, in the O"Trigger line, that would furnish the new room; every one of whom had killed his man! — For though the mansion-house and dirty acres have slipped through my fingers, I thank heaven our honour and the family-pictures are as fresh as ever.

Acres. O, Sir Lucius! I have had ancestors too! — every man of 'em colonel or captain in the militia!—Odds balls and barrels! say no more—I'm braced for it. The thunder of your words has soured the milk of human kindness in my breast;— Zounds! as the man in the play says, *I could do such deeds!*

Sir Luc. Come, come, there must be no passion at all in the case — these things should always be done civilly.

Acres. I must be in a passion, Sir Lucius — I must be in a rage. — Dear Sir Lucius, let me be in a rage, if you love me. Come, here's pen and paper. — [*Sits down to write.*] I would the ink were red! — Indite, I say indite! — How shall I begin? Odds bullets and blades! I'll write a good bold hand, however.

Sir Luc. Pray compose yourself.

Acres. Come — now, shall I begin with an oath? Do, Sir Lucius, let me begin with a damme.

Sir Luc. Pho! pho! do the thing decently, and like a Christian. Begin now — *Sir* ——

Acres. That's too civil by half.

Sir Luc. *To prevent the confusion that might arise* ——

Acres. Well ——

Sir Luc. *From our both addressing the same lady* ——

Acres. Ay, there's the reason — *same lady* — well ——

Sir Luc. *I shall expect the honour of your company* ——

Acres. Zounds! I'm not asking him to dinner.

Sir Luc. Pray be easy.

Acres. Well then, *honour of your company* ——

Sir Luc. *To settle our pretensions* ——

Acres. Well.

Sir Luc. Let me see, ay, King's-Mead-Field will do — *in King's-Mead-Fields.*

Acres. So, that's done — Well, I'll fold it up presently; my own crest — a hand and dagger shall be the seal.

Sir Luc. You see now this little explanation will put a stop at once to all confusion or misunderstanding that might arise between you.

Acres. Ay, we fight to prevent any misunderstanding.

Sir Luc. Now, I'll leave you to fix your own time. — Take my advice, and you'll decide it this evening if you can; then let the worst come of it, 'twill be off your mind to-morrow.

Acres. Very true.

Sir Luc. So I shall see nothing more of you, unless it be by letter, till the evening. — I would do myself the honour to carry your message; but, to tell you a secret, I believe I shall have just such another affair on my own hands. There is a gay captain here, who put a jest on me lately, at the expense of my country, and I only want to fall in with the gentleman, to call him out.

Acres. By my valour, I should like to see you fight first!

Odds life! I should like to see you kill him, if it was only to
get a little lesson.

Sir Luc. I shall be very proud of instructing you. — Well
for the present — but remember now, when you meet your
antagonist, do everything in a mild and agreeable manner.
Let your courage be as keen, but at the same time as polished,
as your sword.   [*Exeunt severally.*

ACT IV.

Scene I. — Acres' *Lodgings.*

Acres and David.

Dav. Then, by the mass, sir! I would do no such thing
— ne'er a Sir Lucius O'Trigger in the kingdom should make
me fight, when I wa'n't so minded. Oons! what will the old
lady say, when she hears o't?

Acres. Ah! David, if you had heard Sir Lucius! — Odds
sparks and flames! he would have roused your valour.

Dav. Not he, indeed. I hate such bloodthirsty cormorants.
Look'ee, master, if you'd wanted a bout at boxing, quarter-
staff, or short-staff, I should never be the man to bid you cry
off: but for your curst sharps and snaps, I never knew any
good come of 'em.

Acres. But my honour, David, my honour! I must be very
careful of my honour.

Dav. Ay, by the mass! and I would be very careful of it;
and I think in return my honour couldn't do less than to be
very careful of me.

Acres. Odds blades! David, no gentleman will ever risk
the loss of his honour!

Dav. I say then, it would be but civil in honour never
to risk the loss of a gentleman. —Look'ee, master, this honour
seems to me to be a marvellous false friend: ay, truly, a very
courtier-like servant. — Put the case, I was a gentleman
(which, thank God, no one can say of me;) well—my honour
makes me quarrel with another gentleman of my acquaintance.
— So — we fight. (Pleasant enough that!) Boh! — I kill

him — (the more's my luck!) now, pray who gets the profit
of it? — Why, my honour. But put the case that he kills
me! — by the mass! I go to the worms, and my honour whips
over to my enemy.

Acres. No, David — in that case! — Odds crowns and
laurels! your honour follows you to the grave.

Dav. Now, that's just the place where I could make a shift
to do without it.

Acres. Zounds! David, you are a coward! — It doesn't
become my valour to listen to you. — What, shall I disgrace
my ancestors? — Think of that, David—think what it would
be to disgrace my ancestors!

Dav. Under favour, the surest way of not disgracing them,
is to keep as long as you can out of their company. Look'ee
now, master, to go to them in such haste — with an ounce of
lead in your brains — I should think might as well be let
alone. Our ancestors are very good kind of folks; but they
are the last people I should choose to have a visiting acquaintance with.

Acres. But, David, now, you don't think there is such
very, very, very great danger, hey?—Odds life! people often
fight without any mischief done!

Dav. By the mass, I think 'tis ten to one against you! —
Oons! here to meet some lion-headed fellow, I warrant, with
his damned double-barrelled swords, and cut-and-thrust
pistols! — Lord bless us! it makes me tremble to think o't!
— Those be such desperate bloody-minded weapons! Well, I
never could abide 'em—from a child I never could fancy 'em!
—I suppose there an't been so merciless a beast in the world
as your loaded pistol!

Acres. Zounds! I won't be afraid! — Odds fire and fury!
you shan't make me afraid. — Here is the challenge, and I
have sent for my dear friend Jack Absolute to carry it for me.

Dav. Ay, i'the name of mischief, let him be the messenger. — For my part, I wouldn't lend a hand to it for the
best horse in your stable. By the mass! it don't look like
another letter! It is, as I may say, a designing and mali-

cious-looking letter; and I warrant smells of gunpowder like a soldier's pouch! — Oons! I wouldn't swear it mayn't go off!

Acres. Out, you poltroon! you ha'n't the valour of a grass-hopper.

Dav. Well, I say no more — 'twill be sad news, to be sure, at Clod-Hall! but I ha' done. — How Phillis will howl when she hears of it! — Ay, poor bitch, she little thinks what shooting her master's going after! And I warrant old Crop, who has carried your honour, field and road, these ten years, will curse the hour he was born.   [*Whimpering.*

Acres. It won't do, David — I am determined to fight — so get along you coward, while I'm in the mind.

Enter SERVANT.

Ser. Captain Absolute, sir.

Acres. Oh! show him up.   [*Exit* SERVANT.

Dav. Well, Heaven send we be all alive this time to-morrow.

Acres. What's that? — Don't provoke me, David!

Dav. Good-bye, master.   [*Whimpering.*

Acres. Get along, you cowardly, dastardly, croaking raven!
    [*Exit* DAVID.

Enter CAPTAIN ABSOLUTE.

Abs. What's the matter, Bob?

Acres. A vile, sheep-hearted blockhead! If I hadn't the valour of St. George and the dragon to boot ——

Abs. But what did you want with me, Bob?

Acres. Oh! — There ——   [*Gives him the challenge.*

Abs. [*Aside.*] *To Ensign Beverley.* — So, what's going on now! — [*Aloud.*] Well, what's this?

Acres. A challenge!

Abs. Indeed! Why, you won't fight him; will you, Bob?

Acres. Egad, but I will, Jack. Sir Lucius has wrought me to it. He has left me full of rage — and I'll fight this evening, that so much good passion mayn't be wasted.

Abs. But what have I to do with this?

Acres. Why, as I think you know something of this fellow,

I want you to find him out for me, and give him this mortal defiance.

Abs. Well, give it to me, and trust me he gets it.

Acres. Thank you, my dear friend, my dear Jack; but it is giving you a great deal of trouble.

Abs. Not in the least — I beg you won't mention it. — No trouble in the world, I assure you.

Acres. You are very kind. — What it is to have a friend! — You couldn't be my second, could you, Jack?

Abs. Why no, Bob — not in this affair — it would not be quite so proper.

Acres. Well, then, I must get my friend Sir Lucius. I shall have your good wishes, however, Jack?

Abs. Whenever he meets you, believe me.

Re-enter SERVANT.

Ser. Sir Anthony Absolute is below, inquiring for the captain.

Abs. I'll come instantly. — [*Exit* SERVANT.] Well, my little hero, success attend you.   [*Going.*

Acres. — Stay — stay, Jack. — If Beverley should ask you what kind of a man your friend Acres is, do tell him I am a devil of a fellow — will you, Jack?

Abs To be sure I shall. I'll say you are a determined dog — hey, Bob!

Acres. Ay, do, do — and if that frightens him, egad, perhaps he mayn't come. So tell him I generally kill a man a week; will you, Jack?

Abs. I will, I will; I'll say you are called in the country Fighting Bob.

Acres. Right — right — 'tis all to prevent mischief; for I don't want to take his life if I clear my honour.

Abs. No! — that's very kind of you.

Acres. Why, you don't wish me to kill him — do you, Jack?

Abs. No, upon my soul, I do not. But a devil of a fellow, hey?   [*Going.*

Acres. True, true — but stay — stay, Jack — you may add

that you never saw me in such a rage before — a most devouring rage!

Abs. I will, I will.

Acres. Remember, Jack — a determined dog!

Abs. Ay, ay, Fighting Bob!   [*Exeunt severally.*

SCENE II. — MRS. MALAPROP's *Lodgings.*

MRS. MALAPROP *and* LYDIA.

Mrs. Mal. Why, thou perverse one! — tell me what you can object to him? Isn't he a handsome man? — tell me that. A genteel man? a pretty figure of a man?

Lyd. [*Aside.*] She little thinks whom she is praising! — [*Aloud.*] So is Beverley, ma'am.

Mrs. Mal. No caparisons, miss, if you please. Caparisons don't become a young woman. No! Captain Absolute is indeed a fine gentleman!

Lyd. Ay, the Captain Absolute you have seen.   [*Aside.*

Mrs. Mal. Then he's so well bred; — so full of alacrity, and adulation! — and has so much to say for himself: — in such good language too! His physiognomy so grammatical! Then his presence is so noble! I protest, when I saw him, I thought of what Hamlet says in the play: —

> "Hesperian curls — the front of Job himself! —
> An eye, like March, to threaten at command! —
> A station, like Harry Mercury, new — "

Something about kissing — on a hill—however, the similitude struck me directly.

Lyd. How enraged she'll be presently, when she discovers her mistake!   [*Aside.*

Enter SERVANT

Ser. Sir Anthony and Captain Absolute are below, ma'am.

Mrs. Mal. Show them up here. — [*Exit* SERVANT.] Now, Lydia, I insist on your behaving as becomes a young woman. Show your good breeding, at least, though you have forgot your duty.

Lyd. Madam, I have told you my resolution! — I shall not

only give him no encouragement, but I won't even speak to,
or look at him.

[Flings herself into a chair, with her face from the door.

Enter SIR ANTHONY ABSOLUTE *and* CAPTAIN ABSOLUTE.

Sir Anth. Here we are, Mrs. Malaprop; come to mitigate
the frowns of unrelenting beauty, — and difficulty enough I
had to bring this fellow. — I don't know what's the matter;
but if I had not held him by force, he'd have given me the
slip.

Mrs. Mal. You have infinite trouble, Sir Anthony, in the
affair. I am ashamed for the cause! — [*Aside to* LYDIA.] Lydia,
Lydia, rise, I beseech you! — pay your respects!

Sir Anth. I hope, madam, that Miss Languish has reflected
on the worth of this gentleman, and the regard due to her
aunt's choice, and my alliance. — [*Aside to* CAPTAIN ABSOLUTE.]
Now, Jack, speak to her.

Abs. [*Aside.*] What the devil shall I do! — *Aside to* SIR
ANTHONY.] You see, sir, she won't even look at me whilst you
are here. I knew she wouldn't! I told you so. Let me entreat
you, sir, to leave us together!

[Seems to expostulate with his father.

Lyd. [*Aside.*] I wonder I ha'n't heard my aunt exclaim yet!
sure she can't have looked at him! — perhaps their regimentals
are alike, and she is something blind.

Sir Anth. I say, sir, I won't stir a foot yet!

Mrs. Mal. I am sorry to say, Sir Anthony, that my affluence over my niece is very small. — [*Aside to* LYDIA.] Turn
round, Lydia: I blush for you!

Sir Anth. May I not flatter myself, that Miss Languish
will assign what cause of dislike she can have to my son! —
[*Aside to* CAPTAIN ABSOLUTE.] Why don't you begin, Jack? —
Speak, you puppy — speak!

Mrs. Mal. It is impossible, Sir Anthony, she can have any.
She will not say she has. — [*Aside to* LYDIA.] Answer, hussy!
why don't you answer?

Sir Anth. Then, madam, I trust that a childish and hasty

predilection will be no bar to Jack's happiness. — [*Aside to* CAPTAIN ABSOLUTE.] — Zounds! sirrah! why don't you speak!

Lyd. [*Aside.*] I think my lover seems as little inclined to conversation as myself. — How strangely blind my aunt must be!

Abs. Hem! hem! madam — hem! — *Attempts to speak, then returns to* SIR ANTHONY.] Faith! sir, I am so confounded! — and — so — so — confused! — I told you I should be so, sir — I knew it. — The — the — tremor of my passion entirely takes away my presence of mind.

Sir Anth. But it don't take away your voice, fool, does it? — Go up, and speak to her directly!

[CAPTAIN ABSOLUTE *makes signs to* MRS. MALAPROP *to leave them together.*

Mrs. Mal. Sir Anthony, shall we leave them together? — [*Aside to* LYDIA.] Ah! you stubborn little vixen!

Sir Anth. Not yet, ma'am, not yet! — [*Aside to* CAPTAIN ABSOLUTE.] What the devil are you at? unlock your jaws, sirrah, or —

Abs. [*Aside.*] Now Heaven send she may be too sullen to look round! — I must disguise my voice. — [*Draws near* LYDIA, *and speaks in a low hoarse tone.*] Will not Miss Languish lend an ear to the mild accents of true love? Will not —

Sir Anth. What the devil ails the fellow? Why don't you speak out? — not stand croaking like a frog in a quinsy!

Abs. The — the — excess of my awe, and my — my — my modesty, quite choke me!

Sir Anth. Ah! your modesty again! — I'll tell you what, Jack; if you don't speak out directly, and glibly too, I shall be in such a rage! — Mrs. Malaprop, I wish the lady would favour us with something more than a side-front.

[MRS. MALAPROP *seems to chide* LYDIA.

Abs. [*Aside.*] So all will out, I see! — [*Goes up to* LYDIA, *speaks softly.*] Be not surprised, my Lydia, suppress all surprise at present.

Lyd. [*Aside.*] Heavens! 'tis Beverley's voice! Sure he can't have imposed on Sir Anthony too! — [*Looks round by degrees, then starts up.*] Is this possible! — my Beverley! — how can this be? — my Beverley?

Abs. Ah! 'tis all over.   [*Aside.*

Sir Anth. Beverley! — the devil — Beverley! — What can the girl mean? — This is my son, Jack Absolute.

Mrs. Mal. For shame, hussy! for shame! your head runs so on that fellow, that you have him always in your eyes! — beg Captain Absolute's pardon directly.

Lyd. I see no Captain Absolute, but my loved Beverley!

Sir Anth. Zounds! the girl's mad! — her brain's turned by reading.

Mrs. Mal. O' my conscience, I believe so! — What do you mean by Beverley, hussy? — You saw Captain Absolute before to-day; there he is — your husband that shall be.

Lyd. With all my soul, ma'am — when I refuse my Beverley ——

Sir Anth. Oh! she's as mad as Bedlam! — or has this fellow been playing us a rogue's trick! — Come here, sirrah, who the devil are you?

Abs. Faith, sir, I am not quite clear myself; but I'll endeavour to recollect.

Sir Anth. Are you my son or not? — answer for your mother, you dog, if you won't for me.

Mrs. Mal. Ay, sir, who are you? O mercy! I begin to suspect! —

Abs. [*Aside.*] Ye powers of impudence, befriend me! — [*Aloud.*] Sir Anthony, most assuredly I am your wife's son: and that I sincerely believe myself to be your's also, I hope my duty has always shown. — Mrs. Malaprop, I am your most respectful admirer, and shall be proud to add affectionate nephew. — I need not tell my Lydia, that she sees her faithful Beverley, who, knowing the singular generosity of her temper, assumed that name and station, which has proved a test of the most disinterested love, which he now hopes to enjoy in a more elevated character.

Lyd. So! — there will be no elopement after all! [*Sullenly.*

Sir Anth. Upon my soul, Jack, thou art a very impudent

fellow! to do you justice, I think I never saw a piece of more consummate assurance!

Abs. Oh, you flatter me, sir — you compliment — 'tis my modesty you know, sir, — my modesty that has stood in my way.

Sir Anth. Well, I am glad you are not the dull, insensible varlet you pretended to be, however! — I'm glad you have made a fool of your father, you dog — I am. So this was your *penitence*, your *duty* and *obedience!* — I thought it was damned sudden! — *You never heard their names before*, not you! — *what the Languishes of Worcestershire*, hey? — *if you could please me in the affair it was all you desired!* — Ah! you dissembling villain! — What! — [*Pointing to* LYDIA] *she squints, don't she?* -- *a little red-haired girl!* — hey? — Why, you hypocritical young rascal! — I wonder you an't ashamed to hold up your head!

Abs. 'Tis with difficulty, sir. — I am confused — very much confused, as you must perceive.

Mrs. Mal. O Lud! Sir Anthony! — a new light breaks in upon me! — hey! — how! what! captain, did you write the letters then? — What — am I to thank you for the elegant compilation of *an old weather-beaten she-dragon* — hey! — O mercy! — was it you that reflected on my parts of speech?

Abs. Dear sir! my modesty will be overpowered at last, if you don't assist me — I shall certainly not be able to stand it!

Sir Anth. Come, come, Mrs. Malaprop, we must forget and forgive; — odds life! matters have taken so clever a turn all of a sudden, that I could find in my heart to be so good-humoured! and so gallant! hey! Mrs. Malaprop!

Mrs. Mal. Well, sir Anthony, since you desire it, we will not anticipate the past! — so mind, young people — our retrospection will be all to the future.

Sir Anth. Come, we must leave them together; Mrs. Malaprop, they long to fly into each other's arms, 1 warrant! — Jack — isn't the cheek as I said, hey? — and the eye; you rogue! — and the lip — hey? Come, Mrs. Malaprop, we'll not disturb their tenderness — theirs is the time of life for happi-

ness! — *Youth's the season made for joy* — [*Sings*] — hey! —
Odds life! I'm in such spirits, — I don't know what I could not
do! — Permit me, ma'am — [*Gives his hand to* Mrs. MALAPROP.]
Tol-de-rol — 'gad, I should like to have a little fooling myself
— Tol-de-rol! de-rol.

    [*Exit, singing and handing* Mrs. MALAPROP. — LYDIA *sits*
       sullenly in her chair.

    Abs. [*Aside.*] So much thought bodes me no good. — [*Aloud.*]
So grave, Lydia!

    Lyd. Sir!

    Abs. [*Aside*] So! — egad! I thought as much! — that
damned monosyllable has froze me! — [*Aloud.*] What, Lydia,
now that we are as happy in our friends' consent, as in our
mutual vows ——

    Lyd. Friends' consent indeed!   [*Peevishly.*

    Abs. Come, come, we must lay aside some of our romance
— a little wealth and comfort may be endured after all. And
for your fortune, the lawyers shall make such settlements
as ——

    Lyd. Lawyers! I hate lawyers!

    Abs. Nay, then, we will not wait for their lingering forms,
but instantly procure the licence, and ——

    Lyd. The licence! — I hate licence!

    Abs. Oh my love! be not so unkind! — thus let me en-
treat ——   [*Kneeling.*

    Lyd. Psha! — what signifies kneeling, when you know I
must have you?

    Abs. [*Rising.*] Nay, madam, there shall be no constraint
upon your inclinations, I promise you. — If I have lost your
heart — I resign the rest — [*Aside.*] 'Gad, I must try what a
little spirit will do.

    Lyd. [*Rising.*] Then, sir, let me tell you, the interest you
had there was acquired by a mean, unmanly imposition, and
deserves the punishment of fraud. — What, you have been
treating me like a child! — humouring my romance! and
laughing, I suppose, at your success!

    Abs. You wrong me, Lydia, you wrong me, — only hear——

Lyd. So, while I fondly imagined we were deceiving my relations, and flattered myself that I should outwit and incense them all — behold my hopes are to be crushed at once, by my aunt's consent and approbation — and I am myself the only dupe at last! — [*Walking about in a heat.*] But here, sir, here is the picture — Beverley's picture! [*taking a miniature from her bosom*] which I have worn, night and day, in spite of threats and entreaties! — There, sir; [*flings it to him*] and be assured I throw the original from my heart as easily.

Abs. Nay, nay, ma'am, we will not differ as to that.—Here, [*taking out a picture*] here is Miss Lydia Languish. — What a difference! — ay, there is the heavenly assenting smile that first gave soul and spirit to my hopes! — those are the lips which sealed a vow, as yet scarce dry in Cupid's calendar! and there the half-resentful blush, that would have checked the ardour of my thanks! — Well, all that's past! — all over indeed! — There, madam — in beauty, that copy is not equal to you, but in my mind its merit over the original, in being still the same, is such — that — I cannot find in my heart to part with it.　　　　[*Puts it up again.*

Lyd. [*Softening.*] 'Tis your own doing, sir — I, I, I suppose you are perfectly satisfied.

Abs. O, most certainly—sure, now, this is much better than being in love! — ha! ha! ha! — there's some spirit in this! — What signifies breaking some scores of solemn promises:—all that's of no consequence, you know. — To be sure people will say, that miss don't know her own mind — but never mind that! Or, perhaps, they may be ill-natured enough to hint, that the gentleman grew tired of the lady and forsook her — but don't let that fret you.

Lyd. There is no bearing his insolence. [*Bursts into tears.*

Re-enter MRS. MALAPROP *and* SIR ANTHONY ABSOLUTE.

Mrs. Mal. Come, we must interrupt your billing and cooing awhile.

Lyd. This is worse than your treachery and deceit, you base ingrate!　　　　[*Sobbing.*

5*

Sir Anth. What the devil's the matter now! — Zounds! Mrs. Malaprop, this is the oddest billing and cooing I ever heard! — but what the deuce is the meaning of it? — I am quite astonished!

Abs. Ask the lady, sir.

Mrs. Mal. Oh mercy! — I'm quite analysed, for my part! — Why, Lydia, what is the reason of this?

Lyd. Ask the gentleman, ma'am.

Sir Anth. Zounds! I shall be in a frenzy! — Why, Jack, you are not come out to be any one else, are you?

Mrs. Mal. Ay, sir, there's no more trick, is there? — you are not like Cerberus, three gentlemen at once, are you?

Abs. You'll not let me speak — I say the lady can account for this much better than I can.

Lyd. Ma'am, you once commanded me never to think of Beverley again — there is the man — I now obey you: for, from this moment, I renounce him for ever.   [*Exit.*

Mrs. Mal. O mercy! and miracles! what a turn here is — why sure, captain, you haven't behaved disrespectfully to my niece.

Sir Anth. Ha! ha! ha! — ha! ha! ha! — now I see it. Ha! ha! ha! — now I see it — you have been too lively, Jack.

Abs. Nay, sir, upon my word ——

Sir Anth. Come, no lying, Jack — I'm sure 'twas so.

Mrs. Mal. O Lud! Sir Anthony! — O fy, captain!

Abs. Upon my soul, ma'am ——

Sir Anth. Come, no excuses, Jack; why, your father, you rogue, was so before you: — the blood of the Absolutes was always impatient. — Ha! ha! ha! poor little Lydia! why, you've frightened her, you dog, you have.

Abs. By all that's good, sir ——

Sir Anth. Zounds! say no more, I tell you — Mrs. Malaprop shall make your peace. — You must make his peace, Mrs. Malaprop: — you must tell her 'tis Jack's way — tell her 'tis all our ways — it runs in the blood of our family! — Come away, Jack — Ha! ha! ha! Mrs. Malaprop — a young villain!

                              [*Pushing him out.*

Mrs. Mal. O! Sir Anthony! — O fy, captain!

[*Exeunt severally.*

SCENE III. — *The North Parade.*

Enter SIR LUCIUS O'TRIGGER.

Sir Luc. I wonder where this Captain Absolute hides himself! Upon my conscience! these officers are always in one's way in love affairs: — I remember I might have married lady Dorothy Carmine, if it had not been for a little rogue of a major, who ran away with her before she could get a sight of me! And I wonder too what it is the ladies can see in them to be so fond of them — unless it be a touch of the old serpent in 'em, that makes the little creatures be caught, like vipers, with a bit of red cloth. Ha! isn't this the captain coming? — faith it is! — There is a probability of succeeding about that fellow, that is mighty provoking! Who the devil is he talking to?   [*Steps aside.*

Enter CAPTAIN ABSOLUTE.

Abs. [*Aside.*] To what fine purpose I have been plotting! a noble reward for all my schemes, upon my soul! — a little gipsy! — I did not think her romance could have made her so damned absurd either. 'Sdeath, I never was in a worse humour in my life! — I could cut my own throat, or any other person's, with the greatest pleasure in the world!

Sir Luc. Oh, faith! I'm in the luck of it. I never could have found him in a sweeter temper for my purpose — to be sure I'm just come in the nick! Now to enter into conversation with him, and so quarrel genteelly. — [*Goes up to* CAPTAIN ABSOLUTE.] With regard to that matter, captain, I must beg leave to differ in opinion with you.

Abs. Upon my word, then, you must be a very subtle disputant: — because, sir, I happened just then to be giving no opinion at all.

Sir Luc. That's no reason. For give me leave to tell you, a man may think an untruth as well as speak one.

Abs. Very true, sir; but if a man never utters his thoughts,

I should think they might stand a chance of escaping controversy.

Sir Luc. Then, sir, you differ in opinion with me, which amounts to the same thing.

Abs. Hark'ee, Sir Lucius; if I had not before known you to be a gentleman, upon my soul, I should not have discovered it at this interview: for what you can drive at, unless you mean to quarrel with me, I cannot conceive!

Sir Luc. I humbly thank you, sir, for the quickness of your apprehension. — [*Bowing.*] You have named the very thing I would be at.

Abs. Very well, sir; I shall certainly not balk your inclinations. — But I should be glad you would please to explain your motives.

Sir Luc. Pray sir, be easy; the quarrel is a very pretty quarrel as it stands; we should only spoil it by trying to explain it. However, your memory is very short, or you could not have forgot an affront you passed on me within this week. So, no more, but name your time and place.

Abs. Well, sir, since you are so bent on it, the sooner the better; let it be this evening — here, by the Spring Gardens. We shall scarcely be interrupted.

Sir Luc. Faith! that same interruption in affairs of this nature shows very great ill-breeding. I don't know what's the reason, but in England, if a thing of this kind gets wind, people make such a pother, that a gentleman can never fight in peace and quietness. However, if it's the same to you, captain, I should take it as a particular kindness if you'd let us meet in King's-Mead-Fields, as a little business will call me there about six o'clock, and I may despatch both matters at once.

Abs. 'Tis the same to me exactly. A little after six, then, we will discuss this matter more seriously.

Sir Luc. If you please, sir; there will be very pretty small-sword light, though it won't do for a long shot   So that matter's settled, and my mind's at ease!   [*Exit.*

Enter FAULKLAND.

Abs. Well met! I was going to look for you. O Faulkland! all the demons of spite and disappointment have conspired against me! I'm so vexed, that if I had not the
prospect of a resource in being knocked o' the head by-and-
by, I should scarce have spirits to tell you the cause.

Faulk. What can you mean? — Has Lydia changed her
mind?—I should have thought her duty and inclination would
now have pointed to the same object.

Abs. Ay, just as the eyes do of a person who squints:
when her love-eye was fixed on me, t'other, her eye of duty,
was finely obliqued: but when duty bid her point that the
same way, off t'other turned on a swivel, and secured its retreat with a frown!

Faulk. But what's the resource you ——

Abs. Oh, to wind up the whole, a good-natured Irishman
here has — [*Mimicking* SIR LUCIUS] — begged leave to have
the pleasure of cutting my throat; and I mean to indulge
him — that's all.

Faulk. Prithee, be serious!

Abs. 'Tis fact, upon my soul! Sir Lucius O'Trigger—you
know him by sight — for some affront, which I am sure I
never intended, has obliged me to meet him this evening at
six o'clock: 'tis on that account I wished to see you; you must
go with me.

Faulk. Nay, there must be some mistake, sure. Sir Lucius
shall explain himself, and I dare say matters may be accom-
modated. But this evening did you say? I wish it had been
any other time.

Abs. Why? there will be light enough: there will (as Sir
Lucius says) be very pretty small-sword light, though it will
not do for a long shot. Confound his long shots.

Faulk. But I am myself a good deal ruffled by a difference I have had with Julia. My vile tormenting temper has
made me treat her so cruelly, that I shall not be myself till
we are reconciled.

Abs. By heavens! Faulkland, you don't deserve her!

Enter Servant, *gives* Faulkland *a letter, and exit.*

Faulk. Oh, Jack! this is from Julia. I dread to open it!
I fear it may be to take a last leave! — perhaps to bid me
return her letters, and restore —— Oh, how I suffer for my
folly!

Abs. Here, let me see. — [*Takes the letter and opens it.*]
Ay, a final sentence, indeed! — 'tis all over with you, faith!

Faulk. Nay, Jack, don't keep me in suspense!

Abs. Hear then. — [Reads.] *As I am convinced that my
dear Faulkland's own reflections have already upbraided him for
his last unkindness to me, I will not add a word on the subject.
I wish to speak with you as soon as possible.   Yours ever and
truly,* Julia. There's stubbornness and resentment for you! —
[*Gives him the letter.*] Why, man, you don't seem one whit
the happier at this!

Faulk. O yes, I am; but — but ——

Abs. Confound your buts! you never hear any thing that
would make another man bless himself, but you immediately
damn it with a but!

Faulk. Now, Jack, as you are my friend, own honestly —
don't you think there is something forward, something indelicate, in this haste to forgive?   Women should never sue
for reconciliation: that should always come from us.   They
should retain their coldness till wooed to kindness; and their
pardon, like their love, should "not unsought be won."

Abs. I have not patience to listen to you! thou'rt incorrigible! so say no more on the subject.   I must go to settle
a few matters.   Let me see you before six, remember, at my
lodgings.   A poor industrious devil like me, who have toiled,
and drudged, and plotted to gain my ends, and am at last
disappointed by other people's folly, may in pity be allowed
to swear and grumble a little; but a captious sceptic in love,
a slave to fretfulness and whim, who has no difficulties but of
his own creating, is a subject more fit for ridicule than compassion!   [*Exit.*

Faulk. I feel his reproaches; yet I would not change this
too exquisite nicety for the gross content with which he

tramples on the thorns of love! His engaging me in this duel has started an idea in my head, which I will instantly pursue. I'll use it as the touchstone of Julia's sincerity and disinterestedness. If her love prove pure and sterling ore, my name will rest on it with honour; and once I've stamped it there, I lay aside my doubts for ever! But if the dross of selfishness, the alloy of pride, predominate, 'twill be best to leave her as a toy for some less cautious fool to sigh for!

[*Exit.*]

ACT V.

Scene I. — Julia's *Dressing-Room.*

Julia *discovered alone.*

Jul. How this message has alarmed me! what dreadful accident can he mean? why such charge to be alone? — O Faulkland! — how many unhappy moments — how many tears have you cost me.

Enter Faulkland.

Jul. What means this? — why this caution, Faulkland?

Faulk. Alas! Julia, I am come to take a long farewell.

Jul. Heavens! what do you mean?

Faulk. You see before you a wretch, whose life is forfeited. Nay, start not! — the infirmity of my temper has drawn all this misery on me. I left you fretful and passionate — an untoward accident drew me into a quarrel — the event is, that I must fly this kingdom instantly. O Julia, had I been so fortunate as to have called you mine entirely, before this mischance had fallen on me, I should not so deeply dread my banishment!

Jul. My soul is oppressed with sorrow at the nature of your misfortune: had these adverse circumstances arisen from a less fatal cause, I should have felt strong comfort in the thought that I could now chase from your bosom every doubt of the warm sincerity of my love. My heart has long known no other guardian — I now entrust my person to your honour — we will fly together. When safe from pursuit, my father's

will may be fulfilled — and I receive a legal claim to be tho
partner of your sorrows, and tenderest comforter. Then on
the bosom of your wedded Julia, you may lull your keen regret to slumbering; while virtuous love, with a cherub's hand,
shall smooth the brow of upbraiding thought, and pluck the
thorn from compunction.

Faulk. O Julia! I am bankrupt in gratitude! but the time
is so pressing, it calls on you for so hasty a resolution. —
Would you not wish some hours to weigh the advantages you
forego, and what little compensation poor Faulkland can
make you beside his solitary love?

Jul. I ask not a moment. No, Faulkland, I have loved
you for yourself: and if I now, more than ever, prize the
solemn engagement which so long has pledged us to each
other, it is because it leaves no room for hard aspersions on
my fame, and puts the seal of duty to an act of love. But let
us not linger. Perhaps this delay ——

Faulk. 'Twill be better I should not venture out again till
dark. Yet am I grieved to think what numberless distresses
will press heavy on your gentle disposition!

Jul. Perhaps your fortune may be forfeited by this unhappy act. — I know not whether 'tis so; but sure that alone
can never make us unhappy. The little I have will be sufficient to support us; and exile never should be splendid.

Faulk. Ay, but in such an abject state of life, my wounded
pride perhaps may increase the natural fretfulness of my
temper, till I become a rude, morose companion, beyond your
patience to endure. Perhaps the recollection of a deed my
conscience cannot justify may haunt me in such gloomy and
unsocial fits, that I shall hate the tenderness that would
relieve me, break from your arms, and quarrel with your
fondness!

Jul. If your thoughts should assume so unhappy a bent,
you will the more want some mild and affectionate spirit to
watch over and console you: one who, by bearing your infirmities with gentleness and resignation, may teach you so
to bear the evils of your fortune.

Faulk. Julia, I have proved you to the quick! and with this useless device I throw away all my doubts. How shall I plead to be forgiven this last unworthy effect of my restless, unsatisfied disposition?

Jul. Has no such disaster happened as you related?

Faulk. I am ashamed to own that it was pretended; yet in pity, Julia, do not kill me with resenting a fault which never can be repeated: but sealing, this once, my pardon, let me to-morrow, in the face of Heaven, receive my future guide and monitress, and expiate my past folly by years of tender adoration.

Jul. Hold, Faulkland! — that you are free from a crime, which I before feared to name, Heaven knows how sincerely I rejoice! These are tears of thankfulness for that! But that your cruel doubts should have urged you to an imposition that has wrung my heart, gives me now a pang more keen than I can express!

Faulk. By Heavens! Julia ——

Jul. Yet hear me. — My father loved you, Faulkland! and you preserved the life that tender parent gave me; in his presence I pledged my hand — joyfully pledged it — where before I had given my heart. When, soon after, I lost that parent, it seemed to me that Providence had, in Faulkland, shown me whither to transfer, without a pause, my grateful duty, as well as my affection: hence I have been content to bear from you what pride and delicacy would have forbid me from another. I will not upbraid you, by repeating how you have trifled with my sincerity ——

Faulk. I confess it all! yet hear ——

Jul. After such a year of trial, I might have flattered myself that I should not have been insulted with a new probation of my sincerity, as cruel as unnecessary! I now see it is not in your nature to be content or confident in love. With this conviction — I never will be yours. While I had hopes that my persevering attention, and unreproaching kindness, might in time reform your temper, I should have been happy to have gained a dearer influence over you; but I will

not furnish you with a licensed power to keep alive an incorrigible fault, at the expense of one who never would contend
with you.

Faulk. Nay, but, Julia, by my soul and honour, if after
this ——

Jul. But one word more. — As my faith has once been
given to you, I never will barter it with another. — I shall
pray for your happiness with the truest sincerity; and the
dearest blessing I can ask of Heaven to send you will be to
charm you from that unhappy temper, which alone has prevented the performance of our solemn engagement. All I
request of you is, that you will yourself reflect upon this infirmity, and when you number up the many true delights it
has deprived you of, let it not be your least regret, that it lost
you the love of one who would have followed you in beggary
through the world!   [*Exit.*

Faulk. She's gone — for ever! — There was an awful resolution in her manner, that riveted me to my place. — O fool!
— dolt! — barbarian! Cursed as I am, with more imperfections than my fellow wretches, kind Fortune sent a heaven-
gifted cherub to my aid, and, like a ruffian, I have driven her
from my side! — I must now haste to my appointment. Well,
my mind is tuned for such a scene. I shall wish only to become a principal in it, and reverse the tale my cursed folly
put me upon forging here. — O Love! — tormentor! — fiend! —
whose influence, like the moon's, acting on men of dull souls,
makes idiots of them, but meeting subtler spirits, betrays
their course, and urges sensibility to madness!   [*Exit.*

Enter LYDIA *and* MAID.

Maid. My mistress, ma'am, I know, was here just now —
perhaps she is only in the next room.   [*Exit.*

Lyd. Heigh-ho! Though he has used me so, this fellow
runs strangely in my head. I believe one lecture from my
grave cousin will make me recall him. [*Re-enter* JULIA.]
O Julia, I am come to you with such an appetite for consolation. — Lud! child, what's the matter with you? You have

been crying! — I'll be hanged if that Faulkland has not been tormenting you!

Jul. You mistake the cause of my uneasiness!—Something has flurried me a little. Nothing that you can guess at. — [*Aside.*] I would not accuse Faulkland to a sister!

Lyd. Ah! whatever vexations you may have, I can assure you mine surpass them. You know who Beverley proves to be?

Jul. I will now own to you, Lydia, that Mr. Faulkland had before informed me of the whole affair. Had young Absolute been the person you took him for, I should not have accepted your confidence on the subject, without a serious endeavour to counteract your caprice.

Lyd. So, then, I see I have been deceived by every one! But I don't care — I'll never have him.

Jul. Nay, Lydia ——

Lyd. Why, is it not provoking? when I thought we were coming to the prettiest distress imaginable, to find myself made a mere Smithfield bargain of at last! There, had I projected one of the most sentimental elopements!—so becoming a disguise!— so amiable a ladder of ropes! — Conscious moon — four horses — Scotch parson — with such surprise to Mrs. Malaprop — and such paragraphs in the newspapers!— Oh, I shall die with disappointment!

Jul. I don't wonder at it!

Lyd. Now — sad reverse!—what have I to expect, but, after a deal of flimsy preparation with a bishop's licence, and my aunt's blessing, to go simpering up to the altar; or perhaps be cried three times in a country church, and have an unmannerly fat clerk ask the consent of every butcher in the parish to join John Absolute and Lydia Languish, spinster! Oh that I should live to hear myself called spinster!

Jul. Melancholy indeed!

Lyd. How mortifying, to remember the dear delicious shifts I used to be put to, to gain half a minute's conversation with this fellow! How often have I stole forth, in the coldest night in January, and found him in the garden, stuck like a dripping

statue! There would he kneel to me in the snow, and sneeze
and cough so pathetically! he shivering with cold and I with
apprehension! and while the freezing blast numbed our joints,
how warmly would he press me to pity his flame, and glow
with mutual ardour! — Ah, Julia, that was something like
being in love.

Jul. If I were in spirits, Lydia, I should chide you only
by laughing heartily at you; but it suits more the situation of
my mind, at present, earnestly to entreat you not to let a man,
who loves you with sincerity, suffer that unhappiness from
your caprice, which I know too well caprice can inflict.

Lyd. O Lud! what has brought my aunt here?

Enter MRS. MALAPROP, FAG, *and* DAVID.

Mrs. Mal. So! so! here's fine work! — here's fine suicide,
parricide, and simulation, going on in the fields! and Sir Anthony not to be found to prevent the antistrophe!

Jul. For Heaven's sake, madam, what's the meaning of
this?

Mrs. Mal. That gentleman can tell you — 'twas he enveloped the affair to me.

Lyd. Do, sir, will you, inform us?   [*To* FAG.

Fag. Ma'am, I should hold myself very deficient in every
requisite that forms the man of breeding, if I delayed a moment to give all the information in my power to a lady so
deeply interested in the affair as you are.

Lyd. But quick! quick sir!

Fag. True, ma'am, as you say, one should be quick in di-
vulging matters of this nature; for should we be tedious,
perhaps while we are flourishing on the subject, two or three
lives may be lost!

Lyd. O patience! — Do, ma'am, for Heaven's sake! tell us
what is the matter?

Mrs. Mal. Why, murder's the matter! slaughter's the
matter; killing 's the matter! — but he can tell you the per-
pendiculars.

Lyd. Then, prithee, sir, be brief.

Fag. Why then, ma'am, as to murder — I cannot take upon me to say — and as to slaughter, or manslaughter, that will be as the jury finds it.

Lyd. But who, sir — who arc engaged in this?

Fag. Faith, ma'am, one is a young gentleman whom I should be very sorry any thing was to happen to — a very pretty behaved gentleman! We have lived much together, and always on terms.

Lyd. But who is this? who! who! who?

Fag. My master, ma'am — my master — I speak of my master.

Lyd. Heavens! What, Captain Absolute!

Mrs. Mal. Oh, to be sure, you are frightened now!

Jul. But who are with him, sir?

Fag. As to the rest, ma'am, this gentleman can inform you better than I.

Jul. Do speak, friend.   ·   [*To* DAVID.

Dav. Look'ee, my lady — by the mass! there's mischief going on. Folks don't use to meet for amusement with fire-arms, firelocks, fire-engines, fire-screens, fire-office, and the devil knows what other crackers beside! — This, my lady, I say, has an angry favour.

Jul. But who is there beside Captain Absolute, friend?

Dav. My poor master — under favour for mentioning him first. You know me, my lady — I am David — and my master of course is, or was, Squire Acres. Then comes Squire Faulkland.

Jul. Do, ma'am, let us instantly endeavour to prevent mischief.

Mrs. Mal. O fy! — it would be very inelegant in us:—we should only participate things.

Dav. Ah! do, Mrs. Aunt, save a few lives — they are desperately given, believe me. — Above all, there is that blood-thirsty Philistine, Sir Lucius O"Trigger.

Mrs. Mal. Sir Lucius O"Trigger? O mercy! have they drawn poor little dear Sir Lucius into the scrape? — Why, how you stand, girl! you have no more feeling than one of the Derbyshire petrifactions!

Lyd. What are we to do, madam?

Mrs. Mal. Why fly with the utmost felicity, to be sure, to prevent mischief! — Here, friend, you can show us the place?

Fag. If you please, ma'am, I will conduct you. — David, do you look for Sir Anthony.   [*Exit* DAVID.

Mrs. Mal. Come, girls! this gentleman will exhort us. — Come, sir, you're our envoy — lead the way, and we'll precede.

Fag. Not a step before the ladies for the world!

Mrs. Mal. You're sure you know the spot?

Fag. I think I can find it, ma'am; and one good thing is, we shall hear the report of the pistols as we draw near, so we can't well miss them; — never fear, ma'am, never fear.

[*Exeunt, he talking.*

SCENE II. — *The South Parade.*

Enter CAPTAIN ABSOLUTE, *putting his sword under his great coat.*

Abs. A sword seen in the streets of Bath would raise as great an alarm as a mad dog. — How provoking this is in Faulkland! — never punctual! I shall be obliged to go without him at last. — Oh, the devil! here's Sir Anthony! how shall I escape him?

[*Muffles up his face, and takes a circle to go off.*

Enter SIR ANTHONY ABSOLUTE.

Sir Anth. How one may be deceived at a little distance! only that I see he don't know me, I could have sworn that was Jack! — Hey! Gad's life! it is. — Why, Jack, what are you afraid of? hey! — sure I'm right. — Why Jack, Jack Absolute!   [*Goes up to him.*

Abs. Really, sir, you have the advantage of me: — I don't remember ever to have had the honour — my name is Saunderson, at your service.

Sir Anth. Sir, I beg your pardon — I took you — hey? — why, zounds! it is — Stay — [*Looks up to his face.*] So, so — your humble servant, Mr. Saunderson! Why, you scoundrel, what tricks are you after now?

Abs. Oh, a joke, sir, a joke! I came here on purpose to look for you, sir.

Sir Anth. You did! well, I am glad you were so lucky: — but what are you muffled up so for? — what's this for? — hey!

Abs. 'Tis cool, sir; isn't? — rather chilly somehow: — but I shall be late — I have a particular engagement.

Sir Anth. Stay! — Why, I thought you were looking for me? — Pray, Jack, where is't you are going?

Abs. Going, sir!

Sir Anth. Ay, where are you going?

Abs. Where am I going?

Sir Anth. You unmannerly puppy!

Abs. I was going, sir, to—to—to—to Lydia—sir, to Lydia — to make matters up if I could; — and I was looking for you, sir, to—to—

Sir Anth. To go with you, I suppose. — Well, come along.

Abs. Oh! zounds! no, sir, not for the world!—I wished to meet with you, sir, — to—to—to — You find it cool, I'm sure, sir — you'd better not stay out.

Sir Anth. Cool! — not at all. — Well, Jack — and what will you say to Lydia?

Abs. Oh, sir, beg her pardon, humour her — promise and vow: but I detain you, sir — consider the cold air on your gout.

Sir Anth. Oh, not at all! — not at all! I'm in no hurry. — Ah! Jack, you youngsters, when once you are wounded here [*Putting his hand to* CAPTAIN ABSOLUTE'S *breast.*] Hey! what the deuce have you got here?

Abs. Nothing, sir — nothing;

Sir Anth. What's this? — here's something damned hard.

Abs. Oh, trinkets, sir! trinkets! — a bauble for Lydia!

Sir Anth. Nay, let me see your taste.—[*Pulls his coat open, the sword falls.*] Trinkets! — a bauble for Lydia!—Zounds! sirrah, you are not going to cut her throat, are you?

Sheridan.   6

Abs. Ha! ha! ha! — I thought it would divert you, sir, though I didn't mean to tell you till afterwards.

Sir Anth. You didn't? — Yes, this is a very diverting trinket, truly!

Abs. Sir, I'll explain to you. — You know, sir, Lydia is romantic, devilish romantic, and very absurd of course: now, sir, I intend, if she refuses to forgive me, to unsheath this sword, and swear — I'll fall upon its point, and expire at her feet!

Sir Anth. Fall upon a fiddlestick's end! — why, I suppose it is the very thing that would please her. — Get along, you fool!

Abs. Well, sir, you shall hear of my success — you shall hear. — *O Lydia! — forgive me, or this pointed steel —* says I.

Sir Anth. O, booby! stab away and welcome — says she. — Get along! and damn your trinkets! [*Exit* CAPTAIN ABSOLUTE.

Enter DAVID, *running.*

Dav. Stop him! stop him! Murder! Thief! Fire! — Stop fire! Stop fire! — O Sir Anthony — call! call! bid 'm stop! Murder! Fire!

Sir Anth. Fire! Murder! — Where?

Dav. Oons! he's out of sight! and I'm out of breath! for my part! O Sir Anthony, why didn't you stop him? why didn't you stop him?

Sir Anth. Zounds! the fellow's mad! — Stop whom? stop Jack?

Dav. Ay, the captain, sir! — there's murder and slaughter ——

Sir Anth. Murder!

Dav. Ay, please you, Sir Anthony, there's all kinds of murder, all sorts of slaughter to be seen in the fields: there's fighting going on, sir — bloody sword-and-gun fighting!

Sir Anth. Who are going to fight, dunce?

Dav. Every body that I know of, Sir Anthony: — every body is going to fight, my poor master, Sir Lucius O'Trigger, your son, the captain ——

Sir Anth. Oh, the dog! I see his tricks. — Do you know the place?

Dav. King's-Mead-Fields.

Sir Anth. You know the way?

Dav. Not an inch; but I'll call the mayor — aldermen — constables — churchwardens — and beadles — we can't be too many to part them.

Sir Anth. Come along — give me your shoulder! we'll get assistance as we go — the lying villain! — Well, I shall be in such a frenzy! — So — this was the history of his trinkets! I'll bauble him!   [*Exeunt.*

SCENE III. — *King's-Mead-Fields.*

Enter Sir Lucius O'Trigger *and* Acres, *with pistols.*

Acres. By my valour! then, Sir Lucius, forty yards is a good distance. Odds levels and aims! — I say it is a good distance.

Sir Luc. Is it for muskets or small field-pieces? Upon my conscience, Mr. Acres, you must leave those things to me. — Stay now — I'll show you. — [*Measures paces along the stage.*] There now, that is a very pretty distance — a pretty gentleman's distance.

Acres. Zounds! we might as well fight in a sentry-box! I tell you, Sir Lucius, the farther he is off, the cooler I shall take my aim.

Sir Luc. Faith! then I suppose you would aim at him best of all if he was out of sight!

Acres. No, Sir Lucius; but I should think forty or eight-and-thirty yards ——

Sir Luc. Pho! pho! nonsense! three or four feet between the mouths of your pistols is as good as a mile.

Acres. Odds bullets, no! — by my valour! there is no merit in killing him so near: do, my dear Sir Lucius, let me bring him down at a long shot: — a long shot, Sir Lucius, if you love me!

Sir Luc. Well, the gentleman's friend and I must settle

6*

that. — But tell me now, Mr. Acres, in case of an accident, is there any little will or commission I could execute for you?

Acres. I am much obliged to you, Sir Lucius—but I don't understand ——

Sir Luc. Why, you may think there's no being shot at without a little risk — and if an unlucky bullet should carry a quietus with it—I say it will be no time then to be bothering you about family matters.

Acres. A quietus!

Sir Luc. For instance, now—if that should be the case — would you choose to be pickled and sent home?—or would it be the same to you to lie here in the Abbey? — I'm told there is very snug lying in the Abbey.

Acres. Pickled! — Snug lying in the Abbey! — Odds tremors! Sir Lucius, don't talk so!

Sir Luc. I suppose, Mr. Acres, you never were engaged in an affair of this kind before?

Acres. No, Sir Lucius, never before.

Sir Luc. Ah! that's a pity! — there's nothing like being used to a thing. — Pray now, how would you receive the gentleman's shot?

Acres. Odds files!—I've practised that—there, Sir Lucius — there. — [*Puts himself in an attitude.*] A side-front, hey? Odd! I'll make myself small enough: I'll stand edgeways.

Sir Luc. Now — you're quite out — for if you stand so when I take my aim —— [*Levelling at him.*

Acres. Zounds! Sir Lucius—are you sure it is not cocked?

Sir Luc. Never fear.

Acres. But — but — you don't know — it may go off of its own head!

Sir Luc. Pho! be easy. — Well, now if I hit you in the body, my bullet has a double chance — for if it misses a vital part of your right side — 'twill be very hard if it don't succeed on the left!

Acres. A vital part!

Sir Luc. But, there — fix yourself so —[*Placing him*]—let him see the broad-side of your full front —there—now a ball or two may pass clean through your body, and never do any harm at all.

Acres. Clean through me! — a ball or two clean through me!

Sir Luc. Ay — may they — and it is much the genteelest attitude into the bargain.

Acres. Look'ee! Sir Lucius — I'd just as lieve be shot in an awkward posture as a genteel one; so, by my valour! I will stand edgeways.

Sir Luc. [*Looking at his watch.*] Sure they don't mean to disappoint us — Hah! — no, faith — I think I see them coming.

Acres. Hey! — what! — coming! ——

Sir Luc. Ay. — Who are those yonder getting over the stile?

Acres. There are two of them indeed! — well — let them come — hey, Sir Lucius! — we — we — we — we — won't run.

Sir Luc. Run!

Acres. No — I say — we won't run, by my valour!

Sir Luc. What the devil's the matter with you?

Acres. Nothing — nothing — my dear friend — my dear Sir Lucius — but I — I — I don't feel quite so bold, somehow, as I did.

Sir Luc. O fy! — consider your honour.

Acres. Ay — true — my honour. Do, Sir Lucius, edge in a word or two every now and then about my honour.

Sir Luc. Well, here they're coming. 　　　　 [*Looking.*

Acres. Sir Lucius — if I wa'n't with you, I should almost think I was afraid. — If my valour should leave me! — Valour will come and go.

Sir Luc. Then pray keep it fast, while you have it.

Acres. Sir Lucius — I doubt it is going — yes — my valour is certainly going! — it is sneaking off! — I feel it oozing out as it were at the palms of my hands!

Sir Luc. Your honour — your honour. — Here they are.

Acres. O mercy! — now — that I was safe at Clod-Hall! or could be shot before I was aware!

Enter FAULKLAND *and* CAPTAIN ABSOLUTE.

Sir Luc. Gentlemen, your most obedient. — Hah! — what, Captain Absolute! — So, I suppose, sir, you are come here, just like myself — to do a kind office, first for your friend — then to proceed to business on your own account.

Acres. What, Jack! — my dear Jack! — my dear friend!

Abs. Hark'ee, Bob, Beverley's at hand.

Sir Luc. Well, Mr. Acres — I don't blame your saluting the gentleman civilly. — [*To* FAULKLAND.] So, Mr. Beverley, if you'll choose your weapons, the captain and I will measure the ground.

Faulk. My weapons, sir!

Acres. Odds life! Sir Lucius, I'm not going to fight Mr. Faulkland; these are my particular friends.

Sir Luc. What, sir, did you not come here to fight Mr. Acres?

Faulk. Not I, upon my word, sir.

Sir Luc. Well, now, that's mighty provoking! But I hope, Mr. Faulkland, as there are three of us come on purpose for the game, you won't be so cantankerous as to spoil the party by sitting out.

Abs. O pray, Faulkland, fight to oblige Sir Lucius.

Faulk. Nay, if Mr. Acres is so bent on the matter ——

Acres. No, no, Mr. Faulkland; — I'll bear my disappointment like a Christian. — Look'ee, Sir Lucius, there's no occasion at all for me to fight; and if it is the same to you, I'd as lieve let it alone.

Sir Luc. Observe me, Mr. Acres — I must not be trifled with. You have certainly challenged somebody — and you came here to fight him. Now, if that gentleman is willing to represent him — I can't see, for my soul, why it isn't just the same thing.

Acres. Why no — Sir Lucius — I tell you, 'tis one Beverley I've challenged — a fellow, you see, that dare not show his face! — If he were here, I'd make him give up his pretensions directly!

Abs. Hold, Bob — let me set you right — there is no such man as Beverley in the case. — The person who assumed that name is before you; and as his pretensions are the same in both characters, he is ready to support them in whatever way you please.

Sir Luc. Well, this is lucky. — Now you have an opportunity ——

Acres. What, quarrel with my dear friend Jack Absolute? — not if he were fifty Beverleys! Zounds! Sir Lucius, you would not have me so unnatural.

Sir Luc. Upon my conscience, Mr. Acres, your valour has oozed away with a vengeance!

Acres. Not in the least! Odds backs and abettors! I'll be your second with all my heart — and if you should get a quietus, you may command me entirely. I'll get you snug lying in the Abbey here; or pickle you, and send you over to Blunderbuss-hall, or any thing of the kind, with the greatest pleasure.

Sir Luc. Pho! pho! you are little better than a coward.

Acres. Mind, gentlemen, he calls me a coward; coward was the word, by my valour!

Sir Luc. Well, sir?

Acres. Look'ee, Sir Lucius, 'tisn't that I mind the word coward — coward may be said in joke — But if you had called me a poltroon, odds daggers and balls ——

Sir Luc. Well, sir?

Acres. I should have thought you a very ill-bred man.

Sir Luc. Pho! you are beneath my notice.

Abs. Nay, Sir Lucius, you can't have a better second than my friend Acres — He is a most determined dog — called in the country, Fighting Bob. — He generally kills a man a week — don't you, Bob?

Acres. Ay — at home!

Sir Luc. Well, then, captain, 'tis we must begin — so come out, my little counsellor — [*Draws his sword*] — and ask the gentleman, whether he will resign the lady, without forcing you to proceed against him?

Abs. Come on then, sir — [*Draws*]; since you won't let it be an amicable suit, here's my reply.

Enter SIR ANTHONY ABSOLUTE, DAVID, MRS. MALAPROP, LYDIA, *and* JULIA.

Dav. Knock 'em all down, sweet Sir Anthony; knock down my master in particular; and bind his hands over to their good behaviour!

Sir Anth. Put up, Jack, put up, or I shall be in a frenzy — how came you in a duel, sir?

Abs. Faith, sir, that gentleman can tell you better than I; 'twas he called on me, and you know, sir, I serve his majesty.

Sir Anth. Here's a pretty fellow; I catch him going to cut a man's throat, and he tells me, he serves his majesty!— Zounds! sirrah, then how durst you draw the king's sword against one of his subjects?

Abs. Sir, I tell you! that gentleman called me out, without explaining his reasons.

Sir Anth. Gad! sir, how came you to call my son out, without explaining your reasons?

Sir Luc. Your son, sir, insulted me in a manner which my honour could not brook.

Sir Anth. Zounds! Jack, how durst you insult the gentleman in a manner which his honour could not brook?

Mrs. Mal. Come, come, let's have no honour before ladies — Captain Absolute, come here — How could you intimidate us so? — Here's Lydia has been terrified to death for you.

Abs. For fear I shoud be killed, or escape, ma'am?

Mrs. Mal. Nay, no delusions to the past — Lydia is convinced; speak, child.

Sir Luc. With your leave, ma'am, I must put in a word here: I believe I could interpret the young lady's silence. Now, mark ——

Lyd. What is it you mean, sir?

Sir Luc. Come, come, Delia, we must be serious now — this is no time for trifling.

Lyd. 'Tis true, sir; and your reproof bids me offer this gentleman my hand, and solicit the return of his affections.

Abs. O! my little angel, say you so! — Sir Lucius — I perceive there must be some mistake here, with regard to the affront which you affirm I have given you. I can only say, that it could not have been intentional. And as you must be convinced, that I should not fear to support a real injury — you shall now see that I am not ashamed to atone for an inadvertency — I ask your pardon. — But for this lady, while honoured with her approbation, I will support my claim against any man whatever.

Sir Anth. Well said, Jack, and I'll stand by you, my boy.

Acres. Mind, I give up all my claim — I make no pretensions to any thing in the world; and if I can't get a wife without fighting for her, by my valour! I'll live a bachelor.

Sir Luc. Captain, give me your hand: an affront handsomely acknow!edged becomes an obligation; and as for the lady, if she chooses to deny her own hand-writing, here ——
                                        [*Takes out letters.*

Mrs. Mal. O, he will dissolve my mystery! — Sir Lucius, perhaps there's some mistake — perhaps I can illuminate ——

Sir Luc. Pray, old gentlewoman, don't interfere where you have no business. — Miss Languish, are you my Delia, or not?

Lyd. Indeed, Sir Lucius, I am not.
                              [*Walks aside with* CAPTAIN ABSOLUTE.

Mrs. Mal. Sir Lucius O'Trigger — ungrateful as you are — I own the soft impeachment — pardon my blushes, I am Delia.

Sir Luc. You Delia — pho! pho! be easy.

Mrs. Mal. Why, thou barbarous Vandyke — those letters are mine — When you are more sensible of my benignity — perhaps I may be brought to encourage your addresses.

Sir Luc. Mrs. Malaprop, I am extremely sensible of your

condescension; and whether you or Lucy have put this trick
on me, I am equally beholden to you. — And, to show you I
am not ungrateful, Captain Absolute, since you have taken
that lady from me, I'll give you my Delia into the bargain.

Abs. I am much obliged to you, Sir Lucius; but here's
my friend, Fighting Bob, unprovided for.

Sir Luc. Hah! little Valour — here, will you make your
fortune?

Acres. Odds wrinkles! No. — But give me your hand,
Sir Lucius, forget and forgive; but if ever I give you a
chance of pickling me again, say Bob Acres is a dunce,
that's all.

Sir Anth. Come, Mrs. Malaprop, don't be cast down —
you are in your bloom yet.

Mrs. Mal. O Sir Anthony — men are all barbarians.

               [*All retire but* JULIA *and* FAULKLAND.

Jul. [*Aside.*] He seems dejected and unhappy — not sullen;
there was some foundation, however, for the tale he told me
— O woman! how true should be your judgment, when your
resolution is so weak!

Faulk. Julia! — how can I sue for what I so little deserve?
I dare not presume — yet Hope is the child of Penitence.

Jul. Oh! Faulkland, you have not been more faulty in your
unkind treatment of me, than I am now in wanting inclination
to resent it. As my heart honestly bids me place my weakness to the account of love, I should be ungenerous not to admit the same plea for yours.

Faulk. Now I shall be blest indeed!

Sir Anth. [*Coming forward.*] What's going on here? — So
you have been quarrelling too, I warrant! Come, Julia, I
never interfered before; but let me have a hand in the matter
at last. — All the faults I have ever seen in my Friend Faulkland seemed to proceed from what he calls the delicacy and
warmth of his affection for you — There, marry him directly,
Julia; you'll find he'll mend surprisingly!

               [*The rest come forward.*

Sir Luc. Come, now, I hope there is no dissatisfied per-

son, but what is content; for as I have been disappointed myself, it will be very hard if I have not the satisfaction of seeing other people succeed better.

Acres. You are right, Sir Lucius. — So Jack, I wish you
joy — Mr. Faulkland the same. — Ladies, — come now, to
show you I'm neither vexed nor angry, odds tabors and pipes!
I'll order the fiddles in half an hour to the New Rooms — and
I insist on your all meeting me there.

Sir Anth. 'Gad! sir, I like your spirit; and at night we
single lads will drink a health to the young couples, and a
husband to Mrs. Malaprop.

Faulk. Our partners are stolen from us, Jack — I hope to
be congratulated by each other — yours for having checked
in time the errors of an ill-directed imagination, which might
have betrayed an innocent heart; and mine, for having, by
her gentleness and candour, reformed the unhappy temper of
one, who by it made wretched whom he loved most, and tortured the heart he ought to have adored.

Abs. Well, Jack, we have both tasted the bitters, as well
as the sweets of love; with this difference only, that you always prepared the bitter cup for yourself, while I ——

Lyd. Was always obliged to me for it, hey! Mr. Modesty?
—— But, come, no more of that — our happiness is now as
unalloyed as general.

Jul. Then let us study to preserve it so: and while Hope
pictures to us a flattering scene of future bliss, let us deny its
pencil those colours which are too bright to be lasting. —
When hearts deserving happiness would unite their fortunes,
Virtue would crown them with an unfading garland of modest
hurtless flowers; but ill judging Passion will force the gaudier rose into the wreath, whose thorn offends them when its
leaves are dropped!   [*Exeunt omnes.*

EPILOGUE.

BY THE AUTHOR.

SPOKEN BY MRS. BULKLEY.

LADIES, for you — I heard our poet say —
He'd try to coax some moral from his play:
"One moral's plain," cried I, "without more fuss;
Man's social happiness all rests on us:
Through all the drama — whether damn'd or not —
Love gilds the scene, and women guide the plot.
From every rank obedience is our due —
D'ye doubt? — The world's great stage shall prove it true."

    The cit, well skill'd to shun domestic strife,
Will sup abroad; but first he'll ask his wife:
John Trot, his friend, for once will do the same,
But then — he'll just step home to tell his dame.

    The surly squire at noon resolves to rule,
And half the day — Zourds! madam is a fool
Convinced at night, the vanquish'd victor says,
Ah, Kate! you women have such coaxing ways.

    The jolly toper chides each tardy blade,
Till reeling Bacchus calls on Love for aid:
Then with each toast he sees fair bumpers swim,
And kisses Chloe on the sparkling brim!

    Nay, I have heard that statesmen — great and wise —
Will sometimes counsel with a lady's eyes!
The servile suitors watch her various face,
She smiles preferment, or she frowns disgrace,
Curtsies a pension here — there nods a place.

    Nor with less awe, in scenes of humbler life,
Is view'd the mistress, or is heard the wife.
The poorest peasant of the poorest soil,
The child of poverty, and heir to toil,
Early from radiant Love's impartial light
Steals one small spark to cheer this world of night:
Dear spark! that oft through winter's chilling woes
Is all the warmth his little cottage knows!

    The wandering tar, who not for years has press'd,
The widow'd partner of his day of rest,
On the cold deck, far from her arms removed,
Still hums the ditty which his Susan loved;
And while around the cadence rude is blown,
The boatswain whistles in a softer tone.

The soldier, fairly proud of wounds and toil,
Pants for the triumph of his Nancy's smile;
But ere the battle should he list her cries,
The lover trembles — and the hero dies!
That heart, by war and honour steel'd to fear,
Droops on a sigh, and sickens at a tear!
But ye more cautious, ye nice-judging few,
Who give to beauty only beauty's due,
Though friends to love — ye view with deep regret
Our conquests marr'd, our triumphs incomplete,
Till polish'd wit more lasting charms disclose,
And judgment fix the darts which beauty throws!
In female breasts did sense and merit rule,
The lover's mind would ask no other school;
Shamed into sense, the scholars of our eyes,
Our beaux from gallantry would soon be wise;
Would gladly light, their homage to improve,
The lamp of knowledge at the torch of love!

ST. PATRICK'S DAY;

OR,

THE SCHEMING LIEUTENANT.

A FARCE.

DRAMATIS PERSONÆ.

AS ORIGINALLY ACTED AT COVENT-GARDEN THEATRE IN 1775.

LIEUTENANT O'CONNOR	*Mr. Clinch.*	LAURETTA	*Mrs. Cargill.*
DOCTOR ROSY . .	. *Mr. Quick.*	MRS. BRIDGET CRE-}	*Mrs. Pitt.*
JUSTICE CREDULOUS	. *Mr. Lee Lewes.*	DULOUS . . . }	
SERJEANT TROUNCE	. *Mr. Booth.*	Drummer, Soldiers, Countrymen, *and*	
CORPORAL FLINT . .		Servant.	

SCENE. — A TOWN IN ENGLAND.

ACT I.

SCENE I. — LIEUTENANT O'CONNOR's *Lodgings.*

Enter SERJEANT TROUNCE, CORPORAL FLINT, *and four*
SOLDIERS.

1 Sol. I say you are wrong; we should all speak together, each for himself, and all at once, that we may be heard the better.

2 Sol. Right, Jack, we'll argue in platoons.

3 Sol. Ay, ay, let him have our grievances in a volley, and if we be to have a spokesman, there's the corporal is the lieutenant's countryman, and knows his humour.

Flint. Let me alone for that. I served three years, within a bit, under his honour, in the Royal Inniskillions, and I never will see a sweeter tempered gentleman, nor one more free with his purse. I put a great shammock in his hat this morning, and I'll be bound for him he'll wear it, was it as big as Steven's Green.

4. *Sol.* I say again then you talk like youngsters, like
militia striplings: there's a discipline, look'ee, in all things,
whereof the serjeant must be our guide; he's a gentleman of
words; he understands your foreign lingo, your figures, and
such like auxiliaries in scoring. Confess now for a reckoning,
whether in chalk or writing, ben't he your only man?

Flint. Why the serjeant is a scholar to be sure, and has
the gift of reading.

Trounce. Good soldiers, and fellow gentlemen, if you make
me your spokesman, you will show the more judgment; and
let me alone for the argument. I'll be as loud as a drum,
and point blank from the purpose.

All. Agreed, agreed.

Flint. Oh, fait! here comes the lieutenant.—Now, serjeant.

Trounce. So then, to order. — Put on your mutiny looks;
every man grumble a little to himself, and some of you hum
the Deserter's March.

Enter LIEUTENANT O'CONNOR.

O'Con. Well, honest lads, what is it you have to complain
of?

Sol. Ahem! hem!

Trounce. So please your honour, the very grievance of the
matter is this: — ever since your honour differed with Justice
Credulous, our inn-keepers use us most scurvily. By my
halbert, their treatment is such, that if your spirit was willing
to put up with it, flesh and blood could by no means agree;
so we humbly petition that your honour would make an end
of the matter at once, by running away with the justice's
daughter, or else get us fresh quarters, — hem! hem!

O'Con. Indeed! Pray which of the houses use you ill?

1 *Sol.* There's the Red Lion an't half the civility of the
old Red Lion.

2 *Sol.* There's the White Horse, if he wasn't casehardened,
ought to be ashamed to show his face.

O'Con. Very well; the Horse and the Lion shall answer
for it at the quarter sessions.

Trounce. The two Magpies are civil enough; but the An-

gel uses us like devils, and the Rising Sun refuses us light to
go to bed by.

O'Con. Then, upon my word, I'll have the Rising Sun put
down, and the Angel shall give security for his good behaviour;
but are you sure you do nothing to quit scores with them?

Flint. Nothing at all, your honour, unless now and then
we happen to fling a cartridge into the kitchen fire, or put a
spatterdash or so into the soup; and sometimes Ned drums up
and down stairs a little of a night.

O'Con. Oh, all that's fair; but hark'ee lads, I must have
no grumbling on St. Patrick's day; so here, take this, and di-
vide it amongst you. But observe me now, — show yourselves men of spirit, and don't spend sixpence of it in drink.

Trounce. Nay, hang it, your honour, soldiers should never
bear malice; we must drink St. Patrick's and your honour's
health.

All. Oh, damn malice! St. Patrick's and his honour's by
all means.

Flint. Come away, then, lads, and first we'll parade round
the Market-cross, for the honour of King George.

1 Sol Thank your honour. — Come along; St. Patrick,
his honour, and strong beer for ever!   [*Exeunt* SOLDIERS.

O'Con. Get along, you thoughtless vagabonds! yet, upon
my conscience, 'tis very hard these poor fellows should
scarcely have bread from the soil they would die to defend.

Enter DOCTOR ROSY.

Ah, my little Dr. Rosy, my Galen a-bridge, what's the news?

Rosy. All things are as they were, my Alexander; the justice is as violent as ever: I felt his pulse on the matter again,
and, thinking his rage began to intermit, I wanted to throw
in the bark of good advice, but it would not do. He says you
and your cut-throats have a plot upon his life, and swears he
had rather see his daughter in a scarlet fever than in the arms
of a soldier.

O'Con. Upon my word the army is very much obliged to
him. Well, then, I must marry the girl first, and ask his
consent afterwards.

Rosy. So, then, the case of her fortune is desperate, hey?

O'Con. Oh, hang fortune, — let that take its chance; there is a beauty in Lauretta's simplicity, so pure a bloom upon her charms.

Rosy. So there is, so there is. You are for beauty as nature made her, hey! No artificial graces, no cosmetic varnish, no beauty in grain, hey!

O'Con. Upon my word, doctor, you are right; the London ladies were always too handsome for me; then they are so defended, such a circumvallation of hoop, with a breast-work of whalebone that would turn a pistol-bullet, much less Cupid's arrows, — then turret on turret on top, with stores of concealed weapons, under pretence of black pins, — and above all, a standard of feathers that would do honour to a knight of the Bath. Upon my conscience, I could as soon embrace an Amazon, armed at all points.

Rosy. Right, right, my Alexander! my taste to a tittle.

O'Con. Then, doctor, though I admire modesty in women, I like to see their faces. I am for the changeable rose; but with one of these quality Amazons, if their midnight dissipations had left them blood enough to raise a blush, they have not room enough in their cheeks to show it. To be sure, bashfulness is a very pretty thing; but, in my mind, there is nothing on earth so impudent as an everlasting blush.

Rosy. My taste, my taste! — Well, Lauretta is none of these. Ay! I never see her but she puts me in mind of my poor dear wife.

O'Con. Ay, faith; in my opinion she can't do a worse thing. Now he is going to bother me about an old hag that has been dead these six years!   [*Aside.*

Rosy. Oh, poor Dolly! I never shall see her like again; such an arm for a bandage — veins that seemed to invite the lancet. Then her skin, smooth and white as a gallipot; her mouth as round and not larger than the mouth of a penny phial; her lips conserve of roses; and then her teeth — none of your sturdy fixtures — ache as they would, it was but a small pull, and out they came. I believe I have drawn half a score of her poor dear pearls — [*weeps*] — But what avails her beauty? Death has no consideration — one must die as well as another.

O'Con. [*Aside.*] Oh, if he begins to moralize ——

[*Takes out his snuff-box.*

Rosy. Fair and ugly, crooked or straight, rich or poor — flesh is grass — flowers fade!

O'Con. Here, doctor, take a pinch, and keep up your spirits.

Rosy. True, true, my friend; grief can't mend the matter— all's for the best; but such a woman was a great loss, lieutenant.

O'Con. To be sure, for doubtless she had mental accomplishments equal to her beauty.

Rosy. Mental accomplishments! she would have stuffed an alligator, or pickled a lizard, with any apothecary's wife in the kingdom. Why, she could decipher a prescription, and invent the ingredients, almost as well as myself: then she was such a hand at making foreign waters!—for Seltzer, Pyrmont, Islington, or Chalybeate, she never had her equal; and her Bath and Bristol springs exceeded the originals. — Ah, poor Dolly! she fell a martyr to her own discoveries.

O'Con. How so, pray?

Rosy. Poor soul! her illness was occasioned by her zeal in trying an improvement on the Spa-water, by an infusion of rum and acid.

O'Con. Ay, Ay, spirits never agree with water-drinkers.

Rosy. No, no, you mistake. Rum agreed with her well enough; it was not the rum that killed the poor dear creature, for she died of a dropsy. Well, she is gone never to return, and has left no pledge of our loves behind. No little babe, to hang like a label round papa's neck. Well, well, we are all mortal — sooner or later — flesh is grass — flowers fade.

O'Con. Oh, the devil! — again!   [*Aside.*

Rosy. Life's a shadow—the world a stage—we strut an hour.

O'Con. Here, doctor.   [*Offers snuff.*

Rosy. True, true, my friend: well, high grief can't cure it. All's for the best, hey! my little Alexander.

O'Con. Right, right; an apothecary should never be out of spirits. But come, faith, 'tis time honest Humphrey should wait on the justice; that must be our first scheme.

Rosy. True, true; you should be ready: the clothes are at my house, and I have given you such a character that he is impatient to have you: he swears you shall be his body-guard. Well, I honour the army, or I should never do so much to serve you.

O'Con. Indeed I am bound to you for ever, doctor; and when once I'm possessed of my dear Lauretta, I will endeavour to make work for you as fast as possible.

Rosy. Now you put me in mind of my poor wife again.

O'Con. Ah, pray forget her a little: we shall be too late.

Rosy. Poor Dolly!

O'Con. 'Tis past twelve.

Rosy. Inhuman dropsy!

O'Con. The justice will wait.

Rosy. Cropped in her prime!

O'Con. For Heaven's sake, come!

Rosy. Well, flesh is grass.

O'Con. O, the devil!

Rosy. We must all die ——

O'Con. Doctor!

Rosy. Kings, lords, and common whores ——

    [*Exeunt,* LIEUTENANT O'CONNOR, *forcing* ROSY *off.*

SCENE II. — *A Room in* JUSTICE CREDULOUS' *House.*

Enter LAURETTA *and* MRS. BRIDGET CREDULOUS.

Lau. I repeat it again, mamma, officers are the prettiest men in the world, and Lieutenant O'Connor is the prettiest officer I ever saw.

Mrs. Bri. For shame, Laura! how can you talk so? — or if you must have a military man, there's Lieutenant Plow, or Captain Haycock, or Major Dray, the brewer, are all your admirers; and though they are peaceable, good kind of men, they have as large cockades, and become scarlet as well as the fighting folks.

Lau. Psha! you know, mamma, I hate militia officers; a set of dunghill cocks with spurs on — heroes scratched off a church door — clowns in military masquerade, wearing the dress without supporting the character. No, give me the bold upright youth, who makes love to-day, and his head shot off to-morrow. Dear! to think how the sweet fellows sleep on the ground, and fight in silk stockings and lace ruffles.

Mrs. Bri. Oh, barbarous! to want a husband that may wed you to-day, and be sent the Lord knows where before night; then in a twelvemonth perhaps to have him come like a Colossus, with one leg at New York and the other at Chelsea Hospital.

Lau. Then I'll be his crutch, mamma.

Mrs. Bri. No, give me a husband that knows where his limbs are, though he want the use of them: — and if he should take you with him, to sleep in a baggage-cart, and stroll about the camp like a gipsy, with a knapsack and two children at your back; — then, by way of entertainment in the evening, to make a party with the serjeant's wife to drink bohea tea, and play at all-fours on a drumhead: — 'tis a precious life, to be sure!

Lau. Nay, mamma, you shouldn't be against my lieutenant, for I heard him say you were the best natured and best looking woman in the world.

Mrs. Bri. Why, child, I never said but that Lieutenant O'Connor was a very well-bred and discerning young man; 'tis your papa is so violent against him.

Lau. Why, Cousin Sophy married an officer.

Mrs. Bri. Ay, Laury, an officer in the militia.

Lau. No, indeed, mamma, a marching regiment.

Mrs. Bri. No, child, I tell you he was major of militia.

Lau. Indeed, mamma, it wasn't.

Enter JUSTICE CREDULOUS.

Just. Bridget, my love, I have had a message.

Lau. It was Cousin Sophy told me so.

Just. I have had a message, love ——

Mrs. Bri. No, child, she would say no such thing.

Just. A message, I say.

Lau. How could he be in the militia, when he was ordered abroad?

Mrs. Bri. Ay, girl, hold your tongue! — Well, my dear.

Just. I have had a message from Doctor Rosy.

Mrs. Bri. He ordered abroad! He went abroad for his health.

Just. Why, Bridget! ——

Mrs. Bri. Well, deary. — Now hold your tongue, miss.

Just. A message from Dr. Rosy, and Doctor Rosy says——

Lau. I'm sure, mamma, his regimentals ——

Just. Damn his regimentals! — Why don't you listen?

Mrs. Bri. Ay, girl, how durst you interrupt your papa?

Lau. Well, papa.

Just. Doctor Rosy says he'll bring ——

Lau. Were blue turned up with red, mamma.

Just. Laury! — says he will bring the young man ——

Mrs. Bri. Red! yellow, if you please, miss.

Just. Bridget! — the young man that is to be hired ——

Mrs. Bri. Besides, miss, it is very unbecoming in you to want to have the last word with your mamma; you should know ——

Just. Why, zounds! will you hear me or no?

Mrs. Bri. I am listening, my love — I am listening! — But what signifies my silence, what good is my not speaking a word, if this girl will interrupt and let nobody speak but herself? — Ay, I don't wonder, my life, at your impatience; your poor dear lips quiver to speak; but I suppose she'll run on, and not let you put in a word. — You may very well be angry; there is nothing, sure, so provoking as a chattering, talking ——

Lau. Nay, I'm sure, mamma, it is you will not let papa speak now.

Mrs. Bri. Why, you little provoking minx ——

Just. Get out of the room directly, both of you — get out!

Mrs. Bri. Ay, go, girl.

Just. Go, Bridget, you are worse than she, you old hag. I wish you were both up to the neck in the canal, to argue there till I took you out.

Enter SERVANT.

Ser. Doctor Rosy, sir.

Just. Show him up.   [*Exit* SERVANT.

Lau. Then you own, mamma, it was a marching regiment?

Mrs. Bri. You're an obstinate fool, I tell you; for if that had been the case ——

Just. You won't go?

Mrs. Bri. We are going, Mr. Surly. — If that had been the case, I say, how could ——

Lau. Nay, mamma, one proof ——

Mrs. Bri. How could Major ——

Lau. And a full proof ——

          [JUSTICE CREDULOUS *drives them off.*

Just. There they go, ding dong in for the day. Good lack! a fluent tongue is the only thing a mother don't like her daughter to resemble her in.

Enter DOCTOR ROSY.

Well, doctor, where's the lad — where's Trusty?

Rosy. At hand; he'll be here in a minute, I'll answer for't. He's such a one as you an't met with, — brave as a lion, gentle as a saline draught.

Just. Ah, he comes in the place of a rogue, a dog that was corrupted by the lieutenant. But this is a sturdy fellow, is he, doctor?

Rosy. As Hercules; and the best back-sword in the country. Egad, he'll make the red-coats keep their distance.

Just. O the villains! this is St. Patrick's day, and the rascals have been parading my house all the morning. I know they have a design upon me; but I have taken all precautions: I have magazines of arms, and if this fellow does but prove faithful, I shall be more at ease.

Rosy. Doubtless he'll be a comfort to you.

Re-enter SERVANT.

Ser. There is a man below, sir, inquires for Doctor Rosy.

Rosy. Show him up.

Just. Hold! a little caution — How does he look?

Ser. A country-looking fellow, your worship.

Just. Oh, well, well, for Doctor Rosy; these rascals try all ways to get in here.

Ser. Yes, please your worship; there was one here this morning wanted to speak to you: he said his name was Corporal Breakbones.

Just. Corporal Breakbones!

Ser. And drummer Crackskull came again.

Just. Ay! did you ever hear of such a damned confounded crew? Well, show the lad in here!   [*Exit* SERVANT.

Rosy. Ay, he'll be your porter; he'll give the rogues an answer.

Enter LIEUTENANT O'CONNOR, *disguised.*

Just. So, a tall — Efacks! what! has lost an eye?

Rosy. Only a bruise he got in taking seven or eight highwaymen.

Just. He has a damned wicked leer somehow with the other.

Rosy. Oh, no, he's bashful — a sheepish look ——

Just. Well, my lad, what's your name?

O'Con. Humphrey Hum.

Just. Hum — I don't like Hum!

O'Con. But I be mostly called honest Humphrey ——

Rosy. There, I told you so, of noted honesty.

Just. Well, honest Humphrey, the doctor has told you my terms, and you are willing to serve, hey?

O'Con. And please your worship I shall be well content.

Just. Well, then, hark'ye, honest Humphrey, — you are sure now you will never be a rogue — never take a bribe, hey, honest Humphrey?

O'Con. A bribe! What's that?

Just. A very ignorant fellow indeed!

Rosy. His worship hopes you will never part with your honesty for money.

O'Con. Noa, noa.

Just. Well said, Humphrey — my chief business with you is to watch the motions of a rake-helly fellow here, one Lieutenant O'Connor.

Rosy. Ay, you don't value the soldiers, do you, Humphrey?

O'Con. Not I; they are but zwaggerers, and you'll see they'll be as much afraid of me as they would of their captain.

Just. And i' faith, Humphrey, you have a pretty cudgel there!

O'Con. Ay, the zwitch is better than nothing, but I should be glad of a stouter: ha' you got such a thing in the house as an old coach-pole, or a spare bed-post?

Just. Oons! what a dragon it is! — Well, Humphrey, come with me. — I'll just show him to Bridget, doctor, and we'll agree. — Come along, honest Humphrey.   [*Exit.*

O'Con. My dear doctor, now remember to bring the justice presently to the walk: I have a scheme to get into his confidence at once.

Rosy. I will, I will.   [*They shake hands.*

Re-enter JUSTICE CREDULOUS.

Just. Why, honest Humphrey, hey! what the devil are you at?

Rosy. I was just giving him a little advice. — Well, I must go for the present. — Good morning to your worship — you need not fear the lieutenant while he is in your house.

Just. Well, get in, Humphrey. Good morning to you, doctor. — [*Exit* DOCTOR ROSY.] Come along, Humphrey. — Now I think I am a match for the lieutenant and all his gang.   [*Exeunt.*

ACT II.

SCENE I. — *A Street.*

Enter SERJEANT TROUNCE, DRUMMER, *and* SOLDIERS.

Trounce. Come, silence your drum — there is no valour stirring to day. I thought St. Patrick would have given us a recruit or two to-day.

Sol. Mark, serjeant!

Enter two COUNTRYMEN.

Trounce. Oh! these are the lads I was looking for; they have the looks of gentlemen — A'n't you single, my lads?

1 Coun. Yes, an please you, I be quite single: my relations be all dead, thank heavens, more or less. I have but one poor mother left in the world, and she's an helpless woman.

Trounce. Indeed! a very extraordinary case — quite your own master then — the fitter to serve his Majesty. — Can you read?

1 Coun. Noa, I was always too lively to take to learning; but John here is main clever at it.

Trounce. So, what you're a scholar, friend?

2 Coun. I was born so, measter. Feyther kept grammar-school.

Trounce. Lucky man—in a campaign or two put yourself down chaplain to the regiment. And I warrant you have read of warriors and heroes?

2 Coun. Yes, that I have: I have read of Jack the Giant-killer, and the Dragon of Wantly, and the — Noa, I believe that's all in the hero way, except once about a comet.

Trounce. Wonderful knowledge! — Well, my heroes, I'll write word to the king of your good intentions, and meet me half an hour hence at the Two Magpies.

Coun. We will, your honour, we will.

Trounce. But stay; for fear I shouldn't see you again in the crowd, clap these little bits of ribbon into your hats.

1 Coun. Our hats are none of the best.

Trounce. Well, meet me at the Magpies, and I'll give you money to buy new ones.

Coun. Bless your honour, thank your honour.   [*Exeunt.*

Trounce. [*Winking at* SOLDIERS.] Jack! [*Exeunt* SOLDIERS.

Enter LIEUTENANT O'CONNOR

So, here comes one would make a grenadier — Stop, friend, will you list?

O'Con. Who shall I serve under?

Trounce. Under me, to be sure.

O'Con. Isn't Lieutenant O'Connor your officer?

Trounce. He is, and I am commander over him.

O'Con. What! be your serjeants greater than your captains?

Trounce. To be sure we are; 'tis our business to keep them in order. For instance now, the general writes to me, dear Serjeant, or dear Trounce, or dear Serjeant Trounce, according to his hurry, if your lieutenant does not demean himself accordingly, let me know. — Yours, General Deluge.   •

O'Con. And do you complain of him often?

Trounce. No, hang him, the lad is good-natured at bottom, so I pass over small things. But hark'ee, between ourselves, he is most confoundedly given to wenching.

Enter CORPORAL FLINT.

Flint. Please your honour, the doctor is coming this way with his worship—We are all ready, and have our cues. [*Exit.*

O'Con. Then, my dear Trounce, or my dear Serjeant, or my dear Serjeant Trounce, take yourself away.

Trounce. Zounds! the lieutenant — I smell of the black hole already.   [*Exit.*

Enter JUSTICE CREDULOUS *and* DOCTOR ROSY.

Just. I thought I saw some of the cut-throats.

Rosy. I fancy not; there's no one but honest Humphrey. Ha! Odds life, here come some of them—we'll stay by these trees, and let them pass.

Just. Oh, the bloody-looking dogs!

[*Walks aside with* DOCTOR ROSY.

Re-enter CORPORAL FLINT *and two* SOLDIERS.

Flint. Halloa, friend! do you serve Justice Credulous?

O'Con. I do.

Flint. Are you rich?

O'Con. Noa.

Flint. Nor ever will be with that old stingy booby. Look here — take it.   [*Gives him a purse.*

O'Con. What must I do for this?

Flint. Mark me, our lieutenant is in love with the old

rogue's daughter: help us to break his worship's bones, and carry off the girl, and you are a made man.

 O'Con. I'll see you hanged first, you pack of skurry villains!   [*Throws away the purse.*

 Flint. What, sirrah, do you mutiny? Lay hold of him.

 O'Con. Nay then, I'll try your armour for you. [*Beats them.*

 All. Oh! oh! — quarter! quarter!

       [*Exeunt* CORPORAL FLINT *and* SOLDIERS.

 Just. [*Coming forward.*] Trim them, trounce them, break their bones, honest Humphrey — What a spirit he has!'

 Rosy. Aquafortis.

 O'Con. Betray your master!

 Rosy. What a miracle of fidelity!

 Just. Ay, and it shall not go unrewarded — I'll give him sixpence on the spot. Here, honest Humphrey, there's for yourself: as for this bribe, [*takes up the purse,*] such trash is best in the hands of justice. Now then, doctor, I think I may trust him to guard the women: while he is with them I may go out with safety.

 Rosy. Doubtless you may—I'll answer for the lieutenant's behaviour whilst honest Humphrey is with your daughter.

 Just. Ay, ay, she shall go nowhere without him. Come along, honest Humphrey. How rare it is to meet with such a servant!   [*Exeunt.*

SCENE II. — *A Garden.*

LAURETTA *discovered.* Enter JUSTICE CREDULOUS *and*

LIEUTENANT O'CONNOR.

 Just. Why, you little truant, how durst you wander so far from the house without my leave? Do you want to invite that scoundrel lieutenant to scale the walls and carry you off?

 Lau. Lud, papa, you are so apprehensive for nothing.

 Just. Why, hussy ——

 Lau. Well then, I can't bear to be shut up all day so like a nun. I am sure it is enough to make one wish to be run away with — and I wish I was run away with — I do — and I wish the lieutenant knew it.

Just. You do, do you, hussy? Well, I think I'll take pretty good care of you. Here, Humphrey, I leave this lady in your care. Now you may walk about the garden, Miss Pert; but Humphrey shall go with you wherever you go. So mind, honest Humphrey, I am obliged to go abroad for a little while; let no one but yourself come near her; don't be shamefaced, you booby, but keep close to her. And now, miss, let your lieutenant or any of his crew come near you if they can. [*Exit.*

Lau. How this booby stares after him! [*Sits down and sings.*
O'Con. Lauretta!
Lau. Not so free, fellow!   [*Sings.*
O'Con. Lauretta! look on me.
Lau. Not so free, fellow!
O'Con. No recollection!
Lau. Honest Humphrey, be quiet.
O'Con. Have you forgot your faithful soldier?
Lau. Ah! Oh preserve me!
O'Con. 'Tis, my soul! your truest slave, passing on your father in this disguise.
Lau. Well now, I declare this is charming—you are so disguised, my dear lieutenant, and you look so delightfully ugly. I am sure no one will find you out, ha! ha! ha! — You know I am under your protection; papa charged you to keep close to me.
O'Con. True, my angel, and thus let me fulfil—
Lau. O pray now, dear Humphrey——
O'Con. Nay, 'tis but what old Mittimus commanded.
[*Offers to kiss her.*

Re-enter JUSTICE CREDULOUS.

Just. Laury, my—hey! what the devil's here?
Lau. Well now, one kiss, and be quiet.
Just. Your very humble servant, honest Humphrey! Don't let me—pray don't let me interrupt you!
Lau. Lud, papa! Now that's so good-natured — indeed there's no harm. You did not mean any rudeness, did you, Humphrey?

Q'Con. No, indeed, miss; his worship knows it is not in me.

Just. I know that you are a lying, canting, hypocritical scoundrel; and if you don't take yourself out of my sight——

Lau. Indeed, papa, now I'll tell you how it was. I was sometime taken with a sudden giddiness, and Humphrey seeing me beginning to totter, ran to my assistance, quite frightened, poor fellow, and took me in his arms.

Just. Oh! was that all—nothing but a little giddiness, hey!

O'Con. That's all, indeed, your worship; for seeing miss change colour, I ran up instantly.

Just. Oh, 'twas very kind in you!

O'Con. And luckily recovered her.

Just. And who made you a doctor, you impudent rascal, hey? Get out of my sight, I say, this instant, or by all the statutes ——

Lau. Oh now, papa, you frighten me, and I am giddy again! — Oh, help!

O'Con. O dear lady, she'll fall! [*Takes her into his arms.*

Just. Zounds! what before my face —why then, thou miracle of impudence! — [*Lays hold of him and discovers him.*] —Mercy on me, who have we here?—Murder! Robbery! Fire! Rape! Gunpowder! Soldiers! John! Susan! Bridget!

O'Con. Good sir, don't be alarmed; I mean you no harm.

Just. Thieves! Robbers! Soldiers!

O'Con. You know my love for your daughter——

Just. Fire! Cut-throats!

O'Con. And that alone ——

Just. Treason! Gunpowder!

Enter a SERVANT *with a blunderbuss.*

Now, scoundrel! let her go this instant.

Lau. O papa, you'll kill me!

Just. Honest Humphrey, be advised. Ay, miss, this way, if you please.

O'Con. Nay, sir, but hear me ——

Just. I'll shoot.

O'Con. And you'll be convinced ——

Just. I'll shoot.

O'Con. How injurious ——

Just. I'll shoot—and so your very humble servant, honest Humphrey Hum.   [*Exeunt separately.*

SCENE III.— *A Walk.*

Enter DOCTOR ROSY.

Rosy. Well, I think my friend is now in a fair way of succeeding. Ah! I warrant he is full of hope and fear, doubt and anxiety; truly he has the fever of love strong upon him: faint, peevish, languishing all day, with burning, restless nights. Ah! just my case when I pined for my poor dear Dolly! when she used to have her daily colics, and her little doctor be sent for. Then would I interpret the language of her pulse—declare my own sufferings in my receipt for her— send her a pearl necklace in a pill-box, or a cordial draught with an acrostic on the label. Well, those days are over: no happiness lasting: all is vanity—now sunshine, now cloudy —we are, as it were, king and beggar—then what avails ——

Enter LIEUTENANT O'CONNOR.

O'Con. O doctor! ruined and undone.

Rosy. The pride of beauty ——

O'Con. I am discovered, and ——

Rosy. The gaudy palace ——

O'Con. The justice is ——

Rosy. The pompous wig ——

O'Con. Is more enraged than ever.

Rosy. The gilded cane ——

O'Con. Why, doctor!   [*Slapping him on the shoulder.*

Rosy. Hey!

O'Con. Confound your morals! I tell you I am discovered, discomfited, disappointed.

Rosy. Indeed! Good lack, good lack, to think of the instability of human affairs! Nothing certain in this world — most deceived when most confident — fools of fortune all.

O'Con. My dear doctor, I want at present a little practical wisdom. I am resolved this instant to try the scheme we were going to put in execution last week. I have the letter ready, and only want your assistance to recover my ground.

Rosy. With all my heart—I'll warrant you I'll bear a part in it: but how the deuce were you discovered?

O'Con. I'll tell you as we go; there's not a moment to be lost.

Rosy. Heaven send we succeed better! — but there's no knowing.

O'Con. Very true.

Rosy. We may, and we may not.

O'Con. Right.

Rosy. Time must show.

O'Con. Certainly.

Rosy. We are but blind guessers.

O'Con. Nothing more.

Rosy. Thick-sighted mortals.

O'Con. Remarkably.

Rosy. Wandering in error.

O'Con. Even so.

Rosy. Futurity is dark.

O'Con. As a cellar.

Rosy. Men are moles.

[*Exeunt*, LIEUTENANT O'CONNOR *forcing out* ROSY.

Scene IV. — *A Room in* JUSTICE CREDULOUS' *House.*

Enter JUSTICE CREDULOUS *and* MRS. BRIDGET CREDULOUS.

Just. Odds life, Bridget, you are enough to make one mad! I tell you he would have deceived a chief justice: the dog seemed as ignorant as my clerk, and talked of honesty as if he had been a churchwarden.

Mrs. Bri. Pho! nonsense, honesty! — what had you to do, pray, with honesty? A fine business you have made of it with your Humphrey Hum; and miss, too, she must have been privy to it. Lauretta! ay, you would have her called so; but for my part I never knew any good come of giving girls these

heathen christian names: if you had called her Deborah, or
Tabitha, or Ruth, or Rebecca, or Joan, nothing of this had
ever happened; but I always knew Lauretta was a runaway
name.

Just. Psha, you're a fool!

Mrs. Bri. No, Mr. Credulous, it is you who are a fool, and
no one but such a simpleton would be so imposed on.

Just. Why, zounds, madam, how durst you talk so? If
you have no respect for your husband, I should think *unus
quorum* might command a little deference.

Mrs. Bri. Don't tell me! — Unus fiddlestick! you ought to
be ashamed to show your face at the sessions: you'll be a
laughing-stock to the whole bench, and a byword with all the
pig-tailed lawyers and bag-wigged attorneys about town.

Just. Is this language for his majesty's representative? By
the statutes, it's high treason and petty treason, both at once!

Enter SERVANT.

Ser. A letter for your worship.

Just. Who brought it?

Ser. A soldier.

Just. Take it away and burn it.

Mrs. Bri. Stay!—Now you're in such a hurry— it is some
canting scrawl from the lieutenant, I suppose. — [*Takes the
letter.— Exit* SERVANT.] Let me see: — ay, 'tis signed O'Connor.

Just. Well, come read it out.

Mrs. Bri. [Reads.] *Revenge is sweet.*

Just. It begins so, does it? I'm glad of that; I'll let the
dog know I'm of his opinion.

Mrs. Bri. [Reads.] *And though disappointed of my designs
upon your daughter, I have still the satisfaction of knowing I
am revenged on her unnatural father; for this morning, in your
chocolate, I had the pleasure to administer to you a dose of
poison.* — Mercy on us!

Just. No tricks, Bridget; come, you know it is not so; you
know it is a lie.

Mrs. Bri. Read it yourself.

Just. [Reads.] *Pleasure to administer a dose of poison!* —
Oh, horrible! Cut-throat villain! — Bridget!

Mrs. Bri. Lovee, stay, here's a postscript. — [Reads.] *N.B.
'Tis not in the power of medicine to save you.*

Just. Odds my life, Bridget! why don't you call for help?
I've lost my voice. — My brain is giddy — I shall burst, and
no assistance. — John! — Laury! — John!

Mrs.Bri. You see, lovee, what you have brought on yourself.

Re-enter SERVANT.

Ser. Your worship!

Just. Stay, John; did you perceive any thing in my chocolate cup this morning?

Ser. Nothing, your worship, unless it was a little grounds.

Just. What colour were they?

Ser. Blackish, your worship.

Just. Ay, arsenic, black arsenic! — Why don't you run for
Doctor Rosy, you rascal?

Ser. Now, sir?

Mrs. Bri. Oh lovee, you may be sure it is in vain: let him
run for the lawyer to witness your will, my life.

Just. Zounds! go for the doctor, you scoundrel. You are
all confederate murderers.

Ser. Oh, here he is, your worship.   [*Exit.*

Just. Now, Bridget, hold your tongue, and let me see if
my horrid situation be apparent.

Enter DOCTOR ROSY.

Rosy. I have but just called to inform — hey! bless me,
what's the matter with your worship?

Just. There, he sees it already! — Poison in my face, in
capitals! Yes, yes, I'm a sure job for the undertakers indeed!

Mrs. Bri. Oh! oh! alas, doctor!

Just. Peace, Bridget! — Why doctor, my dear old friend,
do you really see any change in me?

Rosy. Change! never was man so altered: how came these
black spots on your nose?

Just. Spots on my nose!

Rosy. And that wild stare in your right eye!

Just. In my right eye!

Rosy. Ay, and alack, alack, how you are swelled!

Just. Swelled!

Rosy. Ay, don't you think he is, madam?

Mrs. Bri. Oh, 'tis in vain to conceal it! — Indeed, lovee, you are as big again as you were this morning.

Just. Yes, I feel it now — I'm poisoned!—Doctor, help me, for the love of justice! Give me life to see my murderer hanged.

Rosy. What?

Just. I'm poisoned, I say!

Rosy. Speak out!

Just. What! can't you hear me?

Rosy. Your voice is so low and hollow, as it were, I can't hear a word you say.

Just. I'm gone then! — *Hic jacet,* many years one of his majesty's justices!

Mrs. Bri. Read, doctor! — Ah, lovee, the will! — Consider, my life, how soon you will be dead.

Just. No, Bridget, I shall die by inches.

Rosy. I never heard such monstrous iniquity. — Oh, you are gone indeed, my friend! the mortgage of your little bit of clay is out, and the sexton has nothing to do but to close. We must all go, sooner or later — high and low — Death's a debt; his mandamus binds all alike — no bail, no demurrer.

Just. Silence, Doctor Croaker! will you cure me or will you not?

Rosy. Alas! my dear friend, it is not in my power, but I'll certainly see justice done on your murderer.

Just. I thank you, my dear friend, but I had rather see it myself.

Rosy. Ay, but if you recover, the villain will escape.

Mrs. Bri. Will he? then indeed it would be a pity you should recover. I am so enraged against the villain, I can't bear the thought of his escaping the halter.

Just. That's very kind in you, my dear; but if it's the same thing to you, my dear, I had as soon recover, notwithstanding. — What, doctor, no assistance!

Rosy. Efacks, I can do nothing, but there's the German quack, whom you wanted to send from town; I met him at the next door, and I know he has antidotes for all poisons.

Just. Fetch him, my dear friend, fetch him! I'll get him a diploma if he cures me.

Rosy. Well, there's no time to be lost; you continue to swell immensely.   [*Exit.*

Mrs. Bri. What, my dear, will you submit to be cured by a quack nostrum-monger? For my part, as much as I love you, I had rather follow you to your grave than see you owe your life to any but a regular-bred physician.

Just. I'm sensible of your affection, dearest; and be assured nothing consoles me in my melancholy situation so much as the thoughts of leaving you behind.

Re-enter DOCTOR ROSY, *with* LIEUTENANT O'CONNOR *disguised.*

Rosy. Great luck; met him passing by the door.

O'Con. Metto dowsei pulsum.

Rosy. He desires me to feel your pulse.

Just. Can't he speak English?

Rosy. Not a word.

O'Con. Palio vivem mortem soonem.

Rosy. He says you have not six hours to live.

Just. O mercy! does he know my distemper?

Rosy. I believe not.

Just. Tell him 'tis black arsenic they have given me.

Rosy. Geneable illi arsneeca.

O'Con. Pisonatus.

Just. What does he say?

Rosy. He says you are poisoned.

Just. We know that; but what will be the effect?

Rosy. Quid effectum?

O'Con. Diable tutellum.

Rosy. He says you'll die presently.   •

Just. Oh horrible! What, no antidote?

O'Con. Curum benakere bono fullum.

8*

Just. What, does he say I must row in a boat to Fulham?

Rosy. He says he'll undertake to cure you for three thousand pounds.

Mrs. Bri. Three thousand pounds! three thousand halters! — No, lovee, you shall never submit to such impositions; die at once, and be a customer to none of them.

Just. I won't die, Bridget — I don't like death.

Mrs. Bri. Psha! there is nothing in it: a moment, and it is over.

Just. Ay, but it leaves a numbness behind that lasts a plaguy long time.

Mrs. Bri. O my dear, pray consider the will.

Enter LAURETTA.

Lau. O my father, what is this I hear?

O'Con. Quiddam seomriam deos tollam rosam.

Rosy. The doctor is astonished at the sight of your fair daughter.

Just. How so?

O'Con. Damsellum livivum suvum rislibani.

Rosy. He says that he has lost his heart to her, and that if you will give him leave to pay his addresses to the young lady, and promise your consent to the union, if he should gain her affections, he will on those conditions cure you instantly, without fee or reward.

Just. The devil! did he say all that in so few words? What a fine language it is! Well, I agree, if he can prevail on the girl. — [*Aside.*] And that I am sure he never will.

Rosy. Greal.

O'Con. Writhum bothum.

Rosy. He says you must give this under your hand, while he writes you a miraculous receipt.

[*Both sit down to write.*

Lau. Do, mamma, tell me the meaning of this.

Mrs. Bri. Don't speak to me, girl. — Unnatural parent!

Just. There, doctor; there's what he requires.

Rosy. And here's your receipt: read it yourself.

Just. Hey! what's here? plain English!

Rosy. Read it out; a wondrous nostrum, I'll answer for it

Just. [Reads.] *In reading this you are cured, by your affectionate son-in-law,* O'CONNOR. — Who, in the name of Beelzebub, sirrah, who are you?

O'Con. Your affectionate son-in-law, O'Connor, and your
very humble servant, Humphrey Hum.

Just. 'Tis false, you dog! you are not my son-in-law; for
I'll be poison'd again, and you shall be hanged. — I'll die,
sirrah, and leave Bridget my estate.

Mrs. Bri. Ay, pray do, my dear, leave me your estate:
I'm sure he deserves to be hanged.

Just. He does, you say! — Hark'ee, Bridget, you showed
such a tender concern for me when you thought me poisoned,
that for the future I am resolved never to take your advice
again in any thing. — [*To* LIEUTENANT O'CONNOR.] So, do you
hear, sir, you are an Irishman and a soldier, an't you?

O'Con. I am, sir, and proud of both.

Just. The two things on earth I most hate; so I'll tell you
what — renounce your country and sell your commission, and
I'll forgive you.

O'Con. Hark'ee, Mr. Justice — if you were not the father
of my Lauretta, I would pull your nose for asking the first,
and break your bones for desiring the second.

Rosy. Ay, ay, you're right.

Just. Is he? then I'm sure I must be wrong. — Here, sir,
I give my daughter to you, who are the most impudent dog I
ever saw in my life.

O'Con. Oh, sir, say what you please; with such a gift as
Lauretta, every word is a compliment.

Mrs. Bri. Well, my lovee, I think this will be a good subject for us to quarrel about the rest of our lives.

Just. Why, truly, my dear, I think so, though we are
seldom at a loss for that.

Rosy. This is all as it should be. — My Alexander, I give
you joy, and you, my little god-daughter; and now my sincere
wish is, that you may make just such a wife as my poor dear
Dolly.   [*Exeunt omnes.*

THE DUENNA.

A COMIC OPERA.

DRAMATIS PERSONÆ.

AS ORIGINALLY ACTED AT COVENT-GARDEN THEATRE, NOV. 21, 1775.

DON FERDINAND . .	*Mr. Mattocks.*	LOPEZ	*Mr. Wewitzer.*
DON JEROME . . .	*Mr. Wilson.*		
DON ANTONIO. . .	*Mr. Dubellamy.*	DONNA LOUISA . .	*Mrs. Mattocks.*
DON CARLOS . . .	*Mr. Leoni.*	DONNA CLARA . .	*Mrs. Cargill.*
ISAAC MENDOZA . .	*Mr. Quick.*	THE DUENNA . . .	*Mrs. Green.*
FATHER PAUL . .	*Mr. Mahon.*		
FATHER FRANCIS .	*Mr. Fox.*	Masqueraders, Friars, Porter, Maid,	
FATHER AUGUSTINE	*Mr. Baker.*	and Servants.	

SCENE. — SEVILLE.

ACT I.

SCENE I. — *The Street before* DON JEROME'S *House.*

Enter LOPEZ, *with a dark lantern.*

Lop. Past three o'clock! — So! a notable hour for one of my regular disposition, to be strolling like a bravo through the streets of Seville! Well, of all services, to serve a young lover is the hardest. — Not that I am an enemy to love; but my love and my master's differ strangely. — Don Ferdinand is much too gallant to eat, drink, or sleep:—now, my love gives me an appetite — then I am fond of dreaming of my mistress, and I love dearly to toast her. — This cannot be done without good sleep and good liquor: hence my partiality to a feather-bed and a bottle. What a pity, now, that I have not further time for reflections! but my master expects thee, honest Lopez, to secure his retreat from Donna Clara's window, as I guess. — [*Music without.*] Hey! sure, I heard music! So, so! who have we here? Oh, Don Antonio, my master's friend, come from the masquerade, to serenade my young mistress, Donna Louisa, I suppose: so! we shall have the old gentleman up presently. — Lest he should miss his son, I had best lose no time in getting to my post.　　　　　　　　　[*Exit.*

Enter DON ANTONIO, *with* MASQUERADERS *and music.*

SONG. — *Don Ant.*

Tell me, my lute, can thy soft strain
　So gently speak thy master's pain?
So softly sing, so humbly sigh,
　That, though my sleeping love shall know
　Who sings — who sighs below,
Her rosy slumbers shall not fly?
　Thus, may some vision whisper more
　Than ever I dare speak before.

1 *Mas.* Antonio, your mistress will never wake, while you sing so dolefully; love, like a cradled infant, is lulled by a sad melody.

Don Ant. I do not wish to disturb her rest.

1 *Mas.* The reason is, because you know she does not regard you enough to appear, if you awaked her.

Don Ant. Nay, then, I'll convince you.　　　　　[*Sings.*

The breath of morn bids hence the night,
Unveil those beauteous eyes, my fair;
For till the dawn of love is there,
I feel no day, I own no light.

DONNA LOUISA — *replies from a window.*

Waking, I heard thy numbers chide,
Waking, the dawn did bless my sight;
'Tis Phœbus sure that woos, I cried,
Who speaks in song, who moves in light.

DON JEROME — *from a window.*

What vagabonds are these, I hear,
Fiddling, fluting, rhyming, ranting,
Piping, scraping, whining, canting,
Fly, scurvy minstrels, fly!

TRIO.

Don. Louisa .　Nay, prithee, father, why so rough?
Don Ant. . .　　An humble lover I.

Don Jer. . .	How durst you, daughter, lend an ear
	To such deceitful stuff?
	Quick, from the window fly!
Don. Louisa .	Adieu, Antonio!
Don Ant. . .	Must you go?
Don. Louisa }	We soon, perhaps, may meet again.
Don Ant. . }	For though hard fortune is our foe,
	The god of love will fight for us.
Don Jer. . .	Reach me the blunderbuss.
Don Ant. . }	
Don. Louisa }	The god of love, who knows our pain —
Don Jer. . .	Hence, or these slugs are through your brain.

[Exeunt severally.

SCENE II. — *A Piazza.*

Enter Don Ferdinand *and* Lopez.

Lop. Truly, sir, I think that a little sleep once in a week or so ——

Don Ferd. Peace, fool! don't mention sleep to me.

Lop. No, no, sir, I don't mention your lowbred, vulgar, sound sleep; but I can't help thinking that a gentle slumber, or half an hour's dozing, if it were only for the novelty of the thing ——

Don Ferd. Peace, booby, I say! — Oh Clara, dear, cruel disturber of my rest!

Lop. And of mine too.   *[Aside.*

Don Ferd. 'Sdeath, to trifle with me at such a juncture as this! — now to stand on punctilios! — Love me! I don't believe she ever did.

Lop. Nor I either.   *[Aside.*

Don Ferd. Or is it, that her sex never know their desires for an hour together?

Lop. Ah, they know them oftener than they'll own them.
[Aside.

Don Ferd. Is there, in the world, so inconstant a creature as Clara?

Lop. I could name one.   *[Aside.*

Don Ferd. Yes; the tame fool who submits to her caprice.

Lop. I thought he couldn't miss it.   *[Aside.*

Don Ferd. Is she not capricious, teasing, tyrannical, obstinate, perverse, absurd? ay, a wilderness of faults and follies; her looks are scorn, and her very smiles — 'Sdeath!— I wish I hadn't mentioned her smiles; for she does smile such beaming loveliness, such fascinating brightness — Oh, death and madness! I shall die if I lose her.

Lop. Oh, those damned smiles have undone all!   [*Aside.*

AIR. — *Don Ferd.*

Could I her faults remember,
Forgetting every charm,
Soon would impartial reason
The tyrant love disarm:
But when enraged I number
Each failing of her mind,
Love still suggests each beauty,
And sees — while reason's blind.

Lop. Here comes Don Antonio, sir.

Don Ferd. Well, go you home—I shall be there presently.

Lop. Ah, those cursed smiles!   [*Exit.*

Enter DON ANTONIO.

Don Ferd. Antonio, Lopez tells me he left you chanting before our door — was my father waked?

Don Ant. Yes, yes; he has a singular affection for music, so I left him roaring at his barred window, like the print of Bajazet in the cage. And what brings you out so early?

Don Ferd. I believe I told you, that to-morrow was the day fixed by Don Pedro and Clara's unnatural stepmother, for her to enter a convent, in order that her brat might possess her fortune: made desperate by this, I procured a key to the door, and bribed Clara's maid to leave it unbolted; at two this morning, I entered, unperceived, and stole to her chamber — I found her waking and weeping.

Don Ant. Happy Ferdinand!

Don Ferd. 'Sdeath! hear the conclusion. — I was rated as the most confident ruffian, for daring to approach her room at that hour of night.

Don Ant. Ay, ay, this was at first.

Don Ferd. No such thing! she would not hear a word from me, but threatened to raise her mother, if I did not instantly leave her.

Don Ant. Well, but at last? ——

Don Ferd. At last! why I was forced to leave the house as I came in.

Don Ant. And did you do nothing to offend her?

Don Ferd. Nothing, as I hope to be saved! — I believe, I might snatch a dozen or two of kisses.

Don Ant. Was that all? well, I think, I never heard of such assurance!

Don Ferd. Zounds! I tell you I behaved with the utmost respect.

Don Ant. O Lord! I don't mean you, but in her. But, hark ye, Ferdinand, did you leave your key with them?

Don Ferd. Yes; the maid, who saw me out, took it from the door.

Don Ant. Then, my life for it, her mistress elopes after you.

Don Ferd. Ay, to bless my rival, perhaps. I am in a humour to suspect every body. — You loved her once, and thought her an angel, as I do now.

Don Ant. Yes, I loved her, till I found she wouldn't love me, and then I discovered that she hadn't a good feature in her face.

Air.

I ne'er could any lustre see
In eyes that would not look on me;
I ne'er saw nectar on a lip,
But where my own did hope to sip.
Has the maid who seeks my heart
Cheeks of rose, untouch'd by art?
I will own the colour true,
When yielding blushes aid their hue.

Is her hand so soft and pure?
I must press it, to be sure;
Nor can I be certain then,
Till it, grateful, press again.

> Must I, with attentive eye,
> Watch her heaving bosom sigh?
> I will do so, when I see
> That heaving bosom sigh for me.

Besides, Ferdinand you have full security in my love for your sister; help me there, and I can never disturb you with Clara.

Don Ferd. As far as I can, consistently with the honour of our family, you know I will; but there must be no eloping.

Don Ant. And yet, now, you would carry off Clara?

Don Ferd. Ay, that's a different case! — we never mean that others should act to our sisters and wives as we do to others'. — But, to-morrow, Clara is to be forced into a convent.

Don Ant. Well, and am not I so unfortunately circumstanced? To-morrow, your father forces Louisa to marry Isaac, the Portuguese — but come with me, and we'll devise something, I warrant.

Don Ferd. I must go home.

Don Ant. Well, adieu!

Don. Ferd. But, Antonio, if you did not love my sister, you have too much honour and friendship to supplant me with Clara? ——

AIR. — *Don Ant.*

> Friendship is the bond of reason;
> But if beauty disapprove,
> Heaven dissolves all other treason
> In the heart that's true to love.
>
> The faith which to my friend I swore,
> As a civil oath I view;
> But to the charms which I adore,
> 'Tis religion to be true.   [*Exit.*

Don Ferd. There is always a levity in Antonio's manner of replying to me on this subject that is very alarming. — 'Sdeath! if Clara should love him after all!

SONG.

> Though cause for suspicion appears,
> Yet proofs of her love, too, are strong;

I'm a wretch if I'm right in my fears,
And unworthy of bliss if I'm wrong.
What heart-breaking torments from jealousy flow,
Ah! none but the jealous — the jealous can know!

When blest with the smiles of my fair,
I know not how much I adore:
Those smiles let another but share,
And I wonder I prized them no more!
Then whence can I hope a relief from my woe,
When the falser she seems, still the fonder I grow!   [*Exit.*

SCENE III. — *A Room in* DON JEROME'S *House.*

Enter DONNA LOUISA *and* DUENNA.

Don. Louisa. But, my dear Margaret, my charming Duenna, do you think we shall succeed?

Duen. I tell you again, I have no doubt on't; but it must be instantly put to the trial. Every thing is prepared in your room, and for the rest we must trust to fortune.

Don. Louisa. My father's oath was, never to see me till I had consented to ——

Duen. 'Twas thus I overheard him say to his friend, Don Guzman, — *I will demand of her to-morrow, once for all, whether she will consent to marry Isaac Mendoza; if she hesitates, I will make a solemn oath never to see or speak to her till she returns to her duty.* — These were his words.

Don. Louisa. And on his known obstinate adherence to what he has once said, you have formed this plan for my escape. — But have you secured my maid in our interest?

Duen. She is a party in the whole; but remember, if we succeed, you resign all right and title in little Isaac, the Jew, over to me.

Don. Louisa. That I do with all my soul; get him, if you can, and I shall wish you joy, most heartily. He is twenty times as rich as my poor Antonio.

AIR.

Thou canst not boast of fortune's store,
My love, while me they wealthy call:
But I was glad to find thee poor —
For with my heart I'd give thee all.

And then the grateful youth shall own
I loved him for himself alone.

But when his worth my hand shall gain,
No word or look of mine shall show
That I the smallest thought retain
Of what my bounty did bestow:
    Yet still his grateful heart shall own
    I loved him for himself alone.

Duen. I hear Don Jerome coming. — Quick, give me the last letter I brought you from Antonio — you know that is to be the ground of my dismission — I must slip out to seal it up, as undelivered.   [*Exit.*

Enter Don Jerome *and* Don Ferdinand.

Don. Jer. What, I suppose you have been serenading too! Eh, disturbing some peaceable neighbourhood with villanous catgut and lascivious piping! Out on't! you set your sister, here, a vile example; but I come to tell you, madam, that I'll suffer no more of these midnight incantations — these amorous orgies, that steal the senses in the hearing; as, they say Egyptian embalmers serve mummies, extracting the brain through the ears. However, there's an end of your frolics — Isaac Mendoza will be here presently, and to-morrow you shall marry him.

Don. Louisa. Never, while I have life!

Don Ferd. Indeed, sir, I wonder how you can think of such a man for a son-in-law.

Don. Jer. Sir, you are very kind to favour me with your sentiments — and pray, what is your objection to him?

Don Ferd. He is a Portuguese, in the first place.

Don Jer. No such thing, boy; he has forsworn his country.

Don. Louisa. He is a Jew.

Don Jer. Another mistake: he has been a Christian these six weeks.

Don Ferd. Ay, he left his old religion for an estate, and has not had time to get a new one.

Don. Louisa. But stands like a dead wall between church and synagogue, or like the blank leaves between the Old and New Testament.

Don Jer. Any thing more?

Don Ferd. But the most remarkable part of his character is his passion for deceit and tricks of cunning.

Don. Louisa. Though at the same time the fool predominates so much over the knave, that I am told he is generally the dupe of his own art.

Don Ferd. True; like an unskilful gunner, he usually misses his aim, and is hurt by the recoil of his own piece.

Don Jer. Any thing more?

Don. Louisa. To sum up all, he has the worst fault a husband can have — he's not my choice.

Don Jer. But you are his; and choice on one side is sufficient — two lovers should never meet in marriage — be you sour as you please, he is sweet-tempered; and for your good fruit, there's nothing like ingrafting on a crab.

Don. Louisa. I detest him as a lover, and shall ten times more as a husband.

Don Jer. I don't know that — marriage generally makes a great change — but, to cut the matter short, will you have him or not?

Don. Louisa. There is nothing else I could disobey you in.

Don Jer. Do you value your father's peace?

Don. Louisa. So much, that I will not fasten on him the regret of making an only daughter wretched.

Don Jer. Very well, ma'am, then mark me — never more will I see or converse with you till you return to your duty — no reply — this and your chamber shall be your apartments; I never will stir out without leaving you under lock and key, and when I'm at home no creature can approach you but through my library: we'll try who can be most obstinate. Out of my sight! — there remain till you know your duty.

[*Pushes her out.*

Don Ferd. Surely, sir, my sister's inclinations should be consulted in a matter of this kind, and some regard paid to Don Antonio, being my particular friend.

Don Jer. That, doubtless, is a very great recommendation! — I certainly have not paid sufficient respect to it.

Don Ferd. There is not a man living I would sooner choose for a brother-in-law.

Don Jer. Very possible; and if you happen to have e'er a sister, who is not at the same time a daughter of mine, I'm sure I shall have no objection to the relationship; but at present, if you please, we'll drop the subject.

Don Ferd. Nay, sir, 'tis only my regard for my sister makes me speak.

Don Jer. Then, pray, sir, in future, let your regard for your father make you hold your tongue.

Don Ferd. I have done, sir. I shall only add a wish that you would reflect what at our age you would have felt, had you been crossed in your affection for the mother of her you are so severe to.

Don Jer. Why, I must confess I had a great affection for your mother's ducats, but that was all, boy. I married her for her fortune, and she took me in obedience to her father, and a very happy couple we were. We never expected any love from one another, and so we were never disappointed. If we grumbled a little now and then, it was soon over, for we were never fond enough to quarrel; and when the good woman died, why, why,— had as lieve she had lived, and I wish every widower in Seville could say the same. I shall now go and get the key of this dressing-room—so, good son, if you have any lecture in support of disobedience to give your sister, it must be brief; so make the best of your time, d'ye hear? [*Exit.*

Don Ferd. I fear, indeed, my friend Antonio has little to hope for; however, Louisa has firmness, and my father's anger will probably only increase her affection. — In our intercourse with the world, it is natural for us to dislike those who are innocently the cause of our distress; but in the heart's attachment a woman never likes a man with ardour till she has suffered for his sake — [*Noise.*] so! What bustle is here! between my father and the Duenna too — I'll e'en get out of the way. [*Exit.*

Re-enter DON JEROME *with a letter, pulling in* DUENNA.

Don Jer. I'm astonished! I'm thunder-struck! here's treachery and conspiracy with a vengeance! You, Antonio's creature, and chief manager of this plot for my daughter's eloping! — you, that I placed here as a scarecrow?

Duen. What?

Don Jer. A scarecrow—to prove a decoy-duck! What have you to say for yourself?

Duen. Well sir, since you have forced that letter from me, and discovered my real sentiments, I scorn to renounce them. — I am Antonio's friend, and it was my intention that your daughter should have served you as all such old tyrannical sots should be served — I delight in the tender passions, and would befriend all under their influence.

Don Jer. The tender passions! yes, they would become those impenetrable features! Why, thou deceitful hag! I placed thee as a guard to the rich blossoms of my daughter's beauty. I thought that dragon's front of thine would cry aloof to the sons of gallantry: steel traps and spring guns seemed writ in every wrinkle of it. — But you shall quit my house this instant. The tender passions, indeed! go, thou wanton sibyl, thou amorous woman of Endor, go!

Duen. You base, scurrilous, old — but I won't demean myself by naming what you are. — Yes, savage, I'll leave your den; but I suppose you don't mean to detain my apparel — I may have my things, I presume?

Don Jer. I took you, mistress, with your wardrobe on — what have you pilfered, eh?

Duen. Sir, I must take leave of my mistress; she has valuables of mine: besides, my cardinal and veil are in her room.

Don Jer. Your veil, forsooth! what, do you dread being gazed at? or are you afraid of your complexion? Well, go take your leave, and get your veil and cardinal! so! you quit the house within these five minutes. — In — in — quick!—[*Exit* DUENNA.] Here was a precious plot of mischief! — these are the comforts daughters bring us!

AIR.

If a daughter you have, she's the plague of your life,
No peace shall you know, though you've buried your wife!
At twenty she mocks at the duty you taught her. —
Oh, what a plague is an obstinate daughter!
Sighing and whining,
Dying and pining,
Oh, what a plague is an obstinate daughter!

When scarce in their teens, they have wit to perplex us,
With letters and lovers for ever they vex us;
While each still rejects the fair suitor you've brought her;
Oh, what a plague is an obstinate daughter!
Wrangling and jangling,
Flouting and pouting,
Oh, what a plague is an obstinate daughter!

Re-enter DONNA LOUISA, *dressed as* DUENNA, *with cardinal and veil, seeming to cry.*

This way, mistress, this way. — What, I warrant, a tender parting; so! tears of turpentine down those deal cheeks. — Ay, you may well hide your head—yes, whine till your heart breaks; but I'll not hear one word of excuse — so you are right to be dumb. This way, this way.   [*Exeunt.*

Re-enter DUENNA.

Duen. So, speed you well, sagacious Don Jerome! Oh, rare effects of passion and obstinacy! Now shall I try whether I can't play the fine lady as well as my mistress, and if I succeed, I may be a fine lady for the rest of my life—I'll lose no time to equip myself.   [*Exit.*

SCENE IV. — *The Court before* DON JEROME'S *House.*

Enter DON JEROME *and* DONNA LOUISA.

Don Jer. Come, mistress, there is your way — the world lies before you, so troop, thou antiquated Eve, thou original sin! Hold, yonder is some fellow skulking; perhaps it is Antonio — go to him, d'ye hear, and tell him to make you amends, and as he has got you turned away, tell him I say it is but just he should take you himself; go. — [*Exit* DONNA LOUISA.] So! I am rid of her, thank heaven! and now I shall be able to keep my oath, and confine my daughter with better security.   [*Exit.*

Scene V. — *The Piazza.*

Enter Donna Clara *and* Maid.

Maid. But where, madam, is it you intend to go?

Don. Clara. Any where to avoid the selfish violence of my mother-in-law, and Ferdinand's insolent importunity.

Maid. Indeed, ma'am, since we have profited by Don Ferdinand's key, in making our escape, I think we had best find him, if it were only to thank him.

Don. Clara. No—he has offended me exceedingly. [*Retire.*

Enter Donna Louisa.

Don. Louisa. So I have succeeded in being turned out of doors — but how shall I find Antonio? I dare not inquire for him, for fear of being discovered; I would send to my friend Clara, but that I doubt her prudery would condemn me.

Maid. Then suppose, ma'am, you were to try if your friend Donna Louisa would not receive you?

Don. Clara. No, her notions of filial duty are so severe, she would certainly betray me.

Don. Louisa. Clara is of a cold temper, and would think this step of mine highly forward.

Don. Clara. Louisa's respect for her father is so great, she would not credit the unkindness of mine.

[Donna Louisa *turns, and sees* Donna Clara *and* Maid.

Don. Louisa. Ha! who are those? sure one is Clara—if it be, I'll trust her. Clara! [*Advances.*

Don. Clara. Louisa! and in masquerade too!

Don. Louisa. You will be more surprised when I tell you, that I have run away from my father.

Don. Clara. Surprised indeed! and I should certainly chide you most horridly, only that I have just run away from mine.

Don. Louisa. My dear Clara! [*Embrace.*

Don. Clara. Dear sister truant! and whither are you going?

Don. Louisa. To find the man I love, to be sure: and, I presume, you would have no aversion to meet with my brother?

Don Clara. Indeed I should: he has behaved so ill to me, I don't believe I shall ever forgive him.

AIR.

When sable night, each drooping plant restoring,
  Wept o'er the flowers her breath did cheer,
As some sad widow o'er her babe deploring,
  Wakes its beauty with a tear;
When all did sleep whose weary hearts did borrow
  One hour from love and care to rest,
Lo! as I press'd my couch in silent sorrow.
  My Lover caught me to his breast!
    He vow'd he came to save me
  From those who would enslave me!
      Then kneeling,
      Kisses stealing,
Endless faith he swore;
  But soon I chid him thence,
  For had his fond pretence
  Obtain'd one favour then,
  And he had press'd again,
I fear'd my treacherous heart might grant him more.

Don. Louisa. Well, for all this, I would have sent him to plead his pardon, but that I would not yet a while have him know of my flight. And where do you hope to find protection?

Don. Clara. The Lady Abbess of the convent of St. Catharine is a relation and kind friend of mine — I shall be secure with her, and you had best go thither with me.

Don. Louisa. No; I am determined to find Antonio first; and, as I live, here comes the very man I will employ to seek him for me.

Don. Clara. Who is he? he's a strange figure!

Don. Louisa. Yes; that sweet creature is the man whom my father has fixed on for my husband.

Don Clara. And will you speak to him? are you mad?

Don. Louisa. He is the fittest man in the world for my purpose; for, though I was to have married him to-morrow, he is the only man in Seville, who, I am sure, never saw me in his life.

9*

Don. Clara. And how do you know him?

Don. Louisa. He arrived but yesterday, and he was shown to me from the window, as he visited my father.

Don. Clara. Well, I'll begone.

Don Louisa. Hold, my dear Clara — a thought has struck me: will you give me leave to borrow your name, as I see occasion?

Don. Clara. It will but disgrace you; but use it as you please: I dare not stay. —[*Going.*]—But, Louisa, if you should see your brother, be sure you don't inform him that I have taken refuge with the Dame Prior of the convent of St. Catharine, on the left hand side of the piazza, which leads to the church of St. Anthony.

Don. Louisa. Ha! ha! ha! I'll be very particular in my directions where he may not find you. — [*Exeunt* DONNA CLARA *and* MAID.] — So! my swain, yonder, has done admiring himself, and draws nearer.   [*Retires.*

Enter ISAAC *and* DON CARLOS.

Isaac. [*Looking in a pocket-glass.*] I tell you, friend Carlos, I will please myself in the habit of my chin.

Don Car. But, my dear friend, how can you think to please a lady with such a face?

Isaac. Why, what's the matter with the face! I think it is a very engaging face; and, I am sure, a lady must have very little taste who could dislike my beard. —[*Sees* DONNA LOUISA.] — See now! I'll die if here is not a little damsel struck with it already.

Don. Louisa. Signor, are you disposed to oblige a lady who greatly wants your assistance?   [*Unveils.*

Isaac. Egad, a very pretty black-eyed girl! she has certainly taken a fancy to me, Carlos. First, ma'am, I must beg the favour of your name.

Don. Louisa. [*Aside.*] So! it's well I am provided. — [*Aloud.*] — My name, sir, is Donna Clara d'Almanza.

Isaac. What? Don Guzman's daughter? I' faith, I just now heard she was missing.

Don. Louisa. But sure, sir, you have too much gallantry and honour to betray me, whose fault is love?

Isaac. So! a passion for me! poor girl! Why, ma'am, as for betraying you, I don't see how I could get any thing by it; so, you may rely on my honour; but as for your love, I am sorry your case is so desperate.

Don. Louisa. Why so, signor?

Isaac. Because I am positively engaged to another — an't I, Carlos?

Don. Louisa. Nay, but hear me.

Isaac. No, no; what should I hear for? It is impossible for me to court you in an honourable way; and for any thing else, if I were to comply now, I suppose you have some ungrateful brother, or cousin, who would want to cut my throat for my civility — so, truly, you had best go home again.

Don. Louisa. [*Aside.*] Odious wretch! — [*Aloud.*] — But, good signor, it is Antonio d'Ercilla, on whose account I have eloped.

Isaac. How! what! it is not with me, then, that you are in love?

Don. Louisa. No, indeed, it is not.

Isaac. Then you are a forward, impertinent simpleton! and I shall certainly acquaint your father.

Don. Louisa. Is this your gallantry?

Isaac. Yet hold — Antonio d'Ercilla, did you say? egad, I may make something of this — Antonio d'Ercilla?

Don. Louisa. Yes; and, if ever you hope to prosper in love, you will bring me to him.

Isaac. By St. Iago and I will too! — Carlos, this Antonio is one who rivals me (as I have heard) with Louisa — now, if I could hamper him with this girl, I should have the field to myself: hey, Carlos! A lucky thought, isn't it?

Don Car. Yes, very good — very good!

Isaac. Ah! this little brain is never at a loss — cunning Isaac! cunning rogue! Donna Clara, will you trust yourself awhile to my friend's direction?

Don. Louisa. May I rely on you, good signor?

Don Car. Lady, it is impossible I should deceive you.

AIR.

Had I a heart for falsehood framed,
    I ne'er could injure you;
For though your tongue no promise claim'd,
    Your charms would make me true.
To you no soul shall bear deceit,
    No stranger offer wrong;
But friends in all the aged you'll meet,
    And lovers in the young.

But when they learn that you have blest
    Another with your heart,
They'll bid aspiring passion rest,
    And act a brother's part:
Then, lady, dread not here deceit,
    Nor fear to suffer wrong;
For friends in all the aged you'll meet,
    And brothers in the young.

Isaac. Conduct the lady to my lodgings, Carlos; I must haste to Don Jerome. Perhaps you know Louisa, ma'am. She's divinely handsome, isn't she?

Don. Louisa. You must excuse me not joining with you.

Isaac. Why, I have heard it on all hands.

Don. Louisa. Her father is uncommonly partial to her; but I believe you will find she has rather a matronly air.

Isaac. Carlos, this is all envy. — You pretty girls never speak well of one another. — [*To* DON CARLOS.] Hark ye, find out Antonio, and I'll saddle him with this scrape, I warrant. Oh, 'twas the luckiest thought! Donna Clara, your very obedient. Carlos, to your post.

DUET.

Isaac. . . . My mistress expects me, and I must go to her,
                Or how can I hope for a smile?
Don. Louisa. Soon may you return a prosperous wooer,
                But think what I suffer the while!
                Alone, and away from the man whom I love,
                In strangers I'm forced to confide.
Isaac. . . . Dear lady, my friend you may trust, and he'll prove
                Your servant, protector, and guide.

AIR.

Don Car. . Gentle maid, ah! why suspect me?
                Let me serve thee — then reject me.

Canst thou trust, and I deceive thee?
Art thou sad, and shall I grieve thee?
Gentle maid, ah! why suspect me?
Let me serve thee — then reject me.

TRIO.

Don. Louisa. Never mayst thou happy be,
If in aught thou'rt false to me.

Isaac. . . . Never may he happy be,
If in aught he's false to thee.

Don Car. . Never may I happy be,
If in aught I'm false to thee.

Don. Louisa. Never mayst thou, &c.

Isaac. . . . Never may he, &c.

Don Car. . Never may I, &c.   [*Exeunt.*

ACT II.

SCENE I. — *A Library in* DON JEROME'S *House.*

Enter DON JEROME *and* ISAAC.

Don. Jer. Ha! ha! ha! run away from her father! has she given him the slip? Ha! ha! ha! poor Don Guzman!

Isaac. Ay; and I am to conduct her to Antonio; by which means you see I shall hamper him so that he can give me no disturbance with your daughter — this is trap, isn't it? a nice stroke of cunning, hey?

Don Jer. Excellent! excellent! yes, yes, carry her to him, hamper him by all means, ha! ha! ha! poor Don Guzman! an old fool! imposed on by a girl!

Isaac. Nay, they have the cunning of serpents, that's the truth on 't.

Don Jer. Psha! they are cunning only when they have fools to deal with. Why don't my girl play me such a trick — let her cunning over-reach my caution, I say — hey, little Isaac!

Isaac. True, true; or let me see any of the sex make a fool of me! — No, no, egad! little Solomon (as my aunt used to call me) understands tricking a little too well.

Don. Jer. Ay, but such a driveller as Don Guzman!

Isaac. And such a dupe as Antonio!

Don Jer. True; never were seen such a couple of credulous simpletons! But come, 'tis time you should see my daughter — you must carry on the siege by yourself, friend Isaac.

Isaac. Sir, you'll introduce ——

Don Jer. No — I have sworn a solemn oath not to see or speak to her till she renounces her disobedience; win her to that, and she gains a father and a husband at once.

Isaac. Gad, I shall never be able to deal with her alone; nothing keeps me in such awe as perfect beauty — now there is something consoling and encouraging in ugliness.

Song.

Give Isaac the nymph who no beauty can boast,
But health and good humour to make her his toast;
If straight, I don't mind whether slender or fat,
And six feet or four — we'll ne'er quarrel for that.

Whate'er her complexion, I vow I don't care;
If brown, it is lasting — more pleasing, if fair:
And though in her face I no dimples should see,
Let her smile — and each dell is a dimple to me.

Let her locks be the reddest that ever were seen,
And her eyes may be e'en any colour but green;
For in eyes, though so various the lustre and hue,
I swear I've no choice — only let her have two.

'Tis true I'd dispense with a throne on her back,
And white teeth, I own, are genteeler than black;
A little round chin too 's a beauty, I've heard;
But I only desire she mayn't have a beard.

Don Jer. You will change your note, my friend, when you've seen Louisa.

Isaac. Oh, Don Jerome, the honour of your alliance ——

Don Jer. Ay, but her beauty will affect you — she is, though I say it, who am her father, a very prodigy. There you will see features with an eye like mine — yes, i' faith, there is a kind of wicked sparkling — something of a roguish brightness, that shows her to be my own.

Isaac. Pretty rogue!

Don Jer. Then, when she smiles, you'll see a little dimple in one cheek only; a beauty it is certainly, yet you shall not say which is prettiest, the cheek with the dimple, or the cheek without.

Isaac. Pretty rogue!

Don Jer. Then the roses on those cheeks are shaded with a sort of velvet down, that gives a delicacy to the glow of health.

Isaac. Pretty rogue!

Don Jer. Her skin pure dimity, yet more fair, being spangled here and there with a golden freckle.

Isaac. Charming pretty rogue! pray how is the tone of her voice?

Don Jer. Remarkably pleasing—but if you could prevail on her to sing, you would be enchanted—she is a nightingale—a Virginia nightingale! But come, come; her maid shall conduct you to her antechamber.

Isaac. Well, egad, I'll pluck up resolution, and meet her frowns intrepidly.

Don Jer. Ay! woo her briskly—win her, and give me a proof of your address, my little Solomon.

Isaac. But hold—I expect my friend Carlos to call on me here. If he comes, will you send him to me?

Don Jer. I will. Lauretta!—[*Calls.*]—Come—she'll show you to the room. What! do you droop? here's a mournful face to make love with! [*Exeunt.*

SCENE. II.—DONNA LOUISA's *Dressing Room.*

Enter ISAAC *and* MAID.

Maid. Sir, my mistress will wait on you presently.
[*Goes to the door.*

Isaac. When she's at leisure—don't hurry her.—[*Exit* MAID.]—I wish I had ever practised a love-scene—I doubt I shall make a poor figure—I couldn't be more afraid if I was going before the Inquisition. So, the door opens—yes, she's coming—the very rustling of her silk has a disdainful sound.

Enter DUENNA, *dressed as* DONNA LOUISA.

Now dar'n't I look round for the soul of me — her beauty will certainly strike me dumb if I do. I wish she'd speak first.

Duen. Sir, I attend your pleasure.

Isaac. [*Aside.*] So! the ice is broke, and a pretty civil beginning too! — [*Aloud.*] Hem! madam — miss — I'm all attention.

Duen. Nay, sir, 'tis I who should listen, and you propose.

Isaac. [*Aside.*] Egad, this isn't so disdainful neither — I believe I may venture to look. No — I dar'n't — one glance of those roguish sparklers would fix me again.

Duen. You seem thoughtful, sir. Let me persuade you to sit down.

Isaac. [*Aside.*] So, so; she mollifies apace — she's struck with my figure! this attitude has had its effect.

Duen. Come, sir, here's a chair.

Isaac. Madam, the greatness of your goodness overpowers me — that a lady so lovely should deign to turn her beauteous eyes on me so.   [*She takes his hand, he turns and sees her.*

Duen. You seem surprised at my condescension.

Isaac. Why, yes, madam, I am a little surprised at it. — [*Aside.*] Zounds! this can never be Louisa — she's as old as my mother!

Duen. But former prepossessions give way to my father's commands.

Isaac. [*Aside.*] Her father! Yes, 'tis she then. — Lord, Lord; how blind some parents are!

Duen. Signor Isaac!

Isaac. [*Aside.*] Truly, the little damsel was right — she has rather a matronly air, indeed! ah! 'tis well my affections are fixed on her fortune, and not her person.

Duen. Signor, won't you sit?   [*She sits.*

Isaac. Pardon me, madam, I have scarce recovered my astonishment at — your condescension, madam. — [*Aside.*] She has the devil's own dimples, to be sure!

Duen. I do not wonder, sir, that you are surprised at my affability — I own, signor, that I was vastly prepossessed against you, and, being teased by my father, I did give some encouragement to Antonio; but then, sir, you were described to me as quite a different person.

Isaac. Ay, and so you were to me, upon my soul, madam.

Duen. But when I saw you I was never more struck in my life.

Isaac. That was just my case too, madam: I was struck all on a heap, for my part.

Duen. Well, sir, I see our misapprehension has been mutual—you expected to find me haughty and averse, and I was taught to believe you a little black, snub-nosed fellow, without person, manners, or address.

Isaac. Egad, I wish she had answered her picture as well! [*Aside.*

Duen. But, sir, your air is noble—something so liberal in your carriage, with so penetrating an eye, and so bewitching a smile!

Isaac. Egad, now I look at her again, I don't think she is so ugly! [*Aside.*

Duen. So little like a Jew, and so much like a gentleman!

Isaac. Well, certainly, there is something pleasing in the tone of her voice. [*Aside.*

Duen. You will pardon this breach of decorum in praising you thus, but my joy at being so agreeably deceived has given me such a flow of spirits!

Isaac. Oh, dear lady, may I thank those dear lips for this goodness?—[*Kisses her.*] Why she has a pretty sort of velvet down, that's the truth on't. [*Aside.*

Duen. O sir, you have the most insinuating manner, but indeed you should get rid of that odious beard—one might as well kiss a hedgehog.

Isaac. [*Aside.*] Yes, ma'am, the razor wouldn't be amiss —for either of us.—[*Aloud.*] Could you favour me with a song?

Duen. Willingly, sir, though I am rather hoarse—ahem!
[*Begins to sing.*

Isaac. [*Aside.*] Very like a Virginia nightingale!—[*Aloud.*]
Ma'am, I perceive you're hoarse — I beg you will not distress ——

Duen. Oh, not in the least distressed. Now, sir.

Song.

When a tender maid
Is first assay'd
By some admiring swain,
How her blushes rise
If she meet his eyes,
While he unfolds his pain!
If he takes her hand, she trembles quite!
Touch her lips, and she swoons outright!
While a-pit-a-pat, &c.
Her heart avows her fright.

But in time appear
Fewer signs of fear;
The youth she boldly views:
If her hand he grasp
Or her bosom clasp,
No mantling blush ensues!
Then to church well pleased the lovers move
While her smiles her contentment prove;
And a-pit-a-pat, &c.
Her heart avows her love.

Isaac. Charming, ma'am! enchanting! and, truly, your
notes put me in mind of one that's very dear to me — a lady,
indeed, whom you greatly resemble!

Duen. How! is there, then, another so dear to you?

Isaac. Oh, no, ma'am, you mistake; it was my mother I
meant.

Duen. Come, sir, I see you are amazed and confounded at
my condescension, and know not what to say.

Isaac. It is very true, indeed, ma'am; but it is a judgment,
I look on it as a judgment on me, for delaying to urge the
time when you'll permit me to complete my happiness, by acquainting Don Jerome with your condescension.

Duen. Sir, I must frankly own to you, that I can never be
yours with my father's consent.

Isaac. Good lack! how so?

Duen. When my father, in his passion, swore he would never see me again till I acquiesced in his will, I also made a vow, that I would never take a husband from his hand; nothing shall make me break that oath: but, if you have spirit and contrivance enough to carry me off without his knowledge, I'm yours.

Isaac. Hum!

Duen. Nay, sir, if you hesitate ——

Isaac. [*Aside.*] I' faith, no bad whim this! — If I take her at her word, I shall secure her fortune, and avoid making any settlement in return; thus I shall not only cheat the lover, but the father too. Oh, cunning rogue, Isaac! ay, ay, let this little brain alone! Egad, I'll take her in the mind!

Duen. Well, sir, what's your determination?

Isaac. Madam, I was dumb only from rapture—I applaud your spirit, and joyfully close with your proposal; for which thus let me, on this lily hand, express my gratitude.

Duen. Well, sir, you must get my father's consent to walk with me in the garden. But by no means inform him of my kindness to you.

Isaac. No, to be sure, that would spoil all: but, trust me, when tricking is the word — let me alone for a piece of cunning; this very day you shall be out of his power.

Duen. Well, I leave the management of it all to you; I perceive plainly, sir, that you are not one that can be easily outwitted.

Isaac. Egad, you're right, madam — you're right, i' faith.

Re-enter MAID.

Maid. Here's a gentleman at the door, who begs permission to speak with Signor Isaac.

Isaac. A friend of mine, ma'am, and a trusty friend — let him come in — [*Exit* MAID.] He is one to be depended on, ma'am.

Enter DON CARLOS.

So, coz.　　　　　　　　　　[*Talks apart with* DON CARLOS.

Don Car. I have left Donna Clara at your lodgings, but can nowhere find Antonio.

Isaac. Well, I will search him out myself. Carlos, you rogue, I thrive, I prosper!

Don Car. Where is your mistress?

Isaac. There, you booby, there she stands.

Don Car. Why, she's damned ugly!

Isaac. Hush!   [*Stops his mouth.*

Duen. What is your friend saying, signor?

Isaac. Oh, ma'am, he is expressing his raptures at such charms as he never saw before. Eh, Carlos?

Don Car. Ay, such as I never saw before, indeed!

Duen. You are a very obliging gentleman. Well, signor Isaac, I believe we had better part for the present. Remember our plan.

Isaac. Oh, ma'am, it is written in my heart, fixed as the image of those divine beauties. Adieu, idol of my soul! — yet once more permit me ——   [*Kisses her.*

Duen. Sweet, courteous sir, adieu!

Isaac. Your slave eternally! Come, Carlos, say something civil at taking leave.

Don Car. I'faith, Isaac, she is the hardest woman to compliment I ever saw; however, I'll try something I had studied for the occasion.

Song.

Ah! sure a pair was never seen
  So justly form'd to meet by nature!
The youth excelling so in mien,
  The maid in ev'ry grace of feature.
  Oh, how happy are such lovers,
    When kindred beauties each discovers!
      For surely she
      Was made for thee,
  And thou to bless this lovely creature.

So mild your looks, your children thence
  Will early learn the task of duty —
The boys with all their father's sense,
  The girls with all their mother's beauty!
  Oh, how happy to inherit
    At once such graces and such spirit!
      Thus while you live
      May fortune give
  Each blessing equal to your merit!   [*Exeunt.*

SCENE III. — *A Library in* DON JEROME'S *House.*

DON JEROME *and* DON FERDINAND *discovered.*

Don Jer. Object to Antonio! I have said it. His poverty, can you acquit him of that?

Don Ferd. Sir, I own he is not over rich! but he is of as ancient and honourable a family as any in the kingdom.

Don Jer. Yes, I know the beggars are a very ancient family in most kingdoms; but never in great repute, boy.

Don Ferd. Antonio, sir, has many amiable qualities.

Don Jer. But he is poor; can you clear him of that, I say? Is he not a gay, dissipated rake, who has squandered his patrimony?

Don Ferd. Sir, he inherited but little; and that, his generosity, more than his profuseness, has stripped him of; but he has never sullied his honour, which, with his title, has outlived his means.

Don Jer. Psha! you talk like a blockhead! nobility, without an estate, is as ridiculous as gold lace on a frieze coat.

Don Ferd. This language, sir, would better become a Dutch or English trader than a Spaniard.

Don Jer. Yes; and those Dutch and English traders, as you call them, are the wiser people. Why, booby, in England they were formerly as nice, as to birth and family, as we are: but they have long discovered what a wonderful purifier gold is; and now, no one there regards pedigree in any thing but a horse. Oh, here comes Isaac! I hope he has prospered in his suit.

Don Ferd. Doubtless, that agreeable figure of his must have helped his suit surprisingly.

Don Jer. How now?   [DON FERDINAND *walks aside*

Enter ISAAC.

Well, my friend, have you softened her?

Isaac. Oh, yes; I have softened her.

Don Jer. What, does she come to?

Isaac. Why, truly, she was kinder than I expected to find her.

Don Jer. And the dear little angel was civil, eh?

Isaac. Yes, the pretty little angel was very civil.

Don Jer. I'm transported to hear it! Well, and you were astonished at her beauty, hey?

Isaac. I was astonished, indeed! Pray, how old is miss?

Don Jer. How old! let me see — eight and twelve — she is twenty.

Isaac. Twenty?

Don Jer. Ay, to a month.

Isaac. Then, upon my soul, she is the oldest-looking girl of her age in Christendom!

Don Jer. Do you think so? But, I believe, you will not see a prettier girl.

Isaac. Here and there one.

Don Jer. Louisa has the family face.

Isaac. Yes, egad, I should have taken it for a family face, and one that has been in the family some time too.   [*Aside.*

Don Jer. She has her father's eyes.

Isaac. Truly, I should have guessed them to have been so! If she had her mother's spectacles, I believe she would not see the worse.   [*Aside.*

Don Jer. Her aunt Ursula's nose, and her grandmother's forehead, to a hair.

Isaac. Ay, 'faith, and her grandfather's chin, to a hair.
                                                        [*Aside.*

Don Jer. Well, if she was but as dutiful as she's handsome — and hark ye, friend Isaac, she is none of your made-up beauties — her charms are of the lasting kind.

Isaac. I' faith, so they should — for if she be but twenty now, she may double her age before her years will overtake her face.

Don Jer. Why, zounds, Master Isaac! you are not sneering, are you?

Isaac. Why now, seriously, Don Jerome, do you think your daughter handsome?

Don Jer. By this light, she's as handsome a girl as any in Seville.

Isaac. Then, by these eyes, I think her as plain a woman as ever I beheld.

Don Jer. By St. Iago! you must be blind.

Isaac. No, no; 'tis you are partial.

Don Jer. How! have I neither sense nor taste? If a fair skin, fine eyes, teeth of ivory, with a lovely bloom, and a delicate shape — if these, with a heavenly voice, and a world of grace, are not charms, I know not what you call beautiful.

Isaac. Good lack, with what eyes a father sees! As I have life, she is the very reverse of all this: as for the dimity skin you told me of, I swear 'tis a thorough nankeen as ever I saw! for her eyes, their utmost merit is not squinting — for her teeth, where there is one of ivory, its neighbour is pure ebony, black and white alternately, just like the keys of a harpsichord. Then, as to her singing, and heavenly voice — by this hand, she has a shrill, cracked pipe, that sounds, for all the world, like a child's trumpet.

Don Jer. Why, you little Hebrew scoundrel, do you mean to insult me? Out of my house, I say!

Don Ferd. [*Coming forward.*] Dear sir, what's the matter?

Don Jer. Why, this Israelite here has the impudence to say your sister's ugly.

Don Ferd. He must be either blind or insolent.

Isaac. So, I find they are all in a story. Egad, I believe I have gone too far!   [*Aside.*

Don Ferd. Sure, sir, there must be some mistake; it can't be my sister whom he has seen.

Don Jer. 'Sdeath! you are as great a fool as he! What mistake can there be? Did not I lock up Louisa, and haven't I the key in my own pocket? and didn't her maid show him into the dressing room? and yet you talk of a mistake! No, the Portuguese meant to insult me — and, but that this roof protects him, old as I am, this sword should do me justice.

Isaac. I must get off as well as I can — her fortune is not the less handsome.   [*Aside.*

Shrridan.   10

DUET.

Isaac. Believe me, good sir, I ne'er meant to offend;
My mistress I love, and I value my friend:
To win her and wed her is still my request,
For better for worse — and I swear I don't jest.

Don Jer. Zounds! you'd best not provoke me, my rage is so high!

Isaac. Hold him fast, I beseech you, his rage is so high!
Good sir, you're too hot, and this place I must fly.

Don Jer. You're a knave and a sot, and this place you'd best fly.

Isaac. Don Jerome, come now, let us lay aside all joking, and be serious.

Don. Jer. How?

Isaac. Ha! ha! ha! I'll be hanged if you haven't taken my abuse of your daughter seriously.

Don Jer. You meant it so, did not you?

Isaac. O mercy, no! a joke — just to try how angry it would make you,

Don Jer. Was that all, i' faith? I didn't know you had been such a wag. Ha! ha! ha! By St. Iago! you made me very angry, though. Well, and you do think Louisa handsome?

Isaac. Handsome! Venus de Medicis was a sibyl to her.

Don Jer. Give me your hand, you little jocose rogue! Egad, I thought we had been all off.

Don Ferd. So! I was in hopes this would have been a quarrel; but I find the Jew is too cunning.   [*Aside.*

Don Jer. Ay, this gust of passion has made me dry — I am seldom ruffled. Order some wine in the next room — let us drink the poor girl's health. Poor Louisa! ugly, eh! ha! ha! ha! 'twas a very good joke, indeed!

Isaac. And a very true one, for all that.   [*Aside.*

Don Jer. And, Ferdinand, I insist upon your drinking success to my friend.

Don Ferd. Sir, I will drink success to my friend with all my heart.

Don Jer. Come, little Solomon, if any sparks of anger had remained, this would be the only way to quench them.

TRIO.

A bumper of good liquor
Will end a contest quicker
Than justice, judge, or vicar;
  So fill a cheerful glass,
  And let good humour pass.

But if more deep the quarrel,
Why, sooner drain the barrel
Than be the hateful fellow
That's crabbed when he's mellow.
  A bumper, &c.   [*Exeunt.*

SCENE IV. — ISAAC'S *Lodgings.*

Enter DONNA LOUISA.

Don. Louisa. Was ever truant daughter so whimsically
circumstanced as I am? I have sent my intended husband to
look after my lover — the man of my father's choice is gone
to bring me the man of my own: but how dispiriting is this
interval of expectation!

SONG.

What bard, O Time, discover,
  With wings first made thee move?
Ah! sure it was some lover
  Who ne'er had left his love!
  For who that once did prove
The pangs which absence brings,
  Though but one day
  He were away,
Could picture thee with wings?
    What bard, &c.

Enter DON CARLOS.

So, friend, is Antonio found?

Don Car. I could not meet with him, lady; but I doubt
not my friend Isaac will be here with him presently.

Don. Louisa. Oh, shame! you have used no diligence. Is
this your courtesy to a lady, who has trusted herself to your
protection?

Don Car. Indeed, madam, I have not been remiss.

Don. Louisa. Well, well; but if either of you had known
how each moment of delay weighs upon the heart of her who

10*

loves, and waits the object of her love, oh, ye would not then
have trifled thus!

Don Car. Alas, I know it well!

Don. Louisa. Were you ever in love, then?

Don Car. I was, lady; but, while I have life, will never be
again.

Don. Louisa. Was your mistress so cruel?

Don Car. If she had always been so, I should have been
happier.

SONG.

Oh, had my love ne'er smiled on me,
I ne'er had known such anguish;
But think how false, how cruel she,
To bid me cease to languish;
To bid me hope her hand to gain,
Breathe on a flame half perish'd;
And then, with cold and fix'd disdain,
To kill the hope she cherish'd.

Not worse his fate, who on a wrock,
That drove as winds did blow it,
Silent had left the shatter'd deck,
To find a grave below it.
Then land was cried—no more resign'd,
He glow'd with joy to hear it;
Not worse his fate, his woe, to find
The wreck must sink ere near it!

Don. Louisa. As I live, here is your friend coming with
Antonio! I'll retire for a moment to surprise him.   [*Exit.*

Enter ISAAC *and* DON ANTONIO.

Don Ant. Indeed, my good friend, you must be mistaken.
Clara d'Almanza in love with me, and employ you to bring
me to meet her! It is impossible!

Isaac. That you shall see in an instant. Carlos, where is
the lady? — [DON CARLOS *points to the door.*] In the next
room, is she?

Don Ant. Nay, if that lady is really here, she certainly
wants me to conduct her to a dear friend of mine, who has
long been her lover.

Isaac. Psha! I tell you 'tis no such thing — you are the

man she wants, and nobody but you. Here's ado to persuade
you to take a pretty girl that's dying for you!

Don Ant. But I have no affection for this lady.

Isaac. And you have for Louisa, hey? But take my word
for it, Antonio, you have no chance there — so you may as
well secure the good that offers itself to you.

Don Ant. And could you reconcile it to your conscience
to supplant your friend?

Isaac. Pish! Conscience has no more to do with gallantry
than it has with politics. Why, you are no honest fellow if
love can't make a rogue of you—so come, do go in and speak
to her, at least.

Don Ant. Well, I have no objection to that.

Isaac. [*Opens the door.*] There — there she is — yonder
by the window — get in, do. — [*Pushes him in, and half shuts
the door.*] Now, Carlos, now I shall hamper him, I warrant!
Stay, I'll peep how they go on. Egad, he looks confoundedly
posed! Now she's coaxing him. See, Carlos, he begins to
come to — ay, ay, he'll soon forget his conscience.

Don Car. Look — now they are both laughing!

Isaac. Ay, so they are—yes, yes, they are laughing at that
dear friend he talked of — ay, poor devil, they have outwitted
him.

Don Car. Now he's kissing her hand.

Isaac. Yes, yes, 'faith, they're agreed — he's caught, he's
entangled. My dear Carlos, we have brought it about. Oh, this
little cunning head! I'm a Machiavel — a very Machiavel!

Don Car. I hear somebody inquiring for you — I'll see
who it is. [*Exit.*

Re-enter DON ANTONIO *and* DONNA LOUISA.

Don Ant. Well, my good friend, this lady has so entirely
convinced me of the certainty of your success at Don Jerome's,
that I now resign my pretensions there.

Isaac. You never did a wiser thing, believe me; and, as
for deceiving your friend, that's nothing at all — tricking is
all fair in love, isn't it, ma'am?

Don. Louisa. Certainly, sir; and I am particularly glad to find you are of that opinion.

Isaac. O lud! yes, ma'am — let any one outwit me that can, I say! But here, let me join your hands. There, you lucky rogue! I wish you happily married, from the bottom of my soul!

Don. Louisa. And I am sure, if you wish it, no one else should prevent it.

Isaac. Now, Antonio, we are rivals no more; so let us be friends, will you?

Don Ant. With all my heart, Isaac.

Isaac. It is not every man, let me tell you, that would have taken such pains, or been so generous to a rival.

Don Ant. No, 'faith, I don't believe there's another beside yourself in all Spain.

Isaac. Well, but you resign all pretensions to the other lady?

Don Ant. That I do, most sincerely.

Isaac. I doubt you have a little hankering there still.

Don Ant. None in the least, upon my soul.

Isaac. I mean after her fortune.

Don Ant. No, believe me. You are heartily welcome to every thing she has.

Isaac. Well, i' faith, you have the best of the bargain, as to beauty, twenty to one. Now I'll tell you a secret — I am to carry off Louisa this very evening.

Don. Louisa. Indeed!

Isaac. Yes, she has sworn not to take a husband from her father's hand — so I've persuaded him to trust her to walk with me in the garden, and then we shall give him the slip.

Don. Louisa. And is Don Jerome to know nothing of this?

Isaac. O Lud, no! there lies the jest. Don't you see that, by this step, I over-reach him? I shall be entitled to the girl's fortune, without settling a ducat on her. Ha! ha! ha! I'm a cunning dog, an't I? a sly little villain, eh?

Don Ant. Ha! ha! ha! you are indeed!

Isaac. Roguish, you'll say, but keen, hey? devilish keen?

Don Ant. So you are indeed — keen — very keen.

Isaac. And what a laugh we shall have at Don Jerome's when the truth comes out! hey?

Don Louisa. Yes, I'll answer for it, we shall have a good laugh when the truth comes out.   Ha! ha! ha!

Re-enter DON CARLOS.

Don Car. Here are the dancers come to practise the fan dango you intended to have honoured Donna Louisa with.

Isaac. Oh, I shan't want them; but, as I must pay them, I'll see a caper for my money.   Will you excuse me?

Don. Louisa. Willingly.

Isaac. Here's my friend, whom you may command for any service.   Madam, your most obedient — Antonio, I wish you all happiness. — [*Aside.*]   Oh, the easy blockhead! what a tool I have made of him! — This was a masterpiece!   [*Exit.*

Don. Louisa. Carlos, will you be my guard again, and convey me to the convent of St. Catharine?

Don Ant. Why, Louisa — why should you go there?

Don. Louisa. I have my reasons, and you must not be seen to go with me; I shall write from thence to my father; perhaps, when he finds what he has driven me to, he may relent.

Don Ant. I have no hope from him.   O Louisa! in these arms should be your sanctuary.

Don. Louisa. Be patient but for a little while — my father cannot force me from thence.   But let me see you there before evening, and I will explain myself.

Don Ant. I shall obey.

Don Louisa. Come, friend.   Antonio, Carlos has been a lover himself.

Don Ant. Then he knows the value of his trust.

Don Car. You shall not find me unfaithful.

TRIO.

Soft pity never leaves the gentle breast
Where love has been received a welcome guest;
As wandering saints poor huts have sacred made,
He hallows every heart he once has sway'd,
And, when his presence we no longer share,
Still leaves compassion as a relic there.   [*Exeunt.*

ACT III.

Scene I. — *A Library in* Don Jerome's *House.*

Enter Don Jerome *and* Servant.

Don Jer. Why, I never was so amazed in my life! Louisa gone off with Isaac Mendoza! What! steal away with the very man whom I wanted her to marry — elope with her own husband, as it were — it is impossible!

Ser. Her maid says, sir, they had your leave to walk in the garden while you were abroad. The door by the shrubbery was found open, and they have not been heard of since. [*Exit.*

Don Jer. Well, it is the most unaccountable affair! 'sdeath! there is certainly some infernal mystery in it I can't comprehend!

Enter Second Servant, *with a letter.*

Ser. Here is a letter, sir, from Signor Isaac.   [*Exit.*

Don Jer. So, so, this will explain — ay, Isaac Mendoza — let me see ——   [*Reads.*

Dearest Sir,

You must, doubtless, be much surprised at my flight with your daughter! — yes, 'faith, and well I may — *I had the happiness to gain her heart at our first interview.* — The devil you had! — *But, she having unfortunately made a vow not to receive a husband from your hands, I was obliged to comply with her whim!* — So, so! — *We shall shortly throw ourselves at your feet, and I hope you will have a blessing ready for one, who will then be your son-in-law,*   Isaac Mendoza.

A whim, hey? Why, the devil's in the girl, I think! This morning, she would die sooner than have him, and before evening she runs away with him! Well, well, my will's accomplished — let the motive be what it will — and the Portuguese, sure, will never deny to fulfil the rest of the article.

Re-enter Servant, *with another letter.*

Ser. Sir, here's a man below, who says he brought this from my young lady, Donna Louisa.   [*Exit.*

Don Jer. How! yes, it's my daughter's hand, indeed!

Lord, there was no occasion for them both to write; well,
let's see what she says — 　　　　　　　　　　[*Reads.*

My dearest Father,

*How shall I entreat your pardon for the rash step I have
taken — how confess the motive?* — Pish! hasn't Isaac just told
me the motive? — one would think they weren't together
when they wrote. — *If I have a spirit too resentful of ill usage,
I have also a heart as easily affected by kindness.* — So, so, here
the whole matter comes out; her resentment for Antonio's ill
usage has made her sensible of Isaac's kindness — yes, yes,
it is all plain enough. Well. — *I am not married yet, though
with a man, I am convinced, adores me.* — Yes, yes, I dare say
Isaac is very fond of her. — *But I shall anxiously expect your
answer, in which, should I be so fortunate as to receive your consent, you will make completely happy your ever affectionate
daughter,* 　　　　　　　　　　　　　　　　　　Louisa.

My consent! to be sure she shall have it! Egad, I was never
better pleased — I have fulfilled my resolution — I knew I
should. Oh, there's nothing like obstinacy! Lewis! [*Calls.*

Re-enter Servant.

Let the man, who brought the last letter, wait; and get me a
pen and ink below. — [*Exit* Servant.] I am impatient to set
poor Louisa's heart at rest. Holloa! Lewis! Sancho! [*Calls.*

Enter Servants.

See that there be a noble supper provided in the saloon to-
night; serve up my best wines, and let me have music, d'ye
hear?

Ser. Yes, sir.

Don Jer. And order all my doors to be thrown open;
admit all guests, with masks or without masks. — [*Exeunt*
Servants.] I' faith, we'll have a night of it! and I'll let them
see how merry an old man can be.

Song.

Oh, the days when I was young,
When I laugh'd in fortune's spite;
Talk'd of love the whole day long,
And with nectar crown'd the night!

Then it was, old father Care,
    Little reck'd I of thy frown;
Half thy malice youth could bear,
    And the rest a bumper drown.

Truth, they say, lies in a well,
    Why, I vow I ne'er could see;
Let the water-drinkers tell,
    There it always lay for me:
For when sparkling wine went round,
    Never saw I falsehood's mask;
But still honest truth I found
    In the bottom of each flask.

True, at length my vigour's flown,
    I have years to bring decay;
Few the locks that now I own,
    And the few I have are grey.
Yet, old Jerome, thou mayst boast,
    While thy spirits do not tire;
Still beneath thy age's frost
    Glows a spark of youthful fire.   [*Exit.*

SCENE II. — *The New Piazza.*

Enter DON FERDINAND *and* LOPEZ.

Don Ferd. What, could you gather no tidings of her? nor guess where she was gone? O Clara! Clara!

Lop. In truth, sir, I could not. That she was run away from her father, was in everybody's mouth; and that Don Guzman was in pursuit of her, was also a very common report. Where she was gone, or what was become of her, no one could take upon them to say.

Don Ferd. 'Sdeath and fury, you blockhead! she can't be out of Seville.

Lop. So I said to myself, sir. 'Sdeath and fury, you blockhead, says I, she can't be out of Seville. Then some said, she had hanged herself for love; and others have it, Don Antonio had carried her off.

Don Ferd. 'Tis false, scoundrel! no one said that.

Lop. Then I misunderstood them, sir.

Don Ferd. Go, fool, get home! and never let me see you again till you bring me news of her. — [*Exit* LOPEZ.] Oh, how my fondness for this ungrateful girl has hurt my disposition.

Enter ISAAC.

Isaac. So, I have her safe, and have only to find a priest to marry us. Antonio now may marry Clara, or not, if he pleases.

Don Ferd. What! what was that you said of Clara?

Isaac. Oh, Ferdinand! my brother-in-law that shall be, who thought of meeting you?

Don Ferd. But what of Clara?

Isaac. I' faith, you shall hear. This morning, as I was coming down, I met a pretty damsel, who told me her name was Clara d'Almanza, and begged my protection.

Don Ferd. How!

Isaac. She said she had eloped from her father, Don Guzman, but that love for a young gentleman in Seville was the cause.

Don Ferd. Oh, Heavens! did she confess it?

Isaac. Oh, yes, she confessed at once. But then, says she, my lover is not informed of my flight, nor suspects my intention.

Don Ferd. [*Aside.*] Dear creature! no more I did indeed! Oh, I am the happiest fellow! — [*Aloud.*] Well, Isaac?

Isaac. Why then she entreated me to find him out for her, and bring him to her.

Don Ferd. Good Heavens, how lucky! Well, come along; let's lose no time.   [*Pulling him.*

Isaac. Zooks! where are we to go?

Don Ferd. Why, did any thing more pass?

Isaac. Any thing more! yes; the end on't was, that I was moved with her speeches, and complied with her desires.

Don Ferd. Well, and where is she?

Isaac. Where is she! why, don't I tell you? I complied with her request, and left her safe in the arms of her lover.

Don Ferd. 'Sdeath, you trifle with me! — I have never seen her.

Isaac. You! O Lud, no! how the devil should you? 'Twas Antonio she wanted; and with Antonio I left her.

Don Ferd. [*Aside.*] Hell and madness! — [*Aloud.*] What, Antonio d'Ercilla?

Isaac. Ay, ay, the very man; and the best part of it was, he was shy of taking her at first. He talked a good deal about honour, and conscience, and deceiving some dear friend; but, Lord, we soon overruled that!

Don Ferd. You did!

Isaac. Oh, yes, presently.—Such deceit! says he.—Pish! says the lady, tricking is all fair in love. But then, my friend, says he.—Psha! damn your friend, says I. So, poor wretch, he has no chance. — No, no; he may hang himself as soon as he pleases.

Don Ferd. I must go, or I shall betray myself.   [*Aside.*

Isaac. But stay, Ferdinand, you ha'n't heard the best of the joke.

Don Ferd. Curse on your joke!

Isaac. Good lack! what's the matter now? I thought to have diverted you.

Don Ferd. Be racked! tortured! damned!

Isaac. Why, sure you are not the poor devil of a lover, are you? — I' faith, as sure as can be, he is! This is a better joke than t' other. Ha! ha! ha!

Don Ferd. What! do you laugh? you vile, mischievous varlet! — [*Collars him.*]· But that you're beneath my anger, I'd tear your heart out!   [*Throws him from him.*

Isaac. O mercy! here's usage for a brother-in-law!

Don Ferd. But, hark ye, rascal! tell me directly where these false friends are gone, or, by my soul ——   [*Draws.*

Isaac. For Heaven's sake, now, my dear brother-in-law, don't be in a rage! I'll recollect as well as I can.

Don Ferd. Be quick then!

Isaac. I will, I will!—but people's memories differ; some have a treacherous memory: now mine is a cowardly memory — it takes to its heels at sight of a drawn sword, it does, i' faith; and I could as soon fight as recollect.

Don Ferd. Zounds! tell me the truth, and I won't hurt you.

Isaac. No, no, I know you won't, my dear brother-in-law; but that ill-looking thing there ——

Don Ferd. What, then, you won't tell me?

Isaac. Yes, yes, I will; I'll tell you all, upon my soul! — but why need you listen, sword in hand?

Don Ferd. Why, there. — [*Puts up.*] Now.

Isaac. Why, then, I believe they are gone to — that is, my friend Carlos told me, he had left Donna Clara — dear Ferdinand, keep your hands off — at the convent of St. Catharine.

Don Ferd. St. Catharine!

Isaac. Yes; and that Antonio was to come to her there.

Don Ferd. Is this the truth?

Isaac. It is indeed; and all I know, as I hope for life!

Don Ferd. Well, coward, take your life! 'tis that false, dishonourable Antonio, who shall feel my vengeance.

Isaac. Ay, ay, kill him; cut his throat, and welcome.

Don Ferd. But, for Clara! infamy on her! she is not worth my resentment.

Isaac. No more she is, my dear brother-in-law. I' faith, I would not be angry about her; she is not worth it, indeed.

Don Ferd. 'Tis false! she is worth the enmity of princes!

Isaac. True, true, so she is; and I pity you exceedingly for having lost her.

Don Ferd. 'Sdeath, you rascal! how durst you talk of pitying me?

Isaac. Oh, dear brother-in-law, I beg pardon! I don't pity you in the least, upon my soul!

Don Ferd. Get hence, fool, and provoke me no further; nothing but your insignificance saves you!

Isaac. [*Aside.*] I' faith, then, my insignificance is the best friend I have. — [*Aloud.*] I'm going, dear Ferdinand. — [*Aside.*] What a curst hot-headed bully it is!

[*Exeunt severally.*

SCENE III. — *The Garden of the Convent.*

Enter DONNA LOUISA *and* DONNA CLARA.

Don. Louisa. And you really wish my brother may not find you out?

Don. Clara. Why else have I concealed myself under this disguise?

Don. Louisa. Why, perhaps, because the dress becomes you; for you certainly don't intend to be a nun for life.

Don. Clara. If, indeed, Ferdinand had not offended me so last night ——

Don. Louisa. Come, come, it was his fear of losing you made him so rash.

Don. Clara Well, you may think me cruel, but I swear, if he were here this instant, I believe I should forgive him.

SONG.

By him we love offended,
    How soon our anger flies!
One day apart, 'tis ended;
    Behold him, and it dies.

Last night, your roving brother,
    Enraged, I bade depart;
And sure his rude presumption
    Deserved to lose my heart.

Yet, were he now before me,
    In spite of injured pride,
I fear my eyes would pardon
    Before my tongue could chide.

Don. Louisa. I protest, Clara, I shall begin to think you are seriously resolved to enter on your probation.

Don. Clara. And, seriously, I very much doubt whether the character of a nun would not become me best.

Don. Louisa. Why, to be sure, the character of a nun is a very becoming one at a masquerade; but no pretty woman, in her senses, ever thought of taking the veil for above a night.

Don. Clara. Yonder I see your Antonio is returned — I shall only interrupt you; ah, Louisa, with what happy eagerness you turn to look for him!   [*Exit.*

Enter DON ANTONIO.

Don Ant. Well, my Louisa, any news since I left you?

Don. Louisa. None. The messenger is not yet returned from my father.

Don Ant. Well, I confess, I do not perceive what we are to expect from him.

Don. Louisa. I shall be easier, however, in having made the trial: I do not doubt your sincerity, Antonio; but there is a chilling air around poverty, that often kills affection, that was not nursed in it. If we would make love our household god, we had best secure him a comfortable roof.

SONG. — *Don Antonio.*

How oft, Louisa, hast thou told,
　(Nor wilt thou the fond boast disown,)
Thou wouldst not lose Antonio's love
　To reign the partner of a throne.
And by those lips, that spoke so kind,
　And by that hand, I've press'd to mine,
To be the lord of wealth and power,
　By Heavens, I would not part with thine!

Then how, my soul, can we be poor,
　Who own what kingdoms could not buy?
Of this true heart thou shalt be queen,
　In serving thee, a monarch I.
Thus uncontroll'd, in mutual bliss,
　I rich in love's exhaustless mine,
Do thou snatch treasures from my lips,
　And I'll take kingdoms back from thine!

Enter MAID, *with a letter.*

Don. Louisa. My father's answer, I suppose.

Don Ant. My dearest Louisa, you may be assured that it contains nothing but threats and reproaches.

Don. Louisa. Let us see, however.—[Reads.] *Dearest daughter, make your lover happy; you have my full consent to marry as your whim has chosen, but be sure come home and sup with your affectionate father.*

Don. Ant. You jest, Louisa!

Don. Louisa. [*Gives him the letter.*] Read! read!

Don Ant. 'Tis so, by Heavens! Sure there must be some

mistake; but that's none of our business. — Now, Louisa, you
have no excuse for delay.

Don. Louisa. Shall we not then return and thank my father?

Don Ant. But first let the priest put it out of his power to
recall his word. — I'll fly to procure one.

Don. Louisa. Nay, if you part with me again, perhaps you
may lose me.

Don Ant. Come then — there is a friar of a neighbouring
convent is my friend; you have already been diverted by the
manners of a nunnery; let us see whether there is less hypocrisy among the holy fathers.

Don. Louisa. I'm afraid not, Antonio — for in religion, as
in friendship, they who profess most are ever the least sincere.

[*Exeunt.*

Re-enter DONNA CLARA.

Don. Clara. So, yonder they go, as happy as a mutual and
confessed affection can make them, while I am left in solitude.
Heigho! love may perhaps excuse the rashness of an elopement from one's friend, but I am sure nothing but the presence of the man we love can support it. Ha! what do I
see! Ferdinand, as I live, how could he gain admission? By
potent gold, I suppose, as Antonio did. How eager and disturbed he seems! He shall not know me as yet.

[*Lets down her veil.*

Enter DON FERDINAND.

Don. Ferd. Yes, those were certainly they — my information was right.   [*Going.*

Don. Clara. [*Stops him.*] Pray, signor, what is your business here?

Don Ferd. No matter — no matter! Oh, they stop. — *Looks
out.*] Yes, that is the perfidious Clara indeed!

Don. Clara. So, a jealous error — I'm glad to see him so
moved.   [*Aside.*

Don Ferd. Her disguise can't conceal her — no, no, I know
her too well.

Don. Clara. [*Aside.*] Wonderful discernment! — [*Aloud.*] But, signor ——

Don Ferd. Be quiet, good nun; don't tease me! — By Heavens, she leans upon his arm, hangs fondly on it! O woman, woman!

Don. Clara. But, signor, who is it you want?

Don Ferd. Not you, not you, so pr'ythee don't tease me. Yet pray stay—gentle nun, was it not Donna Clara d'Almanza just parted from you?

Don. Clara. Clara d'Almanza, signor, is not yet out of the garden.

Don. Ferd. Ay, ay, I knew I was right! And pray is not that gentleman, now at the porch with her, Antonio d'Ercilla?

Don. Clara. It is indeed, signor.

Don Ferd. So, so; now but one question more — can you inform me for what purpose they have gone away?

Don Clara. They are gone to be married, I believe.

Don Ferd. Very well — enough. Now if I don't mar their wedding!   [*Exit.*

Don. Clara. [*Unveils.*] I thought jealousy had made lovers quick-sighted, but it has made mine blind. Louisa's story accounts to me for this error, and I am glad to find I have power enough over him to make him so unhappy. But why should not I be present at his surprise when undeceived? When he's through the porch, I'll follow him; and, perhaps, Louisa shall not singly be a bride.

SONG

Adieu, thou dreary pile, where never dies
The sullen echo of repentant sighs!
Ye sister mourners of each lonely cell,
Inured to hymns and sorrow, fare ye well!
For happier scenes I fly this darksome grove,
To saints a prison, but a tomb to love!   [*Exit.*

SCENE IV. — *A Court before the Priory.*

Enter ISAAC, *crossing the stage,* DON ANTONIO *following.*

Don Ant. What, my friend Isaac!

Isaac. What, Antonio! wish me joy! I have Louisa safe.

Don Ant. Have you? I wish you joy with all my soul.

Isaac. Yes, I am come here to procure a priest to marry us.

Don Ant. So, then, we are both on the same errand; I am come to look for Father Paul.

Isaac. Ha! I am glad on't — but, i'faith, he must tack me first; my love is waiting.

Don Ant. So is mine — I left her in the porch.

Isaac. Ay, but I am in haste to go back to Don Jerome.

Don Ant. And so am I too.

Isaac. Well, perhaps he'll save time, and marry us both together — or I'll be your father, and you shall be mine. Come along — but you're obliged to me for all this.

Don Ant. Yes, yes.   [*Exeunt.*

SCENE V. — *A Room in the Priory.*

FATHER PAUL, FATHER FRANCIS, FATHER AUGUSTINE, *and other* FRIARS, *discovered at a table drinking.*

GLEE AND CHORUS.

This bottle's the sun of our table,
His beams are rosy wine:
We, planets, that are not able
Without his help to shine.
Let mirth and glee abound!,
You'll soon grow bright
With borrow'd light,
And shine as he goes round.

Paul. Brother Francis, toss the bottle about, and give me your toast.

Fran. Have we drunk the abbess of St. Ursuline?

Paul. Yes, yes; she was the last.

Fran. Then I'll give you the blue-eyed nun of St. Catharine's.

Paul. With all my heart. —[*Drinks.*] Pray, brother Augustine, were there any benefactions left in my absence?

Aug. Don Juan Corduba has left a hundred ducats, to remember him in our masses.

Paul. Has he? let them be paid to our wine-merchant,

and we'll remember him in our cups, which will do just as well. Any thing more?

Aug. Yes; Baptista, the rich miser, who died last week, has bequeathed us a thousand pistoles, and the silver lamp he used in his own chamber, to burn before the image of St. Anthony.

Paul. 'Twas well meant, but we'll employ his money better — Baptista's bounty shall light the living, not the dead. St. Anthony is not afraid to be left in the dark, though he was. — [*Knocking.*] See who's there.

[FATHER FRANCIS *goes to the door and opens it.*

Enter PORTER.

Port. Here's one without, in pressing haste to speak with father Paul.

Fran. Brother Paul!

[FATHER PAUL *comes from behind a curtain, with a glass of wine, and in his hand a piece of cake.*

Paul. Here! how durst you, fellow, thus abruptly break in upon our devotions?

Port. I thought they were finished.

Paul. No, they were not — were they, brother Francis?

Fran. Not by a bottle each.

Paul. But neither you nor your fellows mark how the hours go; no, you mind nothing but the gratifying of your appetites; ye eat and swill, and sleep, and gourmandise, and thrive, while we are wasting in mortification.

Port. We ask no more than nature craves.

Paul. 'Tis false, ye have more appetites than hairs! and your flushed, sleek, and pampered appearance is the disgrace of our order — out on't! If you are hungry, can't you be content with the wholesome roots of the earth? and, if you are dry, isn't there the crystal spring? — [*Drinks.*] Put this away, — [*Gives the glass.*] and show me where I'm wanted. — [PORTER *drains the glass.* — PAUL, *going, turns.*] So, you would have drunk it, if there had been any left! Ah, glutton! glutton!　　　　　　　　　　　　　　　　　[*Exeunt.*

11*

SCENE VI. — *The Court before the Priory.*

Enter ISAAC *and* DON ANTONIO.

Isaac. A plaguy while coming, this same father Paul! —
He's detained at vespers, I suppose, poor fellow.

Don Ant. No, here he comes.

Enter FATHER PAUL.

Good father Paul, I crave your blessing.

Isaac. Yes, good father Paul, we are come to beg a favour.

Paul. What is it, pray?

Isaac. To marry us, good father Paul; and in truth thou
dost look the very priest of Hymen.

Paul. In short, I may be called so; for I deal in repentance and mortification.

Isaac. No, no, thou seemest an officer of Hymen, because
thy presence speaks content and good humour.

Paul. Alas! my appearance is deceitful. Bloated I am,
indeed! for fasting is a windy recreation, and it hath swollen
me like a bladder.

Don Ant. But thou hast a good fresh colour in thy face,
father; rosy, i'faith!

Paul. Yes, I have blushed for mankind, till the hue of my
shame is as fixed as their vices.

Isaac. Good man!

Paul. And I have laboured too, but to what purpose? they
continue to sin under my very nose.

Isaac. Efecks, father, I should have guessed as much, for
your nose seems to be put to the blush more than any other
part of your face.

Paul. Go, you're a wag!

Don Ant. But, to the purpose, father — will you officiate
for us?

Paul. To join young people thus clandestinely is not safe:
and, indeed, I have in my heart many weighty reasons
against it.

Don Ant. And I have in my hand many weighty reasons for it. Isaac, haven't you an argument or two in our favour about you?

Isaac. Yes, yes; here is a most unanswerable purse.

Paul. For shame! you make me angry: you forget who I am, and when importunate people have forced their trash — ay, into this pocket, here — or into this — why, then the sin was theirs. — [*They put money into his pockets.*] Fie, now how you distress me! I would return it, but that I must touch it that way, and so wrong my oath.

Don Ant. Now then, come with us.

Isaac. Ay, now give us our title to joy and rapture.

Paul. Well, when your hour of repentance comes, don't blame me.

Don Ant. [*Aside.*] No bad caution to my friend Isaac. — [*Aloud.*] Well, well, father, do you do your part, and I'll abide the consequence.

Isaac. Ay, and so will I.

      Enter DONNA LOUISA, *running.*

Don. Louisa. O Antonio, Ferdinand is at the porch, and inquiring for us.

Isaac. Who? Don Ferdinand! he's not inquiring for me, I hope.

Don Ant. Fear not, my love; I'll soon pacify him.

Isaac. Egad, you won't. Antonio, take my advice, and run away; this Ferdinand is the most unmerciful dog, and has the cursedest long sword! — and, upon my soul, he comes on purpose to cut your throat.

Don Ant. Never fear, never fear.

Isaac. Well, you may stay if you will; but I'll get some one to marry me; for, by St. Iago, he shall never meet me again, while I am master of a pair of heels.

    [*Runs out.* — DONNA LOUISA *lets down her veil.*

      Enter DON FERDINAND.

Don Ferd. So, sir, I have met with you at last.

Don Ant. Well, sir.

Don. Ferd. Base, treacherous man! whence can a false, deceitful soul, like yours, borrow confidence to look so steadily on the man you've injured?

Don. Ant. Ferdinand, you are too warm: 'tis true you find me on the point of wedding one I loved beyond my life; but no argument of mine prevailed on her to elope — I scorn deceit, as much as you. By heaven I knew not that she had left her father's till I saw her!

Don Ferd. What a mean excuse! You have wronged your friend, then, for one, whose wanton forwardness anticipated your treachery — of this, indeed, your Jew pander informed me; but let your conduct be consistent, and, since you have dared to do a wrong, follow me, and show you have a spirit to avow it.

Don. Louisa. Antonio, I perceive his mistake — leave him to me.

Paul. Friend, you are rude, to interrupt the union of two willing hearts.

Don Ferd. No, meddling priest! the hand he seeks is mine.

Paul. If so, I'll proceed no further. Lady, did you ever promise this youth your hand?

[*To* DONNA LOUISA, *who shakes her head.*

Don Ferd. Clara, I thank you for your silence — I would not have heard your tongue avow such falsity; be't your punishment to remember I have not reproached you.

Enter DONNA CLARA, *veiled.*

Don. Clara. What mockery is this?

Don Ferd. Antonio, you are protected now, but we shall meet.

[*Going,* DONNA CLARA *holds one arm, and* DONNA LOUISA *the other.*

DUET.

Don. Louisa.	Turn thee round, I pray thee.
	Calm awhile thy rage.
Don. Clara.	I must help to stay thee,
	And thy wrath assuage.

Don. Louisa. Couldst thou not discover
One so dear to thee?
Don. Clara. Canst thou be a lover,
And thus fly from me?   [*Both unveil.*

Don Ferd. How's this? My sister! Clara too — I'm confounded.

Don. Louisa. 'Tis even so, good brother.

Paul. How! what impiety? did the man want to marry his own sister?

Don. Louisa. And ar'n't you ashamed of yourself not to know your own sister?

Don. Clara. To drive away your own mistress ——

Don. Louisa. Don't you see how jealousy blinds people?

Don. Clara. Ay, and will you ever be jealous again?

Don Ferd. Never — never! — You, sister, I know will forgive me — but how, Clara, shall I presume ——

Don. Clara. No, no, just now you told me not to tease you — "Who do you want, good signor?" "Not you, not you!" — Oh, you blind wretch! but swear never to be jealous again, and I'll forgive you.

Don Ferd. By all ——

Don. Clara. There, that will do — you'll keep the oath just as well.   [*Gives her hand.*

Don. Louisa. But, brother, here is one to whom some apology is due.

Don Ferd. Antonio, I am ashamed to think ——

Don Ant. Not a word of excuse, Ferdinand — I have not been in love myself without learning that a lover's anger should never be resented. But come — let us retire with this good father, and we'll explain to you the cause of this error.

GLEE AND CHORUS.

Oft does Hymen smile to hear
  Wordy vows of feign'd regard :
Well he knows when they're sincere,
  Never slow to give reward :
For his glory is to prove
Kind to those who wed for love.   [*Exeunt.*

SCENE VII. — *A Grand Saloon in* DON JEROME'S *House.*

Enter DON JEROME, LOPEZ, *and* SERVANTS.

Don Jer. Be sure, now, let every thing be in the best order — let all my servants have on their merriest faces: but tell them to get as little drunk as possible, till after supper. — [*Exeunt* SERVANTS.] So, Lopez, where's your master? sha'n't we have him at supper?

Lop. Indeed, I believe, not, sir — he's mad, I doubt! I'm sure he has frighted me from him.

Don Jer. Ay, ay, he's after some wench, I suppose: a young rake! Well, well, we'll be merry without him. [*Exit* LOPEZ.

Enter a SERVANT.

Ser. Sir, here is Signor Isaac. [*Exit.*

Enter ISAAC.

Don Jer. So, my dear son-in-law — there, take my blessing and forgiveness. But where's my daughter? where's Louisa?

Isaac. She's without, impatient for a blessing, but almost afraid to enter.

Don Jer. Oh, fly and bring her in. — [*Exit* ISAAC.] Poor girl, I long to see her pretty face.

Isaac. [*Without.*] Come, my charmer! my trembling angel!

Re-enter ISAAC *with* DUENNA; DON JEROME *runs to meet them; she kneels.*

Don Jer. Come to my arms, my — [*Starts back.*] Why, who the devil have we here?

Isaac. Nay, Don Jerome, you promised her forgiveness; see how the dear creature droops!

Don Jer. Droops indeed! Why, Gad take me, this is old Margaret! But where's my daughter? where's Louisa?

Isaac. Why, here, before your eyes — nay, don't be abashed, my sweet wife!

Don Jer. Wife with a vengeance! Why, zounds, you have not married the Duenna!

Duen. [*Kneeling.*]   Oh, dear papa! you'll not disown me, sure!

Don. Jer.   Papa! papa! Why, zounds, your impudence is as great as your ugliness! `

Isaac.   Rise, my charmer, go throw your snowy arms about his neck, and convince him you are ——

Duen.   Oh, sir, forgive me!   [*Embraces him.*

Don Jer.   Help! murder!

Enter Servants.

Ser.   What's the matter, sir?

Don Jer.   Why, here, this damned Jew has brought an old harridan to strangle me.

Isaac.   Lord, it is his own daughter, and he is so hard-hearted he won't forgive her!

Enter Don Antonio *and* Donna Louisa; *they kneel.*

Don Jer.   Zounds and fury! what's here now? who sent for you, sir, and who the devil are you?

Don Ant.   This lady's husband, sir.

Isaac.   Ay, that he is, I'll be sworn; for I left them with a priest, and was to have given her away.

Don Jer.   You were?

Isaac.   Ay; that's my honest friend, Antonio; and that's the little girl I told you I had hampered him with.

Don Jer.   Why, you are either drunk or mad — this is my daughter.

Isaac.   No, no; 'tis you are both drunk and mad, I think — here's your daughter.

Don Jer.   Hark ye, old iniquity! will you explain all this, or not?

Duen.   Come then, Don Jerome, I will — though our habits might inform you all. Look on your daughter, there, and on me.

Isaac.   What's this I hear?

Duen.   The truth is, that in your passion this morning you made a small mistake; for you turned your daughter out of doors, and locked up your humble servant.

Isaac. O Lud! O Lud! here's a pretty fellow, to turn his daughter out of doors, instead of an old Duenna!

Don Jer. And, O Lud! O Lud! here's a pretty fellow, to marry an old Duenna instead of my daughter! But how came the rest about?

Duen. I have only to add, that I remained in your daughter's place, and had the good fortune to engage the affections of my sweet husband here.

Isaac. Her husband! why, you old witch, do you think I'll be your husband now? This is a trick, a cheat! and you ought all to be ashamed of yourselves.

Don Ant. Hark ye, Isaac, do you dare to complain of tricking? Don Jerome, I give you my word, this cunning Portuguese has brought all this upon himself, by endeavouring to over-reach you, by getting your daughter's fortune, without making any settlement in return.

Don Jer. Over-reach me!

Don. Louisa. 'Tis so, indeed, sir, and we can prove it to you.

Don Jer. Why, Gad take me, it must be so, or he could never have put up with such a face as Margaret's — so, little Solomon, I wish you joy of your wife, with all my soul.

Don. Louisa. Isaac, tricking is all fair in love — let you alone for the plot!

Don Ant. A cunning dog, ar'n't you? A sly little villain, eh?

Don. Louisa. Roguish, perhaps; but keen, devilish keen!

Don. Jer. Yes, yes; his aunt always called him little Solomon.

Isaac. Why, the plagues of Egypt upon you all! — but do you think I'll submit to such an imposition?

Don Ant. Isaac, one serious word—you'd better be content as you are; for, believe me, you will find that, in the opinion of the world, there is not a fairer subject for contempt and ridicule than a knave become the dupe of his own art.

Isaac. I don't care — I'll not endure this. Don Jerome, 'tis you have done this—you would be so cursed positive about

the beauty of her you locked up, and all the time I told you
she was as old as my mother, and as ugly as the devil.

Duen. Why, you little insignificant reptile! ——

Don. Jer. That's right! — attack him, Margaret.

Duen. Dare such a thing as you pretend to talk of beauty?
— A walking rouleau! — a body that seems to owe all its consequence to the dropsy! — a pair of eyes like two dead beetles
in a wad of brown dough! — a beard like an artichoke, with
dry shrivelled jaws, that would disgrace the mummy of a
monkey!

Don. Jer. Well done, Margaret!

Duen. But you shall know that I have a brother who
wears a sword — and, if you don't do me justice ——

Isaac. Fire seize your brother, and you too! I'll fly to
Jerusalem to avoid you!

Duen. Fly where you will, I'll follow you.

Don Jer. Throw your snowy arms about him, Margaret. —
[*Exeunt* ISAAC *and* DUENNA.] But, Louisa, are you really married to this modest gentleman?

Don. Louisa. Sir, in obedience to your commands, I gave
him my hand within this hour.

Don Jer. My commands!

Don Ant. Yes, sir; here is your consent, under your own
hand.

Don. Jer. How! would you rob me of my child by a trick,
a false pretence? and do you think to get her fortune by
the same means? Why, 'slife, you are as great a rogue as
Isaac!

Don Ant. No, Don Jerome; though I have profited by this
paper in gaining your daughter's hand, I scorn to obtain her
fortune by deceit. There, sir. — [*Gives a letter.*] Now give
her your blessing for a dower, and all the little I possess shall
be settled on her in return. Had you wedded her to a prince,
he could do no more.

Don Jer. Why, Gad take me, but you are a very extraordinary fellow! But have you the impudence to suppose no
one can do a generous action but yourself? Here, Louisa,

tell this proud fool of yours that he's the only man I know that would renounce your fortune; and, by my soul, he's the only man in Spain that's worthy of it. There, bless you both: I'm an obstinate old fellow when I'm in the wrong; but you shall now find me as steady in the right.

Enter DON FERDINAND *and* DONNA CLARA.

Another wonder still! Why, sirrah! Ferdinand, you have not stole a nun, have you?

Don Ferd. She is a nun in nothing but her habit, sir — look nearer, and you will perceive 'tis Clara d'Almanza, Don Guzman's daughter; and, with pardon for stealing a wedding, she is also my wife.

Don Jer. Gadsbud, and a great fortune! Ferdinand, you are a prudent young rogue, and I forgive you: and, ifecks, you are a pretty little damsel. Give your father-in-law a kiss, you smiling rogue!

Don. Clara. There, old gentleman; and now mind you behave well to us.

Don Jer. Ifecks, those lips ha'n't been chilled by kissing beads! Egad, I believe I shall grow the best-humoured fellow in Spain. Lewis! Sancho! Carlos! d'ye hear? are all my doors thrown open? Our children's weddings are the only holidays our age can boast; and then we drain, with pleasure, the little stock of spirits time has left us. — [*Music within.*] But see, here come our friends and neighbours!

Enter MASQUERADERS.

And, i'faith, we'll make a night on't, with wine, and dance, and catches— then old and young shall join us.

FINALE.

Don Jer.. .   Come now for jest and smiling,
       Both old and young beguiling,
         Let us laugh and play, so blithe and gay,
         Till we banish care away.

Don. Louisa.　Thus crown'd with dance and song,
　　　　　　The hours shall glide along,
　　　　　　　With a heart at ease, merry, merry glees
　　　　　　　Can never fail to please.

Don Ferd. .　Each bride with blushes glowing,
　　　　　　Our wine as rosy flowing,
　　　　　　　Let us laugh and play, so blithe and gay,
　　　　　　　Till we banish care away.

Don Ant.. .　Then healths to every friend
　　　　　　The night's repast shall end,
　　　　　　　With a heart at ease, merry, merry glees
　　　　　　　Can never fail to please.

Don. Clara .　Nor, while we are so joyous,
　　　　　　Shall anxious fear annoy us;
　　　　　　　Let us laugh and play, so blithe and gay,
　　　　　　　Till we banish care away.

Don Jer.. .　For generous guests like these
　　　　　　Accept the wish to please,
　　　　　　　So we'll laugh and play, so blithe and gay,
　　　　　　　Your smiles drive care away.　　　　[*Exeunt omnes.*

THE SCHOOL FOR SCANDAL.

· A COMEDY.

DRAMATIS PERSONÆ.

AS ORIGINALLY ACTED AT DRURY-LANE THEATRE IN 1777.

SIR PETER TEAZLE .	*Mr. King.*	CRABTREE . . .	*Mr. Parsons.*
SIR OLIVER SURFACE	*Mr. Yates.*	ROWLEY	*Mr. Aickin.*
SIR HARRY BUMPER .	*Mr. Gawdry.*	MOSES	*Mr. Baddeley.*
SIR BENJAMIN BACK-} BITE . . . . }	*Mr. Dodd.*	TRIP	*Mr. Lamash.*
		LADY TEAZLE . .	*Mrs. Abington.*
JOSEPH SURFACE . .	*Mr. Palmer.*	LADY SNEERWELL	*Miss Sherry.*
CHARLES SURFACE .	*Mr. Smith.*	MRS. CANDOUR . .	*Miss Pope.*
CARELESS	*Mr. Farren.*	MARIA	*Miss P. Hopkins.*
SNAKE	*Mr. Packer.*	Gentlemen, Maid, *and* Servants.	

SCENE. — LONDON.

A PORTRAIT;

ADDRESSED TO MRS. CREWE, WITH THE COMEDY OF THE SCHOOL FOR SCANDAL.

BY R. B. SHERIDAN, ESQ.

TELL me, ye prim adepts in Scandal's school,
Who rail by precept, and detract by rule,
Lives there no character, so tried, so known,
So deck'd with grace, and so unlike your own,
That even you assist her fame to raise,
Approve by envy, and by silence praise!
Attend! — a model shall attract your view —
Daughters of calumny, I summon you!
You shall decide if this a portrait prove,
Or fond creation of the Muse and Love.
Attend, ye virgin critics, shrewd and sage,
Ye matron censors of this childish age,
Whose peering eye and wrinkled front declare
A fix'd antipathy to young and fair;
By cunning, cautious; or by nature, cold,
In maiden madness, virulently bold! —

Attend, ye skill'd to coin the precious tale,
Creating proof, where innendos fail!
Whose practised memories, cruelly exact,
Omit no circumstance, except the fact! —
Attend, all ye who boast, — or old or young, —
The living libel of a slanderous tongue!
So shall my theme as far contrasted be,
As saints by fiends, or hymns by calumny.
Come, gentle Amoret (for 'neath that name
In worthier verse is sung thy beauty's fame);
Come — for but thee who seeks the Muse? and while
Celestial blushes check thy conscious smile,
With timid grace, and hesitating eye,
The perfect model, which I boast, supply: —
Vain Muse! couldst thou the humblest sketch create
Of her, or slightest charm couldst imitate —
Could thy blest strain in kindred colours trace
The faintest wonder of her form and face —
Poets would study the immortal line,
And Reynolds own his art subdued by thine;
That art, which well might added lustre give
To Nature's best, and Heaven's superlative:
On Granby's cheek might bid new glories rise,
Or point a purer beam from Devon's eyes!
Hard is the task to shape that beauty's praise,
Whose judgment scorns the homage flattery pays!
But praising Amoret we cannot err,
No tongue o'ervalues Heaven, or flatters her!
Yet she by fate's perverseness — she alone
Would doubt our truth, nor deem such praise her own!
Adorning fashion, unadorn'd by dress,
Simple from taste, and not from carelessness;
Discreet in gesture, in deportment mild,
Not stiff with prudence, nor uncouthly wild:
No state has Amoret; no studied mien;
She frowns no goddess, and she moves no queen.
The softer charm that in her manner lies
Is framed to captivate, yet not surprise;
It justly suits the expression of her face, —
'Tis less than dignity, and more than grace!
On her pure cheek the native hue is such,
That, form'd by Heaven to be admired so much,
The hand divine, with a less partial care,
Might well have fix'd a fainter crimson there,
And bade the gentle inmate of her breast —
Inshrined Modesty — supply the rest.
But who the peril of her lips shall paint?
Strip them of smiles — still, still all words are faint!

But moving Love himself appears to teach
Their action, though denied to rule her speech;
And thou who seest her speak, and dost not hear,
Mourn not her distant accents 'scape thine ear;
Viewing those lips, thou still may'st make pretence
To judge of what she says, and swear 'tis sense:
Clothed with such grace, with such expression fraught,
They move in meaning, and they pause in thought!
But dost thou farther watch, with charm'd surprise,
The mild irresolution of her eyes,
Curious to mark how frequent they repose,
In brief eclipse and momentary close —
Ah! seest thou not an ambush'd Cupid there,
Too tim'rous of his charge, with jealous care
Veils and unveils those beams of heavenly light,
Too full, too fatal else, for mortal sight?
Nor yet, such pleasing vengeance fond to meet,
In pard'ning dimples hope a safe retreat.
What though her peaceful breast should ne'er allow
Subduing frowns to arm her alter'd brow,
By Love, I swear, and by his gentle wiles,
More fatal still the mercy of her smiles!
Thus lovely, thus adorn'd, possessing all
Of bright or fair that can to woman fall,
The height of vanity might well be thought
Prerogative in her, and Nature's fault.
Yet gentle Amoret, in mind supreme
As well as charms, rejects the vainer theme;
And, half mistrustful of her beauty's store,
She barbs with wit those darts too keen before: —
Read in all knowledge that her sex should reach,
Though Greville, or the Muse, should deign to teach,
Fond to improve, nor timorous to discern
How far it is a woman's grace to learn;
In Millar's dialect she would not prove
Apollo's priestess, but Apollo's love,
Graced by those signs which truth delights to own,
The timid blush, and mild submitted tone:
Whate'er she says, though sense appear throughout,
Displays the tender hue of female doubt;
Deck'd with that charm, how lovely wit appears,
How graceful science, when that robe she wears!
Such too her talents, and her bent of mind,
As speak a sprightly heart by thought refined:
A taste for mirth, by contemplation school'd,
A turn for ridicule, by candour ruled,
A scorn of folly, which she tries to hide;
An awe of talent, which she owns with pride!

Peace, idle Muse! no more thy strain prolong,
But yield a theme, thy warmest praises wrong;
Just to her merit, though thou canst not raise
Thy feeble verse, behold th' acknowledged praise
Has spread conviction through the envious train,
And cast a fatal gloom o'er Scandal's reign!
And lo! each pallid hag, with blister'd tongue,
Mutters assent to all thy zeal has sung —
Owns all the colours just — the outline true;
Thee my inspirer, and my model — CREWE!

PROLOGUE.

WRITTEN BY MR. GARRICK.

A SCHOOL for Scandal! tell me, I beseech you,
Needs there a school this modish art to teach you?
No need of lessons now, the knowing think;
We might as well be taught to eat and drink.
Caused by a dearth of scandal, should the vapours
Distress our fair ones — let them read the papers;
Their powerful mixtures such disorders hit;
Crave what you will — there's *quantum sufficit*.
"Lord!" cries my Lady Wormwood (who loves tattle,
And puts much salt and pepper in her prattle),
Just risen at noon, all night at cards when threshing
Strong tea and scandal — "Bless me, how refreshing!
Give me the papers, Lisp — how bold and free! [*Sips.*
Last night Lord L. [Sips] was caught with Lady D.
For aching heads what charming sal volatile! [*Sips.*
If Mrs. B. will still continue flirting,
We hope she'll DRAW, or we'll UNDRAW the curtain.
Fine satire, poz — in public all abuse it,
But, by ourselves [*Sips*], our praise we can't refuse it.
Now, Lisp, read you — there, at that dash and star:"
"Yes, ma'am — *A certain lord had best beware,*
Who lives not twenty miles from Grosvenor Square;
For, should he Lady W. find willing,
Wormwood is bitter" — "Oh! that's me! the villain!
Throw it behind the fire, and never more
Let that vile paper come within my door."
Thus at our friends we laugh, who feel the dart;
To reach our feelings, we ourselves must smart.
Is our young bard so young, to think that he
Can stop the full spring-tide of calumny?

Knows he the world so little, and its trade?
Alas! the devil's sooner raised than laid.
So strong, so swift, the monster there's no gagging:
Cut Scandal's head off, still the tongue is wagging.
Proud of your smiles once lavishly bestow'd,
Again our young Don Quixote takes the road;
To show his gratitude he draws his pen,
And seeks this hydra, Scandal, in his den.
For your applause all perils he would through —
He'll fight — that's write — a cavalliero true,
Till every drop of blood — that's ink — is spilt for you.

ACT I.

Scene I. — Lady Sneerwell's *Dressing-room.*

Lady Sneerwell *discovered at her toilet;* Snake *drinking chocolate.*

Lady Sneer. The paragraphs, you say, Mr. Snake, were all inserted?

Snake. They were, madam; and, as I copied them myself in a feigned hand, there can be no suspicion whence they came.

Lady Sneer. Did you circulate the report of Lady Brittle's intrigue with Captain Boastall?

Snake. That's in as fine a train as your ladyship could wish. In the common course of things, I think it must reach Mrs. Clackitt's ears within four-and-twenty hours; and then, you know, the business is as good as done.

Lady Sneer. Why, truly, Mrs. Clackitt has a very pretty talent, and a great deal of industry.

Snake. True, madam, and has been tolerably successful in her day. To my knowledge, she has been the cause of six matches being broken off, and three sons being disinherited; of four forced elopements, and as many close confinements; nine separate maintenances, and two divorces. Nay, I have more than once traced her causing a *tête-à-tête* in the "Town and Country Magazine," when the parties, perhaps, had never seen each other's face before in the course of their lives.

Lady Sneer. She certainly has talents, but her manner is gross.

Snake. 'Tis very true. She generally designs well, has a free tongue and a bold invention; but her colouring is too dark, and her outlines often extravagant. She wants that delicacy of tint, and mellowness of sneer, which distinguish your ladyship's scandal.

Lady Sneer. You are partial, Snake.

Snake. Not in the least; every body allows that Lady Sneerwell can do more with a word or look than many can with the most laboured detail, even when they happen to have a little truth on their side to support it.

Lady Sneer. Yes, my dear Snake; and I am no hypocrite to deny the satisfaction I reap from the success of my efforts. Wounded myself, in the early part of my life, by the envenomed tongue of slander, I confess I have since known no pleasure equal to the reducing others to the level of my own reputation.

Snake. Nothing can be more natural. But, Lady Sneerwell, there is one affair in which you have lately employed me, wherein, I confess, I am at a loss to guess your motives.

Lady Sneer. I conceive you mean with respect to my neighbour, Sir Peter Teazle, and his family?

Snake. I do. Here are two young men, to whom Sir Peter has acted as a kind of guardian since their father's death; the eldest possessing the most amiable character, and universally well spoken of — the youngest, the most dissipated and extravagant young fellow in the kingdom, without friends or character: the former an avowed admirer of your ladyship, and apparently your favourite; the latter attached to Maria, Sir Peter's ward, and confessedly beloved by her. Now, on the face of these circumstances, it is utterly unaccountable to me, why you, the widow of a city knight, with a good jointure, should not close with the passion of a man of such character and expectations as Mr. Surface; and more so why you should be so uncommonly earnest to destroy the mutual attachment subsisting between his brother Charles and Maria.

12*

Lady Sneer. Then, at once to unravel this mystery, I must inform you that love has no share whatever in the intercourse between Mr. Surface and me.

Snake. No!

Lady Sneer. His real attachment is to Maria, or her fortune; but, finding in his brother a favoured rival, he has been obliged to mask his pretensions, and profit by my assistance.

Snake. Yet still I am more puzzled why you should interest yourself in his success.

Lady Sneer. Heavens! how dull you are! Cannot you surmise the weakness which I hitherto, through shame, have concealed even from you? Must I confess that Charles — that libertine, that extravagant, that bankrupt in fortune and reputation — that he it is for whom I am thus anxious and malicious, and to gain whom I would sacrifice every thing?

Snake. Now, indeed, your conduct appears consistent: but how came you and Mr. Surface so confidential?

Lady Sneer. For our mutual interest. I have found him out a long time since. I know him to be artful, selfish, and malicious — in short, a sentimental knave; while with Sir Peter, and indeed with all his acquaintance, he passes for a youthful miracle of prudence, good sense, and benevolence.

Snake. Yes; yet Sir Peter vows he has not his equal in England; and, above all, he praises him as a man of sentiment.

Lady Sneer. True; and with the assistance of his sentiment and hypocrisy he has brought Sir Peter entirely into his interest with regard to Maria; while poor Charles has no friend in the house — though, I fear, he has a powerful one in Maria's heart, against whom we must direct our schemes.

Enter SERVANT.

Ser. Mr. Surface.

Lady Sneer. Show him up. [*Exit* SERVANT.] He generally calls about this time. I don't wonder at people giving him to me for a lover.

Enter JOSEPH SURFACE.

Jos. Surf. My dear Lady Sneerwell, how do you do to-day?
Mr. Snake, your most obedient.

Lady Sneer. Sn' ke has just been rallying me on our mutual
attachment: but I have informed him of our real views. You
know how useful he has been to us; and, believe me, the confidence is not ill placed.

Jos. Surf. Madam, it is impossible for me to suspect a man
of Mr. Snake's sensibility and discernment.

Lady Sneer. Well, well, no compliments now; but tell me
when you saw your mistress, Maria—or, what is more material
to me, your brother.

Jos. Surf. I have not seen either since I left you; but I
can inform you that they never meet. Some of your stories
have taken a good effect on Maria.

Lady Sneer. Ah, my dear Snake! the merit of this belongs
to you. But do your brother's distresses increase?

Jos. Surf. Every hour. I am told he has had another execution in the house yesterday. In short, his dissipation and
extravagance exceed any thing I have ever heard of.

Lady Sneer. Poor Charles!

Jos. Surf. True, madam; notwithstanding his vices, one
can't help feeling for him. Poor Charles! I'm sure I wish it
were in my power to be of any essential service to him; for
the man who does not share in the distresses of a brother, even
though merited by his own misconduct, deserves ——

Lady Sneer. O Lud! you are going to be moral, and forget
that you are among friends.

Jos. Surf. Egad, that's true! I'll keep that sentiment till
I see Sir Peter. However, it is certainly a charity to rescue
Maria from such a libertine, who, if he is to be reclaimed, can
be so only by a person of your ladyship's superior accomplishments and understanding.

Snake. I believe, Lady Sneerwell, here's company coming:
I'll go and copy the letter I mentioned to you. Mr. Surface,
your most obedient.

Jos. Surf. Sir, your very devoted. — [*Exit* SNAKE.] Lady

Sneerwell, I am very sorry you have put any farther confidence in that fellow.

Lady Sneer. Why so?

Jos. Surf. I have lately detected him in frequent conference with old Rowley, who was formerly my father's steward, and has never, you know, been a friend of mine.

Lady Sneer. And do you think he would betray us?

Jos. Surf. Nothing more likely: take my word for't, Lady Sneerwell, that fellow hasn't virtue enough to be faithful even to his own villany. Ah, Maria!

Enter MARIA.

Lady Sneer. Maria, my dear, how do you do? What's the matter?

Mar. Oh! there's that disagreeable lover of mine, Sir Benjamin Backbite, has just called at my guardian's, with his odious uncle, Crabtree; so I slipped out, and ran hither to avoid them.

Lady Sneer. Is that all?

Jos. Surf. If my brother Charles had been of the party, madam, perhaps you would not have been so much alarmed.

Lady Sneer. Nay, now you are severe; for I dare swear the truth of the matter is, Maria heard you were here. But, my dear, what has Sir Benjamin done, that you should avoid him so?

Mar. Oh, he has done nothing — but 'tis for what he has said: his conversation is a perpetual libel on all his acquaintance.

Jos. Surf. Ay, and the worst of it is, there is no advantage in not knowing him; for he'll abuse a stranger just as soon as his best friend: and his uncle's as bad.

Lady Sneer. Nay, but we should make allowance; Sir Benjamin is a wit and a poet.

Mar. For my part, I own, madam, wit loses its respect with me, when I see it in company with malice. What do you think, Mr. Surface?

Jos. Surf. Certainly, madam; to smile at the jest which

plants a thorn in another's breast is to become a principal in
the mischief.

Lady Sneer.   Psha! there's no possibility of being witty
without a little ill nature: the malice of a good thing is the
barb that makes it stick.   What's your opinion, Mr. Surface?

Jos. Surf.   To be sure, madam; that conversation, where
the spirit of raillery is suppressed, will ever appear tedious
and insipid.

Mar.   Well, I'll not debate how far scandal may be allow-
able; but in a man, I am sure, it is always contemptible.   We
have pride, envy, rivalship, and a thousand motives to depre-
ciate each other; but the male slanderer must have the cow-
ardice of a woman before he can traduce one.

Re-enter SERVANT.

Ser.   Madam, Mrs. Candour is below, and, if your ladyship's at leisure, will leave her carriage.

Lady Sneer.   Beg her to walk in. — [*Exit* SERVANT.]   Now,
Maria, here is a character to your taste; for, though Mrs.
Candour is a little talkative, every body allows her to be the
best natured and best sort of woman.

Mar.   Yes, with a very gross affectation of good nature
and benevolence, she does more mischief than the direct
malice of old Crabtree.

Jos. Surf.   I' faith that's true, Lady Sneerwell: whenever
I hear the current running against the characters of my
friends, I never think them in such danger as when Candour
undertakes their defence.

Lady Sneer.   Hush! — here she is!

Enter MRS. CANDOUR.

Mrs. Can.   My dear Lady Sneerwell, how have you been
this century? — Mr. Surface, what news do you hear? —
though indeed it is no matter, for I think one hears nothing
else but scandal.

Jos. Surf.   Just so, indeed, ma'am.

Mrs. Can.   Oh, Maria! child, — what, is the whole affair

off between you and Charles? His extravagance, I presume
—- the town talks of nothing else.

Mar. I am very sorry, ma'am, the town has so little
to do.

Mrs. Can. True, true, child: but there's no stopping
people's tongues. I own I was hurt to hear it, as I indeed
was to learn, from the same quarter, that your guardian, Sir
Peter, and Lady Teazle have not agreed lately as well as
could be wished.

Mar. 'Tis strangely impertinent for people to busy themselves so.

Mrs. Can. Very true, child: but what's to be done?
People will talk — there's no preventing it. Why, it was
but yesterday I was told that Miss Gadabout had eloped with
Sir Filigree Flirt. But, Lord! there's no minding what
one hears; though, to be sure, I had this from very good
authority.

Mar. Such reports are highly scandalous.

Mrs. Can. So they are, child — shameful, shameful! But
the world is so censorious, no character escapes. Lord, now
who would have suspected your friend, Miss Prim, of an indiscretion? Yet such is the ill nature of people, that they
say her uncle stopped her last week, just as she was stepping
into the York Mail with her dancing-master.

Mar. I'll answer for't there are no grounds for that
report.

Mrs. Can. Ah, no foundation in the world, I dare swear;
no more, probably, than for the story circulated last month,
of Mrs. Festino's affair with Colonel Cassino — though, to be
sure, that matter was never rightly cleared up.

Jos. Surf. The licence of invention some people take is
monstrous indeed.

Mar. 'Tis so; but, in my opinion, those who report such
things are equally culpable.

Mrs. Can. To be sure they are; tale-bearers are as bad
as the tale-makers — 'tis an old observation, and a very true
one: but what's to be done, as I said before? how will you

prevent people from talking? To-day, Mrs. Clackitt assured me, Mr. and Mrs. Honeymoon were at last become mere man and wife, like the rest of their acquaintance. She likewise hinted that a certain widow, in the next street, had got rid of her dropsy and recovered her shape in a most surprising manner. And at the same time Miss Tattle, who was by, affirmed, that Lord Buffalo had discovered his lady at a house of no extraordinary fame; and that Sir Harry Bouquet and Tom Saunter were to measure swords on a similar provocation. But, Lord, do you think I would report these things! No, no! tale-bearers, as I said before, are just as bad as the tale-makers.

Jos. Surf. Ah! Mrs. Candour, if every body had your forbearance and good nature!

Mrs. Can. I confess, Mr. Surface, I cannot bear to hear people attacked behind their backs; and when ugly circumstances come out against our acquaintance I own I always love to think the best. By the by, I hope 'tis not true that your brother is absolutely ruined?

Jos. Surf. I am afraid his circumstances are very bad indeed, ma'am.

Mrs. Can. Ah! I heard so — but you must tell him to keep up his spirits; every body almost is in the same way: Lord Spindle, Sir Thomas Splint, Captain Quinze, and Mr. Nickit — all up, I hear, within this week; so, if Charles is undone, he'll find half his acquaintance ruined too, and that, you know, is a consolation.

Jos. Surf. Doubtless, ma'am — a very great one.

Re-enter Servant.

Ser. Mr. Crabtree and Sir Benjamin Backbite.   [*Exit.*

Lady Sneer. So, Maria, you see your lover pursues you; positively you sha'n't escape.

Enter Crabtree and Sir Benjamin Backbite.

Crab. Lady Sneerwell, I kiss your hand. Mrs. Candour, I don't believe you are acquainted with my nephew, Sir Ben-

jamin Backbite? Egad, ma'am, he has a pretty wit, and is a
pretty poet too. Isn't he, Lady Sneerwell?

Sir Ben. Oh, fie, uncle!

Crab. Nay, egad it's true; I back him at a rebus or a
charade against the best rhymer in the kingdom. Has your
ladyship heard the epigram he wrote last week on Lady
Frizzle's feather catching fire? — Do, Benjamin, repeat it, or
the charade you made last night extempore at Mrs. Drowzie's
conversazione. Come now; your first is the name of a fish,
your second a great naval commander, and ——

Sir Ben. Uncle, now — pr'ythee ——

Crab. I' faith, ma'am, 'twould surprise you to hear how
ready he is at all these sort of things.

Lady Sneer. I wonder, Sir Benjamin, you never publish
any thing.

Sir Ben. To say truth, ma'am, 'tis very vulgar to print;
and, as my little productions are mostly satires and lampoons
on particular people, I find they circulate more by giving
copies in confidence to the friends of the parties. However,
I have some love elegies, which, when favoured with the lady's
smiles, I mean to give the public.   [*Pointing to* MARIA.

Crab. [*To* MARIA.] 'Fore heaven, ma'am, they'll immor-
talize you! — you will be handed down to posterity, like Pe-
trarch's Laura, or Waller's Sacharissa.

Sir Ben. [*To* MARIA.] Yes, madam, I think you will like
them, when you shall see them on a beautiful quarto page,
where a neat rivulet of text shall meander through a meadow
of margin. 'Fore Gad they will be the most elegant things
of their kind!

Crab. But, ladies, that's true — have you heard the news?

Mrs. Can. What, sir, do you mean the report of ——

Crab. No, ma'am, that's not it. — Miss Nicely is going to
be married to her own footman.

Mrs. Can. Impossible.

Crab. Ask Sir Benjamin.

Sir Ben. 'Tis very true, ma'am: every thing is fixed, and
the wedding liveries bespoke.

Crab. Yes — and they do say there were pressing reasons for it.

Lady Sneer. Why, I have heard something of this before.

Mrs. Can. It can't be — and I wonder any one should believe such a story of so prudent a lady as Miss Nicely.

Sir Ben. O Lud! ma'am, that's the very reason 'twas believed at once. She has always been so cautious and so reserved, that every body was sure there was some reason for it at bottom.

Mrs. Can. Why, to be sure, a tale of scandal is as fatal to the credit of a prudent lady of her stamp as a fever is generally to those of the strongest constitutions. But there is a sort of puny sickly reputation, that is always ailing, yet will outlive the robuster characters of a hundred prudes.

Sir Ben. True, madam, there are valetudinarians in reputation as well as constitution, who, being conscious of their weak part, avoid the least breath of air, and supply their want of stamina by care and circumspection.

Mrs. Can. Well, but this may be all a mistake. You know, Sir Benjamin, very trifling circumstances often give rise to the most injurious tales.

Crab. That they do, I'll be sworn, ma'am. Did you ever hear how Miss Piper came to lose her lover and her character last summer at Tunbridge? — Sir Benjamin, you remember it?

Sir Ben. Oh, to be sure! — the most whimsical circumstance.

Lady Sneer. How was it, pray?

Crab. Why, one evening, at Mrs. Ponto's assembly, the conversation happened to turn on the breeding Nova Scotia sheep in this country. Says a young lady in company, I have known instances of it; for Miss Letitia Piper, a first cousin of mine, had a Nova Scotia sheep that produced her twins. "What!" cries the Lady Dowager Dundizzy (who you know is as deaf as a post), "has Miss Piper had twins?" This mistake, as you may imagine, threw the whole company into a fit of laughter. However, 'twas the next morning every where reported, and in a few days believed by the whole town, 'that Miss Letitia Piper had actually been brought to bed of a fine boy and a girl: and in less than a week there were some people who could name the father, and the farm-house where the babies were put to nurse.

Lady. Sneer. Strange, indeed!

Crab. Matter of fact, I assure you. O Lud! Mr. Surface, pray is it true that your uncle, Sir Oliver, is coming home?

Jos. Surf. Not that I know of, indeed, sir.

Crab. He has been in the East Indies a long time. You can scarcely remember him, I believe? Sad comfort, when-ever he returns, to hear how your brother has gone on!

Jos. Surf. Charles has been imprudent, sir, to be sure; but I hope no busy people have already prejudiced Sir Oliver against him. He may reform.

Sir Ben. To be sure he may: for my part, I never believed him to be so utterly void of principle as people say; and, though he has lost all his friends, I am told nobody is better spoken of by the Jews.

Crab. That's true, egad, nephew. If the Old Jewry was a ward, I believe Charles would be an alderman: no man more popular there, 'fore Gad! I hear he pays as many an-nuities as the Irish tontine; and that, whenever he is sick, they have prayers for the recovery of his health in all the synagogues.

Sir Ben. Yet no man lives in greater splendour. They tell me, when he entertains his friends he will sit down to dinner with a dozen of his own securities; have a score of tradesmen waiting in the antechamber, and an officer behind every guest's chair.

Jos. Surf. This may be entertainment to you, gentlemen, but you pay very little regard to the feelings of a brother.

Mar. [*Aside.*] Their malice is intolerable!—[*Aloud.*] Lady Sneerwell, I must wish you a good morning: I'm not very well.   [*Exit.*

Mrs. Can. O dear! she changes colour very much.

Lady Sneer. Do, Mrs. Candour, follow her: she may want your assistance.

Mrs. Can. That I will, with all my soul, ma'am. — Poor dear girl, who knows what her situation may be!   [*Exit.*

Lady Sneer. 'Twas nothing but that she could not bear to hear Charles reflected on, notwithstanding their difference.

Sir Ben. The young lady's *penchant* is obvious.

Crab. But, Benjamin, you must not give up the pursuit for that: follow her, and put her into good humour. Repeat her some of your own verses. Come, I'll assist you.

Sir Ben. Mr. Surface, I did not mean to hurt you; but depend on't your brother is utterly undone.

Crab. O Lud, ay! undone as ever man was — can't raise a guinea!

Sir Ben. And every thing sold, I'm told, that was movable.

Crab. I have seen one that was at his house. Not a thing left but some empty bottles that were overlooked, and the family pictures, which I believe are framed in the wainscots.

Sir Ben. And I'm very sorry also to hear some bad stories against him.   [*Going.*

Crab. Oh, he has done many mean things, that's certain.

Sir Ben. But, however, as he's your brother—— [*Going.*

Crab. We'll tell you all another opportunity.

[*Exeunt* CRABTREE *and* SIR BENJAMIN.

Lady Sneer. Ha! ha! 'tis very hard for them to leave a subject they have not quite run down.

Jos. Surf. And I believe the abuse was no more acceptable to your ladyship than Maria.

Lady Sneer. I doubt her affections are farther engaged than we imagine. But the family are to be here this evening, so you may as well dine where you are, and we shall have an opportunity of observing farther; in the meantime, I'll go and plot mischief, and you shall study sentiment.   [*Exeunt.*

SCENE II. — *A Room in* SIR PETER TEAZLE'S *House.*

Enter SIR PETER TEAZLE.

Sir Pet. When an old bachelor marries a young wife, what is he to expect? 'Tis now six months since Lady Teazle made me the happiest of men — and I have been the most miserable dog ever since! We tift a little going to church, and fairly quarrelled before the bells had done ringing. I was more than once nearly choked with gall during the honeymoon, and had lost all comfort in life before my friends had done wishing me joy. Yet I chose with caution — a girl bred wholly in the country, who never knew luxury beyond one silk gown, nor dissipation above the annual gala of a race ball. Yet she now plays her part in all the extravagant fopperies of fashion and the town, with as ready a grace as if she never had seen a bush or a grass-plot out of Grosvenor Square! I am sneered at by all my acquaintance, and para-graphed in the newspapers. She dissipates my fortune, and contradicts all my humours; yet the worst of it is, I doubt I love her, or I should never bear all this. However, I'll never be weak enough to own it.

Enter ROWLEY.

Row. Oh! Sir Peter, your servant: how is it with you, sir?

Sir Pet. Very bad, Master Rowley, very bad. I meet with nothing but crosses and vexations.

Row. What can have happened since yesterday?

Sir Pet. A good question to a married man!

Row. Nay, I'm sure, Sir Peter, your lady can't be the cause of your uneasiness.

Sir Pet. Why, has any body told you she was dead?

Row. Come, come, Sir Peter, you love her, notwithstanding your tempers don't exactly agree.

Sir Pet. But the fault is entirely hers, Master Rowley. I am, myself, the sweetest-tempered man alive, and hate a teas-ing temper; and so I tell her a hundred times a day.

Row. Indeed!

Sir Pet. Ay; and what is very extraordinary, in all our disputes she is always in the wrong! But Lady Sneerwell, and the set she meets at her house, encourage the perverseness of her disposition. Then, to complete my vexation, Maria, my ward, whom I ought to have the power of a father over, is determined to turn rebel too, and absolutely refuses the man whom I have long resolved on for her husband; meaning, I suppose, to bestow herself on his profligate brother.

Row. You know, Sir Peter, I have always taken the liberty to differ with you on the subject of these two young gentlemen. I only wish you may not be deceived in your opinion of the elder. For Charles, my life on't! he will retrieve his errors yet. Their worthy father, once my honoured master, was, at his years, nearly as wild a spark; yet, when he died, he did not leave a more benevolent heart to lament his loss.

Sir Pet. You are wrong, Master Rowley. On their father's death, you know, I acted as a kind of guardian to them both, till their uncle Sir Oliver's liberality gave them an early independence: of course, no person could have more opportunities of judging of their hearts, and I was never mistaken in my life. Joseph is indeed a model for the young men of the age. He is a man of sentiment, and acts up to the sentiments he professes; but, for the other, take my word for't, if he had any grain of virtue by descent, he has dissipated it with the rest of his inheritance. Ah! my old friend, Sir Oliver, will be deeply mortified when he finds how part of his bounty has been misapplied.

Row. I am sorry to find you so violent against the young man, because this may be the most critical period of his fortune. I came hither with news that will surprise you.

Sir Pet. What! let me hear.

Row. Sir Oliver is arrived, and at this moment in town.

Sir Pet. How! you astonish me! I thought you did not expect him this month.

Row. I did not: but his passage has been remarkably quick.

Sir Pet. Egad, I shall rejoice to see my old friend. 'Tis

sixteen years since we met. We have had many a day together:—but does he still enjoin us not to inform his nephews
of his arrival?

Row. Most strictly. He means, before it is known, to
make some trial of their dispositions.

Sir Pet. Ah! there needs no art to discover their merits
— however he shall have his way; but, pray, does he know I
am married?

Row. Yes, and will soon wish you joy.

Sir Pet. What, as we drink health to a friend in a consumption! Ah! Oliver will laugh at me. We used to rail at
matrimony together, but he has been steady to his text. Well,
he must be soon at my house, though — I'll instantly give
orders for his reception. But, Master Rowley, don't drop a
word that Lady Teazle and I ever disagree.

Row. By no means.

Sir Pet. For I should never be able to stand Noll's jokes;
so I'll have him think, Lord forgive me! that we are a very
happy couple.

Row. I understand you:—but then you must be very careful not to differ while he is in the house with you.

Sir Pet. Egad, and so we must — and that's impossible.
Ah! Master Rowley, when an old bachelor marries a young
wife, he deserves — no — the crime carries its punishment
along with it.   [*Exeunt.*

ACT II.

Scene I. — *A Room in* Sir Peter Teazle's *House.*

Enter Sir Peter *and* Lady Teazle.

Sir Pet. Lady Teazle, Lady Teazle, I'll not bear it!

Lady Teaz. Sir Peter, Sir Peter, you may bear it or not,
as you please; but I ought to have my own way in every thing,
and, what's more, I will too. What! though I was educated
in the country, I know very well that women of fashion in
London are accountable to nobody after they are married.

Sir Pet. Very well, ma'am, very well; so a husband is to have no influence, no authority?

Lady Teaz. Authority! No, to be sure: — if you wanted authority over me, you should have adopted me, and not married me: I am sure you were old enough.

Sir Pet. Old enough! — ay, there it is. Well, well, Lady Teazle, though my life may be made unhappy by your temper, I'll not be ruined by your extravagance!

Lady Teaz. My extravagance! I'm sure I'm not more extravagant than a woman of fashion ought to be.

Sir Pet. No, no, madam, you shall throw away no more sums on such unmeaning luxury. 'Slife! to spend as much to furnish your dressing-room with flowers in winter as would suffice to turn the Pantheon into a greenhouse, and give a *fête champêtre* at Christmas.

Lady Teaz. And am I to blame, Sir Peter, because flowers are dear in cold weather? You should find fault with the climate, and not with me. For my part, I'm sure I wish it was spring all the year round, and that roses grew under our feet!

Sir Pet. Oons! madam — if you had been born to this, I shouldn't wonder at your talking thus; but you forget what your situation was when I married you.

Lady Teaz. No, no, I don't; 'twas a very disagreeable one, or I should never have married you.

Sir Pet. Yes, yes, madam, you were then in somewhat a humbler style — the daughter of a plain country squire. Recollect, Lady Teazle, when I saw you first sitting at your tambour, in a pretty figured linen gown, with a bunch of keys at your side, your hair combed smooth over a roll, and your apartment hung round with fruits in worsted, of your own working.

Lady Teaz. Oh, yes! I remember it very well, and a curious life I led. My daily occupation to inspect the dairy, superintend the poultry, make extracts from the family receipt-book, and comb my aunt Deborah's lapdog.

Sir Pet. Yes, yes, ma'am, 'twas so indeed.

Lady Teaz. And then you know, my evening amusements!

To draw patterns for ruffles, which I had not materials to make up; to play Pope Joan with the curate; to read a sermon to my aunt; or to be stuck down to an old spinet to strum my father to sleep after a fox-chase.

Sir Pet. I am glad you have so good a memory. Yes, madam, these were the recreations I took you from; but now you must have your coach — *vis-à-vis* — and three powdered footmen before your chair; and, in the summer, a pair of white cats to draw you to Kensington Gardens. No recollection, I suppose, when you were content to ride double, behind the butler, on a docked coach-horse.

Lady Teaz. No — I swear I never did that: I deny the butler and the coach-horse.

Sir Pet. This, madam, was your situation; and what have I done for you? I have made you a woman of fashion, of fortune, of rank — in short, I have made you my wife.

Lady Teaz. Well, then, and there is but one thing more you can make me to add to the obligation, that is ——

Sir Pet. My widow, I suppose?

Lady Teaz. Hem! hem!

Sir Pet. I thank you, madam — but don't flatter yourself; for, though your ill conduct may disturb my peace of mind, it shall never break my heart, I promise you: however, I am equally obliged to you for the hint.

Lady Teaz. Then why will you endeavour to make yourself so disagreeable to me, and thwart me in every little elegant expense?

Sir Pet. 'Slife, madam, I say, had you any of these little elegant expenses when you married me?

Lady Teaz. Lud, Sir Peter! would you have me be out of the fashion?

Sir Pet. The fashion, indeed! what had you to do with the fashion before you married me?

Lady Teaz. For my part, I should think you would like to have your wife thought a woman of taste.

Sir Pet. Ay — there again — taste! Zounds! madam, you had no taste when you married me!

Lady Teaz. That's very true, indeed, Sir Peter! and, after having married you, I should never pretend to taste again, I allow.   But now, Sir Peter, since we have finished our daily jangle, I presume I may go to my engagement at Lady Sneerwell's.

Sir Pet. Ay, there's another precious circumstance — a charming set of acquaintance you have made there!

Lady Teaz. Nay, Sir Peter, they are all people of rank and fortune, and remarkably tenacious of reputation.

Sir Pet. Yes, egad, they are tenacious of reputation with a vengeance; for they don't choose any body should have a character but themselves!   Such a crew!   Ah! many a wretch has rid on a hurdle who has done less mischief than these utterers of forged tales, coiners of scandal, and clippers of reputation.

Lady Teaz. What, would you restrain the freedom of speech?

Sir Pet. Ah! they have made you just as bad as any one of the society.

Lady Teaz. Why, I believe I do bear a part with a tolerable grace.

Sir Pet. Grace indeed!

Lady Teaz. But I vow I bear no malice against the people I abuse: when I say an ill-natured thing, 'tis out of pure good humour; and I take it for granted they deal exactly in the same manner with me.   But, Sir Peter, you know you promised to come to Lady Sneerwell's too.

Sir Pet. Well, well, I'll call in, just to look after my own character.

Lady Teaz. Then, indeed, you must make haste after me, or you'll be too late.   So good by to ye.   [*Exit.*

Sir Pet. So — I have gained much by my intended expostulation!   Yet with what a charming air she contradicts every thing I say, and how pleasantly she shows her contempt for my authority!   Well, though I can't make her love me, there is great satisfaction in quarrelling with her; and I think she never appears to such advantage as when she is doing every thing in her power to plague me.   [*Exit.*

13*

SCENE II. — *A Room in* LADY SNEERWELL'S *House.*

LADY SNEERWELL, MRS. CANDOUR, CRABTREE, SIR BENJAMIN
BACKBITE, *and* JOSEPH SURFACE, *discovered.*

Lady Sneer. Nay, positively, we will hear it.

Jos Surf. Yes, yes, the epigram, by all means.

Sir Ben. O plague on't, uncle! 'tis mere nonsense.

Crab. No, no; 'fore Gad, very clever for an extempore!

Sir Ben. But, ladies, you should be acquainted with the
circumstance. You must know, that one day last week, as
Lady Betty Curricle was taking the dust in Hyde Park, in a
sort of duodecimo phaeton, she desired me to write some verses
on her ponies; upon which, I took out my pocket-book, and
in one moment produced the following: —

> Sure never were seen two such beautiful ponies;
> Other horses are clowns, but these macaronies:
> To give them this title I'm sure can't be wrong,
> Their legs are so slim, and their tails are so long.

Crab. There, ladies, done in the smack of a whip, and on
horseback too.

Jos. Surf. A very Phœbus, mounted—indeed, Sir Benjamin!

Sir Ben. Oh dear, sir! trifles — trifles.

Enter LADY TEAZLE *and* MARIA.

Mrs. Can. I must have a copy.

Lady Sneer. Lady Teazle, I hope we shall see Sir Peter?

Lady Teaz. I believe he'll wait on your ladyship presently.

Lady Sneer. Maria, my love, you look grave. Come, you
shall sit down to piquet with Mr. Surface.

Mar. I take very little pleasure in cards — however, I'll
do as your ladyship pleases.

Lady Teaz. I am surprised Mr. Surface should sit down
with her; I thought he would have embraced this opportunity
of speaking to me before Sir Peter came.   [*Aside.*

Mrs. Can. Now, I'll die; but you are so scandalous, I'll
forswear your society.

Lady Teaz. What's the matter, Mrs. Candour?

Mrs. Can. They'll not allow our friend Miss Vermilion to be handsome.

Lady Sneer. Oh, surely she is a pretty woman.

Crab. I am very glad you think so, ma'am.

Mrs. Can. She has a charming fresh colour.

Lady Teaz. Yes, when it is fresh put on.

Mrs. Can. Oh, fie! I'll swear her colour is natural: I have seen it come and go!

Lady Teaz. I dare swear you have, ma'am: it goes off at night, and comes again in the morning.

Sir Ben. True, ma'am, it not only comes and goes; but, what's more, egad, her maid can fetch and carry it!

Mrs. Can. Ha! ha! ha! how I hate to hear you talk so! But surely, now, her sister is, or was, very handsome.

Crab. Who? Mrs. Evergreen? O Lord! she's six-and-fifty if she's an hour!

Mrs. Can. Now positively you wrong her; fifty-two or fifty-three is the utmost — and I don't think she looks more.

Sir Ben. Ah! there's no judging by her looks, unless one could see her face.

Lady Sneer. Well, well, if Mrs. Evergreen does take some pains to repair the ravages of time, you must allow she effects it with great ingenuity; and surely that's better than the careless manner in which the widow Ochre caulks her wrinkles.

Sir Ben. Nay, now, Lady Sneerwell, you are severe upon the widow. Come, come, 'tis not that she paints so ill — but, when she has finished her face, she joins it on so badly to her neck, that she looks like a mended statue, in which the connoisseur may see at once that the head is modern, though the trunk's antique.

Crab. Ha! ha! ha! Well said, nephew!

Mrs. Can. Ha! ha! ha! Well, you make me laugh; but I vow I hate you for it. What do you think of Miss Simper?

Sir Ben. Why, she has very pretty teeth.

Lady Teaz. Yes; and on that account, when she is neither speaking nor laughing (which very seldom happens), she never

absolutely shuts her mouth, but leaves it always on a-jar, as
it were — thus.   [*Shows her teeth.*

Mrs. Can. How can you be so ill-natured?

Lady Teaz. Nay, I allow even that's better than the pains
Mrs. Prim takes to conceal her losses in front. She draws her
mouth till it positively resembles the aperture of a poor's-box,
and all her words appear to slide out edgewise, as it were —
thus: *How do you do, madam? Yes, madam.*   [*Mimics.*

Lady Sneer. Very well, Lady Teazle; I see you can be a
little severe.

Lady Teaz. In defence of a friend it is but justice. But
here comes Sir Peter to spoil our pleasantry.

Enter SIR PETER TEAZLE.

Sir Pet. Ladies, your most obedient. — [*Aside.*] Mercy on
me, here is the whole set! a character dead at every word, I
suppose.

Mrs. Can. I am rejoiced you are come, Sir Peter. They
have been so censorious — and Lady Teazle as bad as any
one.

Sir Pet. That must be very distressing to you, indeed,
Mrs. Candour.

Mrs. Can. Oh, they will allow good qualities to nobody;
not even good nature to our friend Mrs. Pursy.

Lady Teaz. What, the fat dowager who was at Mrs Qua-
drille's last night?

Mrs. Can. Nay, her bulk is her misfortune; and, when she
takes so much pains to get rid of it, you ought not to reflect
on her.

Lady Sneer. That's very true, indeed.

Lady Teaz. Yes, I know she almost lives on acids and
small whey; laces herself by pulleys; and often, in the hottest
noon in summer, you may see her on a little squat pony, with
her hair plaited up behind like a drummer's and puffing round
the Ring on a full trot.

Mrs. Can. I thank you, Lady Teazle, for defending her.

Sir Pet. Yes, a good defence, truly.

Mrs. Can. Truly, Lady Teazle is as censorious as Miss Sallow.

Crab. Yes, and she is a curious being to pretend to be censorious — an awkward gawky, without any one good point under heaven.

Mrs. Can. Positively you shall not be so very severe. Miss Sallow is a near relation of mine by marriage, and, as for her person, great allowance is to be made; for, let me tell you, a woman labours under many disadvantages who tries to pass for a girl of six-and-thirty.

Lady Sneer. Though, surely, she is handsome still — and for the weakness in her eyes, considering how much she reads by candlelight, it is not to be wondered at.

Mrs. Can. True, and then as to her manner; upon my word I think it is particularly graceful, considering she never had the least education: for you know her mother was a Welsh milliner, and her father a sugar-baker at Bristol.

Sir Ben. Ah! you are both of you too good-natured!

Sir Pet. Yes, damned good-natured! This their own relation! mercy on me!   [*Aside.*

Mrs. Can. For my part, I own I cannot bear to hear a friend ill spoken of.

Sir Pet. No, to be sure!

Sir Ben. Oh! you are of a moral turn. Mrs. Candour and I can sit for an hour and hear Lady Stucco talk sentiment.

Lady Teaz. Nay, I vow Lady Stucco is very well with the dessert after dinner; for she's just like the French fruit one cracks for mottoes — made up of paint and proverb.

Mrs. Can. Well, I will never join in ridiculing a friend; and so I constantly tell my cousin Ogle, and you all know what pretensions she has to be critical on beauty.

Crab. Oh, to be sure! she has herself the oddest countenance that ever was seen; 'tis a collection of features from all the different countries of the globe.

Sir Ben. So she has, indeed — an Irish front ——

Crab. Caledonian locks ——

Sir Ben. Dutch nose ——

Crab. Austrian lips ——

Sir Ben. Complexion of a Spaniard ——

Crab. And teeth *à la Chinoise* ——

Sir Ben. In short, her face resembles a *table d'hôte* at Spa — where no two guests are of a nation ——

Crab. Or a congress at the close of a general war — wherein all the members, even to her eyes, appear to have a different interest, and her nose and chin are the only parties likely to join issue.

Mrs. Can. Ha! ha! ha!

Sir Pet. Mercy on my life! — a person they dine with twice a week!   [*Aside.*

Mrs. Can. Nay, but I vow you shall not carry the laugh off so — for give me leave to say, that Mrs. Ogle ——

Sir Pet. Madam, madam, I beg your pardon — there's no stopping these good gentlemen's tongues. But when I tell you, Mrs. Candour, that the lady they are abusing is a particular friend of mine, I hope you'll not take her part.

Lady Sneer. Ha! ha! ha! well said, Sir Peter! but you are a cruel creature — too phlegmatic yourself for a jest, and too peevish to allow wit in others.

Sir Pet. Ah, madam, true wit is more nearly allied to good nature than your ladyship is aware of.

Lady Teaz. True, Sir Peter: I believe they are so near akin that they can never be united.

Sir Ben. Or rather, suppose them man and wife, because one seldom sees them together.

Lady Teaz. But Sir Peter is such an enemy to scandal, I believe he would have it put down by parliament.

Sir Pet. 'Fore heaven, madam, if they were to consider the sporting with reputation of as much importance as poaching on manors, and pass an act for the preservation of fame, as well as game, I believe many would thank them for the bill.

Lady Sneer. O Lud! Sir Peter; would you deprive us of our privileges?

Sir Pet. Ay, madam; and then no person should be permitted to kill characters and run down reputations, but qualified old maids and disappointed widows.

Lady Sneer. Go, you monster!

Mrs. Can. But, surely, you would not be quite so severe on those who only report what they hear?

Sir Pet. Yes, madam, I would have law merchant for them too; and in all cases of slander currency, whenever the drawer of the lie was not to be found, the injured parties should have a right to come on any of the indorsers.

Crab. Well, for my part, I believe there never was a scandalous tale without some foundation.

Lady Sneer. Come, ladies, shall we sit down to cards in the next room?

Enter SERVANT *who whispers* SIR PETER.

Sir Pet. I'll be with them directly. — [*Exit* SERVANT.] I'll get away unperceived.   [*Aside.*

Lady Sneer. Sir Peter, you are not going to leave us?

Sir Pet. Your ladyship must excuse me; I'm called away by particular business. But I leave my character behind me.
                                                        [*Exit.*

Sir Ben. Well—certainly, Lady Teazle, that lord of yours is a strange being: I could tell you some stories of him would make you laugh heartily if he were not your husband.

Lady Teaz. Oh, pray don't mind that; come, do let's hear them.   [*Exeunt all but* JOSEPH SURFACE *and* MARIA.

Jos. Surf. Maria, I see you have no satisfaction in this society.

Mar. How is it possible I should? If to raise malicious smiles at the infirmities or misfortunes of those who have never injured us be the province of wit or humour, Heaven grant me a double portion of dulness!

Jos. Surf. Yet they appear more ill-natured than they are; they have no malice at heart.

Mar. Then is their conduct still more contemptible; for, in my opinion, nothing could excuse the intemperance of their tongues but a natural and uncontrollable bitterness of mind.

Jos. Surf. Undoubtedly, madam; and it has always been a
sentiment of mine, that to propagate a malicious truth wan-
tonly is more despicable than to falsify from revenge. But
can you, Maria, feel thus for others, and be unkind to me
alone? Is hope to be denied the tenderest passion?

Mar. Why will you distress me by renewing this subject?

Jos. Surf. Ah, Maria! you would not treat me thus, and
oppose your guardian, Sir Peter's will, but that I see that
profligate Charles is still a favoured rival.

Mar. Ungenerously urged! But, whatever my sentiments
are for that unfortunate young man, be assured I shall not
feel more bound to give him up, because his distresses have
lost him the regard even of a brother.

Jos. Surf. Nay, but, Maria, do not leave me with a frown:
by all that's honest, I swear ——   [*Kneels.*

Re-enter LADY TEAZLE *behind.*

[*Aside.*] Gad's life, here's Lady Teazle. — [*Aloud to* MARIA.]
You must not — no, you shall not — for, though I have the
greatest regard for Lady Teazle——

Mar. Lady Teazle!

Jos. Surf. Yet were Sir Peter to suspect —

Lady Teaz. [*Coming forward.*] What is this, pray? Does
he take her for me? — Child, you are wanted in the next
room. — [*Exit* MARIA.] What is all this, pray?

Jos. Surf. Oh, the most unlucky circumstance in nature!
Maria has somehow suspected the tender concern I have for
your happiness, and threatened to acquaint Sir Peter with
her suspicions, and I was just endeavouring to reason with
her when you came in.

Lady Teaz. Indeed! but you seemed to adopt a very tender mode of reasoning—do you usually argue on your knees?

Jos. Surf. Oh, she's a child, and I thought a little bombast —— But, Lady Teazle, when are you to give me your
judgment on my library, as you promised?

Lady Teaz. No, no; I begin to think it would be imprudent, and you know I admit you as a lover no farther than fashion requires.

Jos. Surf. True — a mere Platonic cicisbeo, what every wife is entitled to.

Lady Teaz. Certainly, one must not be out of the fashion. However, I have so many of my country prejudices left, that, though Sir Peter's ill humour may vex me ever so, it never shall provoke me to ——

Jos. Surf. The only revenge in your power. Well, 1 applaud your moderation.

Lady Teaz. Go—you are an insinuating wretch! But we shall be missed — let us join the company.

Jos. Surf. But we had best not return together.

Lady Teaz. Well, don't stay; for Maria sha'n't come to hear any more of your reasoning, I promise you.   [*Exit.*

Jos. Surf. A curious dilemma, truly, my politics have run me into! I wanted, at first, only to ingratiate myself with Lady Teazle, that she might not be my enemy with Maria; and I have, I don't know how, become her serious lover. Sincerely I begin to wish I had never made such a point of gaining so very good a character, for it has led me into so many cursed rogueries that I doubt I shall be exposed at last.   [*Exit.*

SCENE III. — *A Room in* SIR PETER TEAZLE'S *House.*

Enter SIR OLIVER SURFACE *and* ROWLEY.

Sir Oliv. Ha! ha! ha! so my old friend is married, hey? —a young wife out of the country. Ha! ha! ha! that he should have stood bluff to old bachelor so long, and sink into a husband at last!

Row. But you must not rally him on the subject, Sir Oliver; 'tis a tender point, I assure you, though he has been married only seven months.

Sir Oliv. Then he has been just half a year on the stool of repentance! — Poor Peter! But you say he has entirely given up Charles — never sees him, hey?

Row. His prejudice against him is astonishing, and I am sure greatly increased by a jealousy of him with Lady Teazle,

which he has industriously been led into by a scandalous
society in the neighbourhood, who have contributed not a
little to Charles's ill name. Whereas the truth is, I believe,
if the lady is partial to either of them, his brother is the
favourite.

Sir Oliv. Ay, I know there are a set of malicious, prating,
prudent gossips, both male and female, who murder characters to kill time, and will rob a young fellow of his good
name before he has years to know the value of it. But I am
not to be prejudiced against my nephew by such, I promise
you! No, no; if Charles has done nothing false or mean, I
shall compound for his extravagance.

Row. Then, my life on't, you will reclaim him. Ah, sir,
it gives me new life to find that your heart is not turned
against him, and that the son of my good old master has one
friend, however, left.

Sir Oliv. What! shall I forget, Master Rowley, when I was
at his years myself? Egad, my brother and I were neither
of us very prudent youths; and yet, I believe, you have not
seen many better men than your old master was?

Row. Sir, 'tis this reflection gives me assurance that
Charles may yet be a credit to his family. But here comes
Sir Peter.

Sir Oliv. Egad, so he does! Mercy on me! he's greatly
altered, and seems to have a settled married look! One may
read husband in his face at this distance!

Enter Sir Peter Teazle.

Sir Pet. Ha! Sir Oliver — my old friend! Welcome to
England a thousand times!

Sir Oliv. Thank you, thank you, Sir Peter! and i'faith I
am glad to find you well, believe me!

Sir Pet. Oh! 'tis a long time since we met—fifteen years,
I doubt, Sir Oliver, and many a cross accident in the time.

Sir Oliv. Ay, I have had my share. But, what! I find you
are married, hey, my old boy? Well, well, it can't be helped;
and so — I wish you joy with all my heart!

Sir Pet. Thank you, thank you, Sir Oliver. — Yes, I have entered into — the happy state; but we'll not talk of that now.

Sir Oliv. True, true, Sir Peter; old friends should not begin on grievances at first meeting. No, no, no.

Row. [*Aside to* SIR OLIVER.] Take care, pray, sir.

Sir Oliv. Well, so one of my nephews is a wild rogue, hey?

Sir Pet. Wild! Ah! my old friend, I grieve for your disappointment there; he's a lost young man, indeed. However, his brother will make you amends; Joseph is, indeed, what a youth should be — every body in the world speaks well of him.

Sir Oliv. I am sorry to hear it; he has too good a character to be an honest fellow. Every body speaks well of him! Psha! then he has bowed as low to knaves and fools as to the honest dignity of genius and virtue.

Sir Pet. What, Sir Oliver! do you blame him for not making enemies?

Sir Oliv. Yes, if he has merit enough to deserve them.

Sir Pet. Well, well — you'll be convinced when you know him. 'Tis edification to hear him converse; he professes the noblest sentiments.

Sir Oliv. Oh, plague of his sentiments! If he salutes me with a scrap of morality in his mouth, I shall be sick directly. But, however, don't mistake me, Sir Peter; I don't mean to defend Charles's errors: but, before I form my judgment of either of them, I intend to make a trial of their hearts; and my friend Rowley and I have planned something for the purpose.

Row. And Sir Peter shall own for once he has been mistaken.

Sir Pet. Oh, my life on Joseph's honour!

Sir Oliv. Well — come, give us a bottle of good wine, and we'll drink the lads' health, and tell you our scheme.

Sir Pet. Allons, then!

Sir Oliv. And don't, Sir Peter, be so severe against your

old friend's son.   Odds my life!   I am not sorry that he has
run out of the course a little: for my part, I hate to see
prudence clinging to the green suckers of youth; 'tis like ivy
round a sapling, and spoils the growth of the tree.

[Exeunt.

ACT III.

Scene I. — *A Room in* Sir Peter Teazle's *House.*

Enter Sir Peter Teazle, Sir Oliver Surface, *and* Rowley.

Sir Pet. Well, then, we will see this fellow first, and have
our wine afterwards.   But how is this, Master Rowley?   I
don't see the jet of your scheme.

Row. Why, sir, this Mr. Stanley, whom I was speaking
of, is nearly related to them by their mother.   He was once
a merchant in Dublin, but has been ruined by a series of un-
deserved misfortunes.   He has applied, by letter, since his
confinement, both to Mr. Surface and Charles: from the former
he has received nothing but evasive promises of future service,
while Charles has done all that his extravagance has left him
power to do; and he is, at this time, endeavouring to raise a
sum of money, part of which, in the midst of his own distresses, I know he intends for the service of poor Stanley.

Sir. Oliv. Ah! he is my brother's son.

Sir Pet. Well, but how is Sir Oliver personally to ——

Row. Why, sir, I will inform Charles and his brother that
Stanley has obtained permission to apply personally to his
friends; and, as they have neither of them ever seen him, let
Sir Oliver assume his character, and he will have a fair opportunity of judging, at least, of the benevolence of their dispositions: and believe me, sir, you will find in the youngest
brother one who, in the midst of folly and dissipation, has
still, as our immortal bard expresses it, —

"a heart to pity, and a hand,
Open as day, for melting charity."

Sir Pet. Psha!   What signifies his having an open hand

or purse either, when he has nothing left to give? Well, well, make the trial, if you please. But where is the fellow whom you brought for Sir Oliver to examine, relative to Charles's affairs?

Row. Below, waiting his commands, and no one can give him better intelligence. — This, Sir Oliver, is a friendly Jew, who, to do him justice, has done every thing in his power to bring your nephew to a proper sense of his extravagance.

Sir Pet. Pray let us have him in.

Row. Desire Mr. Moses to walk up stairs.

[*Calls to* Servant.

Sir Pet. But, pray, why should you suppose he will speak the truth?

Row. Oh, I have convinced him that he has no chance of recovering certain sums advanced to Charles but through the bounty of Sir Oliver, who he knows is arrived; so that you may depend on his fidelity to his own interests. I have also another evidence in my power, one Snake, whom I have detected in a matter little short of forgery, and shall shortly produce to remove some of your prejudices, Sir Peter, relative to Charles and Lady Teazle.

Sir Pet. I have heard too much on that subject.

Row. Here comes the honest Israelite.

Enter Moses.

— This is Sir Oliver.

Sir Oliv. Sir, I understand [you have lately had great dealings with my nephew Charles.

Mos. Yes, Sir Oliver, I have done all I could for him; but he was ruined before he came to me for assistance.

Sir Oliv. That was unlucky, truly; for you have had no opportunity of showing your talents.

Mos. None at all; I hadn't the pleasure of knowing his distresses till he was some thousands worse than nothing.

Sir Oliv. Unfortunate, indeed! But I suppose you have done all in your power for him, honest Moses?

Mos. Yes, he knows that. This very evening I was to

have brought him a gentleman from the city, who does not know him, and will, I believe, advance him some money.

Sir Pet. What, one Charles has never had money from before?

Mos. Yes, Mr. Premium, of Crutched Friars, formerly a broker.

Sir Pet. Egad, Sir Oliver, a thought strikes me!—Charles, you say, does not know Mr. Premium?

Mos. Not at all.

Sir Pet. Now then, Sir Oliver, you may have a better opportunity of satisfying yourself than by an old romancing tale of a poor relation: go with my friend Moses, and represent Premium, and then, I'll answer for it, you'll see your nephew in all his glory.

Sir Oliv. Egad, I like this idea better than the other, and I may visit Joseph afterwards as old Stanley.

Sir Pet. True — so you may.

Row. Well, this is taking Charles rather at a disadvantage, to be sure. However, Moses, you understand Sir Peter, and will be faithful?

Mos. You may depend upon me. — [*Looks at his watch.*] This is near the time I was to have gone.

Sir Oliv. I'll accompany you as soon as you please, Moses ——But hold! I have forgot one thing—how the plague shall I be able to pass for a Jew?

Mos. There's no need — the principal is Christian.

Sir Oliv. Is he? I'm very sorry to hear it. But, then again, an't I rather too smartly dressed to look like a money-lender?

Sir Pet. Not at all; 'twould not be out of character, if you went in your own carriage — would it, Moses?

Mos. Not in the least.

Sir Oliv. Well, but how must I talk? there's certainly some cant of usury and mode of treating that I ought to know.

Sir Pet. Oh, there's not much to learn. The great point, as I take it, is to be exorbitant enough in your demands. Hey, Moses?

Mos. Yes, that's a very great point.

Sir Oliv. I'll answer for 't I'll not be wanting in that. I'll ask him eight or ten per cent. on the loan, at least.

Mos. If you ask him no more than that, you'll be discovered immediately.

Sir Oliv. Hey! what, the plague! how much then?

Mos. That depends upon the circumstances. If he appears not very anxious for the supply, you should require only forty or fifty per cent.; but if you find him in great distress, and want the moneys very bad, you may ask double.

Sir Pet. A good honest trade you're learning, Sir Oliver!

Sir Oliv. Truly, I think so — and not unprofitable.

Mos. Then, you know, you haven't the moneys yourself, but are forced to borrow them for him of a friend.

Sir Oliv. Oh! I borrow it of a friend, do I?

Mos. And your friend is an unconscionable dog: but you can't help that.

Sir Oliv. My friend an unconscionable dog, is he?

Mos. Yes, and he himself has not the moneys by him, but is forced to sell stock at a great loss.

Sir Oliv. He is forced to sell stock at a great loss, is he? Well, that's very kind of him.

Sir Pet. I'faith, Sir Oliver — Mr. Premium, I mean — you'll soon be master of the trade. But, Moses! would not you have him run out a little against the annuity bill? That would be in character, I should think.

Mos. Very much.

Row. And lament that a young man now must be at years of discretion before he is suffered to ruin himself?

Mos. Ay, great pity!

Sir Pet. And abuse the public for allowing merit to an act whose only object is to snatch misfortune and imprudence from the rapacious gripe of usury, and give the minor a chance of inheriting his estate without being undone by coming into possession.

Sir Oliv. So, so — Moses shall give me farther instructions as we go together.

Sir Pet. You will not have much time, for your nephew lives hard by.

Sir Oliv. Oh, never fear! my tutor appears so able, that though Charles lived in the next street, it must be my own fault if I am not a complete rogue before I turn the corner.

[Exit with MOSES.

Sir Pet. So, now, I think Sir Oliver will be convinced: you are partial, Rowley, and would have prepared Charles for the other plot.

Row. No, upon my word, Sir Peter.

Sir Pet. Well, go bring me this Snake, and I'll hear what he has to say presently. I see Maria, and want to speak with her. — *[Exit* ROWLEY.] I should be glad to be convinced my suspicions of Lady Teazle and Charles were unjust. I have never yet opened my mind on this subject to my friend Joseph — I am determined I will do it — he will give me his opinion sincerely.

Enter MARIA.

So, child, has Mr. Surface returned with you?

Mar. No, sir; he was engaged.

Sir Pet. Well, Maria, do you not reflect, the more you converse with that amiable young man, what return his partiality for you deserves?

Mar. Indeed, Sir Peter, your frequent importunity on this subject distresses me extremely — you compel me to declare, that I know no man who has ever paid me a particular attention whom I would not prefer to Mr. Surface.

Sir Pet. So — here's perverseness! No, no, Maria, 'tis Charles only whom you would prefer. 'Tis evident his vices and follies have won your heart.

Mar. This is unkind, sir. You know I have obeyed you in neither seeing nor corresponding with him: I have heard enough to convince me that he is unworthy my regard. Yet I cannot think it culpable, if, while my understanding severely condemns his vices, my heart suggests some pity for his distresses.

Sir Pet. Well, well, pity him as much as you please; but give your heart and hand to a worthier object.

Mar. Never to his brother!

Sir Pet. Go, perverse and obstinate! But take care, madam; you have never yet known what the authority of a guardian is: don't compel me to inform you of it.

Mar. I can only say, you shall not have just reason. 'Tis true, by my father's will, I am for a short period bound to regard you as his substitute; but must cease to think you so, when you would compel me to be miserable.   [*Exit.*

Sir Pet. Was ever man so crossed as I am, every thing conspiring to fret me! I had not been involved in matrimony a fortnight, before her father, a hale and hearty man, died, on purpose, I believe, for the pleasure of plaguing me with the care of his daughter. — [*Lady Teazle sings without.*] But here comes my helpmate! She appears in great good humour. How happy I should be if I could tease her into loving me, though but a little!

Lady Teaz. Lud! Sir Peter, I hope you haven't been quarrelling with Maria! It is not using me well to be ill-humoured when I am not by.

Sir Pet. Ah, Lady Teazle, you might have the power to make me good humoured at all times.

Lady Teaz. I am sure I wish I had; for I want you to be in a charming sweet temper at this moment. Do be good-humoured now, and let me have two hundred pounds, will you?

Sir Pet. Two hundred pounds; what an't I to be in a good humour without paying for it! But speak to me thus, and i' faith there's nothing I could refuse you. You shall have it; but seal me a bond for the repayment.

Lady Teaz. Oh, no — there — my note of hand will do as well.   [*Offering her hand.*

Sir Pet. And you shall no longer reproach me with not giving you an independent settlement. I mean shortly to surprise you: but shall we always live thus, hey?

14*

Lady Teaz. If you please. I'm sure I don't care how soon we leave off quarrelling, provided you'll own you were tired first.

Sir Pet. Well — then let our future contest be, who shall be most obliging.

Lady Teaz. I assure you, Sir Peter, good nature becomes you. You look now as you did before we were married, when you used to walk with me under the elms, and tell me stories of what a gallant you were in your youth, and chuck me under the chin, you would; and ask me if I thought I could love an old fellow, who would deny me nothing — didn't you?

Sir Pet. Yes, yes, and you were as kind and attentive——.

Lady Teaz. Ay, so I was, and would always take your part, when my acquaintance used to abuse you, and turn you into ridicule.

Sir Pet. Indeed!

Lady Teaz. Ay, and when my cousin Sophy has called you a stiff, peevish old bachelor, and laughed at me for thinking of marrying one who might be my father, I have always defended you, and said, I didn't think you so ugly by any means.

Sir Pet. Thank you.

Lady Teaz. And I dared say you'd make a very good sort of a husband.

Sir Pet. And you prophesied right; and we shall now be the happiest couple ——

Lady Teaz. And never differ again?

Sir Pet. No, never! — though at the same time, indeed, my dear Lady Teazle, you must watch your temper very seriously; for in all our little quarrels, my dear, if you recollect, my love, you always began first.

Lady Teaz. I beg your pardon, my dear Sir Peter: indeed, you always gave the provocation.

Sir Pet. Now see, my angel! take care — contradicting isn't the way to keep friends.

Lady Teaz. Then don't you begin it, my love!

Sir Pet. There, now! you — you are going on. You don't perceive, my life, that you are just doing the very thing which you know always makes me angry.

Lady Teaz. Nay, you know if you will be angry without any reason, my dear ——

Sir Pet. There! now you want to quarrel again.

Lady Teaz. No, I'm sure I don't: but, if you will be so peevish ——

Sir Pet. There now! who begins first?

Lady Teaz. Why, you, to be sure. I said nothing — but there's no bearing your temper.

Sir Pet. No, no, madam: the fault's in your own temper.

Lady Teaz. Ay, you are just what my cousin Sophy said you would be.

Sir Pet. Your cousin Sophy is a forward, impertinent gipsy.

Lady Teaz. You are a great bear, I'm sure, to abuse my relations.

Sir Pet. Now may all the plagues of marriage be doubled on me, if ever I try to be friends with you any more!

Lady Teaz. So much the better.

Sir Pet. No, no, madam: 'tis evident you never cared a pin for me, and I was a madman to marry you — a pert, rural coquette, that had refused half the honest 'squires in the neighbourhood!

Lady Teaz. And I am sure I was a fool to marry you — an old dangling bachelor, who was single at fifty, only because he never could meet with any one who would have him.

Sir Pet. Ay, ay, madam; but you were pleased enough to listen to me: you never had such an offer before.

Lady Teaz. No! didn't I refuse Sir Tivy Terrier, who every body said would have been a better match? for his estate is just as good as yours, and he has broke his neck since we have been married.

Sir Pet. I have done with you, madam! You are an unfeeling, ungrateful—but there's an end of every thing. I believe you capable of every thing that is bad. Yes, madam, I now believe the reports relative to you and Charles, madam. Yes, madam, you and Charles are, not without grounds ——

Lady Teaz. Take care, Sir Peter! you had better not insinuate any such thing! I'll not be suspected without cause, I promise you.

Sir Pet. Very well, madam! very well! A separate maintenance as soon as you please. Yes, madam, or a divorce! I'll make an example of myself for the benefit of all old bachelors. Let us separate, madam.

Lady Teaz. Agreed! agreed! And now, my dear Sir Peter, we are of a mind once more, we may be the happiest couple, and never differ again, you know: ha! ha! ha! Well, you are going to be in a passion, I see, and I shall only interrupt you — so, bye! bye!   [*Exit.*

Sir Pet. Plagues and tortures! can't I make her angry either! Oh, I am the most miserable fellow! But I'll not bear her presuming to keep her temper: no! she may break my heart, but she shan't keep her temper.   [*Exit.*

Scene II. — *A Room in* Charles Surface's *House.*

Enter Trip, Moses, *and* Sir Oliver Surface.

Trip. Here, Master Moses! if you'll stay a moment, I'll try whether — what's the gentleman's name?

Sir Oliv. Mr. Moses, what is my name? [*Aside to* Moses.

Mos. Mr. Premium.

Trip. Premium — very well.   [*Exit, taking snuff.*

Sir Oliv. To judge by the servants, one wouldn't believe the master was ruined. But what!—sure, this was my brother's house?

Mos. Yes, sir; Mr. Charles bought it of Mr. Joseph, with the furniture, pictures, &c., just as the old gentleman left it. Sir Peter thought it a piece of extravagance in him.

Sir Oliv. In my mind, the other's economy in selling it to him was more reprehensible by half.

Re-enter Trip.

Trip. My master says you must wait, gentlemen: he has company, and can't speak with you yet.

Sir Oliv. If he knew who it was wanted to see him, perhaps he would not send such a message?

Trip. Yes, yes, sir; he knows you are here — I did not forget little Premium: no, no, no.

Sir Oliv. Very well; and I pray, sir, what may be your name?

Trip. Trip, sir; my name is Trip, at your service.

Sir Oliv. Well, then, Mr. Trip, you have a pleasant sort of place here, I guess?

Trip. Why, yes — here are three or four of us pass our time agreeably enough; but then our wages are sometimes a little in arrear—and not very great either — but fifty pounds a year, and find our own bags and bouquets.

Sir Oliv. Bags and bouquets! halters and bastinadoes!
[*Aside.*

Trip. And à propos, Moses, have you been able to get me that little bill discounted?

Sir Oliv. Wants to raise money too! — mercy on me! Has his distresses too, I warrant, like a lord, and affects creditors and duns.   [*Aside.*

Mos. 'Twas not to be done, indeed, Mr. Trip.

Trip. Good lack, you surprise me! My friend Brush has indorsed it, and I thought when he put his name at the back of a bill 'twas the same as cash.

Mos. No, 'twouldn't do.

Trip. A small sum— but twenty pounds. Hark'ee, Moses, do you think you couldn't get it me by way of annuity?

Sir Oliv. An annuity! ha! ha! a footman raise money by way of annuity! Well done, luxury, egad!   ·   [*Aside.*

Mos. Well, but you must insure your place.

Trip. Oh, with all my heart! I'll insure my place, and my life too, if you please.

Sir Oliv. It's more than I would your neck.   [*Aside.*

Mos. But is there nothing you could deposit?

Trip. Why, nothing capital of my master's wardrobe has dropped lately; but I could give you a mortgage on some of his winter clothes, with equity of redemption before November — or you shall have the reversion of the French velvet, or a post-obit on the blue and silver; — these, I should think,

Moses, with a few pair of point ruffles, as a collateral security
— hey, my little fellow?

Mos. Well, well.   [*Bell rings.*

Trip. Egad, I heard the bell! I believe, gentlemen, I can
now introduce you. Don't forget the annuity, little Moses!
This way, gentlemen, I'll insure my place, you know.

Sir Oliv. [*Aside.*] If the man be a shadow of the master,
this is the temple of dissipation indeed!   [*Exeunt.*

Scene III. — *Another Room in the same.*

Charles Surface, Sir Harry Bumper, Careless, *and* Gentlemen, *discovered drinking.*

Chas. Surf. 'Fore heaven, 'tis true! — there's the great
degeneracy of the age. Many of our acquaintance have taste,
spirit, and politeness; but, plague on't, they won't drink.

Care. It is so, indeed, Charles! they give into all the sub-
stantial luxuries of the table, and abstain from nothing but
wine and wit. Oh, certainly society suffers by it intolerably!
for now, instead of the social spirit of raillery that used to
mantle over a glass of bright Burgundy, their conversation
is become just like the Spa-water they drink, which has all
the pertness and flatulency of champagne, without its spirit
or flavour.

1 Gent. But what are they to do who love play better than
wine?

Care. True! there's Sir Harry diets himself for gaming,
and is now under a hazard regimen.

Chas. Surf. Then he'll have the worst of it. What! you
wouldn't train a horse for the course by keeping him from
corn? For my part, egad, I am never so successful as when
I am a little merry: let me throw on a bottle of champagne,
and I never lose.

All. Hey, what?

Care. At least I never feel my losses, which is exactly the
same thing.

2 Gent. Ay, that I believe.

Chas. Surf. And then, what man can pretend to be a believer in love, who is an abjurer of wine? 'Tis the test by which the lover knows his own heart. Fill a dozen bumpers to a dozen beauties, and she that floats at the top is the maid that has bewitched you.

Care. Now then, Charles, be honest, and give us your real favourite.

Chas. Surf. Why, I have withheld her only in compassion to you. If I toast her, you must give a round of her peers, which is impossible — on earth.

Care. Oh! then we'll find some canonised vestals or heathen goddesses that will do, I warrant!

Chas. Surf. Here then, bumpers, you rogues! bumpers! Maria! Maria! ——

Sir Har. Maria who?

Chas. Surf. Oh, damn the surname! — 'tis too formal to be registered in Love's calendar — Maria!

All. Maria!

Chas. Surf. But now, Sir Harry, beware, we must have beauty superlative.

Care. Nay, never study, Sir Harry: we'll stand to the toast, though your mistress should want an eye, and you know you have a song will excuse you.

Sir Har. Egad, so I have! and I'll give him the song instead of the lady.   [*Sings.*

> Here's to the maiden of bashful fifteen;
>   Here's to the widow of fifty;
> Here's to the flaunting extravagant quean,
>   And here's to the housewife that's thrifty.
> *Chorus.* Let the toast pass, —
>   Drink to the lass,
> I'll warrant she'll prove an excuse for the glass.
> Here's to the charmer whose dimples we prize;
>   Now to the maid who has none, sir:
> Here's to the girl with a pair of blue eyes,
>   And here's to the nymph with but one, sir.
> *Chorus.* Let the toast pass, &c.
> Here's to the maid with a bosom of snow:
>   Now to her that's as brown as a berry:
> Here's to the wife with a face full of woe,
>   And now to the damsel that's merry.

Chorus. Let the toast pass, &c.

> For let 'em be clumsy, or let 'em be slim,
>   Young or ancient, I care not a feather;
> So fill a pint bumper quite up to the brim,
> So fill up your glasses, nay, fill to the brim,
>   And let us e'on toast them together.

Chorus. Let the toast pass, &c.

All. Bravo! bravo!

Enter TRIP, *and whispers* CHARLES SURFACE.

Chas. Surf. Gentlemen, you must excuse me a little. — Careless, take the chair, will you?

Care. Nay, pr'ythee, Charles, what now? This is one of your peerless beauties, I suppose, has dropped in by chance?

Chas. Surf. No, faith! To tell you the truth, 'tis a Jew and a broker, who are come by appointment.

Care. Oh, damn it! let's have the Jew in.

1 Gent. Ay, and the broker too, by all means.

2 Gent. Yes, yes, the Jew and the broker.

Chas. Surf. Egad, with all my heart! — Trip, bid the gentlemen walk in. — [*Exit* TRIP.] Though there's one of them a stranger, I can tell you.

Care. Charles, let us give them some generous Burgundy, and perhaps they'll grow conscientious.

Chas. Surf. Oh, hang 'em, no! wine does but draw forth a man's natural qualities; and to make them drink would only be to whet their knavery.

Re-enter TRIP, *with* SIR OLIVER SURFACE *and* MOSES.

Chas. Surf. So, honest Moses; walk in, pray, Mr. Premium — that's the gentleman's name, isn't it, Moses?

Mos. Yes, sir.

Chas. Surf. Set chairs, Trip. — Sit down, Mr. Premium. — Glasses, Trip. — [TRIP *gives chairs and glasses, and exit.*] Sit down, Moses. — Come, Mr. Premium, I'll give you a sentiment; here's *Success to usury!* — Moses, fill the gentleman a bumper.

Mos. Success to usury!   [*Drinks.*

Care. Right, Moses — usury is prudence and industry, and deserves to succeed.

Sir Oliv. Then here's — All the success it deserves! [*Drinks.*

Care. No, no, that won't do! Mr. Premium, you have demurred at the toast, and must drink it in a pint bumper.

1 Gent. A pint bumper, at least.

Mos. Oh, pray, sir, consider—Mr. Premium's a gentleman.

Care. And therefore loves good wine.

2 Gent. Give Moses a quart glass — this is mutiny, and a high contempt for the chair.

Care. Here, now for't! I'll see justice done, to the last drop of my bottle.

Sir Oliv. Nay, pray, gentlemen — I did not expect this usage.

Chas. Surf. No, hang it, you shan't; Mr. Premium's a stranger.

Sir Oliv. Odd! I wish I was well out of their company.
[*Aside.*

Care. Plague on 'em then! if they won't drink, we'll not sit down with them. Come, Harry, the dice are in the next room. — Charles, you'll join us when you have finished your business with the gentlemen?

Chas. Surf. I will! I will! — [*Exeunt* SIR HARRY BUMPER *and* GENTLEMEN; CARELESS *following.*] Careless!

Care. [*Returning.*] Well!

Chas. Surf. Perhaps I may want you.

Care. Oh, you know I am always ready: word, note, or bond, 'tis all the same to me. [*Exit.*

Mos. Sir, this is Mr. Premium, a gentleman of the strictest honour and secrecy; and always performs what he undertakes. Mr. Premium, this is ——

Chas. Surf. Psha! have done. Sir, my friend Moses is a very honest fellow, but a little slow at expression: he'll be an hour giving us our titles. Mr. Premium, the plain state of the matter is this: I am an extravagant young fellow who wants to borrow money; you I take to be a prudent old fellow, who have got money to lend. I am blockhead enough to

give fifty per cent. sooner than not have it; and you, I presume, are rogue enough to take a hundred if you can get it.
Now, sir, you see we are acquainted at once, and may proceed
to business without farther ceremony.

Sir Oliv. Exceeding frank, upon my word. I see, sir, you
are not a man of many compliments.

Chas. Surf. Oh, no, sir! plain dealing in business I always
think best.

Sir Oliv. Sir, I like you the better for it. However, you
are mistaken in one thing; I have no money to lend, but I
believe I could procure some of a friend; but then he's an
unconscionable dog. Isn't he, Moses? And must sell stock
to accommodate you. Mustn't he, Moses?

Mos. Yes, indeed! You know I always speak the truth,
and scorn to tell a lie!

Chas. Surf. Right. People that speak truth generally do.
But these are trifles, Mr. Premium. What! I know money
isn't to be bought without paying for't!

Sir Oliv. Well, but what security could you give? You
have no land, I suppose?

Chas. Surf. Not a mole-hill, nor a twig, but what's in the
bough-pots out of the window!

Sir Oliv. Nor any stock, I presume?

Chas. Surf. Nothing but live stock—and that's only a few
pointers and ponies. But pray, Mr. Premium, are you acquainted at all with any of my connexions?

Sir Oliv. Why, to say truth, I am.

Chas. Surf. Then you must know that I have a devilish
rich uncle in the East Indies, Sir Oliver Surface, from whom
I have the greatest expectations?

Sir Oliv. That you have a wealthy uncle, I have heard;
but how your expectations will turn out is more, I believe,
than you can tell.

Chas. Surf. Oh, no! — there can be no doubt. They tell
me I'm a prodigious favourite, and that he talks of leaving
me every thing.

Sir Oliv. Indeed! this is the first I've heard of it.

Chas. Surf. Yes, yes, 'tis just so. Moses knows 'tis true; don't you, Moses?

Mos. Oh, yes! I'll swear to't.

Sir Oliv. Egad, they'll persuade me presently I'm at Bengal.   [*Aside.*

Chas. Surf. Now I propose, Mr. Premium, if it's agreeable to you, a post-obit on Sir Oliver's life: though at the same time the old fellow has been so liberal to me, that I give you my word, I should be very sorry to hear that any thing had happened to him.

Sir Oliv. Not more than I should, I assure you. But the bond you mention happens to be just the worst security you could offer me — for I might live to a hundred and never see the principal.

Chas. Surf. Oh, yes, you would! the moment Sir Oliver dies, you know, you would come on me for the money.

Sir Oliv. Then I believe I should be the most unwelcome dun you ever had in your life.

Chas. Surf. What! I suppose you're afraid that Sir Oliver is too good a life?

Sir Oliv. No, indeed I am not; though I have heard he is as hale and healthy as any man of his years in Christendom.

Chas. Surf. There again, now, you are misinformed. No, no, the climate has hurt him considerably, poor uncle Oliver. Yes, yes, he breaks apace, I'm told — and is so much altered lately that his nearest relations would not know him.

Sir Oliv. No! Ha! ha! ha! so much altered lately that his nearest relations would not know him! Ha! ha! ha! egad — ha! ha! ha!

Chas. Surf. Ha! ha! — you're glad to hear that, little Premium?

Sir Oliv. No, no, I'm not.

Chas. Surf. Yes, yes, you are — ha! ha! ha! — you know that mends your chance.

Sir Oliv. But I'm told Sir Oliver is coming over; nay, some say he is actually arrived.

Chas. Surf. Psha! sure I must know better than you

whether he's come or not. No, no, rely on't he's at this moment at Calcutta. Isn't he, Moses?

Mos. Oh, yes, certainly.

Sir Oliv. Very true, as you say, you must know better than I, though I have it from pretty good authority. Haven't I, Moses?

Mos. Yes, most undoubted!

Sir Oliv. But, sir, as I understand you want a few hundreds immediately, is there nothing you could dispose of?

Chas. Surf. How do you mean?

Sir Oliv. For instance, now, I have heard that your father left behind him a great quantity of massy old plate.

Chas. Surf. O Lud! that's gone long ago. Moses can tell you how better than I can.

Sir Oliv. [*Aside.*] Good lack! all the family race-cups and corporation-bowls! — [*Aloud.*] Then it was also supposed that his library was one of the most valuable and compact.

Chas. Surf. Yes, yes, so it was — vastly too much so for a private gentleman. For my part, I was always of a communicative disposition, so I thought it a shame to keep so much knowledge to myself.

Sir Oliv. [*Aside.*] Mercy upon me! learning that had run in the family like an heir-loom! — [*Aloud.*] Pray, what are become of the books?

Chas. Surf. You must inquire of the auctioneer, Master Premium, for I don't believe even Moses can direct you.

Mos. I know nothing of books.

Sir Oliv. So, so, nothing of the family property left, I suppose?

Chas. Surf. Not much, indeed; unless you have a mind to the family pictures. I have got a room full of ancestors above; and if you have a taste for old paintings, egad, you shall have 'em a bargain!

Sir Oliv. Hey! what the devil! sure, you wouldn't sell your forefathers, would you?

Chas. Surf. Every man of them, to the best bidder

Sir Oliv. What! your great-uncles and aunts?

Chas. Surf. Ay, and my great-grandfathers and grandmothers too.

Sir Oliv. [*Aside.*] Now I give him up! — [*Aloud.*] What
the plague, have you no bowels for your own kindred? Odd's
life! do you take me for Shylock in the play, that you would
raise money of me on your own flesh and blood?

Chas. Surf. Nay, my little broker, don't be angry: what
need you care, if you have your money's worth?

Sir Oliv. Well, I'll be the purchaser: I think I can dispose of the family canvas. — [*Aside.*] Oh, I'll never forgive
him this! never!

Re-enter CARELESS.

Care. Come, Charles, what keeps you?

Chas. Surf. I can't come yet. I'faith, we are going to
have a sale above stairs; here's little Premium will buy all
my ancestors!

Care. Oh, burn your ancestors!

Chas. Surf. No, he may do that afterwards, if he pleases.
Stay, Careless, we want you: egad, you shall be auctioneer —
so come along with us.

Care. Oh, have with you, if that's the case. I can handle
a hammer as well as a dice-box! Going! going!

Sir Oliv. Oh, the profligates!   [*Aside.*

Chas. Surf. Come, Moses, you shall be appraiser, if we
want one. Gad's life, little Premium, you don't seem to like
the business?

Sir Oliv. Oh, yes, I do, vastly! Ha! ha! ha! yes, yes, I
think it a rare joke to sell one's family by auction — ha! ha!
— [*Aside.*] Oh, the prodigal!

Chas. Surf. To be sure! when a man wants money, where
the plague should he get assistance, if he can't make free
with his own relations?   [*Exeunt.*

Sir Oliv. I'll never forgive him; never! never!

ACT IV.

SCENE I. — *A Picture Room in* CHARLES SURFACE'S *House.*

Enter CHARLES SURFACE, SIR OLIVER SURFACE, MOSES, *and*
CARELESS.

Chas. Surf. Walk in, gentlemen, pray walk in; — here
they are, the family of the Surfaces, up to the Conquest.

Sir Oliv. And, in my opinion, a goodly collection.

Chas. Surf. Ay, ay, these are done in the true spirit of
portrait-painting; no *volontière grace* or expression. Not like
the works of your modern Raphaels, who give you the
strongest resemblance, yet contrive to make your portrait independent of you; so that you may sink the original and not
hurt the picture. No, no; the merit of these is the inveterate
likeness — all stiff and awkward as the originals, and like
nothing in human nature besides.

Sir Oliv. Ah! we shall never see such figures of men
again.

Chas. Surf. I hope not. Well, you see, Master Premium,
what a domestic character I am; here I sit of an evening surrounded by my family. But come, get to your pulpit, Mr.
Auctioneer; here's an old gouty chair of my grandfather's
will answer the purpose.

Care. Ay, ay, this will do. But, Charles, I haven't a
hammer; and what's an auctioneer without his hammer?

Chas. Surf. Egad, that's true. What parchment have we
here? Oh, our genealogy in full. [*Taking pedigree down.*]
Here, Careless, you shall have no common bit of mahogany,
here's the family tree for you, you rogue! This shall be your
hammer, and now you may knock down my ancestors with
their own pedigree.

Sir Oliv. What an unnatural rogue! — an *ex post facto*
parricide! [*Aside.*

Care. Yes, yes, here's a list of your generation indeed;
— faith, Charles, this is the most convenient thing you could
have found for the business, for 'twill not only serve as a

hammer, but a catalogue into the bargain. Come, begin —
A-going, a-going, a-going!

Chas. Surf. Bravo, Careless! Well, here's my great-
uncle, Sir Richard Raveline, a marvellous good general in
his day, I assure you. He served in all the Duke of Marl-
borough's wars, and got that cut over his eye at the battle of
Malplaquet. What say you, Mr. Premium? look at him —
— there's a hero! not cut out of his feathers, as your modern
clipped captains are, but enveloped in wig and regimentals,
as a general should be. What do you bid?

Sir Oliv. [*Aside to Moses.*] Bid him speak.

Mos. Mr. Premium would have you speak.

Chas. Surf. Why, then, he shall have him for ten pounds,
and I'm sure that's not dear for a staff-officer.

Sir Oliv. [*Aside.*] Heaven deliver me! his famous uncle
Richard for ten pounds! — [*Aloud.*] Very well, sir, I take him
at that.

Chas. Surf. Careless, knock down my uncle Richard. —
Here, now, is a maiden sister of his, my great-aunt Deborah,
done by Kneller, in his best manner, and esteemed a very
formidable likeness. There she is, you see, a shepherdess
feeding her flock. You shall have her for five pounds ten
— the sheep are worth the money.

Sir Oliv. [*Aside.*] Ah! poor Deborah! a woman who set
such a value on herself! — [*Aloud.*] Five pounds ten — she's
mine.

Chas. Surf. Knock down my aunt Deborah! Here, now,
are two that were a sort of cousins of theirs. — You see,
Moses, these pictures were done some time ago, when beaux
wore wigs, and the ladies their own hair.

Sir Oliv. Yes, truly, head-dresses appear to have been a
little lower in those days.

Chas. Surf. Well, take that couple for the same.

Mos. 'Tis a good bargain.

Chas. Surf. Careless! — This, now, is a grandfather of
my mother's, a learned judge, well known on the western cir-
cuit. — What do you rate him at, Moses?

Mos. Four guineas.

Chas. Surf. Four guineas! Gad's life, you don't bid me
the price of his wig. — Mr. Premium, you have more respect
for the woolsack; do let us knock his lordship down at
fifteen.

Sir Oliv. By all means.

Care. Gone!

Chas. Surf. And there are two brothers of his, William
and Walter Blunt, Esquires, both members of parliament,
and noted speakers; and, what's very extraordinary, I believe,
this is the first time they were ever bought or sold.

Sir Oliv. That is very extraordinary, indeed! I'll take
them at your own price, for the honour of parliament.

Care. Well said, little Premium! I'll knock them down
at forty.

Chas. Surf. Here's a jolly fellow — I don't know what
relation, but he was mayor of Norwich: take him at eight
pounds

Sir Oliv. No, no; six will do for the mayor.

Chas. Surf. Come, make it guineas, and I'll throw you the
two aldermen there into the bargain.

Sir Oliv. They're mine.

Chas. Surf. Careless, knock down the mayor and aldermen. But, plague on't! we shall be all day retailing in this
manner; do let us deal wholesale: what say you, little Premium? Give me three hundred pounds for the rest of the
family in the lump.

Care. Ay, ay, that will be the best way.

Sir Oliv. Well, well, any thing to accommodate you; they
are mine. But there is one portrait which you have always
passed over.

Care. What, that ill-looking little fellow over the settee?

Sir Oliv. Yes, sir, I mean that; though I don't think him
so ill-looking a little fellow, by any means.

Chas. Surf. What, that? Oh; that's my uncle Oliver!
'twas done before he went to India.

Care. Your uncle Oliver! Gad, then you'll never be friends,

Charles. That, now, to me, is as stern a looking rogue as ever I saw; an unforgiving eye, and a damned disinheriting countenance! an inveterate knave, depend on't. Don't you think so, little Premium?

Sir Oliv. Upon my soul, sir, I do not; I think it is as honest a looking face as any in the room, dead or alive. But I suppose uncle Oliver goes with the rest of the lumber?

Chas. Surf. No, hang it! I'll not part with poor Noll. The old fellow has been very good to me, and, egad, I'll keep his picture while I've a room to put it in.

Sir Oliv. [*Aside.*] The rogue's my nephew after all! — [*Aloud.*] But, sir, I have somehow taken a fancy to that picture.

Chas. Surf. I'm sorry for 't, for you certainly will not have it. Oons, haven't you got enough of them?

Sir Oliv. [*Aside.*] I forgive him every thing! — [*Aloud.*] But, sir, when I take a whim in my head, I don't value money. I'll give you as much for that as for all the rest.

Chas. Surf. Don't tease me, master broker; I tell you I'll not part with it, and there's an end of it.

Sir Oliv. [*Aside.*] How like his father the dog is! — [*Aloud.*] Well, well, I have done. — [*Aside.*] I did not perceive it before, but I think I never saw such a striking resemblance. — [*Aloud.*] Here is a draught for your sum.

Chas. Surf. Why, 'tis for eight hundred pounds!

Sir Oliv. You will not let Sir Oliver go?

Chas. Surf. Zounds! no! I tell you, once more.

Sir Oliv. Then never mind the difference, we'll balance that another time. But give me your hand on the bargain; you are an honest fellow, Charles — I beg pardon, sir, for being so free. — Come, Moses.

Chas. Surf. Egad, this is a whimsical old fellow! — But hark'ee, Premium, you'll prepare lodgings for these gentlemen.

Sir Oliv. Yes, yes, I'll send for them in a day or two.

Chas. Surf. But hold; do now send a genteel conveyance for them, for, I assure you, they were most of them used to ride in their own carriages.

15*

Sir Oliv. I will, I will — for all but Oliver.

Chas. Surf. Ay, all but the little nabob.

Sir Oliv. You're fixed on that?

Chas. Surf. Peremptorily.

Sir Oliv. [*Aside.*] A dear extravagant rogue! — [*Aloud.*] Good day! — Come, Moses. — [*Aside.*] Let me hear now who dares call him profligate!   [*Exit with* Moses.

Care. Why, this is the oddest genius of the sort I ever met with!

Chas. Surf. Egad, he's the prince of brokers, I think. I wonder how the devil Moses got acquainted with so honest a fellow. — Ha! here's Rowley. — Do, Careless, say I'll join the company in a few moments.

Care. I will — but don't let that old blockhead persuade you to squander any of that money on old musty debts, or any such nonsense; for tradesmen, Charles, are the most exorbitant fellows.

Chas. Surf. Very true, and paying them is only encouraging them.

Care. Nothing else.

Chas. Surf. Ay, ay, never fear. — [*Exit* CARELESS.] So! this was an odd old fellow, indeed. Let me see, two-thirds of these five hundred and thirty odd pounds are mine by right. 'Fore Heaven! I find one's ancestors are more valuable relations than I took them for! — Ladies and gentlemen, your most obedient and very grateful servant.

[*Bows ceremoniously to the pictures.*

Enter ROWLEY.

Ha! old Rowley! egad, you are just come in time to take leave of your old acquaintance.

Row. Yes, I heard they were a-going. But I wonder you can have such spirits under so many distresses.

Chas. Surf. Why, there's the point! my distresses are so many, that I can't afford to part with my spirits; but I shall be rich and splenetic, all in good time. However, I suppose you are surprised that I am not more sorrowful at parting

with so many near relations; to be sure, 'tis very affecting:
but you see they never move a muscle, so why should I?

Row. There's no making you serious a moment.

Chas. Surf. Yes, faith, I am so now. Here, my honest
Rowley, here, get me this changed directly, and take a hundred pounds of it immediately to old Stanley.

Row. A hundred pounds! Consider only ——

Chas. Surf. Gad's life, don't talk about it! poor Stanley's
wants are pressing, and, if you don't make haste, we shall
have some one call that has a better right to the money.

Row. Ah! there's the point! I never will cease dunning
you with the old proverb ——

Chas. Surface. Be just before you're generous. — Why, so I
would if I could; but Justice is an old, hobbling beldame,
and I can't get her to keep pace with Generosity, for the soul
of me.

Row. Yet, Charles, believe me, one hour's reflection ——

Chas. Surf. Ay, ay, it's very true; but, hark'ee, Rowley,
while I have, by Heaven I'll give; so, damn your economy!
and now for hazard.   [*Exeunt.*

SCENE II. — *Another room in the same.*

Enter SIR OLIVER SURFACE *and* MOSES.

Mos. Well, sir, I think, as Sir Peter said, you have seen
Mr. Charles in high glory; 'tis great pity he's so extravagant.

Sir Oliv. True, but he would not sell my picture.

Mos. And loves wine and women so much.

Sir Oliv. But he would not sell my picture.

Mos. And games so deep.

Sir Oliv. But he would not sell my picture. Oh, here's
Rowley.

Enter ROWLEY.

Row. So, Sir Oliver, I find you have made a purchase ——

Sir Oliv. Yes, yes, our young rake has parted with his ancestors like old tapestry.

Row. And here has he commissioned me to re-deliver you

part of the purchase money — I mean, though, in your neces-
sitous character of old Stanley.

Mos. Ah! there is the pity of all; he is so damned charitable.

Row. And I left a hosier and two tailors in the hall, who,
I'm sure, won't be paid, and this hundred would satisfy them.

Sir Oliv. Well, well, I'll pay his debts, and his benevolence
too. But now I am no more a broker, and you shall introduce me to the elder brother as old Stanley.

Row. Not yet awhile; Sir Peter, I know, means to call
there about this time.

Enter TRIP.

Trip. Oh, gentlemen, I beg pardon for not showing you
out; this way — Moses, a word.   [*Exit with* MOSES.

Sir Oliv. There's a fellow for you! Would you believe it,
that puppy intercèpted the Jew on our coming, and wanted to
raise money before he got to his master!

Row. Indeed!

Sir Oliv. Yes, they are now planning an annuity business.
Ah, Master Rowley, in my days servants were content with
the follies of their masters, when they were worn a little thread-
bare; but now they have their vices, like their birthday
clothes, with the gloss on.   [*Exeunt.*

SCENE III. — *A Library in* JOSEPH SURFACE'S *House.*

Enter JOSEPH SURFACE *and* SERVANT.

Jos. Surf. No letter from Lady Teazle?

Ser. No, sir.

Jos. Surf. [*Aside.*] I am surprised she has not sent, if she
is prevented from coming. Sir Peter certainly does not suspect me. Yet I wish I may not lose the heiress, through
the scrape I have drawn myself into with the wife; however,
Charles's imprudence and bad character are great points in
my favour.   [*Knocking without.*

Ser. Sir, I believe that must be Lady Teazle.

Jos. Surf. Hold! See whether it is or not, before you go

to the door: I have a particular message for you if it should
be my brother.

Ser. 'Tis her ladyship, sir; she always leaves her chair at
the milliner's in the next street.

Jos. Surf. Stay, stay; draw that screen before the window
— that will do; — my opposite neighbour is a maiden lady of
so curious a temper. — [SERVANT *draws the screen, and exit.*]
I have a difficult hand to play in this affair. Lady Teazle
has lately suspected my views on Maria; but she must by no
means be let into that secret, — at least, till I have her more
in my power.

Enter LADY TEAZLE.

Lady Teaz. What, sentiment in soliloquy now? Have you
been very impatient? O Lud! don't pretend to look grave.
I vow I couldn't come before.

Jos. Surf. O madam, punctuality is a species of constancy
very unfashionable in a lady of quality.

[*Places chairs, and sits after* LADY TEAZLE *is seated.*

Lady Teaz. Upon my word, you ought to pity me. Do you
know Sir Peter is grown so ill-natured to me of late, and so
jealous of Charles too — that's the best of the story, isn't it?

Jos. Surf. I am glad my scandalous friends keep that up.
[*Aside.*

Lady Teaz. I am sure I wish he would let Maria marry
him, and then perhaps he would be convinced; don't you,
Mr. Surface?

Jos. Surf. [*Aside.*] Indeed I do not. — [*Aloud.*] Oh, certainly I do! for then my dear Lady Teazle would also be
convinced how wrong her suspicions were of my having any
design on the silly girl.

Lady Teaz. Well, well, I'm inclined to believe you. But
isn't it provoking, to have the most ill-natured things said of
one? And there's my friend Lady Sneerwell has circulated
I don't know how many scandalous tales of me, and all without
any foundation too; that's what vexes me.

Jos. Surf. Ay, madam, to be sure, that is the provoking
circumstance — without foundation; yes, yes, there's the

mortification, indeed; for, when a scandalous story is believed against one, there certainly is no comfort like the consciousness of having deserved it.

Lady Teaz. No, to be sure, then I'd forgive their malice; but to attack me, who am really so innocent, and who never say an ill-natured thing of any body — that is, of any friend; and then Sir Peter, too, to have him so peevish, and so suspicious, when I know the integrity of my own heart—indeed 'tis monstrous!

Jos. Surf. But, my dear Lady Teazle, 'tis your own fault if you suffer it. When a husband entertains a groundless suspicion of his wife, and withdraws his confidence from her, the original compact is broken, and she owes it to the honour of her sex to endeavour to outwit him.

Lady Teaz. Indeed! So that, if he suspects me without cause, it follows, that the best way of curing his jealousy is to give him reason for 't?

Jos. Surf. Undoubtedly — for your husband should never be deceived in you: and in that case it becomes you to be frail in compliment to his discernment.

Lady Teaz. To be sure, what you say is very reasonable, and when the consciousness of my innocence ——

Jos. Surf. Ah, my dear madam, there is the great mistake! 'tis this very conscious innocence that is of the greatest prejudice to you. What is it makes you negligent of forms, and careless of the world's opinion? why, the consciousness of your own innocence. What makes you thoughtless in your conduct, and apt to run into a thousand little imprudences? why, the consciousness of your own innocence. What makes you impatient of Sir Peter's temper, and outrageous at his suspicions? why, the consciousness of your innocence.

Lady Teaz. 'Tis very true!

Jos. Surf. Now, my dear Lady Teazle, if you would but once make a trifling *faux pas*, you can't conceive how cautious you would grow, and how ready to humour and agree with your husband.

Lady Teaz. Do you think so?

Jos. Surf. Oh, I am sure on 't; and then you would find all scandal would cease at once, for—in short, your character at present is like a person in a plethora, absolutely dying from too much health.

Lady Teaz. So, so; then I perceive your prescription is, that I must sin in my own defence, and part with my virtue to preserve my reputation?

Jos. Surf. Exactly so, upon my credit, ma'am.

Lady Teaz. Well, certainly this is the oddest doctrine, and the newest receipt for avoiding calumny!

Jos. Surf. An infallible one, believe me. Prudence, like experience, must be paid for.

Lady Teaz. Why, if my understanding were once convinced ——

Jos. Surf. Oh, certainly, madam, your understanding should be convinced. Yes, yes — Heaven forbid I should persuade you to do any thing you thought wrong. No, no, I have too much honour to desire it.

Lady Teaz. Don't you think we may as well leave honour out of the argument?   [*Rises.*

Jos. Surf. Ah, the ill effects of your country education, I see, still remain with you.

Lady Teaz. I doubt they do indeed; and I will fairly own to you, that if I could be persuaded to do wrong, it would be by Sir Peter's ill usage sooner than your honourable logic, after all.

Jos. Surf. Then, by this hand, which he is unworthy of—
                                    [*Taking her hand.*

Re-enter SERVANT.

'Sdeath, you blockhead — what do you want?

Ser. I beg your pardon, sir, but I thought you would not choose Sir Peter to come up without announcing him.

Jos. Surf. Sir Peter! — Oons — the devil!

Lady Teaz. Sir Peter! O Lud! I'm ruined! I'm ruined!

Ser. Sir, 'twasn't I let him in.

Lady Teaz. Oh! I'm quite undone! What will become of

me? Now, Mr. Logic — Oh! mercy, sir, he's on the stairs —
I'll get behind here—and if ever I'm so imprudent again——

[Goes behind the screen.

Jos. Surf. Give me that book.

[Sits down. SERVANT *pretends to adjust his chair.*

Enter SIR PETER TEAZLE.

Sir Pet. Ay, ever improving himself — Mr. Surface, Mr.
Surface —— *[Pats* JOSEPH *on the shoulder.*

Jos. Surf. Oh, my dear Sir Peter, I beg your pardon. —
[Gaping, throws away the book.] I have been dozing over a
stupid book. Well, I am much obliged to you for this call.
You haven't been here, I believe, since I fitted up this room.
Books, you know, are the only things I am a coxcomb in.

Sir Pet. 'Tis very neat indeed. Well, well, that's proper;
and you can make even your screen a source of knowledge —
hung, I perceive, with maps.

Jos. Surf. Oh, yes, I find great use in that screen.

Sir Pet. I dare say you must, certainly, when you want to
find any thing in a hurry.

Jos. Surf. Ay, or to hide any thing in a hurry either.

[Aside.

Sir Pet. Well, I have a little private business ——

Jos. Surf. You need not stay. . *[To* SERVANT.

Ser. No, sir. *[Exit.*

Jos. Surf. Here's a chair, Sir Peter — I beg ——

Sir Pet. Well, now we are alone, there is a subject, my
dear friend, on which I wish to unburden my mind to you —
a point of the greatest moment to my peace; in short, my
good friend, Lady Teazle's conduct of late has made me very
unhappy.

Jos. Surf. Indeed! I am very sorry to hear it.

Sir Pet. Yes, 'tis but too plain she has not the least regard
for me; but, what's worse, I have pretty good authority to
suppose she has formed an attachment to another.

Jos. Surf. Indeed! you astonish me!

Sir Pet. Yes! and, between ourselves, I think I've discovered the person.

Jos. Surf. How! you alarm me exceedingly.

Sir Pet. Ay, my dear friend, I knew you would sympathise with me!

Jos. Surf. Yes, believe me, Sir Peter, such a discovery would hurt me just as much as it would you.

Sir Pet. I am convinced of it. Ah! it is a happiness to have a friend whom we can trust even with one's family secrets. But have you no guess who I mean?

Jos. Surf. I haven't the most distant idea. It can't be Sir Benjamin Backbite!

Sir Pet. Oh, no! What say you to Charles?

Jos. Surf. My brother! impossible!

Sir Pet. Oh, my dear friend, the goodness of your own heart misleads you. You judge of others by yourself.

Jos. Surf. Certainly, Sir Peter, the heart that is conscious of its own integrity is ever slow to credit another's treachery.

Sir Pet. True; but your brother has no sentiment — you never hear him talk so.

Jos. Surf. Yet I can't but think Lady Teazle herself has too much principle.

Sir Pet. Ay; but what is principle against the flattery of a handsome, lively young fellow?

Jos. Surf. That's very true.

Sir Pet. And then, you know, the difference of our ages makes it very improbable that she should have any great affection for me; and if she were to be frail, and I were to make it public, why the town would only laugh at me, the foolish old bachelor, who had married a girl.

Jos. Surf. That's true, to be sure — they would laugh.

Sir Pet. Laugh! ay, and make ballads, and paragraphs, and the devil knows what of me.

Jos. Surf. No, you must never make it public.

Sir Pet. But then again—that the nephew of my old friend, Sir Oliver, should be the person to attempt such a wrong, hurts me more nearly.

Jos. Surf. Ay, there's the point. When ingratitude barbs the dart of injury, the wound has double danger in it.

Sir Pet. Ay — I, that was, in a manner, left his guardian; in whose house he had been so often entertained; who never in my life denied him — my advice!

Jos. Surf. Oh, 'tis not to be credited! There may be a man capable of such baseness, to be sure; but, for my part, till you can give me positive proofs, I cannot but doubt it. However, if it should be proved on him, he is no longer a brother of mine — I disclaim kindred with him: for the man who can preak the laws of hospitality, and tempt the wife of his friend, deserves to be branded as the pest of society.

Sir Pet. What a difference there is between you! What noble sentiments!

Jos. Surf. Yet I cannot suspect Lady Teazle's honour.

Sir Pet. I am sure I wish to think well of her, and to remove all ground of quarrel between us. She has lately reproached me more than once with having made no settlement on her; and, in our last quarrel, she almost hinted that she should not break her heart if I was dead. Now, as we seem to differ in our ideas of expense, I have resolved she shall have her own way, and be her own mistress in that respect for the future; and, if I were to die, she will find I have not been inattentive to her interest while living. Here, my friend, are the drafts of two deeds, which I wish to have your opinion on. By one, she will enjoy eight hundred a year independent while I live; and, by the other, the bulk of my fortune at my death.

Jos. Surf. This conduct, Sir Peter, is indeed truly generous. [*Aside.*] I wish it may not corrupt my pupil.

Sir Pet. Yes, I am determined she shall have no cause to complain, though I would not have her acquainted with the latter instance of my affection yet awhile.

Jos. Surf. Nor I, if I could help it. [*Aside.*

Sir Pet. And now, my dear friend, if you please, we will talk over the situation of your hopes with Maria.

Jos. Surf. [*Softly.*] Oh, no, Sir Peter; another time, if you please.

Sir Pet. I am sensibly chagrined at the little progress you seem to make in her affections.

Jos. Surf. [*Softly.*] I beg you will not mention it. What are my disappointments when your happiness is in debate! — [*Aside.*] 'Sdeath, I shall be ruined every way!

Sir Pet. And though you are averse to my acquainting Lady Teazle with your passion, I'm sure she's not your enemy in the affair.

Jos. Surf. Pray, Sir Peter, now oblige me. I am really too much affected by the subject we have been speaking of to bestow a thought on my own concerns. The man who is entrusted with his friend's distresses can never ——

Re-enter SERVANT.

Well, sir?

Ser. Your brother, sir, is speaking to a gentleman in the street, and says he knows you are within.

Jos. Surf. 'Sdeath, blockhead, I'm not within — I'm out for the day.

Sir Pet. Stay — hold — a thought has struck me: — you shall be at home.

Jos. Surf. Well, well, let him up. — [*Exit* SERVANT.] He'll interrupt Sir Peter, however.   [*Aside.*

Sir Pet. Now, my good friend, oblige me, I entreat you. Before Charles comes, let me conceal myself somewhere, then do you tax him on the point we have been talking, and his answer may satisfy me at once.

Jos. Surf. Oh, fie, Sir Peter! would you have me join in so mean a trick? — to trepan my brother too?

Sir Pet. Nay, you tell me you are sure he is innocent; if so, you do him the greatest service by giving him an opportunity to clear himself, and you will set my heart at rest. Come, you shall not refuse me: [*Going up,*] here, behind the screen will be — Hey! what the devil! there seems to be one listener here already — I'll swear I saw a petticoat!

Jos. Surf. Ha! ha! ha! Well, this is ridiculous enough.
I'll tell you, Sir Peter, though I hold a man of intrigue to be
a most despicable character, yet, you know, it does not follow
that one is to be an absolute Joseph either! Hark'ee, 'tis a
little French milliner, a silly rogue that plagues me; and
having some character to lose, on your coming, sir, she ran behind the screen.

Sir Pet. Ah, Joseph! Joseph! Did I ever think that
you —— But, egad, she has overheard all I have been saying
of my wife.

Jos. Surf. Oh, 'twill never go any farther, you may depend
upon it!

Sir Pet. No! then, faith, let her hear it out. — Here's a
closet will do as well.

Jos. Surf. Well, go in there.

Sir Pet. Sly, rogue! sly rogue!   [*Goes into the closet.*

Jos. Surf. A narrow escape, indeed! and a curious situation I'm in, to part man and wife in this manner.

Lady Teaz. [*Peeping.*] Couldn't I steal off?

Jos. Surf. Keep close, my angel!

Sir Pet. [*Peeping.*] Joseph, tax him home.

Jos. Surf. Back, my dear friend!

Lady Teaz. [*Peeping.*] Couldn't you lock Sir Peter in?

Jos. Surf. Be still, my life!

Sir Pet. [*Peeping.*] You're sure the little milliner won't
blab?

Jos. Surf. In, in, my dear Sir Peter! — 'Fore Gad, I wish
I had a key to the door.

Enter CHARLES SURFACE.

Chas. Surf. Holla! brother, what has been the matter?
Your fellow would not let me up at first. What! have you
had a Jew or a wench with you?

Jos. Surf. Neither, brother, I assure you.

Chas. Surf. But what has made Sir Peter steal off? I
thought he had been with you.

Jos. Surf. He was, brother; but, hearing you were coming, he did not choose to stay.

Chas. Surf. What! was the old gentleman afraid I wanted to borrow money of him?

Jos. Surf. No, sir: but I am sorry to find, Charles, you have lately given that worthy man grounds for great uneasiness.

Chas. Surf. Yes, they tell me I do that to a great many worthy men. But how so, pray?

Jos. Surf. To be plain with you, brother, he thinks you are endeavouring to gain Lady Teazle's affections from him.

Chas. Surf. Who, I? O Lud! not I, upon my word.— Ha! ha! ha! ha! so the old fellow has found out that he has got a young wife, has he?—or, what is worse, Lady Teazle has found out she has an old husband?

Jos. Surf. This is no subject to jest on, brother. He who can laugh ——

Chas. Surf. True, true, as you were going to say — then, seriously, I never had the least idea of what you charge me with, upon my honour.

Jos. Surf. Well, it will give Sir Peter great satisfaction to hear this.   [*Raising his voice.*

Chas. Surf. To be sure, I once thought the lady seemed to have taken a fancy to me; but, upon my soul, I never gave her the least encouragement. Besides, you know my attachment to Maria.

Jos. Surf. But sure, brother, even if Lady Teazle had betrayed the fondest partiality for you ——

Chas. Surf. Why, look'ee, Joseph, I hope I shall never deliberately do a dishonourable action; but if a pretty woman was purposely to throw herself in my way — and that pretty woman married to a man old enough to be her father ——

Jos. Surf. Well!

Chas. Surf. Why, I believe I should be obliged to ——

Jos. Surf. What?

Chas. Surf. To borrow a little of your morality, that's all. But, brother, do you know now that you surprise me exceedingly, by naming me with Lady Teazle; for, i'faith, I always understood you were her favourite.

Jos. Surf. Oh, for shame, Charles! This retort is foolish.

Chas. Surf. Nay, I swear I have seen you exchange such significant glances ——

Jos. Surf. Nay, nay, sir, this is no jest.

Chas. Surf. Egad, I'm serious! Don't you remember one day, when I called here ——

Jos. Surf. Nay, pr'ythee, Charles ——

Chas. Surf. And found you together ——

Jos. Surf. Zounds, sir, I insist ——

Chas. Surf. And another time when your servant ——

Jos. Surf. Brother, brother, a word with you! — [*Aside.*] Gad, I must stop him.

Chas. Surf. Informed, I say, that ——

Jos. Surf. Hush! I beg your pardon, but Sir Peter has overheard all we have been saying. I knew you would clear yourself, or I should not have consented.

Chas. Surf. How, Sir Peter! Where is he?

Jos. Surf. Softly, there! [*Points to the closet.*

Chas. Surf. Oh, 'fore Heaven, I'll have him out. Sir Peter, come forth!

Jos. Surf. No, no ——

Chas. Surf. I say, Sir Peter, come into court. — [*Pulls in* SIR PETER.] What! my old guardian! — What! turn inquisitor, and take evidence incog.? Oh, fie! Oh, fie!

Sir Pet. Give me your hand, Charles — I believe I have suspected you wrongfully; but you mustn't be angry with Joseph — 'twas my plan!

Chas. Surf. Indeed!

Sir Pet. But I acquit you. I promise you I don't think near so ill of you as I did: what I have heard has given me great satisfaction.

Chas. Surf. Egad, then, 'twas lucky you didn't hear any more. Wasn't it, Joseph?

Sir Pet. Ah! you would have retorted on him.

Chas. Surf. Ah, ay, that was a joke.

Sir Pet. Yes, yes, I know his honour too well.

Chas. Surf. But you might as well have suspected him as me in this matter, for all that. Mightn't he, Joseph?

Sir Pet. Well, well, I believe you.

Jos. Surf. Would they were both out of the room! [*Aside.*

Sir Pet. And in future, perhaps, we may not be such strangers.

Re-enter SERVANT, *and whispers* JOSEPH SURFACE.

Serv. Lady Sneerwell is below, and says she will come up.

Jos. Surf. Lady Sneerwell! Gad's life! she must not come here. [*Exit* SERVANT.] Gentlemen, I beg pardon — I must wait on you down stairs: here is a person come on particular business.

Chas. Surf. Well, you can see him in another room. Sir Peter and I have not met a long time, and I have something to say to him.

Jos. Surf. [*Aside.*] They must not be left together.—[*Aloud.*] I'll send Lady Sneerwell away, and return directly. — [*Aside to* SIR PETER.] Sir Peter, not a word of the French milliner.

Sir Pet. [*Aside to* JOSEPH SURFACE.] I! not for the world! —[*Exit* JOSEPH SURFACE.] Ah, Charles, if you associated more with your brother, one might indeed hope for your reformation. He is a man of sentiment. Well, there is nothing in the world so noble as a man of sentiment!

Chas. Surf. Psha! he is too moral by half; and so apprehensive of his good name, as he calls it, that I suppose he would as soon let a priest into his house as a wench.

Sir Pet. No, no,— come, come,—you wrong him. No, no! Joseph is no rake, but he is no such saint either, in that respect. — [*Aside.*] I have a great mind to tell him — we should have such a laugh at Joseph.

Chas. Surf. Oh, hang him! he's a very anchorite, a young hermit!

Sir Pet. Hark'ee — you must not abuse him: he may chance to hear of it again, I promise you.

Chas. Surf. Why, you won't tell him?

Sir Pet. No—but—this way.—[*Aside.*] Egad, I'll tell him.
—[*Aloud.*] Hark'ee — have you a mind to have a good laugh
at Joseph?

Chas. Surf. I should like it of all things.

Sir Pet. Then, i'faith, we will! I'll be quit with him for
discovering me. He had a girl with him when I called.

[Whispers.

Chas. Surf. What! Joseph? you jest.

Sir Pet. Hush! — a little French milliner — and the best
of the jest is — she's in the room now.

Chas. Surf. The devil she is!

Sir Pet. Hush! I tell you.   [*Points to the screen.*]

Chas. Surf. Behind the screen! 'Slife, let's unveil her!

Sir Pet. No, no, he's coming: — you sha'n't, indeed!

Chas. Surf. Oh, egad, we'll have a peep at the little
milliner!

Sir Pet. Not for the world!—Joseph will never forgive me.

Chas. Surf. I'll stand by you ——

Sir Pet. Odds, here he is!

[CHARLES SURFACE throws down the screen.

Re-enter JOSEPH SURFACE.

Chas. Surf. Lady Teazle, by all that's wonderful!

Sir Pet. Lady Teazle, by all that's damnable!

Chas. Surf. Sir Peter, this is one of the smartest French
milliners I ever saw. Egad, you seem all to have been
diverting yourselves here at hide and seek, and I don't see
who is out of the secret. Shall I beg your ladyship to inform
me? Not a word! — Brother, will you be pleased to explain
this matter? What! is Morality dumb too? — Sir Peter
though I found you in the dark, perhaps you are not so now
All mute! — Well—though I can make nothing of the affair,
I suppose you perfectly understand one another; so I'll leave
you to yourselves. — [*Going.*] Brother, I'm sorry to find you
have given that worthy man grounds for so much uneasiness.
— Sir Peter! there's nothing in the world so noble as a man
of sentiment!   [*Exit.*]

Jos. Surf. Sir Peter — notwithstanding — I confess — that appearances are against me — if you will afford me your patience — I make no doubt — but I shall explain every thing to your satisfaction.

Sir Pet. If you please, sir.

Jos. Surf. The fact is, sir, that Lady Teazle, knowing my pretensions to your ward Maria — I say, sir, Lady Teazle, being apprehensive of the jealousy of your temper — and knowing my friendship to the family — she, sir, I say — called here — in order that — I might explain these pretensions — but on your coming — being apprehensive — as I said — of your jealousy — she withdrew — and this, you may depend on it, is the whole truth of the matter.

Sir Pet. A very clear account, upon my word; and I dare swear the lady will vouch for every article of it.

Lady Teaz. For not one word of it, Sir Peter!

Sir Pet. How! don't you think it worth while to agree in the lie?

Lady Teaz. There is not one syllable of truth in what that gentleman has told you.

Sir Pet. I believe you, upon my soul, ma'am!

Jos. Surf. [*Aside to* LADY TEAZLE.] 'Sdeath, madam, will you betray me?

Lady Teaz. Good Mr. Hypocrite, by your leave, I'll speak for myself.

Sir Pet. Ay, let her alone, sir; you'll find she'll make out a better story than you, without prompting.

Lady Teaz. Hear me, Sir Peter! — I came here on no matter relating to your ward, and even ignorant of this gentleman's pretensions to her. But I came, seduced by his insidious arguments, at least to listen to his pretended passion, if not to sacrifice your honour to his baseness.

Sir Pet. Now, I believe, the truth is coming, indeed!

Jos. Surf. The woman's mad!

Lady Teaz. No, sir; she has recovered her senses, and your own arts have furnished her with the means. — Sir Peter, I do not expect you to credit me — but the tenderness you

16*

expressed for me, when I am sure you could not think I was a witness to it, has so penetrated to my heart, that had I left the place without the shame of this discovery, my future life should have spoken the sincerity of my gratitude. As for that smooth-tongued hypocrite, who would have seduced the wife of his too credulous friend, while he affected honourable addresses to his ward — I behold him now in a light so truly despicable, that I shall never again respect myself for having listened to him.   [*Exit.*

Jos. Surf. Notwithstanding all this, Sir Peter, Heaven knows ——

Sir Pet. That you are a villain! and so I leave you to your conscience.

Jos. Surf. You are too rash, Sir Peter; you shall hear me. The man who shuts out conviction by refusing to ——

Sir Pet. Oh, damn your sentiments!

[*Exeunt* SIR PETER *and* JOSEPH SURFACE, *talking.*

ACT V.

SCENE I. — *The Library in* JOSEPH SURFACE'S *House.*

Enter JOSEPH SURFACE *and* SERVANT.

Jos. Surf. Mr. Stanley! and why should you think I would see him? you must know he comes to ask something.

Ser. Sir, I should not have let him in, but that Mr. Rowley came to the door with him.

Jos. Surf. Psha! blockhead! to suppose that I should now be in a temper to receive visits from poor relations! — Well, why don't you show the fellow up?

Ser. I will, sir. — Why, sir, it was not my fault that Sir Peter discovered my lady ——

Jos. Surf. Go, fool! — [*Exit* SERVANT.] Sure Fortune never played a man of my policy such a trick before! My character with Sir Peter, my hopes with Maria, destroyed in a moment! I'm in a rare humour to listen to other people's distresses! I sha'n't be able to bestow even a benevolent sentiment on

Stanley. — So! here he comes, and Rowley with him. I must try to recover myself, and put a little charity into my face, however.   [*Exit.*

    Enter SIR OLIVER SURFACE *and* ROWLEY.

Sir Oliv. What! does he avoid us? That was he, was it not?

Row. It was, sir. But I doubt you are come a little too abruptly. His nerves are so weak, that the sight of a poor relation may be too much for him. I should have gone first to break it to him.

Sir Oliv. Oh, plague of his nerves! Yet this is he whom Sir Peter extols as a man of the most benevolent way of thinking!

Row. As to his way of thinking, I cannot pretend to decide; for, to do him justice, he appears to have as much speculative benevolence as any private gentleman in the kingdom, though he is seldom so sensual as to indulge himself in the exercise of it.

Sir Oliv. Yet he has a string of charitable sentiments at his fingers' ends.

Row. Or, rather, at his tongue's end, Sir Oliver; for I believe there is no sentiment he has such faith in as that *Charity begins at home.*

Sir Oliv. And his, I presume, is of that domestic sort which never stirs abroad at all.

Row. I doubt you'll find it so; — but he's coming. I mustn't seem to interrupt you; and you know, immediately as you leave him, I come in to announce your arrival in your real character.

Sir Oliv. True; and afterwards you'll meet me at Sir Peter's.

Row. Without losing a moment. ·   [*Exit.*

Sir Oliv. I don't like the complaisance of his features.

    Re-enter JOSEPH SURFACE.

Jos. Surf. Sir, I beg you ten thousand pardons for keeping you a moment waiting. — Mr. Stanley, I presume.

Sir Oliv. At your service.

Jos. Surf. Sir, I beg you will do me the honour to sit down —I entreat you, sir.

Sir Oliv. Dear sir — there's no occasion. — [*Aside.*] Too civil by half!

Jos. Surf. I have not the pleasure of knowing you, Mr. Stanley; but I am extremely happy to see you look so well. You were nearly related to my mother, I think, Mr. Stanley?

Sir Oliv. I was, sir; so nearly that my present poverty, I fear, may do discredit to her wealthy children, else I should not have presumed to trouble you.

Jos. Surf. Dear sir, there needs no apology; — he that is in distress, though a stranger, has a right to claim kindred with the wealthy. I am sure I wish I was one of that class, and had it in my power to offer you even a small relief.

Sir Oliv. If your uncle, Sir Oliver, were here, I should have a friend.

Jos. Surf. I wish he was, sir, with all my heart: you should not want an advocate with him, believe me, sir.

Sir Oliv. I should not need one — my distresses would recommend me. But I imagined his bounty would enable you to become the agent of his charity.

Jos. Surf. My dear sir, you were strangely misinformed. Sir Oliver is a worthy man, a very worthy man; but avarice, Mr. Stanley, is the vice of age. I will tell you, my good sir, in confidence, what he has done for me has been a mere nothing; though people, I know, have thought otherwise, and, for my part, I never chose to contradict the report.

Sir Oliv. What! has he never transmitted you bullion — rupees — pagodas?

Jos. Surf. Oh, dear sir, nothing of the kind! No, no; a few presents now and then—china, shawls, congou tea, avadavats, and Indian crackers — little more, believe me.

Sir Oliv. Here's gratitude for twelve thousand pounds! — Avadavats and Indian crackers!   [*Aside.*

Jos. Surf. Then, my dear sir, you have heard, I doubt not, of the extravagance of my brother: there are very few would credit what I have done for that unfortunate young man.

Sir Oliv. Not I, for one! [*Aside.*

Jos. Surf. The sums I have lent him! Indeed I have been exceedingly to blame; it was an amiable weakness; however, I don't pretend to defend it — and now I feel it doubly culpable, since it has deprived me of the pleasure of serving you, Mr. Stanley, as my heart dictates.

Sir Oliv. [*Aside.*] Dissembler!—[*Aloud.*] Then, sir, you can't assist me?

Jos. Surf. At present, it grieves me to say, I cannot; but, whenever I have the ability, you may depend upon hearing from me.

Sir Oliv. I am extremely sorry ——

Jos. Surf. Not more than I, believe me; to pity, without the power to relieve, is still more painful than to ask and be denied.

Sir Oliv. Kind sir, your most obedient humble servant.

Jos. Surf. You leave me deeply affected, Mr. Stanley. — William, be ready to open the door. [*Calls to* SERVANT.

Sir. Oliv. Oh, dear sir, no ceremony.

Jos. Surf. Your very obedient.

Sir Oliv. Your most obsequious.

Jos. Surf. You may depend upon hearing from me, whenever I can be of service.

Sir Oliv. Sweet sir, you are too good!

Jos. Surf. In the meantime I wish you health and spirits.

Sir Oliv. Your ever grateful and perpetual humble servant.

Jos. Surf. Sir, yours as sincerely. ·

Sir Oliv. [*Aside.*] Now I am satisfied. [*Exit.*

Jos. Surf. This is one bad effect of a good character; it invites application from the unfortunate, and there needs no small degree of address to gain the reputation of benevolence without incurring the expense. The silver ore of pure charity is an expensive article in the catalogue of a man's good qualities; whereas the sentimental French plate I use instead of it makes just as good a show, and pays no tax.

Re-enter ROWLEY.

Row. Mr. Surface, your servant: I was apprehensive of interrupting you, though my business demands immediate attention, as this note will inform you.

Jos. Surf. Always happy to see Mr. Rowley, — a rascal. — [*Aside. Reads the letter.*] Sir Oliver Surface! — My uncle arrived!

Row. He is, indeed: we have just parted — quite well, after a speedy voyage, and impatient to embrace his worthy nephew.

Jos. Surf. I am astonished! — William! stop Mr. Stanley, if he's not gone.   [*Calls to* SERVANT.

Row. Oh! he's out of reach, I believe.

Jos. Surf. Why did you not let me know this when you came in together?

Row. I thought you had particular business. But I must be gone to inform your brother, and appoint him here to meet your uncle. He will be with you in a quarter of an hour.

Jos. Surf. So he says. Well, I am strangely overjoyed at his coming. — [*Aside.*] Never, to be sure, was any thing so damned unlucky!

Row. You will be delighted to see how well he looks.

Jos. Surf. Oh! I'm overjoyed to hear it. — [*Aside.*] Just at this time!

Row. I'll tell him how impatiently you expect him.

Jos. Surf. Do, do; pray give my best duty and affection. Indeed, I cannot express the sensations I feel at the thought of seeing him. — [*Exit* ROWLEY.] Certainly his coming just at this time is the cruellest piece of ill fortune.   [*Exit.*

SCENE II. — *A Room in* SIR PETER TEAZLE'S *House.*

Enter MRS. CANDOUR *and* MAID.

Maid. Indeed, ma'am, my lady will see nobody at present.

Mrs. Can. Did you tell her it was her friend Mrs. Candour?

Maid. Yes, ma'am; but she begs you will excuse her.

Mrs. Can. Do go again; I shall be glad to see her, if it be

only for a moment, for I am sure she must be in great distress.
—[*Exit* Maid.] Dear heart, how provoking! I'm not mistress
of half the circumstances! We shall have the whole affair in
the newspapers, with the names of the parties at length, before I have dropped the story at a dozen houses.

Enter Sir Benjamin Backbite.

Oh, dear Sir Benjamin! you have heard, I suppose ——

Sir Ben. Of Lady Teazle and Mr. Surface ——

Mrs. Can. And Sir Peter's discovery ——

Sir Ben. Oh, the strangest piece of business, to be sure!

Mrs. Can. Well, I never was so surprised in my life. I
am so sorry for all parties, indeed.

Sir Ben. Now, I don't pity Sir Peter at all: he was so
extravagantly partial to Mr. Surface.

Mrs. Can. Mr. Surface! Why, 'twas with Charles Lady
Teazle was detected.

Sir Ben. No, no, I tell you: Mr. Surface is the gallant.

Mrs. Can. No such thing! Charles is the man. 'Twas Mr.
Surface brought Sir Peter on purpose to discover them.

Sir Ben. I tell you I had it from one ——

Mrs. Can. And I have it from one ——

Sir Ben. Who had it from one, who had it ——

Mrs. Can. From one immediately. But here comes Lady
Sneerwell; perhaps she knows the whole affair.

Enter Lady Sneerwell.

Lady Sneer. So, my dear Mrs. Candour, here's a sad affair
of our friend Lady Teazle!

Mrs. Can. Ay, my dear friend, who would have
thought ——

Lady Sneer. Well, there is no trusting appearances;
though, indeed, she was always too lively for me.

Mrs. Can. To be sure, her manners were a little too free;
but then she was so young!

Lady Sneer. And had, indeed, some good qualities.

Mrs. Can. So she had, indeed. But have you heard the
particulars?

Lady Sneer. No; but every body says that Mr. Surface——

Sir Ben. Ay, there; I told you Mr. Surface was the man.

Mrs. Can. No, no: indeed the assignation was with Charles.

Lady Sneer. With Charles! You alarm me, Mrs. Candour!

Mrs. Can. Yes, yes; he was the lover. Mr. Surface, to do him justice, was only the informer.

Sir Ben. Well, I'll not dispute with you, Mrs. Candour; but, be it which it may, I hope that Sir Peter's wound will not ——

Mrs. Can. Sir Peter's wound! Oh, mercy! I didn't hear a word of their fighting.

Lady Sneer. Nor I, a syllable.

Sir Ben. No! what, no mention of the duel?

Mrs. Can. Not a word.

Sir Ben. Oh, yes: they fought before they left the room.

Lady Sneer. Pray, let us hear.

Mrs. Can. Ay, do oblige us with the duel.

Sir Ben. "*Sir,*" says Sir Peter, immediately after the discovery, "*you are a most ungrateful fellow.*"

Mrs. Can. Ay, to Charles ——

Sir Ben. No, no — to Mr. Surface — *a most ungrateful fellow; and old as I am, sir,* says he, *I insist on immediate satisfaction.*

Mrs. Can. Ay, that must have been to Charles; for 'tis very unlikely Mr. Surface should fight in his own house.

Sir Ben. Gad's life, ma'am, not at all — *giving me immediate satisfaction.* — On this, ma'am, Lady Teazle, seeing Sir Peter in such danger, ran out of the room in strong hysterics, and Charles after her, calling out for hartshorn and water; then, madam, they began to fight with swords ——

Enter CRABTREE.

Crab. With pistols, nephew — pistols! I have it from undoubted authority.

Mrs. Can. Oh, Mr. Crabtree, then it is all true!

Crab. Too true, indeed, madam, and Sir Peter is dangerously wounded ——

Sir Ben. By a thrust in segoon quite through his left side ——

Crab. By a bullet lodged in the thorax.

Mrs. Can. Mercy on me! Poor Sir Peter!

Crab. Yes, madam; though Charles would have avoided the matter, if he could.

Mrs. Can. I told you who it was; I knew Charles was the person.

Sir Ben. My uncle, I see, knows nothing of the matter.

Crab. But Sir Peter taxed him with the basest ingratitude ——

Sir Ben. That I told you, you know ——

Crab. Do, nephew, let me speak! — and insisted on immediate ——

Sir Ben. Just as I said ——

Crab. Odds life, nephew, allow others to know something too! A pair of pistols lay on the bureau (for Mr. Surface, it seems, had come home the night before late from Salthill, where he had been to see the Montem with a friend, who has a son at Eton), so, unluckily, the pistols were left charged.

Sir Ben. I heard nothing of this.

Crab. Sir Peter forced Charles to take one, and they fired, it seems, pretty nearly together. Charles's shot took effect, as I tell you, and Sir Peter's missed; but, what is very extraordinary, the ball struck against a little bronze Shakspeare that stood over the fire-place, grazed out of the window at a right angle, and wounded the postman, who was just coming to the door with a double letter from Northamptonshire.

Sir Ben. My uncle's account is more circumstantial, I confess; but I believe mine is the true one, for all that.

Lady Sneer. [*Aside.*] I am more interested in this affair than they imagine, and must have better information. [*Exit.*

Sir Ben. Ah! Lady Sneerwell's alarm is very easily accounted for.

Crab. Yes, yes, they certainly do say — but that's neither here nor there.

Mrs. Can. But, pray, where is Sir Peter at present?

Crab. Oh! they brought him home, and he is now in the house, though the servants are ordered to deny him.

Mrs. Can. I believe so, and Lady Teazle, I suppose, attending him.

Crab. Yes, yes; and I saw one of the faculty enter just before me.

Sir Ben. Hey! who comes here?

Crab. Oh, this is he: the physician, depend on't.

Mrs. Can. Oh, certainly! it must be the physician; and now we shall know.

Enter SIR OLIVER SURFACE.

Crab. Well, doctor, what hopes?

Mrs. Can. Ay, doctor, how's your patient?

Sir Ben. Now, doctor, isn't it a wound with a small-sword?

Crab. A bullet lodged in the thorax, for a hundred!

Sir Oliv. Doctor! a wound with a small-sword! and a bullet in the thorax! — Oons! are you mad, good people?

Sir Ben. Perhaps, sir, you are not a doctor?

Sir Oliv. Truly, I am to thank you for my degree, if I am.

Crab. Only a friend of Sir Peter's, then, I presume. But, sir, you must have heard of his accident?

Sir Oliv. Not a word!

Crab. Not of his being dangerously wounded?

Sir Oliv. The devil he is!

Sir Ben. Run through the body ——

Crab. Shot in the breast ——

Sir Ben. By one Mr. Surface ——

Crab. Ay, the younger.

Sir Oliv. Hey! what the plague! you seem to differ strangely in your accounts: however, you agree that Sir Peter is dangerously wounded.

Sir Ben. Oh, yes, we agree in that.

Crab. Yes, yes, I believe there can be no doubt of that.

Sir Oliv. Then, upon my word, for a person in that situation, he is the most imprudent man alive; for here he comes, walking as if nothing at all was the matter.

Enter SIR PETER TEAZLE.

Odds heart, Sir Peter! you are come in good time, I promise you; for we had just given you over!

Sir Ben. [*Aside to* CRABTREE.] Egad, uncle, this is the most sudden recovery!

Sir Oliv. Why, man! what do you out of bed with a small-sword through your body, and a bullet lodged in your thorax?

Sir Pet. A small-sword and a bullet!

Sir Oliv. Ay; these gentlemen would have killed you without law or physic, and wanted to dub me a doctor, to make me an accomplice.

Sir Pet. Why, what is all this?

Sir Ben. We rejoice, Sir Peter, that the story of the duel is not true, and are sincerely sorry for your other misfortune.

Sir Pet. So, so; all over the town already!   [*Aside.*

Crab. Though, Sir Peter, you were certainly vastly to blame to marry at your years.

Sir Pet. Sir, what business is that of yours?

Mrs. Can. Though, indeed, as Sir Peter made so good a husband, he's very much to be pitied.

Sir Pet. Plague on your pity, ma'am! I desire none of it.

Sir Ben. However, Sir Peter, you must not mind the laughing and jests you will meet with on the occasion.

Sir Pet. Sir, sir! I desire to be master in my own house.

Crab. 'Tis no uncommon case, that's one comfort.

Sir Pet. I insist on being left to myself: without ceremony, I insist on your leaving my house directly!

Mrs. Can. Well, well, we are going; and depend on't, we'll make the best report of it we can.   [*Exit.*

Sir Pet. Leave my house!

Crab. And tell how hardly you've been treated.   [*Exit.*

Sir Pet. Leave my house!

Sir Ben. And how patiently you bear it   [*Exit.*

Sir Pet. Fiends! vipers! furies! Oh! that their own venom would choke them!

Sir Oliv. They are very provoking indeed, Sir Peter.

Enter ROWLEY.

Row. I heard high words: what has ruffled you, sir?

Sir Pet. Psha! what signifies asking? Do I ever pass a day without my vexations?

Row. Well, I'm not inquisitive.

Sir Oliv. Well, Sir Peter, I have seen both my nephews in the manner we proposed.

Sir Pet. A precious couple they are!

Row. Yes, and Sir Oliver is convinced that your judgment was right, Sir Peter.

Sir Oliv. Yes, I find Joseph is indeed the man, after all.

Row. Ay, as Sir Peter says, he is a man of sentiment.

Sir Oliv. And acts up to the sentiments he professes.

Row. It certainly is edification to hear him talk.

Sir Oliv. Oh, he's a model for the young men of the age! —But how's this, Sir Peter? you don't join us in your friend Joseph's praise, as I expected.

Sir Pet. Sir Oliver, we live in a damned wicked world, and the fewer we praise the better.

Row. What! do you say so, Sir Peter, who were never mistaken in your life?

Sir Pet. Psha! plague on you both! I see by your sneering you have heard the whole affair. I shall go mad among you!

Row. Then, to fret you no longer, Sir Peter, we are indeed acquainted with it all. I met Lady Teazle coming from Mr. Surface's so humbled, that she deigned to request me to be her advocate with you.

Sir Pet. And does Sir Oliver know all this?

Sir Oliv. Every circumstance.

Sir Pet. What of the closet and the screen, hey?

Sir Oliv. Yes, yes, and the little French milliner. Oh, I have been vastly diverted with the story! ha! ha! ha!

Sir Pet. 'Twas very pleasant.

Sir Oliv. I never laughed more in my life, I assure you. ha! ha! ha!

Sir Pet. Oh, vastly diverting! ha! ha! ha!

Row. To be sure, Joseph with his sentiments! ha! ha! ha!

Sir Pet. Yes, yes, his sentiments! ha! ha! ha! Hypocritical villain!

Sir Oliv. Ay, and that rogue Charles to pull Sir Peter out of the closet: ha! ha! ha!

Sir Pet. Ha! ha! 'twas devilish entertaining, to be sure!

Sir Oliv. Ha! ha! ha! Egad, Sir Peter, I should like to have seen your face when the screen was thrown down: ha! ha!

Sir Pet. Yes, yes, my face when the screen was thrown down: ha! ha! ha! Oh, I must never show my head again!

Sir Oliv. But come, come, it isn't fair to laugh at you neither, my old friend; though, upon my soul, I can't help it.

Sir Pet. Oh, pray don't restrain your mirth on my account: it does not hurt me at all! I laugh at the whole affair myself. Yes, yes, I think being a standing jest for all one's acquaintance a very happy situation. Oh, yes, and then of a morning to read the paragraphs about Mr. S——, Lady T——, and Sir P——, will be so entertaining!

Row. Without affectation, Sir Peter, you may despise the ridicule of fools. But I see Lady Teazle going towards the next room; I am sure you must desire a reconciliation as earnestly as she does.

Sir Oliv. Perhaps my being here prevents her coming to you. Well, I'll leave honest Rowley to mediate between you; but he must bring you all presently to Mr. Surface's, where I am now returning, if not to reclaim a libertine, at least to expose hypocrisy.

Sir Pet. Ah, I'll be present at your discovering yourself there with all my heart; though 'tis a vile unlucky place for discoveries.

Row. We'll follow.   [*Exit* SIR OLIVER SURFACE.

Sir Pet. She is not coming here, you see, Rowley.

Row. No, but she has left the door of that room open, you perceive. See, she is in tears.

Sir Pet. Certainly a little mortification appears very becoming in a wife. Don't you think it will do her good to let her pine a little?

Row. Oh, this is ungenerous in you!

Sir Pet. Well, I know not what to think. You remember the letter I found of hers evidently intended for Charles?

Row. A mere forgery, Sir Peter! laid in your way on purpose. This is one of the points which I intend Snake shall give you conviction of.

Sir Pet. I wish I were once satisfied of that. She looks this way. What a remarkably elegant turn of the head she has! Rowley, I'll go to her.

Row. Certainly.

Sir Pet. Though, when it is known that we are reconciled, people will laugh at me ten times more.

Row. Let them laugh, and retort their malice only by showing them you are happy in spite of it.

Sir Pet. I' faith, so I will! and, if I'm not mistaken, we may yet be the happiest couple in the country.

Row. Nay, Sir Peter, he who once lays aside suspicion——

Sir Pet. Hold, Master Rowley! if you have any regard for me, never let me hear you utter any thing like a sentiment: I have had enough of them to serve me the rest of my life.   [*Exeunt.*

SCENE III. — *The Library in* JOSEPH SURFACE'S *House.*

Enter JOSEPH SURFACE *and* LADY SNEERWELL.

Lady Sneer. Impossible! Will not Sir Peter immediately be reconciled to Charles, and of course no longer oppose his union with Maria? The thought is distraction to me.

Jos. Surf. Can passion furnish a remedy?

Lady Sneer. No, nor cunning either. Oh, I was a fool, an idiot, to league with such a blunderer!

Jos. Surf. Sure, Lady Sneerwell, I am the greatest sufferer; yet you see I bear the accident with calmness.

Lady Sneer. Because the disappointment doesn't reach your heart; your interest only attached you to Maria. Had you felt for her what I have for that ungrateful libertine, neither your temper nor hypocrisy could prevent your showing the sharpness of your vexation.

Jos. Surf. But why should your reproaches fall on me for this disappointment?

Lady Sneer. Are you not the cause of it? Had you not a sufficient field for your roguery in imposing upon Sir Peter, and supplanting your brother, but you must endeavour to seduce his wife? I hate such an avarice of crimes; 'tis an unfair monopoly, and never prospers.

Jos. Surf. Well, I admit I have been to blame. I confess I deviated from the direct road of wrong, but I don't think we're so totally defeated neither.

Lady Sneer. No!

Jos. Surf. You tell me you have made a trial of Snake since we met, and that you still believe him faithful to us?

Lady Sneer. I do believe so.

Jos. Surf. And that he has undertaken, should it be necessary, to swear and prove, that Charles is at this time contracted by vows and honour to your ladyship, which some of his former letters to you will serve to support?

Lady Sneer. This, indeed, might have assisted.

Jos. Surf. Come, come; it is not too late yet. — [*Knocking at the door.*] But hark! this is probably my uncle, Sir Oliver: retire to that room; we'll consult farther when he is gone.

Lady Sneer. Well, but if he should find you out too?

Jos. Surf. Oh, I have no fear of that. Sir Peter will hold his tongue for his own credit's sake — and you may depend on it I shall soon discover Sir Oliver's weak side!

Lady Sneer. I have no diffidence of your abilities: only be constant to one roguery at a time.

Jos. Surf. I will, I will! — [*Exit* LADY SNEERWELL.] So! 'tis confounded hard, after such bad fortune, to be baited by

Sheridan.   17

one's confederate in evil. Well, at all events, my character
is so much better than Charles's, that I certainly — hey! —
what — this is not Sir Oliver, but old Stanley again. Plague
on't that he should return to tease me just now! I shall have
Sir Oliver come and find him here — and ——

Enter Sir Oliver Surface.

Gad's life, Mr. Stanley, why have you come back to plague
me at this time? You must not stay now, upon my word.

Sir Oliv. Sir, I hear your uncle Oliver is expected here,
and though he has been so penurious to you, I'll try what
he'll do for me.

Jos. Surf. Sir, 'tis impossible for you to stay now, so I
must beg —— Come any other time, and I promise you, you
shall be assisted.

Sir Oliv. No: Sir Oliver and I must be acquainted.

Jos. Surf. Zounds, sir! then I insist on your quitting the
room directly.

Sir Oliv. Nay, sir ——

Jos. Surf. Sir, I insist on't! — Here, William! show this
gentleman out. Since you compel me, sir, not one moment
— this is such insolence.   [*Going to push him out.*

Enter Charles Surface.

Chas. Surf. Heyday! what's the matter now? What the
devil, have you got hold of my little broker here? Zounds,
brother, don't hurt little Premium. What's the matter, my
little fellow?

Jos. Surf. So! he has been with you too, has he?

Chas. Surf. To be sure, he has. Why, he's as honest a
little — But sure, Joseph, you have not been borrowing money
too, have you?

Jos. Surf. Borrowing! no! But, brother, you know we
expect Sir Oliver here every ——

Chas. Surf. O Gad, that's true! Noll mustn't find the little
broker here, to be sure.

Jos. Surf. Yet Mr. Stanley insists ——

Chas. Surf. Stanley! why his name's Premium.

Jos. Surf. No, sir, Stanley.

Chas. Surf. No, no, Premium.

Jos. Surf. Well, no matter which — but ——

Chas. Surf. Ay, ay, Stanley or Premium, 'tis the same thing, as you say; for I suppose he goes by half a hundred names, besides A. B. at the coffee-house.   [*Knocking.*

Jos. Surf. 'Sdeath! here's Sir Oliver at the door. — Now I beg, Mr. Stanley ——

Chas. Surf. Ay, ay, and I beg, Mr. Premium ——

Sir Oliv. Gentlemen ——

Jos. Surf. Sir, by Heaven you shall go!

Chas. Surf. Ay, out with him, certainly!

Sir Oliv. This violence ——

Jos. Surf. Sir, 'tis your own fault.

Chas. Surf. Out with him, to be sure.

[*Both forcing* SIR OLIVER *out.*

Enter SIR PETER *and* LADY TEAZLE, MARIA, *and* ROWLEY.

Sir Pet. My old friend, Sir Oliver — hey! What in the name of wonder — here are dutiful nephews — assault their uncle at a first visit!

Lady Teaz. Indeed, Sir Oliver, 'twas well we came in to rescue you.

Row. Truly it was; for I perceive, Sir Oliver, the character of old Stanley was no protection to you.

Sir Oliv. Nor of Premium either: the necessities of the former could not extort a shilling from that benevolent gentleman: and with the other I stood a chance of faring worse than my ancestors, and being knocked down without being bid for.

Jos. Surf. Charles!

Chas. Surf. Joseph!

Jos. Surf. 'Tis now complete!

Chas. Surf. Very.

Sir Oliv. Sir Peter, my friend, and Rowley too — look on that elder nephew of mine. You know what he has already received from my bounty; and you also know how gladly I

17*

would have regarded half my fortune as held in trust for him: judge then my disappointment in discovering him to be destitute of truth, charity, and gratitude!

Sir Pet. Sir Oliver, I should be more surprised at this declaration, if I had not myself found him to be mean, treacherous, and hypocritical.

Lady Teaz. And if the gentleman pleads not guilty to these, pray let him call me to his character.

Sir Pet. Then, I believe, we need add no more: if he knows himself, he will consider it as the most perfect punishment, that he is known to the world.

Chas. Surf. If they talk this way to Honesty, what will they say to me, by and by? [*Aside.*

[Sir PETER, LADY TEAZLE, *and* MARIA *retire.*

Sir Oliv. As for that prodigal, his brother, there ——

Chas. Surf. Ay, now comes my turn: the damned family pictures will ruin me! [*Aside.*

Jos. Surf. Sir Oliver — uncle, will you honour me with a hearing?

Chas. Surf. Now, if Joseph would make one of his long speeches, I might recollect myself a little. [*Aside.*

Sir Oliv. I suppose you would undertake to justify yourself? [*To* JOSEPH SURFACE.

Jos. Surf. I trust I could.

Sir Oliv. [*To* CHARLES SURFACE.] Well, sir! — and you could justify yourself too, I suppose?

Chas. Surf. Not that I know of, Sir Oliver.

Sir Oliv. What! — Little Premium has been let too much into the secret, I suppose?

Chas. Surf. True, sir; but they were family secrets, and should not be mentioned again, you know.

Row. Come, Sir Oliver, I know you cannot speak of Charles's follies with anger.

Sir Oliv. Odd's heart, no more I can; nor with gravity either. Sir Peter, do you know the rogue bargained with me for all his ancestors; sold me judges and generals by the foot, and maiden aunts as cheap as broken china.

Chas. Surf. To be sure, Sir Oliver, I did make a little free with the family canvas, that's the truth on't. My ancestors may rise in judgment against me, there's no denying it; but believe me sincere when I tell you — and upon my soul I would not say so if I was not — that if I do not appear mortified at the exposure of my follies, it is because I feel at this moment the warmest satisfaction in seeing you, my liberal benefactor.

Sir Oliv. Charles, I believe you. Give me your hand again: the ill-looking little fellow over the settee has made your peace.

Chas. Surf. Then, sir, my gratitude to the original is still increased.

Lady Teaz. [*Advancing.*] Yet, I believe, Sir Oliver, here is one whom Charles is still more anxious to be reconciled to.

[*Pointing to* MARIA.

Sir Oliv. Oh, I have heard of his attachment there; and, with the young lady's pardon, if I construe right—that blush——

Sir Pet. Well, child, speak your sentiments!

Mar. Sir, I have little to say, but that I shall rejoice to hear that he is happy; for me, whatever claim I had to his attention, I willingly resign to one who has a better title.

Chas. Surf. How, Maria!

Sir Pet. Heyday! what's the mystery now? While he appeared an incorrigible rake, you would give your hand to no one else; and now that he is likely to reform I'll warrant you won't have him!

Mar. His own heart and Lady Sneerwell know the cause.

Chas. Surf. Lady Sneerwell!

Jos. Surf. Brother, it is with great concern I am obliged to speak on this point, but my regard to justice compels me, and Lady Sneerwell's injuries can no longer be concealed.

[*Opens the door.*

Enter LADY SNEERWELL.

Sir Pet. So! another French milliner! Egad, he has one in every room in the house, I suppose!

Lady Sneer. Ungrateful Charles! Well may you be surprised, and feel for the indelicate situation your perfidy has forced me into.

Chas. Surf. Pray, uncle, is this another plot of yours? For, as I have life, I don't understand it.

Jos. Surf. I believe, sir, there is but the evidence of one person more necessary to make it extremely clear.

Sir Pet. And that person, I imagine, is Mr. Snake.—Rowley, you were perfectly right to bring him with us, and pray let him appear.

Row. Walk in, Mr. Snake.

Enter SNAKE.

I thought his testimony might be wanted: however, it happens unluckily, that he comes to confront Lady Sneerwell, not to support her.

Lady Sneer. A villain! Treacherous to me at last! Speak, fellow, have you too conspired against me!

Snake. I beg your ladyship ten thousand pardons: you paid me extremely liberally for the lie in question; but I unfortunately have been offered double to speak the truth.

Sir Pet. Plot and counter-plot, egad! I wish your ladyship joy of your negotiation.

Lady Sneer. The torments of shame and disappointment on you all!   [*Going.*

Lady Teaz. Hold, Lady Sneerwell—before you go, let me thank you for the trouble you and that gentleman have taken, in writing letters from me to Charles, and answering them yourself; and let me also request you to make my respects to the scandalous college, of which you are president, and inform them, that Lady Teazle, licentiate, begs leave to return the diploma they granted her, as she leaves off practice, and kills characters no longer.

Lady Sneer. You too, madam!—provoking — insolent! May your husband live these fifty years!   [*Exit.*

Sir Pet. Oons! what a fury!

Lady Teaz. A malicious creature, indeed!

Sir Pet. What! not for her last wish?

Lady Teaz. Oh, no!

Sir Oliv. Well, sir, and what have you to say now?

Jos. Surf. Sir, I am so confounded, to find that Lady Sneerwell could be guilty of suborning Mr. Snake in this manner, to impose on us all, that I know not what to say! however, lest her revengeful spirit should prompt her to injure my brother, I had certainly better follow her directly. For the man who attempts to ——   [*Exit.*

Sir Pet. Moral to the last!

Sir Oliv. Ay, and marry her, Joseph, if you can. Oil and vinegar! — egad you'll do very well together.

Row. I believe we have no more occasion for Mr. Snake at present?

Snake. Before I go, I beg pardon once for all, for whatever uneasiness I have been the humble instrument of causing to the parties present.

Sir Pet. Well, well, you have made atonement by a good deed at last.

Snake. But I must request of the company, that it shall never be known.

Sir Pet. Hey! what the plague! are you ashamed of having done a right thing once in your life?

Snake. Ah, sir, consider—I live by the badness of my character; and, if it were once known that I had been betrayed into an honest action, I should lose every friend I have in the world.

Sir Oliv. Well, well—we'll not traduce you by saying any thing in your praise, never fear.   [*Exit* SNAKE.

Sir Pet. There's a precious rogue!

Lady Teaz. See, Sir Oliver, there needs no persuasion now to reconcile your nephew and Maria.

Sir Oliv. Ay, ay, that's as it should be, and, egad, we'll have the wedding to-morrow morning.

Chas. Surf. Thank you, dear uncle.

Sir Pet. What, you rogue! don't you ask the girl's consent first?

Chas. Surf. Oh, I have done that a long time — a minute ago — and she has looked yes.

Mar. For shame, Charles! — I protest, Sir Peter, there has not been a word ——

Sir Oliv. Well, then, the fewer the better; may your love for each other never know abatement.

Sir Pet. And may you live as happily together as Lady Teazle and I intend to do!

Chas. Surf. Rowley, my old friend, I am sure you congratulate me; and I suspect that I owe you much.

Sir Oliv. You do, indeed, Charles.

Sir Pet. Ay, honest Rowley always said you would reform.

Chas. Surf. Why, as to reforming, Sir Peter, I'll make no promises, and that I take to be a proof that I intend to set about it. But here shall be my monitor — my gentle guide. — Ah! can I leave the virtuous path those eyes illumine?

> Though thou, dear maid, shouldst waive thy beauty's sway,
> Thou still must rule, because I will obey:
> An humble fugitive from Folly view,
> No sanctuary near but Love and you: [*To the audience.*
> You can, indeed, each anxious fear remove,
> For even Scandal dies, if you approve.   [*Exeunt omnes.*

EPILOGUE.

BY MR. COLMAN.

SPOKEN BY LADY TEAZLE.

> I, WHO was late so volatile and gay,
> Like a trade-wind must now blow all one way,
> Bend all my cares, my studies, and my vows,
> To one dull rusty weathercock — my spouse!
> So wills our virtuous bard — the motley Bayes
> Of crying epilogues and laughing plays!
> Old bachelors, who marry smart young wives,
> Learn from our play to regulate your lives:
> Each bring his dear to town, all faults upon her —
> London will prove the very source of honour.
> Plunged fairly in, like a cold bath it serves,
> When principles relax, to brace the nerves:
> Such is my case; and yet I must deplore
> That the gay dream of dissipation 's o'er.

And say, ye fair! was ever lively wife,
Born with a genius for the highest life,
Like me untimely blasted in her bloom,
Like me condemn'd to such a dismal doom?
Save money — when I just knew how to waste it!
Leave London — just as I began to taste it!
  Must I then watch the early crowing cock,
The melancholy ticking of a clock;
In a lone rustic hall for ever pounded,
With dogs, cats, rats, and squalling brats surrounded
With humble curate can I now retire,
(While good Sir Peter boozes with the squire,)
And at backgammon mortify my soul,
That pants for loo, or flutters at a vole?
Seven 's the main! Dear sound that must expire,
Lost at hot cockles round a Christmas fire;
The transient hour of fashion too soon spent,
Farewell the tranquil mind, farewell content!
Farewell the plumèd head, the cushion'd tête,
That takes the cushion from its proper seat!
That spirit-stirring drum! — card drums I mean,
Spadille — odd trick — pam — basto — king and queen!
And you, ye knockers, that, with brazen throat,
The welcome visitors' approach denote;
Farewell all quality of high renown,
Pride, pomp, and circumstance of glorious town!
Farewell! your revels I partake no more,
And Lady Teazle's occupation 's o'er!
All this I told our bard; he smiled, and said 'twas clear,
I ought to play deep tragedy next year.
Meanwhile he drew wise morals from his play,
And in these solemn periods stalk'd away: —
"Bless'd were the fair like you; her faults who stopp'd,
And closed her follies when the curtain dropp'd!
No more in vice or error to engage,
Or play the fool at large on life's great stage."

THE CRITIC;

OR,

A TRAGEDY REHEARSED.

A DRAMATIC PIECE IN THREE ACTS.

TO MRS. GREVILLE.

MADAM,—In requesting your permission to address the following pages to you, which, as they aim themselves to be critical, require every protection and allowance that approving taste or friendly prejudice can give them, I yet ventured to mention no other motive than the gratification of private friendship and esteem. Had I suggested a hope that your implied approbation would give a sanction to their defects, your particular reserve, and dislike to the reputation of critical taste, as well as of poetical talent, would have made you refuse the protection of your name to such a purpose. However, I am not so ungrateful as now to attempt to combat this disposition in you. I shall not here presume to argue that the present state of poetry claims and expects every assistance that taste and example can afford it; nor endeavour to prove that a fastidious concealment of the most elegant productions of judgment and fancy is an ill return for the possession of those endowments. Continue to deceive yourself in the idea that you are known only to be eminently admired and regarded for the valuable qualities that attach private friendships, and the graceful talents that adorn conversation. Enough of what you have written has stolen into full public notice to answer my purpose; and you will, perhaps, be the only person, conversant in elegant literature, who shall read this address and not perceive that by publishing your particular approbation (of the following drama, I have a more interested object than to boast the true respect and regard with which I have the honour to be, Madam, your very sincere and obedient humble servant,

R. B. SHERIDAN.

DRAMATIS PERSONÆ,

AS ORIGINALLY ACTED AT DRURY LANE THEATRE IN 1779.

SIR FRETFUL PLAGIARY	Mr. Parsons.	MR. HOPKINS.	Mr. Hopkins.
PUFF	Mr. King.	MRS. DANGLE	Mrs. Hopkins.
DANGLE	Mr. Dodd.	SIGNORE PASTICCIO RITORNELLO	Miss Field and the Miss Abrams.
SNEER	Mr. Palmer.		
SIGNOR PASTICCIO RITORNELLO	Mr. Delpini.		
INTERPRETER	Mr. Baddeley.	Scenemen, Musicians, and Servants.	
UNDER PROMPTER	Mr. Phillimore.		

CHARACTERS OF THE TRAGEDY.

Lord Burleigh . .	*Mr. Moody.*	Son	*Mr. Lamash.*
Governor of Til- } bury Fort . . }	*Mr. Wrighten.*	Constable . . .	*Mr. Fawcett.*
		Thames	*Mr. Gawdry.*
Earl of Leicester .	*Mr. Farren.*	Tilburina . . .	*Miss Pope.*
Sir Walter Raleigh	*Mr. Burton.*	Confidant . . .	*Mrs. Bradshaw.*
Sir Christopher } Hatton. . . . }	*Mr. Waldron.*	Justice's Lady . .	*Mrs. Johnston.*
		First Niece . . .	*Miss Collett.*
Master of the Horse	*Mr. Kenny.*	Second Niece . .	*Miss Kirby.*
Don Ferolo Whis- } kerandos . . . }	*Mr. Bannis- ter, jun.*	Knights, Guards, Constables, Senti-	
Beefeater . . .	*Mr. Wright.*	nels, Servants, Chorus, Rivers, At-	
Justice	*Mr. Packer.*	tendants, &c., &c.	

SCENE — London: *in* Dangle's *House during the First Act, and throughout the rest of the Play in* Drury Lane Theatre.

PROLOGUE,

BY THE HONOURABLE RICHARD FITZPATRICK.

The sister muses, whom these realms obey,
Who o'er the drama hold divided sway,
Sometimes, by evil counsellers, 'tis said,
Like earth-born potentates have been mislod.
In those gay days of wickedness and wit,
When Villiers criticised what Dryden writ,
The tragic queen, to please a tasteless crowd,
Had learn'd to bellow, rant, and roar so loud,
That frighten'd Nature, her best friend before,
The blustering beldam's company forswore;
Her comic sister, who had wit 'tis true,
With all her merits, had her failings too;
And would sometimes in mirthful moments use
A style too flippant for a well-bred muse;
Then female modesty abash'd began
To seek the friendly refuge of the fan,
A while behind that slight intrenchment stood,
Till driven from thence, she left the stage for good.
In our more pious, and far chaster times,
These sure no longer are the Muse's crimes!
But some complain that, former faults to shun,
The reformation to extremes has run.
The frantic hero's wild delirium past,
Now insipidity succeeds bombast;
So slow Melpomene's cold numbers creep,
Here dulness seems her drowsy court to keep.
And we are scarce awake, whilst you are fast asleep.

Thalia, once so ill-behaved and rude,
Reform'd, is now become an arrant prude;
Retailing nightly to the yawning pit
The purest morals, undefiled by wit!
Our author offers, in these motley scenes,
A slight remonstrance to the drama's queens:
Nor let the goddesses be over nice;
Free-spoken subjects give the best advice.
Although not quite a novice in his trade,
His cause to-night requires no common aid.
To this, a friendly, just, and powerful court,
I come ambassador to beg support.
Can he undaunted brave the critic's rage?
In civil broils with brother bards engage?
Hold forth their errors to the public eye,
Nay more, e'en newspapers themselves defy?
Say, must his single arm encounter all?
By numbers vanquish'd, e'en the brave may fall;
And though no leader should success distrust,
Whose troops are willing, and whose cause is just;
To bid such hosts of angry foes defiance,
His chief dependence must be, your alliance.

ACT I.

Scene I. — *A Room in* Dangle's *House.*

Mr. and Mrs. Dangle *discovered at breakfast, and reading newspapers.*

Dang. [Reading.] *Brutus to Lord North. — Letter the second on the State of the Army* — Psha! *To the first L dash D of the A dash Y. — Genuine extract of a Letter from St. Kitt's. — Coxheath Intelligence. — It is now confidently asserted that Sir Charles Hardy* — Psha! nothing but about the fleet and the nation! — and I hate all politics but theatrical politics. — Where's the Morning Chronicle?

Mrs. Dang. Yes, that's your Gazette.

Dang. So, here we have it. — [Reads.] *Theatrical intelligence extraordinary. — We hear there is a new tragedy in rehearsal at Drury Lane Theatre, called the Spanish Armada, said to be written by Mr. Puff, a gentleman well known in the theatrical world. If we may allow ourselves to give credit to the report of the performers, who, truth to say, are in general but indifferent judges, this piece abounds with the most striking and received beauties of modern composition.* — So! I am very glad my friend Puff's tragedy is in such forwardness. — Mrs. Dangle, my dear, you will be very glad to hear that Puff's tragedy ——

Mrs. Dang. Lord, Mr. Dangle, why will you plague me about such nonsense? — Now the plays are begun I shall have no peace. — Isn't it sufficient to make yourself ridiculous by your passion for the theatre, without continually teasing me to join you? Why can't you ride your hobby-horse without desiring to place me on a pillion behind you, Mr. Dangle?

Dang. Nay, my dear, I was only going to read ——

Mrs. Dang. No, no; you will never read anything that's worth listening to. You hate to hear about your country; there are letters every day with Roman signatures, demonstrating the certainty of an invasion, and proving that the nation is utterly undone. But you never will read any thing to entertain one.

Dang. What has a woman to do with politics, Mrs. Dangle?

Mrs. Dang. And what have you to do with the theatre, Mr. Dangle? Why should you affect the character of a critic? I have no patience with you! — haven't you made yourself the jest of all your acquaintance by your interference in matters where you have no business? Are you not called a theatrical Quidnunc, and a mock Mæcenas to second-hand authors?

Dang. True; my power with the managers is pretty notorious. But is it no credit to have applications from all quarters for my interest — from lords to recommend fiddlers, from ladies to get boxes, from authors to get answers, and from actors to get engagements?

Mrs. Dang. Yes, truly; you have contrived to get a share in all the plague and trouble of theatrical property, without the profit, or even the credit of the abuse that attends it.

Dang. I am sure, Mrs. Dangle, you are no loser by it, however; you have all the advantages of it. Mightn't you, last winter, have had the reading of the new pantomime a fortnight previous to its performance? And doesn't Mr. Fosbrook let you take places for a play before it is advertised, and set you down for a box for every new piece through the season? And didn't my friend, Mr. Smatter, dedicate his last farce to you at my particular request, Mrs. Dangle?

Mrs. Dang. Yes; but wasn't the farce damned, Mr. Dangle? And to be sure it is extremely pleasant to have one's house made the motley rendezvous of all the lackeys of literature; the very high 'Change of trading authors and jobbing critics? — Yes, my drawing-room is an absolute register office for candidate actors, and poets without character. — Then to be continually alarmed with misses and ma'ams piping hysteric changes on Juliets and Dorindas, Pollys, and Ophelias; and the very furniture trembling at the probationary starts and unprovoked rants of would-be Richards and Hamlets!—And what is worse than all, now that the manager has monopolized the Opera House, haven't we the signors and signoras calling here, sliding their smooth semibreves, and gargling glib divisions in their outlandish throats — with foreign emissaries and French spies, for aught I know, disguised like fiddlers and figure-dancers?

Dang. Mercy! Mrs. Dangle

Mrs. Dang. And to employ yourself so idly at such an alarming crisis as this too—when, if you had the least spirit, you would have been at the head of one of the Westminster associations — or trailing a volunteer pike in the Artillery Ground! But you—o' my conscience, I believe, if the French were landed to-morrow, your first inquiry would be, whether they had brought a theatrical troop with them.

Dang. Mrs. Dangle, it does not signify—I say the stage is *the Mirror of Nature,* and the actors are *the Abstract and brief Chronicles of the Time:* and pray what can a man of sense study better?—Besides, you will not easily persuade me that there is no credit or importance in being at the head of a band of critics, who take upon them to decide for the whole town,

whose opinion and patronage all writers solicit, and whose recommendation no manager dares refuse.

Mrs. Dang. Ridiculous! — Both managers and authors of
the least merit laugh at your pretensions. — The public is their
critic — without whose fair approbation they know no play
can rest on the stage, and with whose applause they welcome
such attacks as yours, and laugh at the malice of them, where
they can't at the wit.

Dang. Very well, madam — very well!

Enter SERVANT.

Ser. Mr. Sneer, sir, to wait on you.

Dang. Oh, show Mr. Sneer up. — [*Exit* SERVANT.] Plague
on't, now we must appear loving and affectionate, or Sneer
will hitch us into a story.

Mrs. Dang. With all my heart; you can't be more ridiculous than you are.

Dang. You are enough to provoke ——

Enter SNEER.

Ha! my dear Sneer, I am vastly glad to see you. — My dear,
here's Mr. Sneer.

Mrs. Dang. Good morning to you, sir.

Dang. Mrs. Dangle and I have been diverting ourselves
with the papers. Pray, Sneer, won't you go to Drury Lane
Theatre the first night of Puff's tragedy?

Sneer. Yes; but I suppose one shan't be able to get in, for
on the first night of a new piece they always fill the house
with orders to support it. But here, Dangle, I have brought
you two pieces, one of which you must exert yourself to make
the managers accept, I can tell you that; for 'tis written by a
person of consequence.

Dang. So! now my plagues are beginning.

Sneer. Ay, I am glad of it, for now you'll be happy. Why,
my dear Dangle, it is a pleasure to see how you enjoy your
volunteer fatigue, and your solicited solicitations.

Dang. It's a great trouble — yet, egad, it's pleasant too.
— Why, sometimes of a morning I have a dozen people call

on me at breakfast-time, whose faces I never saw before, nor ever desire to see again.

Sneer. That must be very pleasant indeed!

Dang. And not a week but I receive fifty letters, and not a line in them about any business of my own.

Sneer. An amusing correspondence!

Dang. [Reading.] *Bursts into tears, and exit.* — What, is this a tragedy?

Sneer. No, that's a genteel comedy, not a translation — only taken from the French: it is written in a style which they have lately tried to run down; the true sentimental, and nothing ridiculous in it from the beginning to the end.

Mrs. Dang. Well, if they had kept to that, I should not have been such an enemy to the stage; there was some edification to be got from those pieces, Mr. Sneer!

Sneer. I am quite of your opinion, Mrs. Dangle: the theatre, in proper hands, might certainly be made the school of morality; but now, I am sorry to say it, people seem to go there principally for their entertainment!

Mrs. Dang. It would have been more to the credit of the managers to have kept it in the other line.

Sneer. Undoubtedly, madam; and hereafter perhaps to have had it recorded, that in the midst of a luxurious and dissipated age, they preserved two houses in the capital, where the conversation was always moral at least, if not entertaining!

Dang. Now, egad, I think the worst alteration is in the nicety of the audience! — No *double-entendre*, no smart innuendo admitted; even Vanbrugh and Congreve obliged to undergo a bungling reformation!

Sneer. Yes, and our prudery in this respect is just on a par with the artificial bashfulness of a courtesan, who increases the blush upon her cheek in an exact proportion to the diminution of her modesty.

Dang. Sneer can't even give the public a good word! But what have we here? — This seems a very odd——

Sneer. Oh, that's a comedy, on a very new plan; replete

with wit and mirth, yet of a most serious moral! You see it
is called *The Reformed House-breaker;* where, by the mere
force of humour, house-breaking is put into so ridiculous a
light, that if the piece has its proper run, I have no doubt
but that bolts and bars will be entirely useless by the end of
the season.

Dang. Egad, this is new indeed!

Sneer. Yes; it is written by a particular friend of mine,
who has discovered that the follies and foibles of society are
subjects unworthy the notice of the comic muse, who should
be taught to stoop only at the greater vices and blacker
crimes of humanity — gibbeting capital offences in five acts,
and pillorying petty larcenies in two. — In short, his idea is
to dramatise the penal laws, and make the stage a court of
ease to the Old Bailey.

Dang. It is truly moral.

Re-enter SERVANT.

Ser. Sir Fretful Plagiary, sir.

Dang. Beg him to walk up.—[*Exit* SERVANT.] Now, Mrs.
Dangle, Sir Fretful Plagiary is an author to your own taste.

Mrs. Dang. I confess he is a favourite of mine, because
everybody else abuses him.

Sneer. Very much to the credit of your charity, madam,
if not of your judgment.

Dang. But, egad, he allows no merit to any author but
himself, that's the truth on't — though he's my friend.

Sneer. Never. — He is as envious as an old maid verging
on the desperation of six-and-thirty; and then the insidious
humility with which he seduces you to give a free opinion on
any of his works, can be exceeded only by the petulant ar-
rogance with which he is sure to reject your observations.

Dang. Very true, egad — though he's my friend.

Sneer. Then his affected contempt of all newspaper strictures; though, at the same time, he is the sorest man alive,
and shrinks like scorched parchment from the fiery ordeal of

true criticism: yet is he so covetous of popularity, that he had rather be abused than not mentioned at all.

Dang. There's no denying it — though he is my friend.

Sneer. You have read the tragedy he has just finished, haven't you?

Dang. O yes; he sent it to me yesterday.

Sneer. Well, and you think it execrable, don't you?

Dang. Why, between ourselves, egad, I must own — though he is my friend — that it is one of the most — He's here — [*Aside*] — finished and most admirable perform——

Sir Fret. [*Without.*] Mr. Sneer with him, did you say?

Enter SIR FRETFUL PLAGIARY.

Dang. Ah, my dear friend! — Egad, we were just speaking of your tragedy. — Admirable, Sir Fretful, admirable!

Sneer. You never did any thing beyond it, Sir Fretful — never in your life.

Sir Fret. You make me extremely happy; for without a compliment, my dear Sneer, there isn't a man in the world whose judgment I value as I do yours and Mr. Dangle's.

Mrs. Dang. They are only laughing at you, Sir Fretful; for it was but just now that——

Dang. Mrs. Dangle! — Ah, Sir Fretful, you know Mrs. Dangle. — My friend Sneer was rallying just now: — he knows how she admires you, and ——

Sir Fret. O Lord, I am sure Mr. Sneer has more taste and sincerity than to — [*Aside*] A damned double-faced fellow!

Dang. Yes, yes — Sneer will jest — but a better humoured ——

Sir Fret. Oh, I know ——

Dang. He has a ready turn for ridicule — his wit costs him nothing.

Sir Fret. No, egad — or I should wonder how he came by it.   [*Aside.*

Mrs. Dang. Because his jest is always at the expense of his friend.   [*Aside.*

Dang. But, Sir Fretful, have you sent your play to the managers yet? — or can I be of any service to you?

Sir Fret. No, no, I thank you: I believe the piece had sufficient recommendation with it. — I thank you though. — I sent it to the manager of Covent Garden Theatre this morning.

Sneer. I should have thought now, that it might have been cast (as the actors call it) better at Drury Lane.

Sir Fret. O lud! no — never send a play there while I live — hark'ee!   [*Whispers* SNEER.

Sneer. Writes himself! — I know he does.

Sir Fret. I say nothing — I take away from no man's merit · -- am hurt at no man's good fortune — I say nothing. — But this I will say — through all my knowledge of life, I have observed — that there is not a passion so strongly rooted in the human heart as envy.

Sneer. I believe you have reason for what you say, indeed.

Sir Fret. Besides — I can tell you it is not always so safe to leave a play in the hands of those who write themselves.

Sneer. What, they may steal from them, hey, my dear Plagiary?

Sir Fret. Steal! — to be sure they may; and, egad, serve your best thoughts as gypsies do stolen children, disfigure them to make 'em pass for their own.

Sneer. But your present work is a sacrifice to Melpomene, and he, you know, never ——

Sir Fret. That's no security: a dexterous plagiarist may do any thing. Why, sir, for aught I know, he might take out some of the best things in my tragedy, and put them into his own comedy.

Sneer. That might be done, I dare be sworn.

Sir Fret. And then, if such a person gives you the least hint or assistance, he is devilish apt to take the merit of the whole ——

Dang. If it succeeds.

Sir Fret. Ay, but with regard to this piece, I think I can hit that gentleman, for I can safely swear he never read it.

Sneer. I'll tell you how you may hurt him more.

Sir Fret. How?

Sneer. Swear he wrote it.

Sir Fret. Plague on't now, Sneer, I shall take it ill! — I believe you want to take away my character as an author.

Sneer. Then I am sure you ought to be very much obliged to me.

Sir Fret. Hey! — sir! ——

Dang. Oh, you know, he never means what he says.

Sir Fret. Sincerely then — you do like the piece?

Sneer. Wonderfully!

Sir Fret. But come now, there must be something that you think might be mended, hey? — Mr. Dangle, has nothing struck you?

Dang. Why, faith, it is but an ungracious thing, for the most part, to ——

Sir Fret. With most authors it is just so indeed; they are in general strangely tenacious! But, for my part, I am never so well pleased as when a judicious critic points out any defect to me; for what is the purpose of showing a work to a friend, if you don't mean to profit by his opinion?

Sneer. Very true. — Why then, though I seriously admire the piece upon the whole, yet there is one small objection; which, if you'll give me leave, I'll mention.

Sir Fret. Sir, you can't oblige me more.

Sneer. I think it wants incident.

Sir Fret. Good God! you surprise me! — wants incident!

Sneer. Yes; I own I think the incidents are too few.

Sir Fret. Good God! Believe me, Mr. Sneer, there is no person for whose judgment I have a more implicit deference. But I protest to you, Mr. Sneer, I am only apprehensive that the incidents are too crowded. — My dear Dangle, how does it strike you?

Dang. Really I can't agree with my friend Sneer. I think the plot quite sufficient; and the four first acts by many degrees the best I ever read or saw in my life. If I might venture to suggest any thing, it is that the interest rather falls off in the fifth.

Sir Fret. Rises, I believe you mean, sir.

Dang. No, I don't, upon my word.

Sir Fret. Yes, yes, you do, upon my soul! — it certainly don't fall off, I assure you. — No, no; it don't fall off.

Dang. Now, Mrs. Dangle, didn't you say it struck you in the same light?

Mrs. Dang. No, indeed, I did not — I did not see a fault in any part of the play, from the beginning to the end.

Sir Fret. Upon my soul, the women are the best judges after all!

Mrs. Dang. Or, if I made any objection, I am sure it was to nothing in the piece; but that I was afraid it was, on the whole, a little too long.

Sir Fret. Pray, madam, do you speak as to duration of time; or do you mean that the story is tediously spun out?

Mrs. Dang. O lud! no. — I speak only with reference to the usual length of acting plays.

Sir Fret. Then I am very happy — very happy indeed — because the play is a short play, a remarkably short play. I should not venture to differ with a lady on a point of taste; but, on these occasions, the watch, you know, is the critic.

Mrs. Dang. Then, I suppose, it must have been Mr. Dangle's drawling manner of reading it to me.

Sir Fret. Oh, if Mr. Dangle read it, that's quite another afiair! — But I assure you, Mrs. Dangle, the first evening you can spare me three hours and a half, I'll undertake to read you the whole from beginning to end, with the prologue and epilogue, and allow time for the music between the acts.

Mrs. Dang. I hope to see it on the stage next.

Dang. Well, Sir Fretful, I wish you may be able to get rid as easily of the newspaper criticisms as you do of ours.

Sir Fret. The newspapers! Sir, they are the most villanous — licentious — abominable — infernal — Not that I ever read them — no — I make it a rule never to look into a newspaper.

Dang. You are quite right; for it certainly must hurt an author of delicate feelings to see the liberties they take.

Sir Fret. No, quite the contrary! their abuse is, in fact, the best panegyric — I like it of all things. An author's reputation is only in danger from their support.

Sneer. Why that's true — and that attack, now, on you the other day ——

Sir Fret. What? where?

Dang. Ay, you mean in a paper of Thursday: it was completely ill-natured, to be sure.

Sir Fret. Oh, so much the better. — Ha! ha! ha! I wouldn't have it otherwise.

Dang. Certainly it is only to be laughed at; for ——

Sir. Fret. You don't happen to recollect what the fellow said, do you?

Sneer. Pray, Dangle, — Sir Fretful seems a little anxious ——

Sir Fret. O lud, — no! — anxious! — not I, — not the least. . – I — but one may as well hear, you know.

Dang. Sneer, do you recollect? — [*Aside to* Sneer.] Make out something.

Sneer. [*Aside to* Dangle.] I will. — [*Aloud.*] Yes, yes, I remember perfectly.

Sir Fret. Well, — and pray now — not that it signifies— what might the gentleman say?

Sneer. Why, he roundly asserts that you have not the slightest invention or original genius whatever; though you are the greatest traducer of all other authors living.

Sir Fret. Ha! ha! ha! — very good.

Sneer. That as to comedy, you have not one idea of your own, he believes, even in your common-place-book — where stray jokes and pilfered witticisms are kept with as much method as the ledger of the lost and stolen office.

Sir Fret. Ha! ha! ha! — very pleasant!

Sneer. Nay, that you are so unlucky as not to have the skill even to steal with taste: — but that you glean from the refuse of obscure volumes, where more judicious plagiarists have been before you; so that the body of your work is a composition of dregs and sediments — like a bad tavern's worst wine.

Sir Fret. Ha! ha!

Sneer. In your more serious efforts, he says, your bombast would be less intolerable, if the thoughts were ever suited to the expression; but the homeliness of the sentiment stares through the fantastic encumbrance of its fine language, like a clown in one of the new uniforms!

Sir Fret. Ha! ha!

Sneer. That your occasional tropes and flowers suit the general coarseness of your style, as tambour sprigs would a ground of linsey-woolsey; while your imitations of Shakspeare resemble the mimicry of Falstaff's page, and are about as near the standard of the original.

Sir Fret. Ha!

Sneer. In short, that even the finest passages you steal are of no service to you; for the poverty of your own language prevents their assimilating; so that they lie on the surface like lumps of marl on a barren moor, encumbering what it is not in their power to fertilise!

Sir Fret. [*After great agitation.*] Now, another person would be vexed at this.

Sneer. Oh! but I wouldn't have told you — only to divert you.

Sir Fret. I know it — I am diverted. — Ha! ha! ha! — not the least invention! — Ha! ha! ha! — very good — very good!

Sneer. Yes — no genius! ha! ha! ha!

Dang. A severe rogue! ha! ha! ha! But you are quite right, Sir Fretful, never to read such nonsense.

Sir Fret. To be sure — for if there is anything to one's praise, it is a foolish vanity to be gratified at it; and, if it is abuse, — why one is always sure to hear of it from one damned good-natured friend or another!

Enter SERVANT.

Ser. Sir, there is an Italian gentleman, with a French

interpreter, and three young ladies, and a dozen musicians, who say they are sent by Lady Rondeau and Mrs. Fugue.

Dang. Gadso! they come by appointment! — Dear Mrs. Dangle, do let them know I'll see them directly.

Mrs. Dang. You know, Mr. Dangle, I shan't understand a word they say.

Dang. But you hear there's an interpreter.

Mrs. Dang. Well, I'll try to endure their complaisance till you come.   [*Exit.*

Ser. And Mr. Puff, sir, has sent word that the last rehearsal is to be this morning, and that he'll call on you presently.

Dang. That's true — I shall certainly be at home. — [*Exit* SERVANT.] Now, Sir Fretful, if you have a mind to have justice done you in the way of answer, egad, Mr. Puff's your man.

Sir Fret. Psha! Sir, why should I wish to have it answered, when I tell you I am pleased at it?

Dang. True, I had forgot that. But I hope you are not fretted at what Mr. Sneer ——

Sir Fret. Zounds! no, Mr. Dangle; don't I tell you these things never fret me in the least?

Dang. Nay, I only thought ——

Sir Fret. And let me tell you, Mr. Dangle, 'tis damned affronting in you to suppose that I am hurt when I tell you I am not.

Sneer. But why so warm, Sir Fretful?

Sir Fret. Gad's life! Mr. Sneer, you are as absurd as Dangle: how often must I repeat it to you, that nothing can vex me but your supposing it possible for me to mind the damned nonsense you have been repeating to me! — and, let me tell you, if you continue to believe this, you must mean to insult me, gentlemen — and, then, your disrespect will affect me no more than the newspaper criticisms — and I shall treat it with exactly the same calm indifference and philosophic contempt — and so your servant.   [*Exit.*

Sneer. Ha! ha! ha! poor Sir Fretful! Now will he go and vent his philosophy in anonymous abuse of all modern critics and authors. — But, Dangle, you must get your friend Puff to take me to the rehearsal of his tragedy.

Dang. I'll answer for't, he'll thank you for desiring it. But come and help me to judge of this musical family: they are recommended by people of consequence, I assure you.

Sneer. I am at your disposal the whole morning; — but I thought you had been a decided critic in music as well as in literature.

Dang. So I am — but I have a bad ear. I' faith, Sneer, though, I am afraid we were a little too severe on Sir Fretful — though he is my friend.

Sneer. Why 'tis certain, that unnecessarily to mortify the vanity of any writer is a cruelty which mere dulness never can deserve; but where a base and personal malignity usurps the place of literary emulation, the aggressor deserves neither quarter nor pity.

Dang. That's true, egad! — though he's my friend!

Scene II. — *A Drawing-room in* Dangle's *House.*

Mrs. Dangle, Signor Pasticcio Ritornello, Signore Pasticcio Ritornello, Interpreter, *and* Musicians, *discovered.*

Interp. Je dis, madame, j'ai l'honneur to introduce et de vous demander votre protection pour le signor Pasticcio Ritornello et pour sa charmante famille.

Signor Past. Ah! vosignoria, noi vi preghiamo di favoritevi colla vostra protezione.

1 *Signora Past.* Vosignoria fatevi questi grazie.

2 *Signora Past.* Si, signora.

Interp. Madame — me interpret. — C'est à dire — in English — qu'ils vous prient de leur faire l'honneur ——

Mrs. Dang. I say again, gentleman, I don't understand a word you say.

Signor Past. Questo signore spiegherò ——

Interp. Oui — me interpret. — Nous avons les lettres de recommendation pour monsieur Dangle de ——

Mrs. Dang. Upon my word, sir, I don't understand you.

Signor Past. La contessa Rondeau è nostra padrona.

3 *Signora Past.* Si, padre, et miladi Fugue.

Interp. O! — me interpret. — Madame, ils disent — in English — Qu'ils ont l'honneur d'être protégés de ces dames. — You understand?

Mrs. Dang. No, sir, — no understand.

     Enter DANGLE *and* SNEER.

Interp. Ah, voici monsieur Dangle!

All Italians. Ah! signor Dangle!

Mrs. Dang. Mr. Dangle, here are two very civil gentlemen trying to make themselves understood, and I don't know which is the interpreter.

Dang. Eh, bien!

  [*The* INTERPRETER *and* SIGNOR PASTICCIO *here speak at the same time.*

Interp. Monsieur Dangle, le grand bruit de vos talens pour la critique, et de votre intérêt avec messieurs les directeurs à tous les théâtres ——

Signor Past. Vosignoria siete si famoso par la vostra conoscenza, e vostra interessa colla le direttore da ——

Dang. Egad, I think the interpreter is the hardest to be understood of the two!

Sneer. Why, I thought, Dangle, you had been an admirable linguist!

Dang. So I am, if they would not talk so damned fast.

Sneer. Well, I'll explain that — the less time we lose in hearing them the better — for that, I suppose, is what they are brought here for.

  [*Speaks to* SIGNOR PASTICCIO — *they sing trios, &c.,* DANGLE *beating out of time.* ·

    Enter SERVANT *and whispers* DANGLE.

Dang. Show him up. — [*Exit* SERVANT.] Bravo! admirable! bravissimo! admirablissimo! — Ah! Sneer! where will you find voices such as these in England?

Sneer. Not easily.

Dang. But Puff is coming. — Signor and little signoras

obligatissimo! — Sposa signora Danglena — Mrs. Dangle, shall I beg you to offer them some refreshments, and take their address in the next room.

[*Exit* MRS. DANGLE *with* SIGNOR PASTICCIO, SIGNORE PAS-TICCIO, MUSICIANS, *and* INTERPRETER, *ceremoniously.*

[*Re-enter* SERVANT.

Ser. Mr. Puff, sir.   [*Exit.*

Enter PUFF.

Dang. My dear Puff!

Puff. My dear Dangle, how is it with you?

Dang. Mr. Sneer, give me leave to introduce Mr. Puff to you.

Puff. Mr. Sneer is this? — Sir, he is a gentleman whom I have long panted for the honour of knowing — a gentleman whose critical talents and transcendent judgment — —

Sneer. Dear Sir — —

Dang. Nay, don't be modest, Sneer; my friend Puff only talks to you in the style of his profession.

Sneer. His profession!

Puff. Yes, sir; I make no secret of the trade I follow: among friends and brother authors, Dangle knows I love to be frank on the subject, and to advertise myself *vivâ voce.* — I am, sir, a practitioner in panegyric, or, to speak more plainly, a professor of the art of puffing, at your service — or anybody else's.

Sneer. Sir, you are very obliging! — I believe, Mr. Puff, I have often admired your talents in the daily prints.

Puff. Yes, sir, I flatter myself I do as much business in that way as any six of the fraternity in town. — Devilish hard work all the summer, friend Dangle, — never worked harder! But, hark'ee, — the winter managers were a little sore, I believe.

Dang. No; I believe they took it all in good part.

Puff. Ay! then that must have been affectation in them; for, egad, there were some of the attacks which there was no laughing at!

Sneer. Ay, the humorous ones. — But I should think, Mr.
Puff, that authors would in general be able to do this sort of
work for themselves.

Puff. Why, yes — but in a clumsy way. Besides, we
look on that as an encroachment, and so take the opposite
side. I dare say, now, you conceive half the very civil paragraphs and advertisements you see to be written by the parties
concerned, or their friends? No such thing: nine out of ten
manufactured by me in the way of business.

Sneer. Indeed!

Puff. Even the auctioneers now — the auctioneers, I say
— though the rogues have lately got some credit for their
language — not an article of the merit theirs: take them out
of their pulpits, and they are as dull as catalogues! — No,
sir; 'twas I first enriched their style — 'twas I first taught
them to crowd their advertisements with panegyrical super-
latives, each epithet rising above the other, like the bidders
in their own auction-rooms! From me they learned to inlay
their phraseology with variegated chips of exotic metaphor:
by me too their inventive faculties were called forth: — yes,
sir, by me they were instructed to clothe ideal walls with
gratuitous fruits — to insinuate obsequious rivulets into
visionary groves — to teach courteous shrubs to nod their
approbation of the grateful soil; or on emergencies to raise
upstart oaks, where there never had been an acorn; to create
a delightful vicinage without the assistance of a neighbour;
or fix the temple of Hygeia in the fens of Lincolnshire!

Dang. I am sure you have done them infinite service; for
now, when a gentleman is ruined, he parts with his house
with some credit.

Sneer. Service! if they had any gratitude, they would
erect a statue to him; they would figure him as a presiding
Mercury, the god of traffic and fiction, with a hammer in his
hand instead of a caduceus. — But pray, Mr. Puff, what first
put you on exercising your talents in this way?

Puff. Egad, sir, sheer necessity! — the proper parent of
an art so nearly allied to invention. You must know, Mr.

Sneer, that from the first time I tried my hand at an advertisement, my success was such, that for some time after I led a most extraordinary life indeed!

Sneer. How, pray.

Puff. Sir, I supported myself two years entirely by my misfortunes.

Sneer. By your misfortunes!

Puff. Yes, sir, assisted by long sickness, and other occasional disorders; and a very comfortable living I had of it.

Sneer. From sickness and misfortunes! You practised as a doctor and an attorney at once?

Puff. No, egad; both maladies and miseries were my own.

Sneer. Hey! what the plague!

Dang. 'Tis true, i' faith.

Puff. Hark'ee! — By advertisements — *To the charitable and humane!* and *To those whom Providence hath blessed with affluence!*

Sneer. Oh, I understand you.

Puff. And, in truth, I deserved what I got; for I suppose never man went through such a series of calamities in the same space of time. Sir, I was five times made a bankrupt, and reduced from a state of affluence, by a train of unavoidable misfortunes: then, sir, though a very industrious tradesman, I was twice burned out, and lost my little all both times: I lived upon those fires a month. I soon after was confined by a most excruciating disorder, and lost the use of my limbs: that told very well; for I had the case strongly attested, and went about to collect the subscriptions myself.

Dang. Egad, I believe that was when you first called on me.

Puff. In November last? — O no; I was at that time a close prisoner in the Marshalsea, for a debt benevolently contracted to serve a friend. I was afterwards twice tapped for a dropsy, which declined into a very profitable consumption. I was then reduced to — O no — then, I became a widow with six helpless children, after having had eleven husbands

pressed, and being left every time eight months gone with
child, and without money to get me into an hospital!

Sneer. And you bore all with patience, I make no doubt?

Puff. Why, yes; though I made some occasional attempts
at *felo de se;* but as I did not find those rash actions answer,
I left off killing myself very soon. Well, sir, at last, what
with bankruptcies, fires, gouts, dropsies, imprisonments, and
other valuable calamities, having got together a pretty handsome sum, I determined to quit a business which had always
gone rather against my conscience, and in a more liberal
way still to indulge my talents for fiction and embellishments,
through my favourite channels of diurnal communication —
and so, sir, you have my history.

Sneer. Most obligingly communicative indeed! and your
confession, if published, might certainly serve the cause of
true charity, by rescuing the most useful channels of appeal
to benevolence from the cant of imposition. But surely, Mr.
Puff, there is no great mystery in your present profession?

Puff. Mystery, sir! I will take upon me to say the matter
was never scientifically treated nor reduced to rule before.

Sneer. Reduced to rule!

Puff. O lud, sir, you are very ignorant, I am afraid! —
Yes, sir, puffing is of various sorts; the principal are, the
puff direct, the puff preliminary, the puff collateral, the puff
collusive, and the puff oblique, or puff by implication. These
all assume, as circumstances require, the various forms of
Letter to the Editor, Occasional Anecdote, Impartial Critique,
Observation from Correspondent, or Advertisement from the
Party.

Sneer. The puff direct, I can conceive ——

Puff. O yes, that's simple enough! For instance,—a new
comedy or farce is to be produced at one of the theatres
(though by-the-by they don't bring out half what they ought
to do) — the author, suppose Mr. Smatter, or Mr. Dapper,
or any particular friend of mine — very well; the day before
it is to be performed, I write an account of the manner in
which it was received; I have the plot from the author, and

only add — "characters strongly drawn — highly coloured — hand of a master — fund of genuine humour — mine of invention — neat dialogue — Attic salt." Then for the performance — "Mr. Dodd was astonishingly great in the character of Sir Harry. That universal and judicious actor, Mr. Palmer, perhaps never appeared to more advantage than in the colonel;—but it is not in the power of language to do justice to Mr. King: indeed he more than merited those repeated bursts of applause which he drew from a most brilliant and judicious audience. As to the scenery — the miraculous powers of Mr. De Loutherbourg's pencil are universally acknowledged. In short, we are at a loss which to admire most, the unrivalled genius of the author, the great attention and liberality of the managers, the wonderful abilities of the painter, or the incredible exertions of all the performers."

Sneer. That's pretty well indeed, sir.

Puff. Oh, cool! — quite cool! — to what I sometimes do.

Sneer. And do you think there are any who are influenced by this?

Puff. O lud, yes, sir! the number of those who undergo the fatigue of judging for themselves is very small indeed.

Sneer. Well, sir, the puff preliminary?

Puff. O, that, sir, does well in the form of a caution. In a matter of gallantry now — Sir Flimsy Gossamer wishes to be well with Lady Fanny Fete — he applies to me — I open trenches for him with a paragraph in the Morning Post. — "It is recommended to the beautiful and accomplished Lady F four stars F dash E to be on her guard against that dangerous character, Sir F dash G; who, however pleasing and insinuating his manners may be, is certainly not remarkable for the *constancy of his attachments!*" — in italics. Here, you see, Sir Flimsy Gossamer is introduced to the particular notice of Lady Fanny, who perhaps never thought of him before — she finds herself publicly cautioned to avoid him, which naturally makes her desirous of seeing him; the observation of their acquaintance causes a pretty kind of mutual embarrassment; this produces a sort of sympathy of interest,

which if Sir Flimsy is unable to improve effectually, he at least
gains the credit of having their names mentioned together,
by a particular set, and in a particular way—which nine times
out of ten is the full accomplishment of modern gallantry.

Dang. Egad, Sneer, you will be quite an adept in the
business!

Puff. Now, sir, the puff collateral is much used as an
appendage to advertisements, and may take the form of anecdote. — "Yesterday, as the celebrated George Bonmot was
sauntering down St. James's Street, he met the lively Lady
Mary Myrtle coming out of the park: — 'Good God, Lady
Mary, I'm surprised to meet you in a white jacket, — for I
expected never to have seen you, but in a full-trimmed uniform
and a light horseman's cap!' — 'Heavens, George, where
could you have learned that?' — 'Why,' replied the wit, 'I
just saw a print of you, in a new publication called the
Camp Magazine; which, by the by, is a devilish clever thing,
and is sold at No. 3, on the right hand of the way, two doors
from the printing-office, the corner of Ivy Lane, Paternoster
Row, price only one shilling.'"

Sneer. Very ingenious indeed!

Puff. But the puff collusive is the newest of any; for it
acts in the disguise of determined hostility. It is much used
by bold booksellers and enterprising poets.— "An indignant
correspondent observes, that the new poem called *Beelzebub's
Cotillon,* or *Proserpine's Fête Champêtre,* is one of the most
unjustifiable performances he ever read. The severity with
which certain characters are handled is quite shocking: and
as there are many descriptions in it too warmly coloured for
female delicacy, the shameful avidity with which this piece is
bought by all people of fashion is a reproach on the taste of
the times, and a disgrace to the delicacy of the age." Here
you see the two strongest inducements are held forth; first,
that nobody ought to read it; and secondly, that everybody
buys it: on the strength of which the publisher boldly prints
the tenth edition, before he had sold ten of the first; and

then establishes it by threatening himself with the pillory, or absolutely indicting himself for *scan. mag.*

Dang. Ha! ha! ha; — 'gad, I know it is so.

Puff. As to the puff oblique, or puff by implication, it is too various and extensive to be illustrated by an instance: it attracts in titles and presumes in patents; it lurks in the limitation of a subscription, and invites in the assurance of crowd and incommodation at public places; it delights to draw forth concealed merit, with a most disinterested assiduity; and sometimes wears a countenance of smiling censure and tender reproach. It has a wonderful memory for parliamentary debates, and will often give the whole speech of a favoured member with the most flattering accuracy. But, above all, it is a great dealer in reports and suppositions. It has the earliest intelligence of intended preferments that will reflect honour on the patrons; and embryo promotions of modest gentlemen, who know nothing of the matter themselves. It can hint a ribbon for implied services in the air of a common report; and with the carelessness of a casual paragraph, suggest officers into commands, to which they have no pretension but their wishes. This, sir, is the last principal class of the art of puffing — an art which I hope you will now agree with me is of the highest dignity, yielding a tablature of benevolence and public spirit; befriending equally trade, gallantry, criticism, and politics: the applause of genius — the register of charity — the triumph of heroism — the self-defence of contractors — the fame of orators — and the gazette of ministers.

Sneer. Sir, I am completely a convert both to the importance and ingenuity of your profession; and now, sir, there is but one thing which can possibly increase my respect for you, and that is, your permitting me to be present this morning at the rehearsal of your new trage——

Puff. Hush, for heaven's sake! — *My* tragedy! — Egad, Dangle, I take this very ill: you know how apprehensive I am of being known to be the author.

Dang. I' faith I would not have told — but it's in the papers, and your name at length in the Morning Chronicle.

Puff. Ah! those damned editors never can keep a secret!
— Well, Mr. Sneer, no doubt you will do me great honour —
I shall be infinitely happy — highly flattered ——

Dang. I believe it must be near the time — shall we go
together?

Puff. No; it will not be yet this hour, for they are always
late at that theatre: besides, I must meet you there, for I
have some little matters here to send to the papers, and a few
paragraphs to scribble before I go. — [*Looking at memorandums.*] Here is *A conscientious Baker, on the subject of the
Army Bread;* and *A Detester of visible Brickwork, in favour
of the new-invented Stucco;* both in the style of Junius, and
promised for to-morrow. The Thames navigation too is at
a stand. Misomud or Anti-shoal must go to work again directly. — Here too are some political memorandums — I see;
ay — *To take Paul Jones, and get the Indiamen out of the
Shannon — reinforce Byron — compel the Dutch to —* so! — I
must do that in the evening papers, or reserve it for the
Morning Herald; for I know that I have undertaken to-morrow, besides, to establish the unanimity of the fleet in the
Public Advertiser, and to shoot Charles Fox in the Morning
Post. — So, egad, I ha'n't a moment to lose!

Dang. Well, we'll meet in the Green Room.

[*Exeunt severally.*

ACT II.

SCENE I. — *The Theatre, before the Curtain.*

Enter DANGLE, PUFF, *and* SNEER.

Puff. No, no, sir; what Shakspeare says of actors may be
better applied to the purpose of plays; they ought to be *the
abstract and brief chronicles of the time.* Therefore when history, and particularly the history of our own country,
furnishes any thing like a case in point, to the time in which
an author writes, if he knows his own interest, he will take
advantage of it; so, sir, I call my tragedy *The Spanish Armada;* and have laid the scene before Tilbury Fort.

Sneer. A most happy thought, certainly!

Dang. Egad it was — I told you so. But pray now, I don't understand how you have contrived to introduce any love into it.

Puff. Love! oh, nothing so easy! for it is a received point among poets, that where history gives you a good heroic outline for a play, you may fill up with a little love at your own discretion: in doing which, nine times out of ten, you only make up a deficiency in the private history of the times. Now I rather think I have done this with some success.

Sneer. No scandal about Queen Elizabeth, I hope?

Puff. O lud! no, no; — I only suppose the governor of Tilbury Fort's daughter to be in love with the son of the Spanish admiral.

Sneer. Oh, is that all!

Dang. Excellent, i' faith! I see at once. But won't this appear rather improbable?

Puff. To be sure it will — but what the plague! a play is not to show occurrences that happen every day, but things just so strange, that though they never did, they might happen.

Sneer. Certainly nothing is unnatural, that is not physically impossible.

Puff. Very true — and for that matter Don Ferolo Whiskerandos, for that's the lover's name, might have been over here in the train of the Spanish Ambassador; or Tilburina, for that is the lady's name, might have been in love with him, from having heard his character, or seen his picture; or from knowing that he was the last man in the world she ought to be in love with — or for any other good female reason. — However, sir, the fact is, that though she is but a knight's daughter, egad! she is in love like any princess!

Dang. Poor young lady! I feel for her already! for I can conceive how great the conflict must be between her passion and her duty; her love for her country, and her love for Don Ferolo Whiskerandos!

Puff. Oh, amazing! — her poor susceptible heart is swayed to and fro by contending passions like ——

19*

Enter UNDER PROMPTER.

Und. Promp. Sir, the scene is set, and every thing is ready to begin, if you please.

Puff. Egad, then we'll lose no time.

Und. Promp. Though, I believe, sir, you will find it very short, for all the performers have profited by the kind permission you granted them.

Puff. Hey! what?

Und. Promp. You know, sir, you gave them leave to cut out or omit whatever they found heavy or unnecessary to the plot, and I must own they have taken very liberal advantage of your indulgence.

Puff. Well, well. — They are in general very good judges, and I know I am luxuriant. — Now, Mr. Hopkins, as soon as you please.

Und. Promp. [*To the* Orchestra.] Gentlemen, will you play a few bars of something, just to —

Puff. Ay, that's right; for as we have the scenes and dresses, egad, we'll go to 't, as if it was the first night's performance; but you need not mind stopping between the acts. — [*Exit* UNDER PROMPTER. — Orchestra *play — then the bell rings.*] So! stand clear, gentlemen. Now you know there will be a cry of Down! down! — Hats off! — Silence! — Then up curtain, and let us see what our painters have done for us.

[*Curtain rises.*

SCENE II. — *Tilbury Fort.*

"*Two* SENTINELS *discovered asleep.*"

Dang. Tilbury Fort! — very fine indeed!

Puff. Now, what do you think I open with?

Sneer. Faith, I can't guess ——

Puff. A clock. — Hark! — [*Clock strikes.*] I open with a clock striking, to beget an awful attention in the audience: it also marks the time, which is four o'clock in the morning, and saves a description of the rising sun, and a great deal about gilding the eastern hemisphere.

Dang. But pray, are the sentinels to be asleep?

Puff. Fast as watchmen.

Sneer. Isn't that odd though at such an alarming crisis?

Puff. To be sure it is, — but smaller things must give way to a striking scene at the opening; that's a rule. And the case is, that two great men are coming to this very spot to begin the piece: now, it is not to be supposed they would open their lips, if these fellows were watching them; so, egad, I must either have sent them off their posts, or set them asleep.

Sneer. Oh, that accounts for it. — But tell us, who are these coming?

Puff. These are they—Sir Walter Raleigh, and Sir Christopher Hatton. You'll know Sir Christopher by his turning out his toes — famous, you know, for his dancing. I like to preserve all the little traits of character. — Now attend.

"*Enter* Sir Walter Raleigh *and* Sir Christopher Hatton.
Sir Christ. True, gallant Raleigh!" —

Dang. What, they had been talking before?

Puff. O yes; all the way as they came along. — [*To the* Actors.] I beg pardon, gentlemen, but these are particular friends of mine, whose remarks may be of great service to us. — [*To* Sneer *and* Dangle.] Don't mind interrupting them whenever any thing strikes you.

"*Sir Christ.* True, gallant Raleigh!
But oh, thou champion of thy country's fame,
There is a question which I yet must ask:
A question which I never ask'd before —
What mean these mighty armaments?
This general muster? and this throng of chiefs?"

Sneer. Pray, Mr. Puff, how came Sir Christopher Hatton never to ask that question before?

Puff. What, before the play began? — how the plague could he?

Dang. That's true, i' faith!

Puff. But you will hear what he thinks of the matter.

"*Sir Christ.* Alas! my noble friend, when I behold
Yon tented plains in martial symmetry

> Array'd; when I count o'er yon glittering lines
> Of crested warriors, where the proud steeds neigh,
> And valour-breathing trumpet's shrill appeal,
> Responsive vibrate on my listening ear;
> When virgin majesty herself I view,
> Like her protecting Pallas, veil'd in steel,
> With graceful confidence exhort to arms!
> When, briefly, all I hear or see bears stamp
> Of martial vigilance and stern defence,
> I cannot but surmise — forgive, my friend,
> If the conjecture's rash — I cannot but
> Surmise the state some danger apprehends!"

Sneer. A very cautious conjecture that.

Puff. Yes, that's his character; not to give an opinion but on secure grounds. — Now then.

"*Sir Walt.* O most accomplish'd Christopher!" ——

Puff. He calls him by his christian name, to show that they are on the most familiar terms.

" *Sir Walt.* O most accomplish'd Christopher! I find
> Thy staunch sagacity still tracks the future,
> In the fresh print of the o'ertaken past."

Puff. Figurative!

" *Sir Walt.* Thy fears are just.

Sir Christ. But where? whence? when? and what
> The danger is, — methinks I fain would learn.

Sir Walt. You know, my friend, scarce two revolving suns,
> And three revolving moons, have closed their course,
> Since haughty Philip, in despite of peace,
> With hostile hand hath struck at England's trade.

Sir Christ. I know it well.

Sir Walt. Philip, you know, is proud Iberia's king!

Sir Christ. He is.

Sir Walt.   His subjects in base bigotry
> And Catholic oppression hold; — while we,
> You know, the Protestant persuasion hold.

Sir Christ. We do.

Sir Walt. You know, beside, his boasted armament,
> The famed Armada, by the Pope baptized,
> With purpose to invade these realms ——

Sir Christ.   Is sailed,
> Our last advices so report.

Sir Walt. While the Iberian admiral's chief hope,
> His darling son ——

Sir Christ.   Ferolo Whiskerandos hight —

Sir Walt.   The same — by chance a prisoner hath been ta'en,
                And in this fort of Tilbury ——

Sir Christ.   Is now
    Confined — 'tis true, and oft from yon tall turret's top
    I've mark'd the youthful Spaniard's haughty mien —
    Unconquer'd, though in chains.

Sir Walt.   You also know " ——

Dang. Mr. Puff, as he knows all this, why does Sir Walter go on telling him?

Puff. But the audience are not supposed to know any thing of the matter, are they?

Sneer. True; but I think you manage ill: for there certainly appears no reason why Sir Walter should be so communicative.

Puff. 'Fore Gad, now, that is one of the most ungrateful observations I ever heard! — for the less inducement he has to tell all this, the more, I think, you ought to be obliged to him; for I am sure you'd know nothing of the matter without it.

Dang. That's very true, upon my word.

Puff. But you will find he was not going on.

" *Sir Christ.* Enough, enough — 'tis plain — and I no more
            Am in amazement lost!" ——

Puff. Here, now you see, Sir Christopher did not in fact ask any one question for his own information.

Sneer. No, indeed: his has been a most disinterested curiosity!

Dang. Really, I find, we are very much obliged to them both.

Puff. To be sure you are. Now then for the commander-in-chief, the Earl of Leicester, who, you know, was no favourite but of the queen's. — We left off — *in amazement lost!*

" *Sir Christ.*   Am in amazement lost.
    But, see where noble Leicester comes! supreme
    In honours and command.

Sir Walt.   And yet, methinks,
    At such a time, so perilous, so fear'd,
    That staff might well become an abler grasp.

Sir Christ. And so, by Heaven! think I; but soft, he's here!"

Puff.   Ay, they envy him!

Sneer.   But who are these with him?

Puff.   Oh! very valiant knights: one is the governor of the fort, the other the master of the horse. And now, I think, you shall hear some better language: I was obliged to be plain and intelligible in the first scene, because there was so much matter of fact in it; but now, i' faith, you have trope, figure, and metaphor, as plenty as noun-substantives.

"*Enter* EARL OF LEICESTER, GOVERNOR, MASTER OF THE HORSE, KNIGHTS, &c.

Leic. ...   How's this, my friends! is't thus your new-fledged zeal
And plumèd valour moulds in roosted sloth?
Why dimly glimmers that heroic flame,
Whose reddening blaze, by patriot spirit fed,
Should be the beacon of a kindling realm?
Can the quick current of a patriot heart
Thus stagnate in a cold and weedy converse,
Or freeze in tideless inactivity?
No! rather let the fountain of your valour
Spring through each stream of enterprise,
Each petty channel of conducive daring,
Till the full torrent of your foaming wrath
O'erwhelm the flats of sunk hostility!"

Puff.   There it is — followed up!

"*Sir Walt.*   No more! — the freshening breath of thy rebuke
Hath fill'd the swelling canvas of our souls!
And thus, though fate should cut the cable of
                                             [*All take hands.*   •
Our topmost hopes, in friendship's closing line
We'll grapple with despair, and if we fall,
We'll fall in glory's wake!

Leic. ...   There spoke old England's genius!
Then, are we all resolved?

All. . . . .   We are — all resolved.

Leic. ...   To conquer — or be free?

All. . . . .   To conquer, or be free.

Leic. ...   All?

All. . . . .   All."

Dang.   *Nem. con.* egad!

Puff.   O yes! — where they do agree on the stage, their unanimity is wonderful!

"*Leic.* . . .   Then let's embrace — and now ——   [*Kneels.*"

Sneer. What the plague, is he going to pray?

Puff. Yes; hush! — in great emergencies, there is nothing like a prayer.

"*Leic.*. . . . O mighty Mars!"

Dang. But why should he pray to Mars?

Puff. Hush!

"*Leic.*. . . .   If in thy homage bred,
    Each point of discipline I've still observed;
    Nor but by due promotion, and the right
    Of service, to the rank of major-general
    Have risen; assist thy votary now!

Gov.	Yet do not rise — hear me!	[*Kneels.*
Mast. . . .	And me!	[*Kneels.*
Knight. . .	And me!	[*Kneels.*
Sir Walt. .	And me!	[*Kneels.*
Sir Christ.	And me!	[*Kneels.*"

Puff. Now pray altogether.

"*All.* . . . Behold thy votaries submissive beg,
    That thou wilt deign to grant them all they ask;
    Assist them to accomplish all their ends,
    And sanctify whatever means they use
    To gain them!".

Sneer. A very orthodox quintetto!

Puff. Vastly well, gentlemen! — Is that well managed or not? Have you such a prayer as that on the stage?

Sneer. Not exactly.

Leic. [*To* PUFF.] But, sir, you haven't settled how we are to get off here.

Puff. You could not go off kneeling, could you?

Sir Walt. [*To* PUFF.] O no, sir; impossible!

Puff. It would have a good effect, i' faith, if you could exeunt praying! — Yes, and would vary the established mode of springing off with a glance at the pit.

Sneer. Oh, never mind, so as you get them off! — I'll answer for it, the audience won't care how.

Puff. Well, then, repeat the last line standing, and go off the old way.

"*All.* . . . And sanctify whatever means we use
    To gain them.   [*Exeunt.*"

Dang. Bravo! a fine exit.

Sneer. Well, really, Mr. Puff——

Puff. Stay a moment!

                    " The SENTINELS *get up.*

1 *Sent.* . . All this shall to Lord Burleigh's ear.

2 *Sent.* . . 'Tis meet it should.   [*Exeunt.*"

Dang. Hey!— why, I thought those fellows had been asleep?

Puff. Only a pretence; there's the art of it: they were spies of Lord Burleigh's.

Sneer. But isn't it odd they never were taken notice of, not even by the commander-in-chief?

Puff. O lud, sir! if people, who want to listen or over-hear, were not always connived at in a tragedy, there would be no carrying on any plot in the world.

Dang. That's certain!

Puff. But take care, my dear Dangle! the morning-gun is going to fire.   [*Cannon fires.*

Dang Well, that will have a fine effect!

Puff. I think so, and helps to realise the scene. — [*Cannon twice.*] What the plague! three morning guns! there never is but one!—Ay, this is always the way at the theatre: give these fellows a good thing, and they never know when to have done with it. — You have no more cannon to fire?

Und. Promp. [*Within.*] No, sir.

Puff. Now, then, for soft music.

Sneer. Pray what's that for?

Puff. It shows that Tilburina is coming; — nothing introduces you a heroine like soft music. Here she comes!

Dang. And her confidant, I suppose?

Puff. To be sure! Here they are — inconsolable to the minuet in Ariadne!   [*Soft music.*

               "Enter TILBURINA *and* CONFIDANT.

Til. . . . . . Now has the whispering breath of gentle morn
            Bid Nature's voice and Nature's beauty rise;
            While orient Phœbus, with unborrow'd hues,
            Clothes the waked loveliness which all night slept
            In heavenly drapery! Darkness is fled.

> Now flowers unfold their beauties to the sun,
> And, blushing, kiss the beam he sends to wake them —
> The striped carnation, and the guarded rose,
> The vulgar wallflower, and smart gillyflower,
> The polyanthus mean — the dapper daisy,
> Sweet-william, and sweet marjoram — and all
> The tribe of single and of double pinks!
> Now, too, the feather'd warblers tune their notes
> Around, and charm the listening grove. The lark!
> The linnet! chaffinch! bullfinch! goldfinch! greenfinch!
> But O, to me no joy can they afford!
> Nor rose, nor wallflower, nor smart gillyflower,
> Nor polyanthus mean, nor dapper daisy,
> Nor William sweet, nor marjoram — nor lark,
> Linnet, nor all the finches of the grove!"

Puff. Your white handkerchief, madam! ——

Tilb. I thought, sir, I wasn't to use that till *heart-rending woe.*

Puff. O yes, madam, at *the finches of the grove*, if you please.

" *Tilb.* . . .   Nor lark,
> Linnet, nor all the finches of the grove!   [*Weeps.*"

Puff. Vastly well, madam!

Dang. Vastly well, indeed!

" *Tilb.* . . .   For, O, too sure, heart-rending woe is now
> The lot of wretched Tilburina!"

Dang. Oh! — 'tis too much!

Sneer. Oh! — it is indeed!

" *Con.* . .   .   Be comforted, sweet lady; for who knows,
> But Heaven has yet some milk-white day in store?

Tilb. . . . . .   Alas! my gentle Nora,
> Thy tender youth as yet hath never mourn'd
> Love's fatal dart. Else wouldst thou know, that when
> The soul is sunk in comfortless despair,
> It cannot taste of merriment."

Dang. That's certain!

" *Con.* . . . .   But see where your stern father comes:
> It is not meet that he should find you thus."

Puff. Hey, what the plague! — what a cut is here! Why, what is become of the description of her first meeting with Don Whiskerandos — his gallant behaviour in the sea fight — and the simile of the canary-bird?

Tilb. Indeed, sir, you'll find they will not be missed.

Puff. Very well, very well!

Tilb. [*To* Confidant.] The cue, ma'am, if you please.

"*Con.* . . . . It is not meet that he should find you thus.
Tilb. . . . . . Thou counsel'st right; but 'tis no easy task
                    For barefaced grief to wear a mask of joy.

Enter Governor.

Gov. . . . . How's this! — in tears? — O Tilburina, shame!
                    Is this a time for maudling tenderness,
                    And Cupid's baby woes? — Hast thou not heard
                    That haughty Spain's pope-consecrated fleet
                    Advances to our shores, while England's fate,
                    Like a clipp'd guinea, trembles in the scale?
Tilb. . . . . . Then is the crisis of my fate at hand!
                    I see the fleets approach — I see —— "

Puff. Now, pray, gentlemen, mind. This is one of the
most useful figures we tragedy writers have, by which a hero
or heroine, in consideration of their being often obliged to
overlook things that are on the stage, is allowed to hear and
see a number of things that are not.

Sneer. Yes; a kind of poetical second-sight!

Puff. Yes. — Now then, madam.

"*Tilb.* . . . .   I see their decks
                    Are clear'd! — I see the signal made!
                    The line is form'd! — a cable's length asunder! —
                    I see the frigates station'd in the rear;
                    And now, I hear the thunder of the guns!
                    I hear the victor's shouts! — I also hear
                    The vanquish'd groan! — and now 'tis smoke — and now
                    I see the loose sails shiver in the wind!
                    I see — I see — what soon you'll see —
Gov. . . . . . Hold, daughter! peace! this love hath turn'd thy brain:
                    The Spanish fleet thou canst not see — because
                    — It is not yet in sight!"

Dang. Egad, though, the governor seems to make no allowance for this poetical figure you talk of.

Puff. No, a plain matter-of-fact man;—that's his character.

"*Tilb.* . . . . But will you then refuse his offer?
Gov. . . . . . I must — I will — I can — I ought — I do.
Tilb. . . . . . Think what a noble price.
Gov. . . . . . No more — you urge in vain.
Tilb. . . . . . His liberty is all he asks."

Sneer. All who asks, Mr. Puff? Who is ——

Puff. Egad, sir, I can't tell! Here has been such cutting and slashing, I don't know where they have got to myself.

Tilb. Indeed, sir, you will find it will connect very well.

　　"— And your reward secure."

Puff. Oh, if they hadn't been so devilish free with their cutting here, you would have found that Don Whiskerandos has been tampering for his liberty, and has persuaded Tilburina to make this proposal to her father. And now, pray observe the conciseness with which the argument is conducted. Egad, the *pro* and *con* goes as smart as hits in a fencing-match. It is indeed a sort of small-sword logic, which we have borrowed from the French.

```
"Tilb.  . . A retreat in Spain!
Gov.. . . . Outlawry here!
Tilb.  . . . Your daughter's prayer?
Gov.. . . . Your father's oath.
Tilb.  . . . My lover!
Gov.. . . . My country!
Tilb.  . . . Tilburina!
Gov.. . . . England!
Tilb.  . . . A title!
Gov.. . . . Honour!
Tilb.  . . . A pension!
Gov.. . . . Conscience!
Tilb.  . . . A thousand pounds!
Gov.. . . . Ha! thou hast touch'd me nearly!"
```

Puff. There you see — she threw in *Tilburina*, Quick, parry quarte with *England!* — Ha! thrust in tierce *a title!* — parried by *honour.* Ha! *a pension* over the arm! — put by by *conscience.* Then flankonade with *a thousand pounds* — and a palpable hit, egad!

```
"Tilb.  . . Canst thou —
          Reject the suppliant, and the daughter too?
Gov.. . . .  No more; I would not hear thee plead in vain:
          The father softens — but the governor
          Is fix'd!                               [Exit."
```

Dang. Ay, that antithesis of persons is a most established figure.

" *Tilb.* . .   'Tis well, — hence then, fond hopes, — fond passion, hence;
                Duty, behold I am all over thine ——
Whisk. . .   [*Without.*] Where is my love — my ——
Tilb. . . . Ha!

Enter DON FEROLO WHISKERANDOS.

Whisk. . .   My beauteous enemy! ——"

Puff. O dear, ma'am, you must start a great deal more
than that! Consider, you had just determined in favour of
duty — when, in a moment, the sound of his voice revives
your passion — overthrows your resolution — destroys your
obedience. If you don't express all that in your start, you
do nothing at all.

Tilb. Well, we'll try again!

Dang. Speaking from within has always a fine effect.

Sneer. Very.

" *Whisk.* .   My conquering Tilburina! How! is't thus
                We meet? why are thy looks averse? what means
                That falling tear — that frown of boding woe?
                Ha! now indeed I am a prisoner!
                Yes, now I feel the galling weight of these
                Disgraceful chains — which, cruel Tilburina!
                Thy doating captive gloried in before. —
                But thou art false, and Whiskerandos is undone!
Tilb. . . . O no! how little dost thou know thy Tilburina!
Whisk. . .   Art thou then true? — Begone cares, doubts, and fears,
                I make you all a present to the winds;
                And if the winds reject you — try the waves."

Puff. The wind, you know, is the established receiver of
all stolen sighs, and cast-off griefs and apprehensions.

" *Tilb.* . . . Yet must we part! — stern duty seals our doom:
                Though here I call yon conscious clouds to witness,
                Could I pursue the bias of my soul,
                All friends, all right of parents, I'd disclaim,
                And thou, my Whiskerandos, shouldst be father
                And mother, brother, cousin, uncle, aunt,
                And friend to me!
Whisk. . .   Oh, matchless excellence! and must we part?
                Well, if — we must — we must — and in that case
                The less is said the better."

Puff. Heyday! here's a cut! — What, are all the mutual
protestations out?

Tilb. Now, pray, sir, don't interrupt us just here: you ruin our feelings.

Puff. Your feelings! — but zounds, my feelings, ma'am!

Sneer. No; pray don't interrupt them.

"*Whisk.* . One last embrace.
Tilb. . . . Now, — farewell, for ever.
Whisk. . . For ever!
Tilb. . . . Ay, for ever!   [*Going.*"

Puff. 'Sdeath and fury! — Gad's life! — sir! madam! if you go out without the parting look, you might as well dance out. Here, here!

Con. But pray, sir, how am I to get off here?

Puff. You! pshaw! what the devil signifies how you get off! edge away at the top, or where you will — [*Pushes the* CONFIDANT *off.*] Now, ma'am, you see ——

Tilb. We understand you, sir.

"Ay, for ever.
Both. . . . Oh! [*Turning back, and exeunt. — Scene closes.*"

Dang. Oh, charming!

Puff. Hey! — 'tis pretty well, I believe: you see I don't attempt to strike out any thing new — but I take it I improve on the established modes.

Sneer. You do, indeed! But pray is not Queen Elizabeth to appear?

Puff. No, not once — but she is to be talked of for ever; so that, egad, you'll think a hundred times that she is on the point of coming in.

Sneer. Hang it, I think it's a pity to keep her in the green-room all the night.

Puff. O no, that always has a fine effect — it keeps up expectation.

Dang. But are we not to have a battle?

Puff. Yes, yes, you will have a battle at last; but, egad, it's not to be by land, but by sea — and that is the only quite new thing in the piece.

Dang. What, Drake at the Armada, hey?

Puff. Yes, i'faith — fire-ships and all; then we shall end with the procession. Hey, that will do, I think?

Sneer. No doubt on't.

Puff. Come, we must not lose time; so now for the under-plot.

Sneer. What the plague, have you another plot?

Puff. O Lord, yes; ever while you live have two plots to your tragedy. The grand point in managing them is only to let your under-plot have as little connection with your main-plot as possible. — I flatter myself nothing can be more dis-tinct than mine; for as in my chief plot the characters are all great people, I have laid my under-plot in low life; and as the former is to end in deep distress, I make the other end as happy as a farce. — Now, Mr. Hopkins, as soon as you please.

Enter UNDER PROMPTER.

Und. Promp. Sir, the carpenter says it is impossible you can go to the park scene yet.

Puff. The park scene! no! I mean the description scene here, in the wood.

Und. Promp. Sir, the performers have cut it out.

Puff. Cut it out!

Under Promp. Yes, sir.

Puff. What! the whole account of Queen Elizabeth?

Under Promp. Yes, sir.

Puff. And the description of her horse and side-saddle?

Under Promp. Yes, sir.

Puff. So, so; this is very fine indeed! — Mr. Hopkins, how the plague could you suffer this?

Mr. Hop. [*Within.*] Sir, indeed the pruning-knife ——

Puff. The pruning-knife — zounds! — the axe! Why, here has been such lopping and topping, I shan't have the bare trunk of my play left presently! — Very well, sir — the performers must do as they please; but, upon my soul, I'll print it every word.

Sneer. That I would, indeed.

Puff. Very well, sir; then we must go on. — Zounds! I would not have parted with the description of the horse! — Well, sir, go on. — Sir, it was one of the finest and most laboured things. — Very well, sir; let them go on. — There you had him and his accoutrements, from the bit to the crupper. — Very well, sir; we must go to the park scene.

Under Promp. Sir, there is the point: the carpenters say, that unless there is some business put in here before the drop, they shan't have time to clear away the fort, or sink Gravesend and the river.

Puff. So! this is a pretty dilemma, truly! — Gentlemen, you must excuse me — these fellows will never be ready, unless I go and look after them myself.

Sneer. O dear, sir, these little things will happen.

Puff. To cut out this scene! — but I'll print it — egad, I'll print it every word!   [*Exeunt.*

ACT III.

SCENE I. — *The Theatre, before the Curtain.*

Enter PUFF, SNEER, *and* DANGLE.

Puff. Well, we are ready; now then for the justices.

[*Curtain rises.*

"JUSTICES, CONSTABLES, &c., *discovered.*"

Sneer. This, I suppose, is a sort of senate scene.

Puff. To be sure; there has not been one yet.

Dang. It is the under-plot, isn't it?

Puff. Yes. — What, gentlemen, do you mean to go at once to the discovery scene?

Just. If you please, sir.

Puff. Oh, very well! — Hark'ee, I don't choose to say any thing more; but, i' faith, they have mangled my play in a most shocking manner.

Dang. It's a great pity!

Puff. Now, then, Mr. Justice, if you please.

"*Just.* . . Are all the volunteers without?
Const.. . . .   They are.
Some ten in fetters, and some twenty drunk.
Just. . . . Attends the youth, whose most opprobrious fame
And clear convicted crimes have stamp'd him soldier?

Sheridan.   20

Const. . . .   He waits your pleasure; eager to repay
               The blest reprieve that sends him to the fields
               Of glory, there to raise his branded hand
               In honour's cause.
Just. . . .   'Tis well — 'tis justice arms him!
               Oh! may he now defend his country's laws
               With half the spirit he has broke them all!
               If 'tis your worship's pleasure, bid him enter.
Const. . . .   I fly, the herald of your will.   [*Exit.*"

     Puff.   Quick, sir.
     Sneer.   But, Mr. Puff, I think not only the Justice, but
the clown seems to talk in as high a style as the first hero
among them.
     Puff.   Heaven forbid they should not in a free country!—
Sir, I am not for making slavish distinctions, and giving all
the fine language to the upper sort of people.
     Dang.   That's very noble in you, indeed.

                    "*Enter* JUSTICE'S LADY."

     Puff.   Now, pray mark this scene.

"Lady. . .   Forgive this interruption, good my love;
               But as I just now pass'd a prisoner youth,
               Whom rude hands hither lead, strange bodings seized
               My fluttering heart, and to myself I said,
               An if our Tom had lived, he'd surely been
               This stripling's height!
Just. . . .   Ha! sure some powerful sympathy directs
               Us both ——

                    Re-enter CONSTABLE *with* SON.
                    What is thy name!
Son. . . . .   My name is Tom Jenkins — *alias* have I none —
               Though orphan'd, and without a friend!
Just. . . .   Thy parents?
Son. . . . .   My father dwelt in Rochester — and was,
               As I have heard — a fishmonger — no more."

     Puff.   What, sir, do you leave out the account of your
birth, parentage and education?
     Son.   They have settled it so, sir, here.
     Puff.   Oh! oh!
"Lady. . .   How loudly nature whispers to my heart!
               Had he no other name?
Son. . . . .   I've seen a bill
               Of his sign'd Tomkins, creditor.

Just. . . . This does indeed confirm each circumstance
      The gipsy told! — Prepare!
Son. . . . . .   I do.
Just. . . . No orphan, nor without a friend art thou —
      I am thy father; here's thy mother; there
      Thy uncle — this thy first cousin, and those
      Are all your near relations!
Lady. . . . O ecstacy of bliss!
Son. . . . . O most unlook'd for happiness!
Just. . . . O wonderful event! [*They faint alternately in each other's arms.*"

Puff. There, you see relationship, like murder, will out.

"*Just.* . . . Now let's revive — else were this joy too much!
      But come — and we'll unfold the rest within;
      And thou, my boy, must needs want rest and food.
      Hence may each orphan hope, as chance directs,
      To find a father — where he least expects!   [*Exeunt.*"

Puff. What do you think of that?

Dang. One of the finest discovery-scenes I ever saw! — Why, this under-plot would have made a tragedy itself.

Sneer. Ay, or a comedy either.

Puff. And keeps quite clear you see of the other.

"*Enter* SCENEMEN, *taking away the seats.*"

Puff. The scene remains, does it?

Sceneman. Yes, sir.

Puff. You are to leave one chair, you know. — But it is always awkward in a tragedy, to have you fellows coming in in your playhouse liveries to remove things. — I wish that could be managed better. — So now for my mysterious yeoman.

"*Enter* BEEFEATER.

Beef. . . . Perdition catch my soul, but I do love thee."

Sneer. Haven't I heard that line before?

Puff. No, I fancy not. — Where, pray?

Dang. Yes, I think there is something like it in Othello.

Puff. Gad! now you put me in mind on't, I believe there is — but that's of no consequence; all that can be said is, that two people happened to hit on the same thought — and Shakspeare made use of it first, that's all.

Sneer. Very true.

20*

Puff. Now, sir, your soliloquy — but speak more to the pit, if you please — the soliloquy always to the pit, that's a rule.

"*Beef.* . . . Though hopeless love finds comfort in despair,
    It never can endure a rival's bliss!
    But soft — I am observed.   [*Exit.*"

Dang. That's a very short soliloquy.

Puff. Yes — but it would have been a great deal longer if he had not been observed.

Sneer. A most sentimental Beefeater that, Mr. Puff!

Puff. Hark'ee — I would not have you be too sure that he is a Beefeater.

Sneer. What, a hero in disguise?

Puff. No matter — I only give you a hint. But now for my principal character. Here he comes — Lord Burleigh in person! Pray, gentlemen step this way — softly — I only hope the Lord High Treasurer is perfect — if he is but perfect!

"*Enter* LORD BURLEIGH, *goes slowly to a chair, and sits.*"

Sneer. Mr. Puff!

Puff. Hush! — Vastly well, sir! vastly well! a most interesting gravity!

Dang. What isn't he to speak at all?

Puff. Egad, I thought you'd ask me that! — Yes, it is a very likely thing — that a minister in his situation, with the whole affairs of the nation on his head, should have time to talk! — But hush! or you'll put him out.

Sneer. Put him out! how the plague can that be, if he's not going to say any thing!

Puff. There's the reason! why, his part is to think; and how the plague do you imagine he can think if you keep talking?

Dang. That's very true, upon my word!

"LORD BURLEIGH *comes forward, shakes his head, and exit.*"

Sneer. He is very perfect indeed! Now, pray what did he mean by that?

Puff. You don't take it?

Sneer. No, I don't, upon my soul.

Puff. Why, by that shake of the head, he gave you to understand that even though they had more justice in their cause, and wisdom in their measures — yet, if there was not a greater spirit shown on the part of the people, the country would at last fall a sacrifice to the hostile ambition of the Spanish monarchy.

Sneer. The devil! did he mean all that by shaking his head?

Puff. Every word of it — if he shook his head as I taught him.

Dang. Ah! there certainly is a vast deal to be done on the stage by dumb show and expression of face; and a judicious author knows how much he may trust to it.

Sneer. Oh, here are some of our old acquaintance.

"*Enter* SIR CHRISTOPHER HATTON *and* SIR WALTER RALEIGH.

Sir Christ. My niece and your niece too!
By Heaven! there's witchcraft in 't. — He could not else
Have gain'd their hearts. — But see where they approach:
Some horrid purpose lowering on their brows!

Sir Walt. Let us withdraw and mark them.   [*They withdraw.*"

Sneer. What is all this?

Puff. Ah! here has been more pruning! — but the fact is, these two young ladies are also in love with Don Whiskerandos. — Now, gentlemen, this scene goes entirely for what we call situation and stage effect, by which the greatest applause may be obtained, without the assistance of language, sentiment, or character: pray mark!

"*Enter the two* NIECES.

1st Niece. Ellena here!
She is his scorn as much as I — that is
Some comfort still!"

Puff. O dear, madam, you are not to say that to her face! — aside, ma'am, aside. — The whole scene is to be aside.

"*1st Niece.* She is his scorn as much as I — that is
Some comfort still!   [*Aside.*

2nd Niece. I know he prizes not Pollina's love;
But Tilburina lords it o'er his heart.   [*Aside.*

1st Niece. But see the proud destroyer of my peace.
Revenge is all the good I've left.   [*Aside.*

2nd Niece.   He comes, the false disturber of my quiet.
Now, vengeance do thy worst.   [*Aside.*

        Enter DON FEROLO WHISKERANDOS.

Whisk. . . . O hateful liberty — if thus in vain
I seek my Tilburina!
Both Nieces. . . And ever shalt!

    SIR CHRISTOPHER HATTON *and* SIR WALTER RALEIGH *come forward.*

Sir Christ. and Sir Walt. Hold! we will avenge you.
Whisk. . . Hold *you* — or see your nieces bleed!

       [*The two* NIECES *draw their two daggers to strike* WHISKER-
       ANDOS: *the two* UNCLES *at the instant, with their two
       swords drawn, catch their two* NIECES' *arms, and turn
       the points of their swords to* WHISKERANDOS, *who imme-
       diately draws two daggers, and holds them to the two
       * NIECES' *bosoms."*

   Puff.   There's situation for you! there's an heroic group!
— You see the ladies can't stab Whiskerandos — he durst
not strike them, for fear of their uncles — the uncles durst
not kill him, because of their nieces — I have them all at
a dead lock! — for every one of them is afraid to let go first.

   Sneer.   Why, then they must stand there for ever!

   Puff.   So they would, if I hadn't a very fine contrivance
for't. — Now mind ——

        "*Enter* BEEFEATER, *with his halberd.*

Beef. . . . In the queen's name I charge you all to drop
Your swords and daggers!

        [*They drop their swords and daggers."*

   Sneer.   That is a contrivance indeed!

   Puff.   Ay — in the queen's name.

"*Sir Christ.* Come, niece!
Sir Walter. Come, niece!   [*Exeunt with the two* NIECES.
Whisk. . . What's he, who bids us thus renounce our guard?
Beef. . . . Thou must do more — renounce thy love!
Whisk. . . Thou liest — base Beefeater!
Beef. . . .   Ha! hell! the lie!
By Heaven thou'st roused the lion in my heart!
Off, yeoman's habit! — base disguise! off! off!

       [*Discovers himself, by throwing off his upper dress, and ap-
       pearing in a very fine waistcoat.*

Am I a Beefeater now?
Or beams my crest as terrible as when
In Biscay's Bay I took thy captive sloop?"

Puff. There, egad! he comes out to be the very captain of the privateer who had taken Whiskerandos prisoner — and was himself an old lover of Tilburina's.

Dang. Admirably managed, indeed!

Puff. Now, stand out of their way.

"*Whisk* .. I thank thee, Fortune, that hast thus bestowed
        A weapon to chastise this insolent. [*Takes up one of the swords.*
Beef. ... I take thy challenge, Spaniard, and I thank thee,
        Fortune, too!   [*Takes up the other sword.*"

Dang. That's excellently contrived! — It seems as if the two uncles had left their swords on purpose for them.

Puff. No, egad, they could not help leaving them.

"*Whisk.*.. Vengeance and Tilburina!
Beef. ...   Exactly so ——

        [*They fight — and after the usual number of wounds given,*
        WHISKERANDOS *falls.*

Whisk. .. O cursèd parry! — that last thrust in tierce
        Was fatal. — Captain, thou hast fencèd well!
        And Whiskerandos quits this bustling scene
        For all eter ——
Beef. ...   —— nity — he would have added, but stern death
        Cut short his being, and the noun at once!"

Puff. Oh, my dear sir, you are too slow: now mind me. — Sir, shall I trouble you to die again?

"*Whisk.* . And Whiskerandos quits this bustling scene
        For all eter ——
Beef. ...   —— nity — he would have added. ——"

Puff. No, sir — that's not it — once more, if you please.

Whisk. I wish, sir, you would practise this without me — I can't stay dying here all night.

Puff. Very well; we'll go over it by-and-by. — [*Exit* WHISKERANDOS.] I must humour these gentlemen!

"*Beef.* .. Farewell, brave Spaniard! and when next"—

Puff. Dear sir, you needn't speak that speech, as the body has walked off.

Beef. That's true, sir — then I'll join the fleet.

Puff. If you please. — [*Exit* BEEFEATER.] Now, who comes on?

"Enter GOVERNOR, *with his hair properly disordered.*

Gov. . . . . A hemisphere of evil planets reign!
And every planet sheds contagious frenzy!
My Spanish prisoner is slain! my daughter,
Meeting the dead corse borne along, has gone
Distract!   [*A loud flourish of trumpets.*
          But hark! I am summon'd to the fort:
Perhaps the fleets have met! amazing crisis!
O Tilburina! from thy aged father's beard
Thou'st pluck'd the few brown hairs which time had left!
          [*Exit.*

Sneer. Poor gentleman!

Puff. Yes — and no one to blame but his daughter!

Dang. And the planets ——

Puff. True. — Now enter Tilburina!

Sneer. Egad, the business comes on quick here.

Puff. Yes, sir — now she comes in stark mad in white satin.

Sneer. Why in white satin?

Puff. O Lord, sir — when a heroine goes mad, she always goes into white satin. — Don't she, Dangle?

Dang. Always — it's a rule.

Puff. Yes — here it is — [*Looking at the book.*] "Enter Tilburina stark mad in white satin, and her confidant stark mad in white linen."

"Enter TILBURINA *and* CONFIDANT, *mad, according to custom."*

Sneer. But, what the deuce, is the confidant to be mad too?

Puff. To be sure she is: the confidant is always to do whatever her mistress does; weep when she weeps, smile when she smiles, go mad when she goes mad. — Now, madam confidant — but keep your madness in the back-ground, if you please.

"Tilb. . . The wind whistles — the moon rises — see
They have kill'd my squirrel in his cage!
Is this a grasshopper? — Ha! no; it is my
Whiskerandos — you shall not keep him —
I know you have him in your pocket —

> An oyster may be cross'd in love! — Who says
> A whale's a bird? — Ha! did you call, my love? —
> He's here! he's there! — He's everywhere!
> Ah me! he's nowhere! 　　　　　　　　　[*Exit.*"

Puff. There, do you ever desire to see any body madder than that?

Sneer. Never, while I live!

Puff. You observed how she mangled the metre?

Dang. Yes—egad, it was the first thing made me suspect she was out of her senses!

Sneer. And pray what becomes of her?

Puff. She is gone to throw herself into the sea, to be sure — and that brings us at once to the scene of action, and so to my catastrophe — my sea-fight, I mean.

Sneer. What, you bring that in at last?

Puff. Yes, yes — you know my play is called *The Spanish Armada;* otherwise, egad, I have no occasion for the battle at all.—Now then for my magnificence!—my battle!—my noise! — and my procession! — You are all ready?

Und. Promp. [*Within.*] Yes, sir.

Puff. Is the Thames dressed?

"*Enter* THAMES *with two* ATTENDANTS."

Thames. Here I am, sir.

Puff. Very well, indeed! — See, gentlemen, there's a river for you! — This is blending a little of the masque with my tragedy — a new fancy, you know — and very useful in my case; for as there must be a procession, I suppose Thames, and all his tributary rivers, to compliment Britannia with a fête in honour of the victory.

Sneer. But pray, who are these gentlemen in green with him?

Puff. Those? — those are his banks.

Sneer. His banks?

Puff. Yes, one crowned with alders, and the other with a villa!—you take the allusions?—But hey! what the plague! you have got both your banks on one side. — Here, sir, come round. — Ever while you live, Thames, go between your banks. — [*Bell rings.*]   There, so! now for't! — Stand aside, my dear friends! — Away, Thames!

> [*Exit* THAMES *between his banks.*
> [*Flourish of drums, trumpets, cannon, &c. &c.   Scene changes to the sea — the fleets engage — the music plays "Britons strike home." — Spanish fleet destroyed by fire-ships, &c. — English fleet advances — music plays "Rule Britannia." — The procession of all the English rivers, and their tribu taries, with their emblems, &c., begins with Handel's water music, ends with a chorus, to the march in Judas Macca- bæus. — During this scene,* PUFF *directs and applauds every thing — then*

Puff. Well, pretty well — but not quite perfect. — So, ladies and gentlemen, if you please, we'll rehearse this piece again to-morrow.   [*Curtain drops.*

A TRIP TO SCARBOROUGH.
A COMEDY.

DRAMATIS PERSONÆ.
AS ORIGINALLY ACTED AT DRURY-LANE THEATRE IN 1777.

Lord Foppington	*Mr. Dodd.*	Shoemaker	*Mr. Carpenter.*
Sir Tunbelly Clumsy	*Mr. Moody.*	Tailor	*Mr. Parker.*
Colonel Townly	*Mr. Brereton.*	Amanda	*Mrs. Robinson.*
Loveless	*Mr. Smith.*	Berinthia	*Miss Farren.*
Tom Fashion	*Mr. J. Palmer.*	Miss Hoyden	*Mrs. Abington.*
La Varole	*Mr. Burton.*	Mrs. Coupler	*Mrs. Booth.*
Lory	*Mr. Baddeley.*	Nurse	*Mrs. Bradshaw.*
Probe	*Mr. Parsons.*	Sempstress, Postilion, Maid, and	
Mendlegs	*Mr. Norris.*	Servants.	
Jeweller	*Mr. Lamash.*		

SCENE — Scarborough and its Neighbourhood.

PROLOGUE,
SPOKEN BY MR. KING.

WHAT various transformations we remark,
From east Whitechapel to the west Hyde Park!
Men, women, children, houses, signs, and fashions,
State, stage, trade, taste, the humours and the passions;
The Exchange, 'Change Alley, wheresoe'er you're ranging,
Court, city, country, all are changed or changing:
The streets, some time ago, were paved with stones,
Which, aided by a hackney-coach, half broke your bones.
The purest lovers then indulged in bliss;
They run great hazard if they stole a kiss.
One chaste salute! — the damsel cried — Oh, fie!
As they approach'd — slap went the coach awry —
Poor Sylvia got a bump, and Damon a black eye.
  But now weak nerves in hackney-coaches roam,
And the cramm'd glutton snores, unjolted, home:
Of former times, that polish'd thing a beau,
Is metamorphosed now from top to too;

Then the full flaxen wig, spread o'er the shoulders,
Conceal'd the shallow head from the beholders!
But now the whole's reversed — each fop appears,
Cropp'd and trimm'd up, exposing head and ears:
The buckle then its modest limits knew,
Now, like the ocean, dreadful to the view,
Hath broke its bounds, and swallows up the shoe;
The wearer's foot, like his once fine estate,
Is almost lost, the encumbrance is so great.
Ladies may smile — are they not in the plot?
The bounds of nature have not they forgot?
Were they design'd to be, when put together,
Made up, like shuttlecocks, of cork and feather?
Their pale-faced grandmammas appear'd with grace,
When dawning blushes rose upon the face;
No blushes now their once-loved station seek;
The foe is in possession of the cheek!
No heads of old, too high in feather'd state,
Hinder'd the fair to pass the lowest gate;
A church to enter now, they must be bent,
If ever they should try the experiment.
    As change thus circulates throughout the nation,
Some plays may justly call for alteration;
At least to draw some slender covering o'er
That *graceless wit** which was too bare before:
Those writers well and wisely use their pens,
Who turn our wantons into Magdalens;
And howsoever wicked wits revile 'em,
We hope to find in you their stage asylum.

ACT I.

Scene I. — *The Hall of an Inn.*

Enter Tom Fashion *and* Lory, Postilion *following with a portmanteau.*

Fash. Lory, pay the postboy, and take the portmanteau.

Lory. [*Aside to* Tom Fashion.] Faith, sir, we had better let the postboy take the portmanteau and pay himself.

Fash. [*Aside to* Lory.] Why, sure, there's something left in it!

Lory. Not a rag, upon my honour, sir! We eat the last

* "And *Van* wants grace, who never wanted wit." — Pope.

of your wardrobe at Newmalton — and, if we had had twenty miles further to go, our next meal must have been of the cloak-bag.

Fash. Why, 'sdeath, it appears full!

Lory. Yes, sir — I made bold to stuff it with hay, to save appearances, and look like baggage.

Fash. [*Aside.*] What the devil shall I do?—[*Aloud.*] Hark'ee, boy, what's the chaise?

Post. Thirteen shillings, please your honour.

Fash. Can you give me change for a guinea?

Post. Oh, yes, sir.

Lory. [*Aside.*] So, what will he do now? — [*Aloud.*] Lord, sir, you had better let the boy be paid below.

Fash. Why, as you say, Lory, I believe it will be as well.

Lory. Yes, yes; I'll tell them to discharge you below, honest friend.

Post. Please your honour, there are the turnpikes too.

Fash. Ay, ay, the turnpikes by all means.

Post. And I hope your honour will order me something for myself.

Fash. To be sure; bid them give you a crown.

Lory. Yes, yes — my master doesn't care what you charge them — so get along, you ——

Post. And there's the hostler, your honour.

Lory. Psha! damn the ostler! — would you impose upon the gentleman's generosity? — [*Pushes him out.*] A rascal, to be so cursed ready with his change!

Fash. Why, faith, Lory, he had nearly posed me.

Lory. Well, sir, we are arrived at Scarborough, not worth a guinea! I hope you'll own yourself a happy man — you have outlived all your cares.

Fash. How so, sir?

Lory. Why you have nothing left to take care of.

Fash. Yes, sirrah, I have myself and you to take care of still.

Lory. Sir, if you could prevail with somebody else to do that for you, I fancy we might both fare the better for it. But now, sir, for my Lord Foppington, your elder brother.

Fash. Damn my eldest brother!

Lory. With all my heart; but get him to redeem your annuity, however. Look you, sir, you must wheedle him, or you must starve.

Fash. Look you, sir, I will neither wheedle him nor starve.

Lory. Why, what will you do, then?

Fash. Cut his throat, or get some one to do it for me.

Lory. 'Gad so, sir, I'm glad to find I was not so well acquainted with the strength of your conscience as with the weakness of your purse.

Fash. Why, art thou so impenetrable a blockhead as to believe he'll help me with a farthing?

Lory. Not if you treat him *de haut en bas*, as you used to do.

Fash. Why, how wouldst have me treat him?

Lory. Like a trout — tickle him.

Fash. I can't flatter.

Lory. Can you starve?

Fash. Yes.

Lory. I can't — good by t'ye, sir.

Fash. Stay — thou'lt distract me. But who comes here? My old friend, Colonel Townly.

Enter COLONEL TOWNLY.

My dear Colonel, I am rejoiced to meet you here.

Col. Town. Dear Tom, this is an unexpected pleasure! What, are you come to Scarborough to be present at your brother's wedding?

Lory. Ah, sir, if it had been his funeral, we should have come with pleasure.

Col. Town. What, honest Lory, are you with your master still?

Lory. Yes, sir, I have been starving with him ever since I saw your honour last.

Fash. Why, Lory is an attached rogue—there's no getting rid of him.

Lory. True, sir, as my master says, there's no seducing me from his service. — [*Aside.*] Till he's able to pay me my wages.

Fash. Go, go, sir — and take care of the baggage.

Lory. Yes, sir — the baggage! — O Lord! [*Takes up the portmanteau.*] I suppose, sir, I must charge the landlord to be very particular where he stows this?

Fash. Get along, you rascal. — [*Exit* LORY, *with the portmanteau.*] But, Colonel, are you acquainted with my proposed sister-in-law?

Col. Town. Only by character — her father, Sir Tunbelly Clumsy, lives within a quarter of a mile of this place, in a lonely old house, which nobody comes near. She never goes abroad, nor sees company at home; to prevent all misfortunes, she has her breeding within doors; the parson of the parish teaches her to play upon the dulcimer, the clerk to sing, her nurse to dress, and her father to dance; — in short, nobody has free admission there but our old acquaintance, Mother Coupler, who has procured your brother this match, and is, I believe, a distant relation of Sir Tunbelly's.

Fash. But is her fortune so considerable?

Col. Town. Three thousand a year, and a good sum of money, independent of her father, beside.

Fash. 'Sdeath! that my old acquaintance, Dame Coupler, could not have thought of me, as well as my brother, for such a prize.

Col. Town. Egad, I wouldn't swear that you are too late — his lordship, I know, hasn't yet seen the lady — and, I believe, has quarrelled with his patroness.

Fash. My dear Colonel, what an idea have you started!

Col. Town. Pursue it, if you can, and I promise you you shall have my assistance; for, besides my natural contempt for his lordship, I have at present the enmity of a rival towards him.

Fash. What, has he been addressing your old flame, the widow Berinthia!

Col. Town. Faith, Tom, I am at present most whimsically circumstanced. I came here a month ago to meet the lady you mention; but she failing in her promise, I, partly from pique and partly from idleness, have been diverting my chagrin by offering up incense to the beauties of Amanda, our friend Loveless's wife.

Fash. I never have seen her, but have heard her spoken of as a youthful wonder of beauty and prudence.

Col. Town. She is so indeed; and, Loveless being too careless and insensible of the treasure he possesses, my lodging in the same house has given me a thousand opportunities of making my assiduities acceptable; so that, in less than a fortnight, I began to bear my disappointment from the widow with the most Christian resignation.

Fash. And Berinthia has never appeared?

Col. Town. Oh, there's the perplexity! for, just as I began not to care whether I ever saw her again or not, last night she arrived.

Fash. And instantly resumed her empire.

Col. Town. No, faith— we met — but, the lady not condescending to give me any serious reasons for having fooled me for a month, I left her in a huff.

Fash. Well, well, I'll answer for it she'll soon resume her power, especially as friendship will prevent your pursuing the other too far. — But my coxcomb of a brother is an admirer of Amanda's too, is he?

Col. Town. Yes, and I believe is most heartily despised by her. But come with me, and you shall see her and your old friend Loveless.

Fash. I must pay my respects to his lordship — perhaps you can direct me to his lodgings.

Col. Town. Come with me; I shall pass by it.

Fash. I wish you could pay this visit for me, or could tell me what I should say to him.

Col. Town. Say nothing to him — apply yourself to his bag, his sword, his feather, his snuff-box; and when you are well with them desire him to lend you a thousand pounds, and I'll engage you prosper.

Fash. 'Sdeath and furies! why was that coxcomb thrust

into the world before me? O Fortune, Fortune, thou art a jilt, by Gad! [*Exeunt.*

SCENE II. — LORD FOPPINGTON'S *Dressing-room.*

Enter LORD FOPPINGTON *in his nightgown, and* LA VAROLE.

Lord Fop. [*Aside.*] Well, 'tis an unspeakable pleasure to be a man of quality — strike me dumb! Even the boors of this northern spa have learned the respect due to a title. — [*Aloud.*] La Varole!

La Var. Milor ——

Lord Fop. You han't yet been at Muddymoat Hall, to announce my arrival, have you?

La Var. Not yet, milor.

Lord Fop. Then you need not go till Saturday — [*Exit* LA VAROLE] as I am in no particular haste to view my intended sposa. I shall sacrifice a day or two more to the pursuit of my friend Loveless's wife. Amanda is a charming creature — strike me ugly! and, if I have any discernment in the world, she thinks no less of my Lord Foppington.

Re-enter LA VAROLE.

La Var. Milor, de shoemaker, de tailor, de hosier, de sempstress, de peru, be all ready, if your lordship please to dress.

Lord Fop. 'Tis well; admit them.

La Var. Hey, messieurs, entrez!

Enter TAILOR, SHOEMAKER, SEMPSTRESS, JEWELLER, *and* MENDLEGS.

Lord Fop. So, gentlemen, I hope you have all taken pains to show yourselves masters in your professions!

Tai. I think I may presume, sir ——

La Var. Milor, you clown, you!

Tai. My lord — I ask your lordship's pardon, my lord. I hope, my lord, your lordship will be pleased to own I have brought your lordship as accomplished a suit of clothes as ever peer of England wore, my lord — will your lordship please to view 'em now?

Lord Fop. Ay; but let my people dispose the glasses so that I may see myself before and behind; for I love to see myself all round.

[*Puts on his clothes.*

Enter TOM FASHION *and* LORY. *They remain behind, conversing apart.*

Fash. Heyday! what the devil have we here? Sure my gentleman's grown a favourite at court, he has got so many people at his levee.

Lory. Sir, these people come in order to make him a favourite at court — they are to establish him with the ladies.

Fash. Good Heaven! to what an ebb of taste are women fallen, that it should be in the power of a laced coat to recommend a gallant to them!

Lory. Sir, tailors and hair-dressers debauch all the women.

Fash. Thou sayest true. But now for my reception.

Lord Fop. [*To Tailor.*] Death and eternal tortures! Sir — I say the coat is too wide here by a foot.

Tai. My lord, if it had been tighter, 'twould neither have hooked nor buttoned.

Lord Fop. Rat the hooks and buttons, sir! Can any thing be worse than this? As Gad shall jedge me, it hangs on my shoulders like a chairman's surtout.

Tai. 'Tis not for me to dispute your lordship's fancy.

Lory. There, sir, observe what respect does.

Fash. Respect! damn him for a coxcomb! — But let's accost him. — [*Coming forward.*] Brother, I'm your humble servant.

Lord Fop. O Lard, Tam! I did not expect you in England — brother, I'm glad to see you. — But what has brought you to Scarborough, Tam? — [*To the* TAILOR.] Look you, sir, I shall never be reconciled to this nauseous wrapping-gown, therefore pray get me another suit with all possible expedition; for this is my eternal aversion. — [*Exit* TAILOR.] Well but, Tam, you don't tell me what has driven you to Scarborough. — Mrs. Calico, are not you of my mind?

Semp. Directly, my lord. — I hope your lordship is pleased with your ruffles?

Lord Fop. In love with them, stap my vitals! — Bring my bill, you shall be paid to-morrow.

Semp. I humbly thank your lordship.   [*Exit.*

Lord Fop. Hark thee, shoemaker, these shoes aren't ugly, but they don't fit me.

Shoe. My lord, I think they fit you very well.

Lord Fop. They hurt me just below the instep.

Shoe. [*Feels his foot.*] No, my lord, they don't hurt you there.

Lord Fop. I tell thee they pinch me execrably.

Shoe. Why then, my lord, if those shoes pinch you, I'll be damned.

Lord Fop. Why, wilt thou undertake to persuade me I cannot feel?

Shoe. Your lordship may please to feel what you think fit, but that shoe does not hurt you — I think I understand my trade.

Lord Fop. Now, by all that's good and powerful, thou art an incomprehensive coxcomb! — but thou makest good shoes, and so I'll bear with thee.

Shoe. My lord, I have worked for half the people of quality in this town these twenty years, and 'tis very hard I shouldn't know when a shoe hurts, and when it don't.

Lord Fop. Well, pr'ythee be gone about thy business. — [*Exit* SHOEMAKER.] Mr. Mendlegs, a word with you. — The calves of these stockings are thickened a little too much; they make my legs look like a porter's.

Mend. My lord, methinks they look mighty well.

Lord Fop. Ay, but you are not so good a judge of those things as I am — I have studied them all my life — therefore pray let the next be the thickness of a crown-piece less.

Mend. Indeed, my lord, they are the same kind I had the honour to furnish your lordship with in town.

Lord Fop. Very possibly, Mr. Mendlegs; but that was in the beginning of the winter, and you should always remember,

21 *

Mr. Hosier, that if you make a nobleman's spring legs as
robust as his autumnal calves, you commit a monstrous im-
propriety, and make no allowance for the fatigues of the
winter.   [*Exit* MENDLEGS.

Jewel. I hope, my lord, these buckles have had the unspeakable satisfaction of being honoured with your lordship's
approbation?

Lord Fop. Why, they are of a pretty fancy; but don't you
think them rather of the smallest?

Jewel. My lord, they could not well be larger, to keep on
your lordship's shoe.

Lord Fop. My good sir, you forget that these matters are
not as they used to be; formerly, indeed, the buckle was a
sort of machine, intended to keep on the shoe; but the case
is now quite reversed, and the shoe is of no earthly use, but
to keep on the buckle. — Now give me my watches, [SERVANT
fetches the watches,] my chapeau, [SERVANT *brings a dress hat,*]
my handkerchief, [SERVANT *pours some scented liquor on a
handkerchief and brings it,*] my snaff-box, [SERVANT *brings snuff-
box.*] There, now the business of the morning is pretty well
over.   [*Exit* JEWELLER.

Fash. [*Aside to* LORY.] Well, Lory, what dost think on't?
— a very friendly reception from a brother, after three years'
absence!

Lory. [*Aside to* TOM FASHION.] Why, sir, 'tis your own
fault — here you have stood ever since you came in, and have
not commended any one thing that belongs to him.

                        [SERVANTS *all go off.*

Fash. [*Aside to* LORY.] Nor ever shall, while they belong
to a coxcomb. — *To* LORD FOPPINGTON.] Now your people of
business are gone, brother, I hope I may obtain a quarter of
an hour's audience of you?

Lord Fop. Faith, Tam, I must beg you'll excuse me at this
time, for I have an engagement which I would not break for
the salvation of mankind. — Hey! — there! — is my carriage
at the door? — You'll excuse me, brother.   '[*Going.*

   Fash. Shall you be back to dinner?

Lord Fop. As Gad shall jedge me, I can't tell; for it is passible I may dine with some friends at Donner's.

Fash. Shall I meet you there? for I must needs talk with you.

Lord Fop. That I'm afraid mayn't be quite so praper; for those I commonly eat with are people of nice conversation; and you know, Tam, your education has been a little at large. — But there are other ordinaries in town — very good beef ordinaries — I suppose, Tam, you can eat beef? — However, dear Tam, I'm glad to see thee in England, stap my vitals!

[*Exit*, LA VAROLE *following*.

Fash. Hell and furies! is this to be borne?

Lory. Faith, sir, I could almost have given him a knock o'the pate myself.

Fash. 'Tis enough; I will now show you the excess of my passion, by being very calm. — Come, Lory, lay your loggerhead to mine, and, in cold blood, let us contrive his destruction.

Lory. Here comes a head, sir, would contrive it better than both our loggerheads, if she would but join in the confederacy.

Fash. By this light, Madam Coupler! she seems dissatisfied at something: let us observe her.

Enter MRS. COUPLER.

Mrs. Coup. So! I am likely to be well rewarded for my services, truly; my suspicions, I find, were but too just. — What! refuse to advance me a petty sum, when I am upon the point of making him master of a galleon! But let him look to the consequences; an ungrateful narrow-minded coxcomb!

Fash. So he is, upon my soul, old lady; it must be my brother you speak of.

Mrs. Coup. Ha! stripling, how came you here? What, hast spent all, eh? And art thou come to dun his lordship for assistance?

Fash. No, I want somebody's assistance to cut his lordship's throat, without the risk of being hanged for him.

Mrs. Coup. Egad, sirrah, I could help thee to do him almost as good a turn, without the danger of being burned in the hand for't.

Fash. How — how, old Mischief?

Mrs. Coup. Why, you must know I have done you the kindness to make up a match for your brother.

Fash. I am very much beholden to you, truly!

Mrs. Coup. You may before the wedding-day yet: the lady is a great heiress, the match is concluded, the writings are drawn, and his lordship is come hither to put the finishing hand to the business.

Fash. I understand as much.

Mrs. Coup. Now, you must know, stripling, your brother's a knave.

Fash. Good.

Mrs. Coup. He has given me a bond of a thousand pounds for helping him to this fortune, and has promised me as much more, in ready money, upon the day of the marriage; which, I understand by a friend, he never designs to pay me; and his just now refusing to pay me a part is a proof of it. If, therefore, you will be a generous young rogue, and secure me five thousand pounds, I'll help you to the lady.

Fash. And how the devil wilt thou do that?

Mrs. Coup. Without the devil's aid, I warrant thee. Thy brother's face not one of the family ever saw; the whole business has been managed by me, and all his letters go through my hands. Sir Tunbelly Clumsy, my relation — for that's the old gentleman's name — is apprised of his lordship's being down here, and expects him to-morrow to receive his daughter's hand; but the peer, I find, means to bait here a few days longer, to recover the fatigue of his journey, I suppose. Now you shall go to Muddymoat Hall in his place. — I'll give you a letter of introduction: and if you don't marry the girl before sunset, you deserve to be hanged before morning.

Fash. Agreed! agreed! and for thy reward ——

Mrs. Coup. Well, well; — though I warrant thou hast not

a farthing of money in thy pocket now — no — one may see it
in thy face.

Fash. Not a sous, by Jupiter!

Mrs. Coup. Must I advance, then? Well, be at my lodgings, next door, this evening, and I'll see what may be done
— we'll sign and seal, and when I have given thee some
further instructions, thou shalt hoist sail and begone.   [*Exit.*

Fash. So, Lory, Fortune, thou seest, at last takes care of
merit! we are in a fair way to be great people.

Lory. Ay, sir, if the devil don't step between the cup and
the lip, as he used to do.

Fash. Why, faith, he has played me many a damned trick
to spoil my fortune; and, egad, I am almost afraid he's at
work about it again now; but if I should tell thee how, thou'dst
wonder at me.

Lory. Indeed, sir, I should not.

Fash. How dost know?

Lory. Because, sir, I have wondered at you so often, I
can wonder at you no more.

Fash. No! What wouldst thou say, if a qualm of conscience should spoil my design?

Lory. I would eat my words, and wonder more than ever.

Fash. Why faith, Lory, though I have played many a
roguish trick, this is so full-grown a cheat, I find I must take
pains to come up to't — I have scruples.

Lory. They are strong symptoms of death. If you find
they increase, sir, pray make your will.

Fash. No, my conscience shan't starve me neither; but
thus far I'll listen to it. Before I execute this project, I'll try
my brother to the bottom. If he has yet so much humanity
about him as to assist me — though with a moderate aid —
I'll drop my project at his feet, and show him how I can do for
him much more than what I'd ask he'd do for me. This one
conclusive trial of him I resolve to make. —

> Succeed or fail, still victory is my lot;
> If I subdue his heart, 'tis well — if not,
> I will subdue my conscience to my plot.   [*Exeunt.*

ACT II.

Scene I. — Loveless's *Lodgings.*

Enter Loveless *and* Amanda.

Love. How do you like these lodgings, my dear? For my part, I am so pleased with them, I shall hardly remove whilst we stay here, if you are satisfied.

Aman. I am satisfied with every thing that pleases you, else I had not come to Scarborough at all.

Love. Oh, a little of the noise and folly of this place will sweeten the pleasures of our retreat; we shall find the charms of our retirement doubled when we return to it.

Aman. That pleasing prospect will be my chiefest entertainment, whilst, much against my will, I engage in those empty pleasures which 'tis so much the fashion to be fond of.

Love. I own most of them are, indeed, but empty; yet there are delights of which a private life is destitute, which may divert an honest man, and be a harmless entertainment to a virtuous woman: good music is one; and truly (with some small allowance) the plays, I think, may be esteemed another.

Aman. Plays, I must confess, have some small charms. What do you think of that you saw last night?

Love. To say truth, I did not mind it much — my attention was for some time taken off to admire the workmanship of nature, in the face of a young lady who sat some distance from me, she was so exquisitely handsome.

Aman. So exquisitely handsome!

Love. Why do you repeat my words, my dear?

Aman. Because you seemed to speak them with such pleasure, I thought I might oblige you with their echo.

Love. Then, you are alarmed, Amanda?

Aman. It is my duty to be so when you are in danger.

Love. You are too quick in apprehending for me. I viewed her with a world of admiration, but not one glance of love.

Aman. Take heed of trusting to such nice distinctions.

But were your eyes the only things that were inquisitive? Had I been in your place, my tongue, I fancy, had been curious too. I should have asked her where she lived — yet still without design — who was she, pray?

Love. Indeed I cannot tell.

Aman. You will not tell.

Love. Upon my honour, then, I did not ask.

Aman. Nor do you know what company was with her?

Love. I do not. But why are you so earnest?

Aman. I thought I had cause.

Love. But you thought wrong, Amanda; for turn the case, and let it be your story: should you come home and tell me you had seen a handsome man, should I grow jealous because you had eyes?

Aman. But should I tell you he was exquisitely so, and that I had gazed on him with admiration, should you not think 'twere possible I might go one step further, and inquire his name?

Love. [*Aside.*] She has reason on her side; I have talked too much; but I must turn off another way. — [*Aloud.*] Will you then make no difference, Amanda, between the language of our sex and yours? There is a modesty restrains your tongues, which makes you speak by halves when you commend; but roving flattery gives a loose to ours, which makes us still speak double what we think.

Enter SERVANT.

Serv. Madam, there is a lady at the door in a chair desires to know whether your ladyship sees company; her name is Berinthia.

Aman. Oh dear! 'tis a relation I have not seen these five years; pray her to walk in. — [*Exit* SERVANT.] Here's another beauty for you; she was, when I saw her last, reckoned extremely handsome.

Love. Don't be jealous now; for I shall gaze upon her too.

Enter BERINTHIA.

Ha! by heavens, the very woman! [*Aside.*

Ber. [*Salutes* AMANDA.] Dear Amanda, I did not expect to meet you in Scarborough.

Aman. Sweet cousin, I'm overjoyed to see you. — Mr. Loveless, here's a relation and a friend of mine, I desire you'll be better acquainted with.

Love. [*Salutes* BERINTHIA.] If my wife never desires a harder thing, madam, her request will be easily granted.

Re-enter SERVANT.

Serv. Sir, my Lord Foppington presents his humble service to you, and desires to know how you do. He's at the next door; and, if it be not inconvenient to you, he'll come and wait upon you.

Love. Give my compliments to his lordship, and I shall be glad to see him.—[*Exit* SERVANT.] If you are not acquainted with his lordship, madam, you will be entertained with his character.

Aman. Now it moves my pity more than my mirth to see a man whom nature has made no fool be so very industrious to pass for an ass.

Love. No, there you are wrong, Amanda; you should never bestow your pity upon those who take pains for your contempt: pity those whom nature abuses, never those who abuse nature.

Enter LORD FOPPINGTON.

Lord Fop. Dear Loveless, I am your most humble servant.

Love. My lord, I'm yours.

Lord Fop. Madam, your ladyship's very obedient slave.

Love. My lord, this lady is a relation of my wife's.

Lord Fop. [*Salutes* BERINTHIA.] The beautifulest race of people upon earth, rat me! Dear Loveless, I am overjoyed that you think of continuing here: I am, stap my vitals! — [*To* AMANDA.] For Gad's sake, madam, how has your ladyship been able to subsist thus long, under the fatigue of a country life?

Aman. My life has been very far from that, my lord; it has been a very quiet one.

Lord Fop. Why, that's the fatigue I speak of, madam; for 'tis impossible to be quiet without thinking: now thinking is to me the greatest fatigue in the world.

Aman. Does not your lordship love reading, then?

Lord Fop. Oh, passionately, madam; but I never think of what I read. For example, madam, my life is a perpetual stream of pleasure, that glides through with such a variety of entertainments, I believe the wisest of our ancestors never had the least conception of any of 'em. I rise, madam, when in tawn, about twelve o'clock. I don't rise sooner, because it is the worst thing in the world for the complexion: nat that I pretend to be a beau; but a man must endeavour to look decent, lest he makes so odious a figure in the side-bax, the ladies should be compelled to turn their eyes upon the play. So at twelve o'clock, I say, I rise. Naw, if I find it is a good day, I resalve to take the exercise of riding; so drink my chocolate, and draw on my boots by two. On my return, I dress; and, after dinner, lounge perhaps to the opera.

Ber. Your lordship, I suppose, is fond of music?

Lord Fop. Oh, passionately, on Tuesdays and Saturdays; for then there is always the best company, and one is not expected to undergo the fatigue of listening.

Aman. Does your lordship think that the case at the opera?

Lord Fop. Most certainly, madam. There is my Lady Tattle, my Lady Prate, my Lady Titter, my Lady Sneer, my Lady Giggle, and my Lady Grin — these have boxes in the front, and while any favourite air is singing, are the prettiest company in the waurld, stap my vitals! — Mayn't we hope for the honour to see you added to our society, madam?

Aman. Alas! my lord, I am the worst company in the world at a concert, I'm so apt to attend to the music.

Lord Fop. Why, madam, that is very pardonable in the country or at church, but a monstrous inattention in a polite assembly. But I am afraid I tire the company?

Love. Not at all. Pray go on.

Lord Fop. Why then, ladies, there only remains to add, that I generally conclude the evening at one or other of the clubs; nat that I ever play deep; indeed I have been for some time tied up from losing above five thousand paunds at a sitting.

Love. But isn't your lordship sometimes obliged to attend the weighty affairs of the nation?

Lord Fop. Sir, as to weighty affairs, I leave them to weighty heads; I never intend mine shall be a burden to my body.

Ber. Nay, my lord, but you are a pillar of the state.

Lord Fop. An ornamental pillar, madam; for sooner than undergo any part of the fatigue, rat me, but the whole building should fall plump to the ground!

Aman. But, my lord, a fine gentleman spends a great deal of his time in his intrigues; you have given us no account of them yet.

Lord Fop. [*Aside.*] So! she would inquire into my amours — that's jealousy, poor soul! — I see she's in love with me. — [*Aloud.*] O Lord, madam, I had like to have forgot a secret I must needs tell your ladyship. — Ned, you must not be so jealous now as to listen.

Love. [*Leading* BERINTHIA *up the stage.*] Not I, my lord; I am too fashionable a husband to pry into the secrets of my wife.

Lord Fop. [*Aside to* AMANDA, *squeezing her hand.*] I am in love with you to desperation, strike me speechless!

Aman. [*Strikes him on the ear.*] Then thus I return your passion. — An impudent fool!

Lord Fop. Gad's curse, madam, I am a peer of the realm!

Love. [*Hastily returning.*] Hey! what the devil, do you affront my wife, sir? Nay, then —— [*Draws. They fight.*

Aman. What has my folly done? — Help! murder! help! Part them, for Heaven's sake.

Lord Fop. [*Falls back and leans on his sword.*] Ah! quite through the body, stap my vitals!

Enter SERVANTS.

Love. [*Runs to* LORD FOPPINGTON.] I hope I han't killed the fool, however. Bear him up. — Call a surgeon there.

Lord Fop. Ay, pray make haste. [*Exit* SERVANT.

Love. This mischief you may thank yourself for.

Lord Fop. I may so; love's the devil indeed, Ned.

Re-enter SERVANT, *with* PROBE.

Ser. Here's Mr. Probe, sir, was just going by the door.

Lord Fop. He's the welcomest man alive.

Probe. Stand by, stand by, stand by; pray, gentlemen, stand by. Lord have mercy upon us, did you never see a man run through the body before? — Pray stand by.

Lord Fop. Ah, Mr. Probe, I'm a dead man.

Probe. A dead man, and I by! I should laugh to see that, egad.

Love. Pr'ythee don't stand prating, but look upon his wound.

Probe. Why, what if I won't look upon his wound this hour, sir?

Love. Why, then he'll bleed to death, sir.

Probe. Why, then I'll fetch him to life again, sir.

Love. 'Slife! he's run through the body, I tell thee.

Probe. I wish he was run through the heart, and I should get the more credit by his cure. Now I hope you are satisfied? Come, now let me come at him — now let me come at him. — [*Viewing his wound.*] Oons! what a gash is here! why, sir, a man may drive a coach and six horses into your body.

Lord Fop. Oh!

Probe. Why, what the devil have you run the gentleman through with a scythe? — [*Aside.*] A little scratch between the skin and the ribs, that's all.

Love. Let me see his wound.

Probe. Then you shall dress it, sir; for if any body looks upon it I won't.

Love. Why thou art the veriest coxcomb I ever saw!

Probe. Sir, I am not master of my trade for nothing.

Lord Fop. Surgeon!

Probe. Sir.

Lord Fop. Are there any hopes?

Probe. Hopes! I can't tell. What are you willing to give for a cure?

Lord Fop. Five hundred paunds with pleasure.

Probe. Why then perhaps there may be hopes; but we must avoid further delay. — Here, help the gentleman into a chair, and carry him to my house presently — that's the properest place — [*Aside*] to bubble him out of his money. — [*Aloud.*] Come, a chair — a chair quickly — there, in with him.   [SERVANTS *put* LORD FOPPINGTON *into a chair.*

Lord Fop. Dear Loveless, adieu! if I die, I forgive thee; and if I live, I hope thou wilt do as much by me. I am sorry you and I should quarrel, but I hope here's an end on't; for, if you are satisfied, I am.

Love. I shall hardly think it worth my prosecuting any further, so you may be at rest, sir.

Lord Fop. Thou art a generous fellow, strike me dumb. — [*Aside.*] But thou hast an impertinent wife, stap my vitals'

Probe. So — carry him off, carry him off! — We shall have him prate himself into a fever by-and-by. — Carry him off!   [*Exit with* LORD FOPPINGTON.

Enter COLONEL TOWNLY.

Col. Town. So, so, I am glad to find you all alive — I met a wounded peer carrying off. For heaven's sake what was the matter?

Love. Oh, a trifle! he would have made love to my wife before my face, so she obliged him with a box o' the ear, and I run him through the body, that was all.

Col. Town. Bagatelle on all sides. But pray, madam, how long has this noble lord been an humble servant of yours?

Aman. This is the first I have heard on't — so, I suppose, 'tis his quality more than his love has brought him into this adventure. He thinks his title an authentic passport to every woman's heart below the degree of a peeress.

Col. Town. He's coxcomb enough to think any thing; but I would not have you brought into trouble for him. I hope there's no danger of his life?

Love. None at all. He's fallen into the hands of a roguish surgeon, who, I perceive, designs to frighten a little money out of him: but I saw his wound — 'tis nothing: he may go to the ball to-night if he pleases.

Col. Town. I am glad you have corrected him without further mischief, or you might have deprived me of the pleasure of executing a plot against his lordship, which I have been contriving with an old acquaintance of yours.

Love. Explain.

Col. Town. His brother, Tom Fashion, is come down here, and we have it in contemplation to save him the trouble of his intended wedding; but we want your assistance. Tom would have called, but he is preparing for his enterprise, so I promised to bring you to him — so sir, if these ladies can spare you——

Love. I'll go with you with all my heart. — [*Aside.*] Though I could wish, methinks, to stay and gaze a little longer on that creature. Good gods! how engaging she is! but what have I to do with beauty? I have already had my portion, and must not covet more.

Aman. Mr. Loveless, pray one word with you before you go. [*Exit* COLONEL TOWNLY.

Love. What would my dear?

Aman. Only a woman's foolish question: how do you like my cousin here?

Love. Jealous already, Amanda?

Aman. Not at all: I ask you for another reason.

Love. [*Aside.*] Whate'er her reason be, I must not tell her true. — [*Aloud.*] Why, I confess, she's handsome: but you must not think I slight your kinswoman, if I own to you, of all the women who may claim that character, she is the last that would triumph in my heart.

Amand. I'm satisfied.

Love. Now tell me why you asked?

Aman. At night I will — adieu!

Love. I'm yours.   [*Kisses her, and exit.*

Aman. I'm glad to find he does not like her, for I have a great mind to persuade her to come and live with me. [*Aside.*

Ber. So! I find my colonel continues in his airs: there must be something more at the bottom of this than the provocation he pretends from me.   [*Aside.*

Aman. For Heaven's sake, Berinthia, tell me what way I shall take to persuade you to come and live with me.

Ber. Why, one way in the world there is, and but one.

Aman. And pray what is that?

Ber. It is to assure me — I shall be very welcome.

Aman. If that be all, you shall e'en sleep here to-night.

Ber. To-night!

Aman. Yes, to-night.

Ber. Why, the people where I lodge will think me mad.

Aman. Let 'em think what they please.

Ber. Say you so, Amanda? Why, then, they shall think what they please: for I'm a young widow, and I care not what any body thinks. — Ah, Amanda, it's a delicious thing to be a young widow!

Aman. You'll hardly make me think so.

Ber. Poh! because you are in love with your husband.

Aman. Pray, 'tis with a world of innocence I would inquire whether you think those we call women of reputation do really escape all other men as they do those shadows of beaux?

Ber. Oh no, Amanda; there are a sort of men make dreadful work amongst 'em, men that may be called the beau's antipathy, for they agree in nothing but walking upon two legs. These have brains, the beau has none. These are in love with their mistress, the beau with himself. They take care of their reputation, the beau is industrious to destroy it. They are decent, he's a fop; in short, they are men, he's an ass.

Aman. If this be their character, I fancy we had here, e'en now, a pattern of 'em both.

Ber. His lordship and Colonel Townly?

Aman. The same.

Ber. As for the lord, he is eminently so; and for the other, I can assure you there's not a man in town who has a better interest with the women, that are worth having an interest with.

Aman. He answers the opinion I had ever of him. — [*Takes her hand.*] I must acquaint you with a secret — 'tis not that fool alone has talked to me of love; Townly has been tampering too.

Ber. [*Aside.*] So, so! here the mystery comes out!—[*Aloud.*] Colonel Townly! impossible, my dear!

Aman. 'Tis true, indeed; though he has done it in vain; nor do I think that all the merit of mankind combined could shake the tender love I bear my husband; yet I will own to you, Berinthia, I did not start at his addresses, as when they came from one whom I contemned.

Ber. [*Aside.*] Oh, this is better and better! — [*Aloud.*] Well said, Innocence! and you really think, my dear, that nothing could abate your constancy and attachment to your husband?

Aman. Nothing, I am convinced.

Ber. What, if you found he loved another woman better? -

Aman. Well!

Ber. Well! — why, were I that thing they call a slighted wife, somebody should run the risk of being that thing they call — a husband. Don't I talk madly?

Aman. Madly indeed!

Ber. Yet I'm very innocent.

Aman. That I dare swear you are. I know how to make allowances for your humour: but you resolve then never to marry again?

Ber. Oh no! I resolve I will.

Aman. How so?

Ber. That I never may.

Aman. You banter me.

Ber. Indeed I don't: but I consider I'm a woman, and form my resolutions accordingly.

Aman. Well, my opinion is, form what resolution you will, matrimony will be the end on't.

Ber. I doubt it — but a —— Heavens! I have business at home, and am half an hour too late.

Aman. As you are to return with me, I'll just give some orders, and walk with you.

Ber. Well, make haste, and we'll finish this subject as we go. — [*Exit* AMANDA.] Ah, poor Amanda! you have led a country life. Well, this discovery is lucky! Base Townly! at once false to me and treacherous to his friend! — And my innocent and demure cousin too! I have it in my power to be revenged on her, however. Her husband, if I have any skill in countenance, would be as happy in my smiles as Townly can hope to be in hers. I'll make the experiment, come what will on't. The woman who can forgive the being robbed of a favoured lover, must be either an idiot or something worse.

[*Exit.*

ACT III.

SCENE I. — LORD FOPPINGTON's *Lodgings.*

Enter LORD FOPPINGTON *and* LA VAROLE.

Lord Fop. Hey, fellow, let my vis-à-vis come to the door.

La Var. Will your lordship venture so soon to expose yourself to the weather?

Lord Fop. Sir, I will venture as soon as I can to expose myself to the ladies.

La Var. I wish your lordship would please to keep house a little longer; I'm afraid your honour does not well consider your wound.

Lord Fop. My wound! — I would not be in eclipse another day, though I had as many wounds in my body as I have had in my heart. So mind, Varole, let these cards be left as directed; for this evening I shall wait on my future father-in-law, Sir Tunbelly, and I mean to commence my devoirs to the lady, by giving an entertainment at her father's expense; and hark thee, tell Mr. Loveless I request he and his company will honour me with their presence, or I shall think we are not friends.

La Var. I will be sure, milor.   [*Exit.*

Enter TOM FASHION.

Fash. Brother, your servant; how do you find yourself today?

Lord Fop. So well that I have ardered my coach to the door — so there's no danger of death this baut, 'Tam.

Fash. I'm very glad of it.

Lord Fop. [*Aside.*] That I believe's a lie. — [*Aloud.*] Pr'ythee, Tam, tell me one thing, — did not your heart cut a caper up to your mauth, when you heard I was run through the bady?

Fash. Why do you think it should?

Lord Fop. Because I remember mine did so, when I heard my uncle was shot through the head.

Fash. It then did very ill.

Lord Fop. Pr'ythee, why so?

Fash. Because he used you very well.

Lord Fop. Well! — Naw, strike me dumb! he starved me; he has let me want a thousand women for want of a thousand paund.

Fash. Then he hindered you from making a great many ill bargains; for I think no woman worth money that will take money.

Lord Fop. If I was a younger brother I should think so too.

Fash. Then you are seldom much in love?

Lord Fop. Never, stap my vitals!

Fash. Why, then, did you make all this bustle about Amanda?

Lord Fop. Because she's a woman of insolent virtue, and I thought myself piqued, in honour, to debauch her.

Fash. Very well. — [*Aside.*] Here's a rare fellow for you,

to have the spending of ten thousand pounds a year! But now
for my business with him. [*Aloud.*] Brother, though I know
to talk of any business (especially of money) is a theme not
quite so entertaining to you as that of the ladies, my necessities are such, I hope you'll have patience to hear me.

Lord Fop. The greatness of your necessities, Tam, is the
worst argument in the waurld for your being patiently heard.
I do believe you are going to make a very good speech, but,
strike me dumb! it has the worst beginning of any speech I
have heard this twelvemonth.

Fash. I'm sorry you think so.

Lord Fop. I do believe thou art: but come, let's know the
affair quickly.

Fash. Why then, my case in a word is this: the necessary
expenses of my travels have so much exceeded the wretched
income of my annuity, that I have been forced to mortgage
it for five hundred pounds, which is spent. So, unless you are
so kind as to assist me in redeeming it, I know no remedy
but to take a purse.

Lord Fop. Why faith, Tam, to give you my sense of the
thing, I do think taking a purse the best remedy in the waurld;
for if you succeed, you are relieved that way, if you are taken,
[*Drawing his hand round his neck,*] you are relieved t'other.

Fash. I'm glad to see you are in so pleasant a humour; I
hope I shall find the effects on't.

Lord Fop. Why, do you then really think it a reasonable
thing, that I should give you five hundred paunds?

Fash. I do not ask it as a due, brother; I am willing to
receive it as a favour.

Lord Fop. Then thou art willing to receive it any how,
strike me speechless! But these are damned times to give
money in; taxes are so great, repairs so exorbitant, tenants
such rogues, and bouquets so dear, that, the devil take me,
I am reduced to that extremity in my cash, I have been
forced to retrench in that one article of sweet pawder, till I
have brought it down to five guineas a maunth — now judge,
Tam, whether I can spare you five hundred paunds.

Fash. If you can't, I must starve, that's all. — [*Aside.*] Damn him!

Lord Fop. All I can say is, you should have been a better husband.

Fash. Ouns! if you can't live upon ten thousand a year, how do you think I should do 't upon two hundred?

Lord Fop. Don't be in a passion, Tam, for passion is the most unbecoming thing in the waurld — to the face. Look you, I don't love to say any thing to you to make you melancholy, but upon this occasion I must take leave to put you in mind that a running horse does require more attendance than a coach-horse. Nature has made some difference 'twixt you and me.

Fash. Yes — she has made you older. — [*Aside.*] Plague take her!

Lord Fop. That is not all, Tam.

Fash. Why, what is there else?

Lord Fop. [*Looks first on himself, and then on his brother.*] Ask the ladies.

Fash. Why, thou essence-bottle, thou musk-cat! dost thou then think thou hast any advantage over me but what Fortune has given thee?

Lord Fop. I do, stap my vitals!

Fash. Now, by all that's great and powerful, thou art the prince of coxcombs!

Lord Fop. Sir, I am proud at being at the head of so prevailing a party.

Fash. Will nothing provoke thee? — Draw, coward!

Lord Fop. Look you, Tam, you know I have always taken you for a mighty dull fellow, and here is one of the foolishest plats broke out that I have seen a lang time. Your poverty makes life so burdensome to you, you would provoke me to a quarrel, in hopes either to slip through my lungs into my estate, or to get yourself run through the guts, to put an end to your pain. But I will disappoint you in both your designs; far with the temper of a philasapher, and the discretion of a statesman — I shall leave the room with my sword in the scabbard.   [*Exit.*

Fash. So! farewell, brother; and now, conscience, I defy thee. Lory!

Enter LORY.

Lory. Sir!

Fash. Here's rare news, Lory; his lordship has given me a pill has purged off all my scruples.

Lory. Then my heart's at ease again: for I have been in a lamentable fright, sir, ever since your conscience had the impudence to intrude into your company.

Fash. Be at peace; it will come there no more: my brother has given it a wring by the nose, and I have kicked it down stairs. So run away to the inn, get the chaise ready quickly, and bring it to Dame Coupler's without a moment's delay.

Lory. Then, sir, you are going straight about the fortune?

Fash. I am. — Away — fly, Lory!

Lory. The happiest day I ever saw. I'm upon the wing already. Now then I shall get my wages.   [*Exeunt.*

SCENE II. — *A Garden behind* LOVELESS'S *Lodgings.*

Enter LOVELESS *and* SERVANT.

Love. Is my wife within?

Serv. No, sir, she has gone out this half hour.

Love. Well, leave me. — [*Exit* SERVANT.] How strangely does my mind run on this widow! — Never was my heart so suddenly seized on before. That my wife should pick out her, of all womankind, to be her playfellow! But what fate does, let fate answer for: I sought it not. So! by Heavens! here she comes.

Enter BERINTHIA.

Ber. What makes you look so thoughtful, sir? I hope you are not ill.

Love. I was debating, madam, whether I was so or not, and that was it which made me look so thoughtful.

Ber. Is it then so hard a matter to decide? I thought all

people were acquainted with their own bodies, though few people know their own minds.

Love. What if the distemper I suspect be in the mind?

Ber. Why then I'll undertake to prescribe you a cure.

Love. Alas! you undertake you know not what.

Ber. So far at least, then, you allow me to be a physician.

Love. Nay, I'll allow you to be so yet further; for I have reason to believe, should I put myself into your hands, you would increase my distemper.

Ber. How?

Love. Oh, you might betray me to my wife.

Ber. And so lose all my practice.

Love. Will you then keep my secret?

Ber. I will.

Love. Well — but swear it.

Ber. I swear by woman.

Love. Nay, that's swearing by my deity; swear by your own, and I shall believe you.

Ber. Well then, I swear by man!

Love. I'm satisfied. Now hear my symptoms, and give me your advice. The first were these; when I saw you at the play, a random glance you threw at first alarmed me. I could not turn my eyes from whence the danger came — I gazed upon you till my heart began to pant — nay, even now, on your approaching me, my illness is so increased that if you do not help me I shall, whilst you look on, consume to ashes.

[*Takes her hand.*

Ber. O lord, let me go! 'tis the plague, and we shall be infected.   [*Breaking from him.*

Love. Then we'll die together, my charming angel.

Ber. O Gad! the devil's in you! Lord, let me go! — here's somebody coming.

Re-enter SERVANT.

Serv. Sir, my lady's come home, and desires to speak with you.

Love. Tell her I'm coming. — [*Exit* SERVANT.] But before
I go, one glass of nectar to drink her health.

[*To* BERINTHIA.

Ber. Stand off, or I shall hate you, by Heavens!

Love. [*Kissing her.*] In matters of love, a woman's oath
is no more to be minded than a man's.   [*Exit.*

Ber. Um!

Enter COLONEL TOWNLY.

Col. Town. [*Aside.*] So! what's here—Berinthia and Loveless—and in such close conversation!—I cannot now wonder
at her indifference in excusing herself to me! — O rare woman! — Well then, let Loveless look to his wife, 'twill be but
the retort courteous on both sides. — [*Aloud.*] Your servant,
madam; I need not ask you how you do, you have got so good
a colour.

Ber. No better than I used to have, I suppose.

Col. Town. A little more blood in your cheeks.

Ber. I have been walking!

Col. Town. Is that all? Pray was it Mr. Loveless went
from here just now?

Ber. O yes — he has been walking with me.

Col. Town. He has!

Ber. Upon my word I think he is a very agreeable man;
and there is certainly something particularly insinuating in
his address!

Col. Town. [*Aside.*] So, so! she hasn't even the modesty
to dissemble! [*Aloud.*] Pray, madam, may I, without impertinence, trouble you with a few serious questions?

Ber. As many as you please; but pray let them be as
little serious as possible.

Col. Town. Is it not near two years since I have presumed to address you?

Ber. I don't know exactly — but it has been a tedious
long time.

Col. Town. Have I not, during that period, had every reason to believe that my assiduities were far from being unac-
ceptable?

Ber. Why, to do you justice, you have been extremely troublesome — and I confess I have been more civil to you than you deserved.

Col. Town. Did I not come to this place at your express desire, and for no purpose but the honour of meeting you? — and after waiting a month in disappointment, have you condescended to explain, or in the slightest way apologise, for your conduct?

Ber. O heavens! apologise for my conduct! — apologise to you! O you barbarian! But pray now, my good serious colonel, have you any thing more to add?

Col. Town. Nothing, madam, but that after such behaviour I am less surprised at what I saw just now; it is not very wonderful that the woman who can trifle with the delicate addresses of an honourable lover should be found coquetting with the husband of her friend.

Ber. Very true: no more wonderful than it was for this honourable lover to divert himself in the absence of this coquette, with endeavouring to seduce his friend's wife! O colonel, colonel, don't talk of honour or your friend, for Heaven's sake!

Col. Town. [*Aside.*] 'Sdeath! how came she to suspect this! — [*Aloud.*] Really, madam, I don't understand you.

Ber. Nay, nay, you saw I did not pretend to misunderstand you. — But here comes the lady: perhaps you would be glad to be left with her for an explanation.

Col. Town. O madam, this recrimination is a poor resource; and to convince you how much you are mistaken, I beg leave to decline the happiness you propose me. — Madam, your servant.

Enter AMANDA. COLONEL TOWNLY *whispers* AMANDA, *and exit.*

Ber. [*Aside.*] He carries it off well, however; upon my word, very well! How tenderly they part! — [*Aloud.*] So, cousin; I hope you have not been chiding your admirer for being with me? I assure you we have been talking of you.

Aman. Fy, Berinthia!—my admirer! will you never learn to talk in earnest of any thing?

Ber. Why this shall be in earnest, if you please; for my part, I only tell you matter of fact.

Aman. I'm sure there's so much jest and earnest in what you say to me on this subject, I scarce know how to take it. I have just parted with Mr. Loveless; perhaps it is fancy, but I think there is an alteration in his manner which alarms me.

Ber. And so you are jealous! is that all?

Aman. That all! is jealousy, then, nothing?

Ber. It should be nothing, if I were in your case.

Aman. Why, what would you do?

Ber. I'd cure myself.

Aman. How?

Ber. Care as little for my husband as he did for me. Look you, Amanda, you may build castles in the air, and fume, and fret, and grow thin, and lean, and pale, and ugly, if you please; but I tell you, no man worth having is true to his wife, or ever was, or ever will be so.

Aman. Do you then really think he's false to me? for I did not suspect him.

Ber. Think so? I am sure of it.

Aman. You are sure on't?

Ber. Positively — he fell in love at the play.

Aman. Right — the very same! But who could have told you this?

Ber. Um!—Oh, Townly! I suppose your husband has made him his confidant.

Aman. O base Loveless! And what did Townly say on't?

Ber. [*Aside.*] So, so! why should she ask that? — [*Aloud.*] Say! why he abused Loveless extremley, and said all the tender things of you in the world.

Aman. Did he? — Oh! my heart! — I'm very ill — dear Berinthia, don't leave me a moment.   [*Exeunt.*

SCENE III. — *Outside of* SIR TUNBELLY CLUMSY'S *House.*

Enter TOM FASHION *and* LORY.

Fash. So, here's our inheritance, Lory, if we can but get into possession. But methinks the seat of our family looks like Noah's ark, as if the chief part on't were designed for the fowls of the air, and the beasts of the field.

Lory. Pray, sir, don't let your head run upon the orders of building here: get but the heiress, let the devil take the house.

Fash. Get but the house, let the devil take the heiress! I say. — But come, we have no time to squander; knock at the door. — [LORY *knocks two or three times at the gate.*] What the devil! have they got no ears in this house? — Knock harder.

Lory. Egad, sir, this will prove some enchanted castle; we shall have the giant come out, by-and-by, with his club, and beat our brains out.   [*Knocks again.*

Fash. Hush, they come.

Serv. [*Within.*] Who is there?

Lory. Open the door and see: is that your country breeding?

Serv. Ay, but two words to that bargain. — Tummas, is the blunderbuss primed?

Fash. Ouns! give 'em good words, Lory, — or we shall be shot here a fortune catching.

Lory. Egad, sir, I think you're in the right on't. — Ho! Mr. What-d'ye-call-'um, will you please to let us in? or are we to be left to grow like willows by your moat side?

SERVANT *appears at the window with a blunderbuss.*

Serv. Well naw, what's ya're business?

Fash. Nothing, sir, but to wait upon Sir Tunbelly, with your leave.

Serv. To weat upon Sir Tunbelly! why you'll find that's just as Sir Tunbelly pleases.

Fash. But will you do me the favour, sir, to know whether Sir Tunbelly pleases or not?

Serv. Why, look you, d'ye see, with good words much may be done. — Ralph, go thy ways, and ask Sir Tunbelly if he pleases to be waited upon — and dost hear, call to nurse, that she may lock up Miss Hoyden before the gates open.

Fash. D'ye hear that, Lory?

Enter Sir Tunbelly Clumsy, *with* Servants, *armed with guns, clubs, pitch-forks, &c.*

Lory. Oh! [*Runs behind his master.*] O Lord! O Lord! Lord! we are both dead men!

Fash. Fool! thy fear will ruin us.   [*Aside to* Lory.

Lory. My fear, sir? 'sdeath, sir, I fear nothing.—[*Aside.*] Would I were well up to the chin in a horsepond!

Sir Tun. Who is it here hath any business with me?

Fash. Sir, 'tis I, if your name be Sir Tunbelly Clumsy.

Sir Tun. Sir, my name is Sir Tunbelly Clumsy, whether you have any business with me or not. — So you see I am not ashamed of my name, nor my face either.

Fash. Sir, you have no cause that I know of.

Sir Tun. Sir, if you have no cause either, I desire to know who you are; for, till I know your name, I shan't ask you to come into my house: and when I do know your name, 'tis six to four I don't ask you then.

Fash. Sir, I hope you'll find this letter an authentic passport.   [*Gives him a letter.*

Sir Tun Cod's my life, from Mrs. Coupler! — I ask your lordship's pardon ten thousand times. — [*To a* Servant.] Here, run in a-doors quickly; get a Scotch coal fire in the parlour, set all the Turkey work chairs in their places, get the brass candlesticks out, and be sure stick the socket full of laurel — run! — [*Turns to* Tom Fashion.] My lord, I ask your lordship's pardon. — [*To* Servant.] And, do you hear, run away to nurse; bid her let Miss Hoyden loose again. — [*Exit* Servant.] I hope your honour will excuse the disorder of my family. We are not used to receive men of your lordship's great quality every day. Pray where are your coaches and servants, my lord?

Fash. Sir, that I might give you and your daughter a proof how impatient I am to be nearer akin to you, I left my equipage to follow me, and came away post with only one servant.

Sir Tun. Your lordship does me too much honour — it was exposing your person to too much fatigue and danger, I protest it was; but my daughter shall endeavour to make you what amends she can; and, though I say it that should not say it, Hoyden has charms.

Fash. Sir, I am not a stranger to them, though I am to her; common fame has done her justice.

Sir Tun. My lord, I am common fame's very grateful, humble servant. My lord, my girl's young — Hoyden is young, my lord: but this I must say for her, what she wants in art she has in breeding; and what's wanting in her age, is made good in her constitution. — So pray, my lord, walk in; pray, my lord, walk in.

Fash. Sir, I wait upon you.   [*Exeunt.*

SCENE IV. — *A Room in* SIR TUNBELLY CLUMSY'S *House.*

MISS HOYDEN *discovered alone.*

Miss Hoyd. Sure, nobody was ever used as I am! I know well enough what other girls do, for all they think to make a fool o'me. It's well I have a husband a-coming, or ecod I'd marry the baker, I would so. Nobody can knock at the gate, but presently I must be locked up; and here's the young greyhound can run loose about the house all the day long, so she can. — 'Tis very well!

Nurse. [*Without, opening the door.*] Miss Hoyden! miss, miss, miss! Miss Hoyden!

Enter NURSE.

Miss Hoyd. Well, what do you make such a noise for, ha? What do you din a body's ears for? Can't one be at quiet for you?

Nurse. What do I din your ears for? Here's one come will din your ears for you.

Miss Hoyd. What care I who's come? I care not a fig who comes, or who goes, so long as I must be locked up like the ale-cellar.

Nurse. That, miss, is for fear you should be drank before you are ripe.

Miss Hoyd. Oh, don't trouble your head about that; I'm as ripe as you, though not so mellow.

Nurse. Very well! Now I have a good mind to lock you up again, and not let you see my lord to-night.

Miss Hoyd. My lord: why, is my husband come?

Nurse. Yes, marry, is he; and a goodly person too.

Miss Hoyd. [*Hugs* Nurse.] Oh, my dear nurse, forgive me this once, and I'll never misuse you again; no, if I do, you shall give me three thumps on the back, and a great pinch by the cheek.

Nurse. Ah, the poor thing! see now it melts; it's as full of good-nature as an egg's full of meat.

Miss Hoyd. But, my dear nurse, don't lie now — is he come, by your troth?

Nurse. Yes, by my truly, is he.

Miss Hoyd. O Lord! I'll go and put on my laced tucker, though I'm locked up for a month for't.

> [*Exeunt.* Miss Hoyden *goes off capering, and twirl-ing her doll by its leg.*

ACT IV.

Scene I. — *A Room in* Sir Tunbelly Clumsy's *House.*

Enter Miss Hoyden *and* Nurse.

Nurse. Well, miss, how do you like your husband that is to be?

Miss Hoyd. O Lord, nurse, I'm so overjoyed I can scarce contain myself!

Nurse. Oh, but you must have a care of being too fond; for men, now-a-days, hate a woman that loves 'em.

Miss Hoyd. Love him! why, do you think I love him, nurse? Ecod, I would not care if he was hanged, so I were but once married to him. No, that which pleases me is to think what work I'll make when I get to London; for when I am a wife and a lady both, ecod, I'll flaunt it with the best of 'em. Ay, and I shall have money enough to do so too, nurse.

Nurse. Ah, there's no knowing that, miss; for though these lords have a power of wealth indeed, yet, as I have heard say, they give it all to their sluts and their trulls, who joggle it about in their coaches, with a murrain to 'em, whilst poor madam sits sighing and wishing, and has not a spare half-crown to buy her a Practice of Piety.

Miss Hoyd. Oh, but for that, don't deceive yourself, nurse; for this I must say of my lord, he's as free as an open house at Christmas; for this very morning he told me I should have six hundred a year to buy pins. Now if he gives me six hundred a year to buy pins, what do you think he'll give me to buy petticoats?

Nurse. Ah, my dearest, he deceives thee foully, and he's no better than a rogue for his pains! These Londoners have got a gibberish with 'em would confound a gipsy. That which they call pin-money, is to buy everything in the versal world, down to their very shoe-knots. Nay, I have heard some folks say that some ladies, if they'll have gallants as they call 'em, are forced to find them out of their pin-money too. — But look, look, if his honour be not coming to you! — Now, if I were sure you would behave yourself handsomely, and not disgrace me that have brought you up, I'd leave you alone together.

Miss Hoyd. That's my best nurse; do as you'd be done by. Trust us together this once, and if I don't show my breeding, I wish I may never be married, but die an old maid.

Nurse. Well, this once I'll venture you. But if you disparage me ——

Miss Hoyd. Never fear.   [*Exit* NURSE.

Enter TOM FASHION.

Fash. Your servant, madam; I'm glad to find you alone, for I have something of importance to speak to you about.

Miss Hoyd. Sir (my lord, I meant), you may speak to me about what you please, I shall give you a civil answer.

Fash. You give so obliging an one, it encourages me to tell you in a few words what I think, both for your interest and mine. Your father, I suppose you know, has resolved to make me happy in being your husband; and I hope I may obtain your consent to perform what he desires.

Miss Hoyd. Sir, I never disobey my father in any thing but eating green gooseberries.

Fash. So good a daughter must needs be an admirable wife. I am therefore impatient till you are mine, and hope you will so far consider the violence of my love, that you won't have the cruelty to defer my happiness so long as your father designs it.

Miss Hoyd. Pray, my lord, how long is that?

Fash. Madam, a thousand years — a whole week.

Miss Hoyd. Why I thought it was to be to-morrow morning, as soon as I was up. I'm sure nurse told me so.

Fash. And it shall be to-morrow morning, if you'll consent.

Miss Hoyd. If I'll consent! Why I thought I was to obey you as my husband?

Fash. That's when we are married. Till then, I'm to obey you.

Miss Hoyd. Why then, if we are to take it by turns, it's the same thing. I'll obey you now, and when we are married, you shall obey me.

Fash. With all my heart. But I doubt we must get nurse on our side, or we shall hardly prevail with the chaplain.

Miss Hoyd. No more we shan't, indeed; for he loves her better than he loves his pulpit, and would always be a-preaching to her by his good will.

Fash. Why then, my dear, if you'll call her hither, we'll persuade her presently.

Miss Hoyd. O Lud! I'll tell you a way how to persuade her to any thing.

Fash. How's that?

Miss. Hoyd. Why tell her she's a handsome comely woman, and give her half-a-crown.

Fash. Nay, if that will do, she shall have half a score of 'em.

Miss Hoyd. O gemini! for half that she'd marry you herself. — I'll run and call her.   [*Exit.*

Fash. So! matters go on swimmingly. This is a rare girl, i'faith. I shall have a fine time on't with her at London.

Enter LORY.

So, Lory, what's the matter?

Lory. Here, sir — an intercepted packet from the enemy; your brother's postillion brought it. I knew the livery, pretended to be a servant of Sir Tunbelly's, and so got possession of the letter.

Fash. [*Looks at the letter.*] Ouns! he tells Sir Tunbelly here that he will be with him this evening, with a large party to supper. — Egad, I must marry the girl directly.

Lory. Oh, zounds, sir, directly to be sure. Here she comes.   [*Exit.*

Fash. And the old Jezebel with her.

Re-enter MISS HOYDEN *and* NURSE.

How do you do, good Mrs. Nurse? I desired your young lady would give me leave to see you, that I might thank you for your extraordinary care and kind conduct in her education: pray accept of this small acknowledgment for it at present, and depend upon my further kindness when I shall be that happy thing her husband.   [*Gives her money.*

Nurse. [*Aside.*] Gold, by the maakins! — [*Aloud.*] Your honour's goodness is too great. Alas! all I can boast of is, I gave her pure good milk, and so your honour would have said, an you had seen how the poor thing thrived, and how it would look up in my face, and crow and laugh, it would.

Miss Hoyd. [*To* NURSE, *taking her angrily aside.*] Pray, one word with you. Pr'ythee, nurse, don't stand ripping up old stories, to make one ashamed before one's love. Do you

think such a fine proper gentleman as he is cares for a fiddle-
come tale of a child? If you have a mind to make him have
a good opinion of a woman, don't tell him what one did then,
tell him what one can do now. — [*To* TOM FASHION.] I hope
your honour will excuse my mis-manners to whisper before
you; it was only to give some orders about the family.

Fash. Oh, every thing, madam, is to give way to business;
besides, good housewifery is a very commendable quality in
a young lady.

Miss Hoyd. Pray, sir, are young ladies good housewives
at London-town? Do they darn their own linen?

Fash. Oh no, they study how to spend money, not to save.

Miss Hoyd. Ecod, I don't know but that may be better
sport, ha, nurse?

Fash. Well, you shall have your choice when you come
there.

Miss Hoyd. Shall I? then, by my troth, I'll get there as
fast as I can. — [*To* NURSE.] His honour desires you'll be so
kind as to let us be married to-morrow.

Nurse. To-morrow, my dear madam?

Fash. Ay, faith, nurse, you may well be surprised at miss's
wanting to put it off so long. To-morrow! no, no; 'tis now,
this very hour, I would have the ceremony performed.

Miss Hoyd. Ecod, with all my heart.

Nurse. O mercy! worse and worse!

Fash. Yes, sweet nurse, now and privately; for all things
being signed and sealed, why should Sir Tunbelly make us
stay a week for a wedding-dinner?

Nurse. But if you should be married now, what will you
do when Sir Tunbelly calls for you to be married?

Miss Hoyd. Why then we will be married again.

Nurse. What twice, my child?

Miss Hoyd. Ecod, I don't care how often I'm married,
not I.

Nurse. Well, I'm such a tender-hearted fool, I find I
can refuse you nothing. So you shall e'en follow your own
inventions.

Miss Hoyd. Shall I? O Lord, I could leap over the moon!

Fash. Dear nurse, this goodness of yours shall be still more rewarded. But now you must employ your power with the chaplain, that he may do his friendly office too, and then we shall be all happy. Do you think you can prevail with him?

Nurse. Prevail with him! or he shall never prevail with me, I can tell him that.

Fash. I'm glad to hear it; however, to strengthen your interest with him, you may let him know I have several fat livings in my gift, and that the first that falls shall be in your disposal.

Nurse. Nay, then, I'll make him marry more folks than one, I'll promise him!

Miss Hoyd. Faith, do, nurse, make him marry you too; I'm sure he'll do't for a fat living.

Fash. Well, nurse, while you go and settle matters with him, your lady and I will go and take a walk in the garden. — [*Exit* NURSE.] Come, madam, dare you venture yourself alone with me? [*Takes* MISS HOYDEN *by the hand.*

Miss Hoyd. Oh dear, yes, sir; I don't think you'll do any thing to me I need be afraid on. [*Exeunt.*

SCENE II. — AMANDA'S *Dressing-room.*

Enter AMANDA, *followed by her* MAID.

Maid. If you please, madam, only to say whether you'll have me buy them or not?

Aman. Yes — no — Go, teaser; I care not what you do. Pr'ythee leave me. [*Exit* MAID.

Enter BERINTHIA.

Ber. What, in the name of Jove, is the matter with you?

Aman. The matter, Berinthia! I'm almost mad; I'm plagued to death.

Ber. Who is it that plagues you?

Aman. Who do you think should plague a wife but her husband?

23*

Ber. O, ho! is it come to that? — We shall have you wish yourself a widow, by-and-by.

Aman. Would I were any thing but what I am! A base, ungrateful man, to use me thus!

Ber. What has he given you fresh reason to suspect his wandering?

Aman. Every hour gives me reason.

Ber. And yet, Amanda, you perhaps at this moment cause in another's breast the same tormenting doubts and jealousies which you feel so sensibly yourself.

Aman. Heaven knows I would not.

Ber. Why, you can't tell but there may be some one as tenderly attached to Townly, whom you boast of as your conquest, as you can be to your husband?

Aman. I'm sure I never encouraged his pretensions.

Ber. Psha! psha! no sensible man ever perseveres to love without encouragement. Why have you not treated him as you have Lord Foppington?

Aman. Because he presumed not so far. But let us drop the subject. Men, not women, are riddles. Mr. Loveless now follows some flirt for variety, whom I'm sure he does not like so well as he does me.

Ber. That's more than you know, madam.

Aman. Why, do you know the ugly thing?

Ber. I think I can guess at the person; but she's no such ugly thing neither.

Aman. Is she very handsome?

Ber. Truly I think so.

Aman. Whate'er she be, I'm sure he does not like her well enough to bestow any thing more than a little outward gallantry upon her.

Ber. [*Aside.*] Outward gallantry! I can't bear this. — [*Aloud.*] Come, come, don't you be too secure, Amanda: while you suffer Townly to imagine that you do not detest him for his designs on you, you have no right to complain that your husband is engaged elsewhere. But here comes the person we were speaking of.

Enter COLONEL TOWNLY.

Col. Town. Ladies, as I come uninvited, I beg, if I intrude, you will use the same freedom in turning me out again.

Aman. I believe it is near the time Loveless said he would be at home. He talked of accepting of Lord Foppington's invitation to sup at Sir Tunbelly Clumsy's.

Col. Town. His lordship has done me the honour to invite me also. If you'll let me escort you, I'll let you into a mystery as we go, in which you must play a part when we arrive.

Aman. But we have two hours yet to spare; the carriages are not ordered till eight, and it is not a five minutes' drive. So, cousin, let us keep the colonel to play at piquet with us, till Mr. Loveless comes home.

Ber. As you please, madam; but you know I have a letter to write.

Col. Town. Madam, you know you may command me, though I am a very wretched gamester.

Aman. Oh, you play well enough to lose your money, and that's all the ladies require; and so, without any more ceremony, let us go into the next room, and call for cards and candles.   [*Exeunt.*

SCENE III. — BERINTHIA'S *Dressing-room.*

Enter LOVELESS.

Love. So, thus far all's well: I have got into her dressing-room, and it being dusk, I think nobody has perceived me steal into the house. I heard Berinthia tell my wife she had some particular letters to write this evening, before she went to Sir Tunbelly's, and here are the implements of correspondence. — How shall I muster up assurance to show myself when she comes? I think she has given me encouragement; and, to do my impudence justice, I have made the most of it. — I hear a door open, and some one coming. If it should be my wife, what the devil should I say? I believe she mistrusts me, and, by my life, I don't deserve her tenderness; however,

I am determined to reform — though not yet. Ha! Berinthia!
— So, I'll step in here, till I see what sort of humour she is in.
[*Goes into the closet.*

Enter BERINTHIA.

Ber. Was ever so provoking a situation! To think I should
sit and hear him compliment Amanda to, my face! I have lost
all patience with them both! I would not for something have
Loveless know what temper of mind they have piqued me
into; yet I can't bear to leave them together. No, I'll put my
papers away, and return to disappoint them. — [*Goes to the
closet.*] — O Lord! a ghost! a ghost! a ghost!

Re-enter LOVELESS.

Love. Peace, my angel! it's no ghost, but one worth a
hundred spirits.

Ber. How, sir, have you had the insolence to presume to
—— run in again, here's somebody coming.
[LOVELESS *goes into the closet.*

Enter MAID.

Maid. O Lord, ma'am! what's the matter?
Ber. O Heavens! I'm almost frightened out of my wits! I
thought verily I had seen a ghost, and 'twas nothing but a
black hood pinned against the wall. You may go again; I
am the fearfullest fool!   [*Exit* MAID.

Re-enter LOVELESS.

Love. Is the coast clear?
Ber. The coast clear! Upon my word, I wonder at your
assurance!
Love. Why then you wonder before I have given you a
proof of it. But where's my wife?
Ber. At cards.
Love. With whom?
Ber. With Townly.
Love. Then we are safe enough.
Ber. You are so! Some husbands would be of another
mind, were he at cards with their wives.

Love. And they'd be in the right on't too; but I dare trust mine.

Ber. Indeed! and she, I doubt not, has the same confidence in you. Yet do you think she'd be content to come and find you here?

Love. Egad, as you say, that's true! — Then, for fear she should come, hadn't we better go into the next room, out of her way?

Ber. What, in the dark?

Love. Ay, or with a light, which you please.

Ber. You are certainly very impudent.

Love. Nay, then — let me conduct you, my angel!

Ber. Hold, hold! you are mistaken in your angel, I assure you.

Love. I hope not; for by this hand I swear——

Ber. Come, come, let go my hand, or I shall hate you! — I'll cry out as I live!

Love. Impossible! you cannot be so cruel.

Ber. Ha! here's some one coming. Begone instantly!

Love. Will you promise to return, if I remain here?

Ber. Never trust myself in a room again with you while I live.

Love. But I have something particular to communicate to you.

Ber. Well, well, before we go to Sir Tunbelly's, I'll walk upon the lawn. If you are fond of a moonlight evening, you'll find me there.

Love. I'faith, they're coming here now! — I take you at your word.   [*Exit into the closet.*

Ber. 'Tis Amanda, as I live! I hope she has not heard his voice; though I mean she should have her share of jealousy in her turn.

Enter AMANDA.

Aman. Berinthia, why did you leave me?

Ber. I thought I only spoiled your party.

Aman. Since you have been gone, Townly has attempted to renew his importunities. I must break with him —

for I cannot venture to acquaint Mr. Loveless with his conduct.

Ber. Oh, no! Mr. Loveless mustn't know of it by any
means.

Aman. Oh, not for the world! — I wish, Berinthia, you
would undertake to speak to Townly on the subject.

Ber. Upon my word, it would be a very pleasant subject
for me to talk upon! But, come, let us go back; and you
may depend on't I'll not leave you together again, if I can
help it.   [*Exeunt.*

Re-enter LOVELESS.

Love. So — so! a pretty piece of business I have overheard! Townly makes love to my wife, and I am not to
know it for all the world. I must inquire into this — and,
by Heaven, if I find that Amanda has, in the smallest degree
— yet what have I been at here! — Oh, 'sdeath! that's no
rule.

> That wife alone unsullied credit wins,
> Whose virtues can atone her husband's sins.
> Thus, while the man has other nymphs in view,
> It suits the woman to be doubly true.   [*Exit.*

ACT V.

SCENE I. — *The Garden behind* LOVELESS's *Lodgings.*

Enter LOVELESS.

Love. Now, does she mean to make a fool of me, or not!
I shan't wait much longer, for my wife will soon be inquiring
for me to set out on our supping party. Suspense is at
all times the devil, but of all modes of suspense, the watching for a loitering mistress is the worst. — But let me accuse
her no longer; she approaches with one smile to o'erpay the
anxieties of a year.

Enter BERINTHIA.

O Berinthia, what a world of kindness are you in my debt!
had you staid five minutes longer ——

Ber. You would have gone, I suppose?

Love. Egad, she's right enough.   [*Aside.*

Ber. And I assure you 'twas ten to one that I came at all. In short, I begin to think you are too dangerous a being to trifle with; and as I shall probably only make a fool of you at last, I believe we had better let matters rest as they are.

Love. You cannot mean it, sure?

Ber. What more would you have me 'give to a married man?

Love. How doubly cruel to remind me of my misfortunes

Ber. A misfortune to be married to so charming a woman as Amanda?

Love. I grant all her merit, but — 'sdeath! now see what you have done by talking of her — she's here, by all that's unlucky, and Townly with her. — I'll observe them.

Ber. O Gad, we had better get out of the way; for I should feel as awkward to meet her as you.

Love. Ay, if I mistake not, I see Townly coming this way also. I must see a little into this matter.   [*Steps aside.*

Ber. Oh, if that's your intention, I am no woman if I suffer myself to be outdone in curiosity.

[*Goes on the other side.*

Enter AMANDA.

Aman. Mr. Loveless come home, and walking on the lawn! I will not suffer him to walk so late, though perhaps it is to show his neglect of me. — Mr. Loveless, I must speak with you. — Ha! Townly again! How I am persecuted!

Enter COLONEL TOWNLY.

Col. Town. Madam, you seem disturbed.

Aman. Sir, I have reason.

Col. Town. Whatever be the cause, I would to Heaven it were in my power to bear the pain, or to remove the malady.

Aman. Your interference can only add to my distress.

Col. Town. Ah, madam, if it be the sting of unrequited love you suffer from, seek for your remedy in revenge: weigh well the strength and beauty of your charms, and rouse up that spirit a woman ought to bear. Disdain the false embraces of a husband. See at your feet a real lover; his zeal may give him title to your pity, although his merit cannot claim your love.

Love. So, so, very fine, i'faith! [*Aside.*

Aman. Why do you presume to talk to me thus? Is this your friendship to Mr. Loveless? I perceive you will compel me at last to acquaint him with your treachery.

Col. Town. He could not upbraid me if you were. — He deserves it from me; for he has not been more false to you than faithless to me.

Aman. To you?

Col. Town. Yes, madam; the lady for whom he now deserts those charms which he was never worthy of, was mine by right; and, I imagined too, by inclination. Yes, madam, Berinthia, who now ——

Aman. Berinthia! Impossible!

Col. Town. 'Tis true, or may I never merit your attention. She is the deceitful sorceress who now holds your husband's heart in bondage.

Aman. I will not believe it.

Col. Town. By the faith of a true lover, I speak from conviction. This very day I saw them together, and overheard ——

Aman. Peace, sir! I will not even listen to such slander — this is a poor device to work on my resentment, to listen to your insidious addresses. No, sir, though Mr. Loveless may be capable of error, I am convinced I cannot be deceived so grossly in him, as to believe what you now report; and for Berinthia, you should have fixed on some more probable person for my rival than her who is my relation and my friend: for while I am myself free from guilt, I will never believe that love can beget injury, or confidence create ingratitude.

Col. Town. If I do not prove to you ——

Aman. You never shall have an opportunity. From the artful manner in which you first showed yourself to me, I might have been led, as far as virtue permitted, to have thought you less criminal than unhappy; but this last unmanly artifice merits at once my resentment and contempt. [*Exit.*

— *Col. Town.* Sure there's divinity about her; and she has dispensed some portion of honour's light to me: yet can I bear to lose Berinthia without revenge or compensation? Perhaps she is not so culpable as I thought her. I was mistaken when I began to think lightly of Amanda's virtue, and may be in my censure of my Berinthia. Surely I love her still, for I feel I should be happy to find myself in the wrong.

[*Exit.*

Re-enter LOVELESS *and* BERINTHIA.

Ber. Your servant, Mr. Loveless.

Love. Your servant, madam.

Ber. Pray what do you think of this?

Love. Truly, I don't know what to say.

Ber. Don't you think we steal forth two contemptible creatures?

Love. Why tolerably so, I must confess.

Ber. And do you conceive it possible for you ever to give Amanda the least uneasiness again?

Love. No, I think we never should indeed.

Ber. Well why, monster, you don't pretend that I ever entertained a thought?

Love. Why then, sincerely and honestly, Berinthia, there is something in my wife's conduct which strikes me so forcibly, that if it were not for shame, and the fear of hurting you in her opinion, I swear I would follow her, confess my error, and trust to her generosity for forgiveness.

Ber. Nay, pr'ythee, don't let your respect for me prevent you; for as my object in trifling with you was nothing more than to pique Townly, and as I perceive he has been actuated by a similar motive, you may depend on't I shall make no mystery of the matter to him.

Love. By no means inform him; for though I may choose to pass by his conduct without resentment, how will he presume to look me in the face again?

Ber. How will you presume to look him in the face again?

Love. He, who has dared to attempt the honour of my wife!

Ber. You, who have dared to attempt the honour of his mistress! Come, come, be ruled by me, who affect more levity than I have, and don't think of anger in this cause. A readiness to resent injuries is a virtue only in those who are slow to injure.

Love. Then I will be ruled by you; and when you shall think proper to undeceive Townly, may your good qualities make as sincere a convert of him as Amanda's have of me. — When truth's extorted from us, then we own the robe of virtue is a sacred habit.

> Could women but our secret counsels scan —
> Could they but reach the deep reserve of man —
> To keep our love they'd rate their virtue high,
> They live together, and together die.   [*Exeunt.*

SCENE II. — *A Room in* SIR TUNBELLY CLUMSY'S *House.*

Enter MISS HOYDEN, NURSE, *and* TOM FASHION.

Fash. This quick despatch of the chaplain's I take so kindly, it shall give him claim to my favour as long as I live, I assure you.

Miss Hoyd. And to mine too, I promise you.

Nurse. I most humbly thank your honours; and may your children swarm about you like bees about a honeycomb!

Miss Hoyd. Ecod, with all my heart — the more the merrier, I say — ha, nurse?

Enter LORY.

Lory. One word with you, for Heaven's sake.

[*Taking* TOM FASHION *hastily aside.*

Fash. What the devil's the matter?

Lory. Sir, your fortune's ruined if you are not married. Yonder's your brother arrived, with two coaches and six horses, twenty footmen, and a coat worth fourscore pounds — so judge what will become of your lady's heart.

Fash. Is he in the house yet?

Lory. No, they are capitulating with him at the gate. Sir Tunbelly luckily takes him for an impostor; and I have told him that we have heard of this plot before.

Fash. That's right.—[*Turning to* Miss HOYDEN.] My dear, here's a troublesome business my man tells me of, but don't be frightened; we shall be too hard for the rogue. Here's an impudent fellow at the gate (not knowing I was come hither incognito) has taken my name upon him, in hopes to run away with you.

Miss Hoyd. Oh, the brazen-faced varlet! it's well we are married, or may be we might never have been so.

Fash. [*Aside.*] Egad, like enough. — [*Aloud.*] Pr'ythee, nurse, run to Sir Tunbelly, and stop him from going to the gate before I speak with him.

Nurse. An't please your honour, my lady and I had best lock ourselves up till the danger be over.

Fash. Do so, if you please.

Miss Hoyd. Not so fast; I won't be locked up any more, now I'm married.

Fash. Yes, pray, my dear, do, till we have seized this rascal.

Miss Hoyd. Nay, if you'll pray me, I'll do any thing.

[*Exit with* NURSE.

Fash. Hark you, sirrah, things are better than you imagine. The wedding's over.

Lory. The devil it is, sir! [*Capers about.*

Fash. Not a word — all's safe — but Sir Tunbelly don't know it, nor must not yet. So I am resolved to brazen the brunt of the business out, and have the pleasure of turning the impostor upon his lordship, which I believe may easily be done.

Enter SIR TUNBELLY CLUMSY.

Did you ever hear, sir, of so impudent an undertaking?

Sir Tun. Never, by the mass; but we'll tickle him, I'll warrant you.

Fash. They tell me, sir, he has a great many people with him, disguised like servants.

Sir Tun. Ay, ay, rogues enow, but we have mastered them. We only fired a few shot over their heads, and the regiment scoured in an instant. — Here, Tummas, bring in your prisoner.

Fash. If you please, Sir Tunbelly, it will be best for me not to confront the fellow yet, till you have heard how far his impudence will carry him.

Sir Tun. Egad, your lordship is an ingenious person. Your lordship then will please to step aside.

Lory [Aside.] 'Fore heaven, I applaud my master's modesty!   [*Exit with* TOM FASHION.

Enter SERVANTS, *with* LORD FOPPINGTON *disarmed.*

Sir Tun. Come, bring him along, bring him along.

Lord Fop. What the plague do you mean, gentlemen? is it fair time, that you are all drunk before supper?

Sir Tun. Drunk, sirrah! here's an impudent rogue for you now. Drunk or sober, bully, I'm a justice o' the peace, and know how to deal with strollers.

Lord Fop. Strollers!

Sir Tun. Ay, strollers. Come, give an account of yourself. What's your name? where do you live? do you pay scot and lot? Come, are you a freeholder or a copyholder?

Lord Fop. And why dost thou ask me so many impertinent questions?

Sir Tun. Because I'll make you answer 'em, before I have done with you, you rascal you!

Lord Fop. Before Gad, all the answers I can make to them is, that you are a very extraordinary old fellow, stap my vitals!

Sir Tun. Nay, if thou art joking deputy lieutenants, we know how to deal with you. — Here, draw a warrant for him immediately.

Lord Fop. A warrant! What the devil is't thou wouldst be at, old gentleman?

Sir Tun. I would be at you, sirrah, (if my hands were not tied as a magistrate,) and with these two double fists beat your teeth down your throat, you dog you!   [*Driving him.*

Lord Fop. And why wouldst thou spoil my face at that rate?

Sir Tun. For your design to rob me of my daughter, villain.

Lord Fop. Rob thee of thy daughter! Now do I begin to believe I am in bed and asleep, and that all this is but a dream. Pr'ythee, old father, wilt thou give me leave to ask thee one question?

Sir Tun. I can't tell whether I will or not, till I know what it is.

Lord Fop. Why, then, it is, whether thou didst not write to my Lord Foppington, to come down and marry thy daughter?

Sir Tun. Yes, marry, did I, and my Lord Foppington is come down, and shall marry my daughter before she's a day older.

Lord Fop. Now give me thy hand, old dad; I thought we should understand one another at last.

Sir Tun. The fellow's mad! — Here, bind him hand and foot.   [*They bind him.*

Lord Fop. Nay, pr'ythee, knight, leave fooling; thy jest begins to grow dull.

Sir Tun. Bind him, I say — he's mad: bread and water, a dark room, and a whip, may bring him to his senses again.

Lord Fop. Pr'ythee, Sir Tunbelly, why should you take such an aversion to the freedom of my address as to suffer the rascals thus to skewer down my arms like a rabbit! — [*Aside.*] Egad, if I don't awake, by all that I can see, this is like to prove one of the most impertinent dreams that ever I dreamt in my life.

Re-enter Miss Hoyden *and* Nurse.

Miss Hoyd. [*Going up to* Lord Foppington.] Is this he that would have run — Fough, how he stinks of sweets! — Pray, father, let him be dragged through the horsepond.

Lord Fop. This must be my wife, by her natural inclination to her husband.   [*Aside.*

Miss Hoyd. Pray, father, what do you intend to do with him — hang him?

Sir Tun. That at least, child.

Nurse. Ay, and it's e'en too good for him too.

Lord Fop. Madame la gouvernante, I presume: hitherto this appears to me to be one of the most extraordinary families that ever man of quality matched into. ` [Aside.

Sir Tun. What's become of my lord, daughter?

Miss Hoyd. He's just coming, sir.

Lord Fop. My lord, what does he mean by that, now! [Aside.

Re-enter Tom Fashion and Lory.

Stap my vitals, Tam, now the dream's out! [Runs.

Fash. Is this the fellow, sir, that designed to trick me of your daughter?

Sir Tun. This is he, my lord; how do you like him; is not he a pretty fellow to get a fortune?

Fash. I find by his dress he thought your daughter might be taken with a beau.

Miss Hoyd. Oh, gemini! is this a beau? let me see him again. [Surveys him.] Ha! I find a beau is no such ugly thing, neither.

Fash. [Aside.] Egad, she'll be in love with him presently — I'll e'en have him sent away to jail. — [To Lord Foppington.] Sir, though your undertaking shows you a person of no extraordinary modesty, I suppose you han't confidence enough to expect much favour from me?

Lord Fop. Strike me dumb, Tam, thou art a very impudent fellow.

Nurse. Look, if the varlet has not the effrontery to call his lordship plain Thomas!

Lord Fop. My Lord Foppington, shall I beg one word with your lordship?

Nurse. Ho, ho, it's my lord with him now! See how afflictions will humble folks.

Miss Hoyd. Pray, my lord — [To Fashion] — don't let him whisper too close, lest he bite your ear off.

Lord Fop. I am not altogether so hungry as your lady-ship is pleased to imagine. — [*Aside to* TOM FASHION.] Look you, Tam, I am sensible I have not been so kind to you as I ought, but I hope you'll forgive what's past, and accept of the five thousand pounds I offer — thou mayst live in extreme splendour with it, stap my vitals!

Fash. It's a much easier matter to prevent a disease than to cure it. A quarter of that sum would have secured your mistress, twice as much cannot redeem her.

[*Aside to* LORD FOPPINGTON.

Sir Tun. Well, what says he?

Fash. Only the rascal offered me a bribe to let him go.

Sir Tun. Ay, he shall go, with a plague to him! — Lead on, constable.

Enter SERVANT.

Serv. Sir, here is Muster Loveless, and Muster Colonel Townly, and some ladies to wait on you.   [*To* TOM FASHION.

Lory. [*Aside to* TOM FASHION.] So, sir, what will you do now?

Fash. [*Aside to* LORY.] Be quiet; they are in the plot. — [*Aloud.*] Only a few friends, Sir Tunbelly, whom I wish to introduce to you.

Lord Fop. Thou art the most impudent fellow, Tam, that ever nature yet brought into the world. — Sir Tunbelly, strike me speechless, but these are my friends and acquaintance, and my guests, and they will soon inform thee whether I am the true Lord Foppington or not.

Enter LOVELESS, COLONEL TOWNLY, AMANDA, *and* BERINTHIA. — LORD FOPPINGTON *accosts them as they pass, but none answer him.*

Fash. So, gentlemen, this is friendly; I rejoice to see you.

Col. Town. My lord, we are fortunate to be the witnesses of your lordship's happiness.

Love. But your lordship will do us the honour to introduce us to Sir Tunbelly Clumsy?

Aman. And us to your lady.

Lord Fop. Gad take me, but they are all in a story!

[*Aside.*

Sir Tun. Gentlemen, you do me much honour; my Lord Foppington's friends will ever be welcome to me and mine.

Fash. My love, let me introduce you to these ladies.

Miss Hoyd. By goles, they look so fine and so stiff, I am almost ashamed to come nigh 'em.

Aman. A most engaging lady, indeed!

Miss Hoyd. Thank ye, ma'am.

Ber. And I doubt not will soon distinguish herself in the beau-monde.

Miss Hoyd. Where is that?

Fash. You'll soon learn, my dear.

Love. But Lord Foppington ——

Lord Fop. Sir!

Love. Sir! I was not addressing myself to you, sir! — Pray who is this gentleman? He seems rather in a singular predicament —

Col. Town. For so well-dressed a person, a little oddly circumstanced, indeed.

Sir Tun. Ha! ha! ha! — So, these are your friends and your guests, ha, my adventurer?

Lord Fop. I am struck dumb with their impudence, and cannot positively say whether I shall ever speak again or not.

Sir Tun. Why, sir, this modest gentleman wanted to pass himself upon me as Lord Foppington, and carry off my daughter.

Love. A likely plot to succeed, truly, ha! ha!

Lord Fop. As Gad shall judge me, Loveless, I did not expect this from thee. Come, pr'ythee confess the joke; tell Sir Tunbelly that I am the real Lord Foppington, who yesterday made love to thy wife; was honoured by her with a slap on the face, and afterwards pinked through the body by thee.

Sir Tun. A likely story, truly, that a peer would behave thus!

Love. A pretty fellow, indeed, that would scandalize the

character he wants to assume; but what will you do with him, Sir Tunbelly?

Sir Tun. Commit him, certainly, unless the bride and bridegroom choose to pardon him.

Lord Fop. Bride and bridegroom! For Gad's sake, Sir Tunbelly, 'tis tarture to me to hear you call 'em so.

Miss Hoyd. Why, you ugly thing, what would you have him call us — dog and cat?

Lord Fop. By no means, miss; for that sounds ten times more like man and wife than t'other.

Sir Tun. A precious rogue this to come a-wooing!

Re-enter Servant.

Serv. There are some gentlefolks below to wait upon Lord Foppington.   [*Exit.*

Col. Town. 'Sdeath, Tom, what will you do now?
                              [*Aside to* Tom Fashion.

Lord Fop. Now, Sir Tunbelly, here are witnesses who I believe are not corrupted.

Sir Tun. Peace, fellow! — Would your lordship choose to have your guests shown here, or shall they wait till we come to 'em?

Fash. I believe, Sir Tunbelly, we had better not have these visitors here yet. — [*Aside.*] Egad, all must out.

Love. Confess, confess; we'll stand by you.
                              [*Aside to* Tom Fashion.

Lord Fop. Nay, Sir Tunbelly, I insist on your calling evidence on both sides — and if I do not prove that fellow an impostor ——

Fash. Brother, I will save you the trouble, by now confessing that I am not what I have passed myself for. — Sir Tunbelly, I am a gentleman, and I flatter myself a man of character; but 'tis with great pride I assure you I am not Lord Foppington.

Sir Tun. Ouns! — what's this? — an impostor? — a cheat? — fire and faggots, sir, if you are not Lord Foppington, who the devil are you?

                                     24*

Fash. Sir, the best of my condition is, I am your son-in-law; and the worst of it is, I am brother to that noble peer

Lord Fop. Impudent to the last, Gad dem me!

Sir Tun. My son-in-law! not yet, I hope.

Fash. Pardon me, sir; thanks to the goodness of your chaplain, and the kind offices of this gentlewoman.

Lory. 'Tis true, indeed, sir; I gave your daughter away, and Mrs. Nurse, here, was clerk.

Sir Tun. Knock that rascal down! — But speak, Jezebel, how's this?

Nurse. Alas! your honour, forgive me; I have been over-reached in this business as well as you. Your worship knows, if the wedding-dinner had been ready, you would have given her away with your own hands.

Sir Tun. But how durst you do this without acquainting me!

Nurse. Alas! if your worship had seen how the poor thing begged and prayed, and clung and twined about me like ivy round an old wall, you would say, I who had nursed it, must have had a heart like stone to refuse it.

Sir Tun. Ouns! I shall go mad! Unloose my lord there, you scoundrels!

Lord Fop. Why, when these gentlemen are at leisure, I should be glad to congratulate you on your son-in-law, with a little more freedom of address.

Miss Hoyd. Egad, though, I don't see which is to be my husband after all.

Love. Come, come, Sir Tunbelly, a man of your understanding must perceive, that an affair of this kind is not to be mended by anger and reproaches.

Col. Town. Take my word for it, Sir Tunbelly, you are only tricked into a son-in-law you may be proud of: my friend Tom Fashion is as honest a fellow as ever breathed.

Love. That he is, depend on't; and will hunt or drink with you most affectionately: be generous, old boy, and forgive them ——

Sir Tun. Never! the hussy! — when I had set my heart on getting her a title.

Lord Fop. Now, Sir Tunbelly, that I am untrussed — give me leave to thank thee for the very extraordinary reception I have met with in thy damned, execrable mansion; and at the same time to assure you, that of all the bumpkins and blockheads I have had the misfortune to meet with, thou art the most obstinate and egregious, strike me ugly!

Sir Tun. What's this? I believe you are both rogues alike.

Lord Fop. No, Sir Tunbelly, thou wilt find to thy unspeakable mortification, that I am the real Lord Foppington, who was to have disgraced myself by an alliance with a clod; and that thou hast matched thy girl to a beggarly younger brother of mine, whose title-deeds might be contained in thy tobacco-box.

Sir Tun. Puppy! puppy! — I might prevent their being beggars, if I chose it; for I could give 'em as good a rent-roll as your lordship.

Lord Fop. Ay, old fellow, but you will not do that — for that would be acting like a Christian, and thou art a barbarian, stap my vitals.

Sir Tun. Udzookers! now six such words more, and I'll forgive them directly.

Love. 'Slife, Sir Tunbelly, you should do it, and bless yourself — Ladies, what say you?

Aman. Good Sir Tunbelly, you must consent.

Ber. Come, you have been young yourself, Sir Tunbelly.

Sir Tun. Well then, if I must, I must; but turn — turn that sneering lord out, however, and let me be revenged on somebody. But first look whether I am a barbarian or not; there, children, I join your hands; and when I'm in a better humour, I'll give you my blessing.

Love. Nobly done, Sir Tunbelly! and we shall see you dance at a grandson's christening yet.

Miss Hoyd. By goles, though, I don't understand this! What, an't I to be a lady after all? only plain Mrs. — What's my husband's name, nurse?

Nurse. Squire Fashion.

Miss Hoyd. Squire, is he? — Well, that's better than nothing.

Lord Fop. [*Aside.*] Now I will put on a philosophic air, and show these people, that it is not possible to put a man of my quality out of countenance. — [*Aloud.*] Dear Tam, since things are fallen out, pr'ythee give me leave to wish thee joy; I do it *de bon cœur*, strike me dumb! You have married into a family of great politeness and uncommon elegance of manners, and your bride appears to be a lady beautiful in person, modest in her deportment, refined in her sentiments, and of nice morality, split my windpipe!

Miss Hoyd. By goles, husband, break his bones, if he calls me names!

Fash. Your lordship may keep up your spirits with your grimace, if you please; I shall support mine by Sir Tunbelly's favour, with this lady and three thousand pounds a year.

Lord Fop. Well, adieu, Tam! — Ladies, I kiss your hands. — Sir Tunbelly, I shall now quit this thy den; but while I retain the use of my arms, I shall ever remember thou art a demned horrid savage; Ged demn me!   [*Exit.*

Sir Tun. By the mass, 'tis well he's gone — for I should ha' been provoked, by-and by, to ha' dun un a mischief. Well, if this is a lord, I think Hoyden has luck o' her side, in troth.

Col. Town. She has indeed, Sir Tunbelly. — But I hear the fiddles; his lordship, I know, had provided 'em.

Love. Oh, a dance and a bottle, Sir Tunbelly, by all means!

Sir Tun. I had forgot the company below; well — what — we must be merry then, ha? and dance and drink, ha? Well, 'fore George, you shan't say I do these things by halves. Son-in-law there looks like a hearty rogue, so we'll have a night on't: and which of these ladies will be the old man's partner, ha? — Ecod, I don't know how I came to be in so good a humour.

Ber. Well, Sir Tunbelly, my friend and I both will

endeavour to keep you so: you have done a generous action,
and are entitled to our attention. If you should be at a loss
to divert your new guests, we will assist you to relate to them
the plot of your daughter's marriage, and his lordship's deserved mortification; a subject which perhaps may afford no
bad evening's entertainment.

Sir Tun. Ecod, with all my heart; though I am a main
bungler at a long story.

Ber. Never fear; we will assist you, if the tale is judged
worth being repeated; but of this you may be assured, that
while the intention is evidently to please, British auditors will
ever be indulgent to the errors of the performance.

[*Exeunt omnes.*

PIZARRO.
A TRAGEDY.

ADVERTISEMENT.

As the two translations which have been published of Kotzebue's "Spaniards in Peru" have, I understand, been very generally read, the public are in possession of all the materials necessary to form a judgment on the merits and defects of the Play performed at Drury-lane Theatre.

DEDICATION.

To her, whose approbation of this Drama, and whose peculiar delight in the applause it has received from the public, have been to *me* the highest gratification derived from its success — I dedicate this Play.

RICHARD BRINSLEY SHERIDAN.

DRAMATIS PERSONÆ.
AS ORIGINALLY ACTED AT DRURY-LANE THEATRE in 1799.

ATALIBA	*Mr. Powell.*	OLD BLIND MAN	*Mr. Cory.*
ROLLA	*Mr. Kemble.*	BOY	*Master Chatterley.*
OROZEMBO	*Mr. Dowton.*	SENTINEL	*Mr. Holland.*
ORANO	*Mr. Archer.*	ATTENDANT	*Mr. Maddocks.*
ALONZO	*Mr. C. Kemble.*	CORA	*Mrs. Jordan.*
PIZARRO	*Mr. Barrymore.*	ELVIRA	*Mrs. Siddons.*
ALMAGRO	*Mr. Caulfield.*	ZULUGA	
GONZALO	*Mr. Wentworth.*	Peruvian Warriors, Women, *and*
DAVILLA	*Mr. Trueman.*	Children, High-priest, Priests, *and*
GOMEZ	*Mr. Surmount.*	Virgins of the Sun, Spanish Officers,
VALVERDE	*Mr. R. Palmer.*	Soldiers, Guards, &c. &c.
LAS-CASAS	*Mr. Aickin.*	

SCENE. — PERU.

PROLOGUE.
WRITTEN BY RICHARD BRINSLEY SHERIDAN.
SPOKEN BY MR. KING.

CHILL'D by rude gales, while yet reluctant May
Withholds the beauties of the vernal day;

As some fond maid, whom matron frowns reprove,
Suspends the smile her heart devotes to love;
The season's pleasures too delay their hour,
And Winter revels with protracted power:
Then blame not, critics, if, thus late, we bring
A Winter Drama — but reproach — the Spring.
What prudent cit dares yet the season trust,
Bask in his whisky, and enjoy the dust?
Horsed in Cheapside, scarce yet the gayer spark
Achieves the Sunday triumph of the Park;
Scarce yet you see him, dreading to be late,
Scour the New Road, and dash through Grosvenor Gate: —
Anxious — yet timorous too — his steed to show,
The hack Bucephalus of Rotten Row.
Careless he seems, yet vigilantly sly,
Woos the gay glance of ladies passing by,
While his off heel, insidiously aside,
Provokes the caper which he seems to chide.
Scarce rural Kensington due honour gains;
The vulgar verdure of her walk remains!
Where night-robed misses amble two by two,
Nodding to booted beaux — "How'do, how'do?"
With generous questions that no answer wait,
"How vastly full! An't you come vastly late?
Isn't it quite charming? When do you leave town?
An't you quite tired? Pray, can't we sit down?"
These suburb pleasures of a London May,
Imperfect yet, we hail the cold delay;
Should our Play please — and you're indulgent ever —
Be your decree — " 'Tis better late than never."

ACT I.

Scene I. — *A Pavilion near* Pizarro's *Tent.*

Elvira *discovered sleeping under a canopy.* Valverde *enters, gazes on* Elvira, *kneels, and attempts to kiss her hand;* Elvira, *awakened, rises and looks at him with indignation.*

Elv. Audacious! Whence is thy privilege to interrupt the few moments of repose my harassed mind can snatch amid the tumults of this noisy camp? Shall I inform thy master, Pizarro, of this presumptuous treachery?

Val. I am his servant, it is true — trusted by him — and I

know him well; and therefore 'tis I ask, by what magic could
Pizarro gain your heart? by what fatality still holds he your
affection?

Elv. Hold! thou trusty secretary!

Val. Ignobly born! in mind and manners rude, ferocious,
and unpolished, though cool and crafty if occasion need — in
youth audacious — ill his first manhood — a licensed pirate —
treating men as brutes, the world as booty; yet now the
Spanish hero is he styled — the first of Spanish conquerors!
and, for a warrior so accomplished, 'tis fit Elvira should leave
her noble family, her fame, her home, to share the dangers,
humours, and the crimes, of such a lover as Pizarro!

Elv. What! Valverde moralising! But grant I am in error,
what is my incentive? Passion, infatuation, call it as you will;
but what attaches thee to this despised, unworthy leader?
Base lucre is thy object, mean fraud thy means. Could you
gain me, you only hope to win a higher interest in Pizarro.
I know you.

Val. On my soul, you wrong me! What else my faults, I
have none towards you. But indulge the scorn and levity of
your nature; do it while yet the time permits; the gloomy
hour, I fear, too soon approaches.

Elv. Valverde a prophet too!

Val. Hear me, Elvira. Shame from his late defeat, and
burning wishes for revenge, again have brought Pizarro to
Peru; but trust me, he overrates his strength, nor measures
well the foe. Encamped in a strange country, where terror
cannot force, nor corruption buy a single friend, what have
we to hope? The army murmuring at increasing hardships,
while Pizarro decorates with gaudy spoil the gay pavilion of
his luxury, each day diminishes our force.

Elv. But are you not the heirs of those that fall?

Val. Are gain and plunder, then, our only purpose? Is
this Elvira's heroism?

Elv. No, so save me Heaven! I abhor the motive, means,
and end of your pursuits; but I will trust none of you. In

your whole army there is not one of you that has a heart, or speaks ingenuously—aged Las-Casas, and he alone, excepted.

Val. He! an enthusiast in the opposite and worst extreme!

Elv. Oh! had I earlier known that virtuous man, how different might my lot have been!

Val. I will grant Pizarro could not then so easily have duped you: forgive me, but at that event I still must wonder.

Elv. Hear me, Valverde. When first my virgin fancy waked to love, Pizarro was my country's idol. Self-taught, self-raised, and self-supported, he became a hero; and I was formed to be won by glory and renown. 'Tis known that, when he left Panama in a slight vessel, his force was not a hundred men. Arrived at the island of Gallo, with his sword he drew a line upon the sands, and said, "Pass those who fear to die or conquer with their leader." Thirteen alone remained, and at the head of these the warrior stood his ground. Even at the moment when my ears first caught this tale, my heart exclaimed, "Pizarro is its lord!" What since I have perceived, or thought, or felt, you must have more worth to win the knowledge of.

Val. I press no further, still assured that, while Alonzo de Molina, our general's former friend and pupil, leads the enemy, Pizarro never more will be a conqueror.

[Trumpets without.

Elv. Silence! I hear him coming; look not perplexed. How mystery and fraud confound the countenance! Quick, put on an honest face, if thou canst.

Piz. [*Without.*] Chain and secure him; I will examine him myself.

Enter PIZARRO. VALVERDE *bows* — ELVIRA *laughs.*

Piz. Why dost thou smile, Elvira?

Elv. To laugh or weep without a reason is one of the few privileges poor women have.

Piz. Elvira, I will know the cause, I am resolved!

Elv. I am glad of that, because I love resolution, and am resolved not to tell you. Now my resolution, I take it, is the

better of the two, because it depends upon myself, and yours
does not.

Piz. Psha! trifler!

Val. Elvira was laughing at my apprehensions that——

Piz. Apprehensions!

Val. Yes — that Alonzo's skill and genius should so have
disciplined and informed the enemy, as to——

Piz. Alonzo! the traitor! How I once loved that man! His
noble mother intrusted him, a boy, to my protection. [ELVIRA
walks about pensively in the background.] At my table did he
feast — in my tent did he repose. I had marked his early
genius, and the valorous spirit that grew with it. Often had
I talked to him of our first adventures — what storms we
struggled with — what perils we surmounted! When landed
with a slender host upon an unknown land — then, when I
told how famine and fatigue, discord and toil, day by day,
did thin our ranks amid close-pressing enemies — how still
undaunted I endured and dared — maintained my purpose and
my power in despite of growling mutiny or bold revolt, till
with my faithful few remaining I became at last victorious! —
when, I say, of these things I spoke, the youth Alonzo, with
tears of wonder and delight, would throw him on my neck,
and swear his soul's ambition owned no other leader.

Val. What could subdue attachment so begun?

Piz. Las-Casas. — He it was, with fascinating craft and
canting precepts of humanity, raised in Alonzo's mind a new
enthusiasm, which forced him, as the stripling termed it, to
forego his country's claims for those of human nature.

Val. Yes, the traitor left you, joined the Peruvians, and
became thy enemy, and Spain's.

Piz. But first with weariless remonstrance he sued to win
me from my purpose, and untwine the sword from my determined grasp. Much he spoke of right, of justice, and
humanity, calling the Peruvians our innocent and unoffending
brethren.

Val. They! Obdurate heathens! They our brethren!

Piz. But, when he found that the soft folly of the pleading tears he dropped upon my bosom fell on marble, he flew and joined the foe: then, profiting by the lessons he had gained in wronged Pizarro's school, the youth so disciplined and led his new allies, that soon he forced me — ha! I burn with shame and fury while I own it! — in base retreat and foul discomfiture to quit the shore.

Val. But the hour of revenge is come.

Piz. It is; I am returned: my force is strengthened, and the audacious boy shall soon know that Pizarro lives, and has — a grateful recollection of the thanks he owes him.

Val. 'Tis doubted whether still Alonzo lives.

Piz. 'Tis certain that he does; one of his armour-bearers is just made prisoner: twelve thousand is their force, as he reports, led by Alonzo and Peruvian Rolla. This day they make a solemn sacrifice on their ungodly altars. We must profit by their security, and attack them unprepared — the sacrificers shall become the victims.

Elv. Wretched innocents! And their own blood shall bedew their altars!

Piz. Right! — [*Trumpets without.*] Elvira, retire!

Elv. Why should I retire?

Piz. Because men are to meet here, and on manly business.

Elv. O men! men! ungrateful and perverse! O woman! still affectionate though wronged! [VALVERDE *retires back.*] The beings to whose eyes you turn for animation, hope, and rapture, through the days of mirth and revelry; and on whose bosoms, in the hour of sore calamity, you seek for rest and consolation; them, when the pompous follies of your mean ambition are the question, you treat as playthings or as slaves! — I shall not retire.

Piz. Remain then; and, if thou canst, be silent.

Elv. They only babble who practise not reflection. I shall think — and thought is silence.

Piz. [*Aside.*] Ha! there's somewhat in her manner lately——
[*Looks sternly and suspiciously at* ELVIRA, *who meets his glance with a commanding and unaltered eye.*

Enter Las-Casas, Almagro, Gonzalo, Davilla, Officers *and*
Soldiers.—*Trumpets without.*

Las-Cas. Pizarro, we attend thy summons.

Piz. Welcome, venerable father! — My friends, most welcome! — Friends and fellow soldiers, at length the hour is arrived, which to Pizarro's hopes presents the full reward of
our undaunted enterprise and long-enduring toils. Confident
in security, this day the foe devotes to solemn sacrifice: it
with bold surprise we strike on their solemnity — trust to your
leader's word — we shall not fail.

Alm. Too long inactive have we been mouldering on the
coast; our stores exhausted, and our soldiers murmuring.
Battle! battle! — then death to the armed, and chains for the
defenceless.

Dav. Death to the whole Peruvian race!

Las-Cas. Merciful Heaven!

Alm. Yes, general, the attack, and instantly! Then shall
Alonzo, basking at his ease, soon cease to scoff our sufferings,
and scorn our force.

Las-Cas. Alonzo! — scorn and presumption are not in his
nature.

Alm. 'Tis fit Las-Casas should defend his pupil.

Piz. Speak not of the traitor! or hear his name but as the
bloody summons to assault and vengeance. It appears we are
agreed?

Alm. Dav. We are.

Gon. All. — Battle! battle!

Las-Cas. Is, then, the dreadful measure of your cruelty
not yet complete? Battle! gracious Heaven! against whom?
Against a king, in whose mild bosom your atrocious injuries even yet have not excited hate! but who, insulted or
victorious, still sues for peace. Against a people who never
wronged the living being their Creator formed: a people
who, children of innocence! received you as cherished guests
with eager hospitality and confiding kindness. Generously
and freely did they share with you their comforts, their treasures, and their homes: you repaid them by fraud, oppres-

sion, and dishonour. These eyes have witnessed all I speak — as gods you were received; as fiends have you acted.

Piz. Cas-Casas!

Las-Cas. Pizarro, hear me! — Hear me, chieftains! —And thou, all-powerful! whose thunders can shiver into sand the adamantine rock — whose lightnings can pierce to the core of the rived and quaking earth — oh! let thy power give effect to thy servant's words, as thy spirit gives courage to his will! — Do not, I implore you, chieftains — countrymen — do not, I implore you, renew the foul barbarities which your insatiate avarice has inflicted on this wretched, unoffending race!—But hush, my sighs!—fall not, drops of useless sorrow! —heart-breaking anguish, choke not my utterance!—All I entreat is, send me once more to those you call your enemies. — Oh! let me be the messenger of penitence from you; I shall return with blessings and with peace from them. — [*Turning to* ELVIRA.] Elvira, you weep!—Alas! and does this dreadful crisis move no heart but thine?

Alm. Because there are no women here but she and thou.

Piz. Close this idle war of words: time flies, and our opportunity will be lost. Chieftains, are ye for instant battle?

Alm. We are.

Las-Cas. Oh, men of blood! — [*Kneels.*] God! thou hast anointed me thy servant — not to curse, but to bless my countrymen: yet now my blessing on their force were blasphemy against thy goodness. — [*Rises.*] No! I curse your purpose, homicides! I curse the bond of blood by which you are united. May fell division, infamy, and rout, defeat your projects and rebuke your hopes! On you, and on your children, be the peril of the innocent blood which shall be shed this day! I leave you, and for ever! No longer shall these aged eyes be seared by the horrors they have witnessed. In caves, in forests, will I hide myself; with tigers and with savage beasts will I commune; and when at length we meet before the blessed tribunal of that Deity, whose mild doctrines and whose mercies ye have this day renounced, then shall

you feel the agony and grief of soul which tear the bosom of
your accuser now!   [*Going.*

Elv. [*Rises and takes the hand of* LAS-CASAS.] Las-Casas!
Oh, take me with thee, Las-Casas!

Las-Cas. Stay! lost, abused lady! I alone am useless here.
Perhaps thy loveliness may persuade to pity, where reason
and religion plead in vain. Oh! save thy innocent fellow-
creatures if thou canst: then shall thy frailty be redeemed,
and thou wilt share the mercy thou bestowest.   [*Exit.*

Piz. How, Elvira! wouldst thou leave me?

Elv. I am bewildered, grown terrified! Your inhumanity
— and that good Las-Casas — oh! he appeared to me just
now something more than heavenly: and you! ye all looked
worse than earthly.

Piz. Compassion sometimes becomes a beauty.

Elv. Humanity always becomes a conqueror.

Alm. Well! Heaven be praised, we are rid of the old
moralist.

Gon. I hope he'll join his preaching pupil, Alonzo.

Piz. [*Turning to* ALMAGRO.] Now to prepare our muster
and our march. At midday is the hour of the sacrifice. [EL-
VIRA *sits.*] Consulting with our guides, the route of your
divisions shall be given to each commander. If we surprise,
we conquer; and, if we conquer, the gates of Quito will be
open to us.

Alm. And Pizarro then be monarch of Peru.

Piz. Not so fast — ambition for a time must take counsel
from discretion. Ataliba still must hold the shadow of a
sceptre in his hand — Pizarro still appear dependent upon
Spain: while the pledge of future peace, his daughter's hand,
[ELVIRA *rises much agitated*,] secures the proud succession to
the crown I seek.

Alm. This is best. In Pizarro's plans observe the statesman's wisdom guides the warrior's valour.

Val. [*Aside to* ELVIRA.] You mark, Elvira?

Elv. Oh, yes — this is best — this is excellent!

Piz. You seem offended. Elvira still retains my heart Think — a sceptre waves me on.

Elv. Offended? — no! Thou knowest thy glory is my idol; and this will be most glorious, most just and honourable.

Piz. What mean you?

Elv. Oh, nothing! — mere woman's prattle — a jealous whim, perhaps: but let it not impede the royal hero's course. — [*Trumpets without.*] The call of arms invites you. — Away! away! you, his brave, his worthy fellow-warriors.

Piz. And go you not with me?

Elv. Undoubtedly! I needs must be first to hail the future monarch of Peru.

Enter GOMEZ.

Alm. How, Gomez! what bringest thou?

Gom. On yonder hill, among the palm-trees, we have surprised an old cacique: escape by flight he could not, and we seized him and his attendant unresisting; yet his lips breathe nought but bitterness and scorn.

Piz. Drag him before us. — [ELVIRA *sits pensively.* GOMEZ *goes out and returns with* OROZEMBO *and* Attendant, *in chains guarded.*] What art thou, stranger?

Oro. First tell me which among you is the captain of this band of robbers.

Piz. Ha!

Alm. Madman! — Tear out his tongue, or else ——

Oro. Thou'lt hear some truth.

Dav. [*Showing his poniard.*] Shall I not plunge this into his heart?

Oro. [*To* PIZARRO.] Does your army boast many such heroes as this?

Piz. Audacious! this insolence has sealed thy doom. Die thou shalt, grey-headed ruffian. But first confess what thou knowest.

Oro. I know that which thou hast just assured me of — that I shall die.

Piz. Less audacity perhaps might have preserved thy life.

Sheridan.   25

Oro. My life is as a withered tree; it is not worth preserving.

Piz. Hear me, old man. Even now we march against the Peruvian army. We know there is a secret path that leads to your stronghold among the rocks: guide us to that, and name thy reward. If wealth be thy wish ——

Oro. Ha! ha! ha! ha!

Piz. Dost thou despise my offer?

Oro. Thee and thy offer! Wealth!— I have the wealth of two dear gallant sons — I have stored in heaven the riches which repay good actions here — and still my chiefest treasure do I bear about me.

Piz. What is that? inform me.

Oro. I will; for it never can be thine — the treasure of a pure, unsullied conscience.

　　　　[ELVIRA *sits, still paying marked attention to* OROZEMBO.

Piz. I believe there is no other Peruvian who dares speak as thou dost.

Oro. Would I could believe there is no other Spaniard who dares act as thou dost!

Gon. Obdurate Pagan! How numerous is your army?

Oro. Count the leaves of yonder forest.

Alm. Which is the weakest part of your camp?

Oro. It has no weak part; on every side 'tis fortified by justice.

Piz. Where have you concealed your wives and your children?

Oro. In the hearts of their husbands and their fathers.

Piz. Knowest thou Alonzo?

Oro. Know him! Alonzo! Know him! Our nation's benefactor! the guardian angel of Peru!

Piz. By what has he merited that title?

Oro. By not resembling thee.

Alm. Who is this Rolla, joined with Alonzo in command?

Oro. I will answer that; for I love to hear and to repeat the hero's name. Rolla, the kinsman of the king, is the idol of our army; in war a tiger, chafed by the hunter's spear;

in peace more gentle than the unweaned lamb. Cora was
once betrothed to him; but, finding she preferred Alonzo, he
resigned his claim, and, I fear, his peace, to friendship and
to Cora's happiness; yet still he loves her with a pure and
holy fire.

Piz. Romantic savage! — I shall meet this Rolla soon.

Oro. Thou hadst better not! the terrors of his noble eye
would strike thee dead.

Dav. Silence, or tremble!

Oro. Beardless robber! I never yet have trembled before
God; why should I tremble before man? Why before thee,
thou less than man?

Dav. Another word, audacious heathen, and I strike!

Oro. Strike, Christian! Then boast among thy fellows —
I too have murdered a Peruvian!

Dav. Hell and vengeance seize thee!   [*Stabs him.*

Piz. Hold!

Dav. Couldst thou longer have endured his insults?

Piz. And therefore should he die untortured?

Oro. True! Observe, young man — [*To* DAVILLA.] Thy
unthinking rashness has saved me from the rack; and thou
thyself hast lost the opportunity of a useful lesson; thou
mightst thyself have seen with what cruelty vengeance would
have inflicted torments — and with what patience virtue
would have borne them.

Elv. [*Supporting* OROZEMBO's *head upon her bosom.*] Oh, ye
are monsters all! Look up, thou martyred innocent—look up
once more, and bless me ere thou diest. God! how I pity thee!

Oro. Pity me! — me! so near my happiness! Bless thee,
lady! — Spaniards — Heaven turn your hearts, and pardon
you as I do.

Piz. Away! — [OROZEMBO *is borne off dying.*] Away! Davilla! if thus rash a second time — —

Dav. Forgive the hasty indignation which — —

Piz. No more! Unbind that trembling wretch — let him
depart: 'tis well he should report the mercy which we show
to insolent defiance — Hark! our troops are moving.

Attend. [*On passing* ELVIRA.] If through your gentle means my master's poor remains might be preserved from insult ——

Elv. I understand thee.

Attend. His sons may yet thank your charity, if not avenge their father's fate.   [*Exit.*

Piz. What says the slave?

Elv. A parting word to thank you for your mercy.

Piz. Our guards and guides approach. — [SOLDIERS *march through the tents.*] Follow me, friends.— each shall have his post assigned, and ere Peruvia's god shall sink beneath the main, the Spanish banner, bathed in blood, shall float above the walls of vanquished Quito.

                        [*Exeunt all but* ELVIRA *and* VALVERDE.

Val. Is it now presumption that my hopes gain strength with the increasing horrors which I see appal Elvira's soul?

Elv. I am mad with terror and remorse! Would I could fly these dreadful scenes!

Val. Might not Valverde's true attachment be thy refuge?

Elv. What wouldst thou do to save or to avenge me?

Val. I dare do all thy injuries may demand — a word — and he lies bleeding at your feet.

Elv. Perhaps we will speak again of this. Now leave me. — [*Exit* VALVERDE.] No! not this revenge — no! not this instrument. Fie, Elvira! even for a moment to counsel with this unworthy traitor! Can a wretch, false to a confiding master, be true to any pledge of love or honour? — Pizarro will abandon me — yes; me — who, for his sake, have sacrificed — oh, God! what have I not sacrificed for him! Yet, curbing the avenging pride that swells this bosom, I still will further try him. Oh, men! ye who, wearied by the fond fidelity of virtuous love, seek in the wanton's flattery a new delight, oh, ye may insult and leave the hearts to which your faith was pledged, and, stifling self-reproach, may fear no other peril; because such hearts, howe'er you injure and desert them, have yet the proud retreat of an unspotted fame — of unreproaching conscience. But beware the desperate libertine

who forsakes the creature whom his arts have first deprived
of all natural protection — of all self-consolation! What has
he left her? Despair and vengeance!   [*Exit.*

ACT II.

Scene I. — *A Bank surrounded by a wild wood, and rocks.*

Cora *is discovered playing with her* Child; Alonzo *hanging over
them with delight.*

Cora. Now confess, does he resemble thee, or not?

Alon. Indeed he is liker thee — thy rosy softness, thy
smiling gentleness.

Cora. But his auburn hair, the colour of his eyes, Alonzo.
— Oh, my lord's image, and my heart's adored!

[*Presses the* Child *to her bosom.*

Alon. The little darling urchin robs me, I doubt, of some
portion of thy love, my Cora. At least he shares caresses,
which till his birth were only mine.

Cora. Oh no, Alonzo! a mother's love for her sweet babe
is not a stealth from the dear father's store; it is a new delight
that turns with quickened gratitude to Him, the author of her
augmented bliss.

Alon. Could Cora think me serious?

Cora. I am sure he will speak soon: then will be the last
of the three holidays allowed by Nature's sanction to the
fond, anxious mother's heart.

Alon. What are those three?

Cora. The ecstasy of his birth I pass; that in part is
selfish: but when first the white blossoms of his teeth appear,
breaking the crimson buds that did incase them, that is a day
of joy; next, when from his father's arms he runs without
support, and clings, laughing and delighted, to his mother's
knees, that is the mother's heart's next holiday; and sweeter
still the third, whene'er his little stammering tongue shall
utter the grateful sound of father! mother! — Oh, that is the
dearest joy of all!

Alon. Beloved Cora!

Cora. Oh, my Alonzo! daily, hourly, do I pour thanks to Heaven for the dear blessing I possess in him and thee.

Alon. To Heaven and Rolla!

Cora. Yes, to Heaven and Rolla: and art thou not grateful to them too, Alonzo? art thou not happy?

Alon. Can Cora ask that question?

Cora. Why then of late so restless on thy couch? Why to my waking, watching ear so often does the stillness of the night betray thy struggling sighs?

Alon. Must not I fight against my country, against my brethren?

Cora. Do they not seek our destruction? and are not all men brethren?

Alon. Should they prove victorious?

Cora. I will fly, and meet thee in the mountains.

Alon. Fly, with thy infant, Cora?

Cora. What! think you a mother, when she runs from danger, can feel the weight of her child?

Alon. Cora, my beloved, do you wish to set my heart at rest?

Cora. Oh yes! yes! yes!

Alon. Hasten then to the concealment in the mountains; where all our matrons and virgins, and our warriors' offspring, are allotted to await the issue of the war. Cora will not alone resist her husband's, her sisters', and her monarch's wish.

Cora. Alonzo, I cannot leave you. Oh! how in every moment's absence would my fancy paint you, wounded, alone, abandoned! No, no, I cannot leave you.

Alon. Rolla will be with me.

Cora. Yes, while the battle rages, and where it rages most, brave Rolla will be found. He may revenge, but cannot save thee. To follow danger, he will leave even thee. But I have sworn never to forsake thee but with life. Dear, dear Alonzo! canst thou wish that I should break my vow?

Alon. Then be it so. Oh! excellence in all that's great and lovely, in courage, gentleness, and truth; my pride, my content, my all! Can there on this earth be fools who seek for happiness, and pass by love in the pursuit?

Cora. Alonzo, I cannot thank thee: silence is the gratitude of true affection: who seeks to follow it by sound will miss the track. — [*Shouts without.*]   Does the king approach?

Alon. No, 'tis the general placing the guard that will surround the temple during the sacrifice.   'Tis Rolla comes, the first and best of heroes.   [*Trumpets sound.*

Rol. [*Without.*] Then place them on the hill fronting the Spanish camp.

Enter ROLLA.

Cora. Rolla! my friend, my brother!

Alon. Rolla! my friend, my benefactor! how can our lives repay the obligations which we owe thee?

Rol. Pass them in peace and bliss.   Let Rolla witness it, he is overpaid.

Cora. Look on this child.   He is the life-blood of my heart; but, if ever he loves or reveres thee less than his own father, his mother's hate fall on him!

Rol. Oh, no more!   What sacrifice have I made to merit gratitude?   The object of my love was Cora's happiness.   I see her happy.   Is not my object gained, and am I not rewarded?   Now, Cora, listen to a friend's advice.   Thou must away; thou must seek the sacred caverns, the unprofaned recess, whither, after this day's sacrifice, our matrons, and e'en the virgins of the sun, retire.

Cora. Not secure with Alonzo and with thee, Rolla?

Rol. We have heard Pizarro's plan is to surprise us.   Thy presence, Cora, cannot aid, but may impede our efforts.

Cora. Impede!

Rol. Yes, yes.   Thou knowest how tenderly we love thee; we, thy husband and thy friend.   Art thou near us? our thoughts, our valour — vengeance will not be our own.   No advantage will be pursued that leads us from the spot where thou art placed; no succour will be given but for thy protection.   The faithful lover dares not be all himself amid the war, until he knows that the beloved of his soul is absent from the peril of the fight.

Alon. Thanks to my friend! 'tis this I would have urged.

Cora. This timid excess of love, producing fear instead of valour, flatters, but does not convince me: the wife is incredulous.

Rol. And is the mother unbelieving too?

Cora. [*Kisses child.*] No more! do with me as you please. My friend, my husband! place me where you will.

Alon. My adored! we thank you both. — [*March without.*] Hark! the king approaches to the sacrifice. You, Rolla, spoke of rumours of surprise. A servant of mine, I hear, is missing; whether surprised or treacherous, I know not.

Rol. It matters not. We are every where prepared. Come, Cora, upon the altar 'mid the rocks thou'lt implore a blessing on our cause. The pious supplication of the trembling wife, and mother's heart, rises to the throne of mercy, the most resistless prayer of human homage.

[*Exeunt.*

SCENE II. — *The Temple of the Sun.*

The HIGH-PRIEST, PRIESTS, *and* VIRGINS *of the* SUN, *discovered. A solemn march.* ATALIBA *and the* PERUVIAN WARRIORS *enter on one side; on the other* ROLLA, ALONZO, *and* CORA *with the* CHILD.

Ata. Welcome, Alonzo! — [*To* ROLLA.] Kinsman, thy hand. — [*To* CORA.] Blessed be the object of the happy mother's love.

Cora. May the sun bless the father of his people!

Ata. In the welfare of his children lives the happiness of their king. — Friends, what is the temper of our soldiers?

Rol. Such as becomes the cause which they support; their cry is, Victory or death! our king! our country! and our God.

Ata. Thou, Rolla, in the hour of peril, hast been wont to animate the spirit of their leaders, ere we proceed to consecrate the banners which thy valour knows so well to guard.

Rol. Yet never was the hour of peril near, when to inspire them words were so little needed. My brave associates — partners of my toil, my feelings, and my fame! — can Rolla's words add vigour to the virtuous energies which inspire your

hearts? No! You have judged, as I have, the foulness of
the crafty plea by which these bold invaders would delude
you. Your generous spirit has compared, as mine has, the
motives which, in a war like this, can animate their minds
and ours. They, by a strange frenzy driven, fight for power,
for plunder, and extended rule: we, for our country, our
altars, and our homes. They follow an adventurer whom they
fear, and obey a power which they hate: we serve a monarch
whom we love — a God whom we adore. Whene'er they
move in anger, desolation tracks their progress! Whene'er
they pause in amity, affliction mourns their friendship. They
boast they come but to improve our state, enlarge our thoughts,
and free us from the yoke of error! Yes: they will give
enlightened freedom to our minds! who are themselves the
slaves of passion, avarice, and pride. They offer us their
protection: yes, such protection as vultures give to lambs —
covering and devouring them! They call on us to barter all
of good we have inherited and proved, for the desperate
chance of something better which they promise. Be our plain
answer this: — The throne we honour is the people's choice;
the laws we reverence are our brave fathers' legacy; the faith
we follow teaches us to live in bonds of charity with all mankind, and die with hope of bliss beyond the grave. Tell your
invaders this, and tell them too, we seek no change; and,
least of all, such change as they would bring us.

[*Loud shouts of the* PERUVIAN WARRIORS.
  Ata. [*Embracing* ROLLA.] Now, holy friends, ever mindful
of these sacred truths, begin the sacrifice. — [*A solemn procession commences. The* PRIESTS *and* VIRGINS *arrange themselves
on either side of the altar, which the* HIGH-PRIEST *approaches,
and the solemnity begins. The invocation of the* HIGH-PRIEST *is
followed by the choruses of the* PRIESTS *and* VIRGINS. *Fire from
above lights upon the altar. The whole assembly rise, and join
in the thanksgiving.*] Our offering is accepted. Now to arms,
my friends; prepare for battle.

Enter ORANO.
  Ora. The enemy.

Ata. How near?

Ora. From the hill's brow, e'en now as I o'erlooked their force, suddenly I perceived the whole in motion: with eager haste they march towards our deserted camp, as if apprised of this most solemn sacrifice.

Rol. They must be met before they reach it.

Ata. And you my daughters, with your dear children, away to the appointed place of safety.

 Cora. Oh, Alonzo!   *[Embracing him.*

 Alon. We shall meet again.

 Cora. Bless us once more ere you leave us.

 Alon. Heaven protect and bless thee, my beloved; and thee, my innocent!

 Ata. Haste, haste! each moment is precious!

 Cora. Farewell, Alonzo! Remember thy life is mine.

 Rol. [*As she is passing him.*] Not one farewell to Rolla?

 Cora. [*Giving him her hand.*] Farewell! The god of war be with you: but bring me back Alonzo.

           [Exit with the Child.

 Ata. [*Draws his sword.*] Now, my brethren, my sons, my friends, I know your valour. Should ill success assail us, be despair the last feeling of your hearts. If successful, let mercy be the first. — Alonzo, to you I give to defend the narrow passage of the mountains. On the right of the wood be Rolla's station. For me straight forwards will I march to meet them, and fight until I see my people saved, or they behold their monarch fall. Be the word of battle — God! and our native land.   *[A march. Exeunt.*

Scene III. — *A Wood between the Temple and the Camp.*

Enter Rolla *and* Alonzo.

 Rol. Here, my friend, we separate — soon, I trust, to meet again in triumph.

 Alon. Or perhaps we part to meet no more. — Rolla, a moment's pause; we are yet before our army's strength; one earnest word at parting.

Rol. There is in language now no word but battle.

Alon. Yes, one word — one — Cora!

Rol. Cora! — speak!

Alon. The next hour brings us ——

Rol. Death or victory!

Alon. It may be victory to one — death to the other.

Rol. Or both may fall.

Alon. If so, my wife and child I bequeath to the protection of Heaven and my king. But should I only fall, Rolla, be thou my heir.

Rol. How!

Alon. Be Cora thy wife — be thou a father to my child.

Rol. Rouse thee, Alonzo! banish these timid fancies.

Alon. Rolla! I have tried in vain, and cannot fly from the foreboding which oppresses me: thou knowest it will not shake me in the fight: but give me the promise I exact.

Rol. If it be Cora's will — yes — I promise.

[Gives his hand.

Alon. Tell her it was my last wish; and bear to her and to my son my last blessing!

Rol. I will. — Now then to our posts, and let our swords speak for us.   [*They draw their swords.*

Alon. For the king and Cora!

Rol. For Cora and the king.

[Exeunt severally. Alarms without.

Scene IV. — *The Peruvian Camp.*

Enter an Old Blind Man *and a* Boy.

Old Man. Have none returned to the camp?

Boy. One messenger alone. From the temple they all marched to meet the foe.

Old Man. Hark! I hear the din of battle. Oh, had I still retained my sight, I might now have grasped a sword, and died a soldier's death! — Are we quite alone?

Boy. Yes! — I hope my father will be safe!

Old Man. He will do his duty. I am more anxious for thee, my child.

Boy. I can stay with you, dear grandfather.

Old Man. But, should the enemy come, they will drag thee from me, my boy.

Boy. Impossible, grandfather! for they will see at once that you are old and blind, and cannot do without me.

Old Man. Poor child! thou little knowest the hearts of these inhuman men. — [*Discharge of cannon heard.*] Hark! the noise is near. I hear the dreadful roaring of the fiery engines of these cruel strangers. — [*Shouts at a distance.*] At every shout, with involuntary haste I clench my hand, and fancy still it grasps a sword! Alas! I can only serve my country by my prayers. Heaven preserve the Inca and his gallant soldiers!

Boy. O father! there are soldiers running ——

Old Man. Spaniards, boy?

Boy. No, Peruvians!

Old Man. How! and flying from the field! — It cannot be.

Enter two PERUVIAN SOLDIERS.

Oh, speak to them, boy! — whence come you? how goes the battle?

Sold. We may not stop; we are sent for the reserve behind the hill. The day's against us.   [*Exeunt* SOLDIERS.

Old Man. Quick, then, quick.

Boy. I see the points of lances glittering in the light.

Old Man. Those are Peruvians. Do they bend this way?

Enter a PERUVIAN SOLDIER.

Boy. Soldier, speak to my blind father.

Sold. I'm sent to tell the helpless father to retreat among the rocks: all will be lost, I fear. The king is wounded.

Old Man. Quick, boy! Lead me to the hill, where thou mayst view the plain.   [*Alarms.*

Enter ATALIBA, *wounded, with* ORANO, OFFICERS, *and* SOLDIERS.

Ata. My wound is bound; believe me, the hurt is nothing: I may return to the fight.

Ora. Pardon your servant; but the allotted priest who attends the sacred banner has pronounced that, the Inca's blood once shed, no blessing can await the day until he leave the field.

Ata. Hard restraint! Oh my poor brave soldiers! Hard that I may no longer be a witness of their valour. — But haste you; return to your comrades; I will not keep one soldier from his post. Go, and avenge your fallen brethren. — [*Exeunt* ORANO, OFFICERS, *and* SOLDIERS.] I will not repine; my own fate is the last anxiety of my heart. It is for you, my people, that I feel and fear.

Old Man. [*Coming forward.*] Did I not hear the voice of an unfortunate? — Who is it complains thus?

Ata. One almost by hope forsaken.

Old Man. Is the king alive?

Ata. The king still lives.

Old Man. Then thou art not forsaken! Ataliba protects the meanest of his subjects.

Ata. And who shall protect Ataliba?

Old Man. The immortal powers, that protect the just. The virtues of our monarch alike secure to him the affection of his people and the benign regard of Heaven.

Ata. How impious, had I murmured! How wondrous, thou supreme Disposer, are thy acts! Even in this moment, which I had thought the bitterest trial of mortal suffering, thou hast infused the sweetest sensation of my life — it is the assurance of my people's love.   [*Aside.*

Boy. [*Turning forward.*] O father! — Stranger! see those hideous men that rush upon us yonder!

Ata. Ha! Spaniards! and I Ataliba — ill-fated fugitive, without a sword even to try the ransom of a monarch's life.

Enter DAVILLA, ALMAGRO, *and* SPANISH SOLDIERS.

Dav. 'Tis he — our hopes are answered — I know him well — it is the king!

Alm. Away! Follow with your prize. Avoid those Peruvians, though in flight. This way we may regain our line.

[*Exeunt* DAVILLA, ALMAGRO, *and* SOLDIERS, *with* ATALIBA *prisoner.*

Old Man. The king! — wretched old man, that could not see his gracious form! — Boy, would thou hadst led me to the reach of those ruffians' swords!

Boy. Father! all our countrymen are flying here for refuge.

Old Man. No — to the rescue of their king — they never will desert him.   [*Alarms without.*

Enter PERUVIAN OFFICERS *and* SOLDIERS, *flying across the stage;* ORANO *following.*

Ora. Hold, I charge you! Rolla calls you.

Officer. We cannot combat with their dreadful engines.

Enter ROLLA.

Rol. Hold! recreants! cowards! What, fear ye death, and fear not shame? By my soul's fury, I cleave to the earth the first of you that stirs, or plunge your dastard swords into your leader's heart, that he no more may witness your disgrace. Where is the king?

Ora. From this old man and boy I learn that the detachment of the enemy, which you observed so suddenly to quit the field, have succeeded in surprising him; they are yet in sight.

Rol. And bear the Inca off a prisoner? — Hear this, ye base, disloyal rout! Look there! The dust you see hangs on the bloody Spaniards' track, dragging with ruffian taunts your king, your father — Ataliba in bondage! Now fly, and seek your own vile safety if you can.

Old Man. Bless the voice of Rolla — and bless the stroke I once lamented, but which now spares these extinguished eyes the shame of seeing the pale, trembling wretches who dare not follow Rolla, though to save their king!

Rol. Shrink ye from the thunder of the foe — and fall ye not at this rebuke? Oh! had ye each but one drop of the loyal blood which gushes to waste through the brave heart of this sightless veteran! Eternal shame pursue you, if you desert me now! — But do — alone I go — alone — to die with glory by my monarch's side!

Soldiers. Rolla! we'll follow thee.

[*Trumpets sound;* ROLLA *rushes out, followed by* ORANO,
OFFICERS *and* SOLDIERS.

Old Man. O godlike Rolla!—And thou sun, send from thy
clouds avenging lightning to his aid! Haste, my boy; ascend
some height, and tell to my impatient terror what thou seest.

Boy. I can climb this rock, and the tree above.—[*Ascends
a rock, and from thence into the tree.*] Oh—now I see them—
now—yes—and the Spaniards turning by the steep.

Old Man. Rolla follows them?

Boy. He does—he does—he moves like an arrow! Now
he waves his arm to our soldiers.—[*Report of cannon heard.*]
Now there is fire and smoke.

Old Man. Yes, fire is the weapon of those fiends.

Boy. The wind blows off the smoke: they are all mixed
together.

Old Man. Seest thou the king?

Boy. Yes—Rolla is near him! His sword sheds fire as
he strikes!

Old Man. Bless thee, Rolla! Spare not the monsters.

Boy. Father! father! the Spaniards fly!—Oh—now I see
the king embracing Rolla.

[*Waves his cap for joy. Shouts of victory, flourish of trumpets, &c.*

Old Man. [*Falls on his knees.*] Fountain of life! how can
my exhausted breath bear to thee thanks for this one moment
of my life!—My boy, come down, and let me kiss thee—my
strength is gone.

Boy. [*Running to the Old Man.*] Let me help you, father—
you tremble so ——

Old Man. 'Tis with transport, boy!

[BOY *leads the* OLD MAN *off. Shouts, flourish, &c.*

Re-enter ATALIBA, ROLLA, *and* PERUVIAN OFFICERS *and* SOLDIERS.

Ata. In the name of my people, the saviour of whose sovereign thou hast this day been, accept this emblem of his gratitude.—[*Giving* ROLLA *his sun of diamonds.*] The tear that

falls upon it may for a moment dim its lustre, yet does it not impair the value of the gift.

Rol. It was the hand of Heaven, not mine, that saved my king.

Enter PERUVIAN OFFICER *and* SOLDIERS.

Rol. Now, soldier, from Alonzo?

Off. Alonzo's genius soon repaired the panic which early broke our ranks; but I fear we have to mourn Alonzo's loss: his eager spirit urged him too far in the pursuit!

Ata. How! Alonzo slain?

1st Sold. I saw him fall.

2nd Sold. Trust me, I beheld him up again and fighting — he was then surrounded and disarmed.

Ata. O victory, dearly purchased!

Rol. O Cora! who shall tell thee this?

Ata. Rolla, our friend is lost — our native country saved! Our private sorrows must yield to the public claim for triumph. Now go we to fulfil the first, the most sacred duty which belongs to victory — to dry the widowed and the orphaned tear of those whose brave protectors have perished in their country's cause.   [*Triumphant march, and exeunt.*

ACT III.

SCENE I. — *A wild Retreat among stupendous rocks.*

CORA *and her* CHILD, *with other* WIVES *and* CHILDREN *of the* PERUVIAN WARRIORS, *discovered. They sing alternately stanzas expressive of their situation, with a Chorus, in which all join.*

1st Wom. Zuluga, seest thou nothing yet?

Zul. Yes, two Peruvian soldiers — one on the hill, the other entering the thicket in the vale.

2nd Wom. One more has passed. — He comes — but pale and terrified.

Cora. My heart will start from my bosom.

Enter a PERUVIAN SOLDIER, *panting for breath.*

Wom. Well! joy or death?

Sold. The battle is against us. The king is wounded and a prisoner.

Wom. Despair and misery!

Cora. [*In a faint voice.*] And Alonzo?

Sold. I have not seen him.

1st Wom. Oh! whither must we fly?

2nd Wom. Deeper into the forest.

Cora. I shall not move.

2nd Sold. [*Without.*] Victory! victory!

Enter another PERUVIAN SOLDIER.

2nd Sold. Rejoice! rejoice! we are victorious!

Wom. [*Springing up.*] Welcome! welcome, thou messenger of joy: — but the king!

2nd Sold. He leads the brave warriors who approach.

[*The triumphant march of the army is heard at a distance. The* WOMEN *and* CHILDREN *join in a strain expressive of anxiety and exultation.*]   •

Enter the PERUVIAN WARRIORS, *singing the Song of Victory.* ATALIBA *and* ROLLA *follow, and are greeted with rapturous shouts.* CORA, *with her* CHILD *in her arms, runs through the ranks searching for* ALONZO.

Ata. Thanks, thanks, my children! I am well, believe it; the blood once stopped, my wound was nothing.

Cora. [*To* ROLLA.] Where is Alonzo? — [ROLLA *turns away in silence.*] Give me my husband; give this child his father.

[*Falls at* ATALIBA'S *feet.*

Ata. I grieve that Alonzo is not here.

Cora. Hoped you to find him?

Ata. Most anxiously.

Cora. Ataliba! is he not dead?

Ata. No! the gods will have heard our prayers.

Cora. Is he not dead, Ataliba?

Ata. He lives — in my heart.

Cora. O king! torture me not thus! Speak out, is this child fatherless?

Sheridan.   26

Ata.   Dearest Cora! do not thus dash aside the little hope
that still remains.

Cora.   The little hope! yet still there is hope! [*Turns to*
Rolla.] Speak to me, Rolla: you are the friend of truth.

Rol.   Alonzo has not been found.

Cora.   Not found! what mean you? will not you, Rolla,
tell me truth? Oh! let me not hear the thunder rolling at a
distance; let the bolt fall and crush my brain at once. Say
not that he is not found: say at once that he is dead.

Rol.   Then should I say false.

Cora.   False! Blessings on thee for that word! But
snatch me from this terrible suspense. — [Cora *and* Child
kneel to Rolla.] Lift up thy little hands, my child; perhaps
thy ignorance may plead better than thy mother's agony.

Rol.   Alonzo is taken prisoner.

Cora.   Prisoner! and by the Spaniards? — Pizarro's prisoner? Then is he dead.

Ata.   Hope better — the richest ransom which our realm
can yield, a herald shall this instant bear.

Peruv. Wom.   Oh! for Alonzo's ransom — our gold, our
gems! — all! all! Here, dear Cora — here! here!

[*The* Peruvian Women *eagerly tear off all their ornaments,
and offer them to* Cora.

Ata.   Yes, for Alonzo's ransom they would give all! — I
thank thee, Father, who has given me such hearts to rule over!

Cora.   Now one boon more, beloved monarch. Let me
go with the herald.

Ata.   Remember, Cora, thou art not a wife only, but a
mother too: hazard not your own honour, and the safety of
your infant. Among these barbarians the sight of thy youth,
thy loveliness, and innocence, would but rivet faster your
Alonzo's chains, and rack his heart with added fears for thee.
Wait, Cora, the return of the herald.

Cora.   Teach me how to live till then.

Ata.   Now we go to offer to the gods thanks for our victory, and prayers for our Alonzo's safety.

[*March and procession.   Exeunt.*

SCENE II. — *The Wood.*

Enter CORA *and* CHILD.

Cora.   Mild innocence, what will become of thee?

Enter ROLLA.

Rol.   Cora, I attend thy summons at the appointed spot.

Cora.   O my child, my boy! hast thou still a father?

Rol.   Cora, can thy child be fatherless, while Rolla lives?

Cora.   Will he not soon want a mother too? For canst thou think I will survive Alonzo's loss?

Rol.   Yes! for his child's sake. Yes, as thou didst love Alonzo, Cora, listen to Alonzo's friend.

Cora.   You bid me listen to the world. — Who was not Alonzo's friend?

Rol.   His parting words ——

Cora.   His parting words! — [*Wildly.*] Oh, speak!

Rol.   Consigned to me two precious trusts — his blessing to his son, and a last request to thee.

Cora.   His last request! his last! — Oh, name it!

Rol.   If I fall, said he (and sad forebodings shook him while he spoke), promise to take my Cora for thy wife; be thou a father to my child. — I pledged my word to him, and we parted. Observe me, Cora, I repeat this only, as my faith to do so was given to Alonzo: for myself, I neither cherish claim nor hope.

Cora.   Ha! does my reason fail me, or what is this horrid light that presses on my brain? O Alonzo! it may be thou hast fallen a victim to thy own guileless heart: hadst thou been silent, hadst thou not made a fatal legacy of these wretched charms ——

Rol.   Cora! what hateful suspicion has possessed thy mind?

Cora.   Yes, yes, 'tis clear! — his spirit was ensnared; he was led to the fatal spot, where mortal valour could not front a host of murderers. He fell — in vain did he exclaim for

26*

help to Rolla. At a distance you looked on and smiled: you
could have saved him — could — but did not.

Rol.   Oh, glorious sun! can I have deserved this?—Cora,
rather bid me strike this sword into my heart.

Cora.   No! — live! live for love!— for that love thou
seekest; whose blossoms are to shoot from the bleeding grave
of thy betrayed and slaughtered friend! But thou hast borne
to me the last words of my Alonzo! now hear mine: sooner
shall this boy draw poison from this tortured breast — sooner
would I link me to the pallid corse of the meanest wretch that
perished with Alonzo, than he call Rolla father — than I call
Rolla husband!

Rol.   Yet call me what I am — thy friend, thy protector!

Cora.   [*Distractedly.*] Away! I have no protector but my
God! With this child in my arms will I hasten to the field
of slaughter: there with these hands will I turn up to the light
every mangled body, seeking, howe'er by death disfigured,
the sweet smile of my Alonzo: with fearful cries I will shriek
out his name till my veins snap! If the smallest spark of
life remain, he will know the voice of his Cora, open for a
moment his unshrouded eyes, and bless me with a last look
But if we find him not — oh! then, my boy, we will to the
Spanish camp — that look of thine will win my passage
through a thousand swords — they too are men. Is there a
heart that could drive back the wife that seeks her bleeding
husband; or the innocent babe that cries for his imprisoned
father? No, no, my child, every where we shall be safe. A
wretched mother, bearing a poor orphan in her arms, has
nature's passport through the world. Yes, yes, my son, we'll
go and seek thy father.   [*Exit with the* CHILD.

Rol.   [*After a pause of agitation.*] Could I have merited
one breath of thy reproaches, Cora, I should be the wretch I
think I was not formed to be. Her safety must be my present purpose — then to convince her she has wronged me!

                                                      [*Exit.*

SCENE III. — PIZARRO's *Tent.*

PIZARRO *discovered, traversing the scene in gloomy and furious agitation.*

Piz. Well, capricious idol, Fortune, be my ruin thy work and boast. To myself I will still be true. Yet, ere I fall, grant me thy smile to prosper in one act of vengeance, and be that smile Alonzo's death.

Enter ELVIRA.

Who's there? who dares intrude? Why does my guard neglect their duty?

Elv. Your guard did what they could — but they knew their duty better than to enforce authority, when I refused obedience.

Piz. And what is it you desire?

Elv. To see how a hero bears misfortune. Thou, Pizarro, art not now collected — nor thyself.

Piz. Wouldst thou I should rejoice that the spears of the enemy, led by accursed Alonzo, have pierced the bravest hearts of my followers?

Elv. No! I would have thee cold and dark as the night that follows the departed storm; still and sullen as the awful pause that precedes nature's convulsion: yet I would have thee feel assured that a new morning shall arise, when the warrior's spirit shall stalk forth — nor fear the future, nor lament the past.

Piz. Woman! Elvira! — why had not all my men hearts like thine?

Elv. Then would thy brows have this day worn the crown of Quito.

Piz. Oh! hope fails me while that scourge of my life and fame, Alonzo, leads the enemy.

Elv. Pizarro, I am come to probe the hero farther: not now his courage, but his magnanimity — Alonzo is your prisoner.

Piz. How!

Elv. 'Tis certain; Valverde saw him even now dragged in chains within your camp. I chose to bring you the intelligence myself.

Piz. Bless thee, Elvira, for the news! — Alonzo in my power! — then I am the conqueror — the victory is mine!

Elv. Pizarro, this is savage and unmanly triumph. Believe me, you raise impatience in my mind to see the man whose valour and whose genius awe Pizarro; whose misfortunes are Pizarro's triumph; whose bondage is Pizarro's safety.

Piz. Guard!

Enter GUARD.

Drag here the Spanish prisoner, Alonzo! Quick, bring the traitor here. . [*Exit* GUARD

Elv. What shall be his fate?

Piz. Death! death! in lingering torments! protracted to the last stretch that burning vengeance can devise, and fainting life sustain.

Elv. Shame on thee. Wilt thou have it said that the Peruvians found Pizarro could not conquer till Alonzo felt that he could murder?

Piz. Be it said — I care not. His fate is sealed.

Elv. Follow then thy will: but mark me, if basely thou dost shed the blood of this brave youth, Elvira's lost to thee for ever.

Piz. Why this interest for a stranger? What is Alonzo's fate to thee?

Elv. His fate, nothing; thy glory, every thing! Thinkest thou I could love thee, stripped of fame, of honour, and a just renown? Know me better.

Piz. Thou shouldst have known me better. Thou shouldst have known, that, once provoked to hate, I am for ever fixed in vengeance.

Re-enter GUARD *with* ALONZO *in chains.*

Welcome, welcome, Don Alonzo de Molina! 'tis long since we have met: thy mended looks should speak a life of rural indolence. How is it that, amid the toils and cares of war, thou

dost preserve the healthful bloom of careless ease? Tell me
thy secret.

Alon. Thou wilt not profit by it. Whate'er the toils or
cares of war, peace still is here.

[*Putting his hand to his heart.*

Piz. Sarcastic boy!

Elv. Thou art answered rightly. Why sport with the
unfortunate?

Piz. And thou art wedded too, I hear; ay, and the father
of a lovely boy—the heir, no doubt, of all his father's loyalty,
of all his mother's faith?

Alon. The heir, I hope, of all his father's scorn of fraud,
oppression, and hypocrisy — the heir, I hope, of all his
mother's virtue, gentleness, and truth — the heir, I am sure,
to all Pizarro's hate.

Piz. Really! Now do I feel for this poor orphan; for
fatherless to-morrow's sun shall see that child Alonzo, thy
hours are numbered.

Elv. Pizarro — no!

Piz. Hence — or dread my anger.

Elv. I will not hence; nor do I dread thy anger.

Alon. Generous loveliness! spare thy unavailing pity. Seek
not to thwart the tiger with the prey beneath his fangs.

Piz. Audacious rebel! thou a renegado from thy monarch
and thy God!

Alon. 'Tis false!

Piz. Art thou not, tell me, a deserter from thy country's
legions — and, with vile heathens leagued, hast thou not
warred against thy native land?

Alon. No! deserter I am none! I was not born among
robbers! pirates! murderers! When those legions, lured by
the abhorred lust of gold, and by thy foul ambition urged,
forgot the honour of Castilians, and forsook the duties of humanity, they deserted me. I have not warred against my
native land, but against those who have usurped its power.
The banners of my country, when first I followed arms beneath
them, were justice, faith, and mercy. If these are beaten

down and trampled under foot, I have no country, nor exists the power entitled to reproach me with revolt.

Piz. The power to judge and punish thee at least exists.

Alon. Where are my judges?

Piz. Thou wouldst appeal to the war council?

Alon. If the good Las-Casas have yet a seat there, yes; if not, I appeal to Heaven!

Piz. And, to impose upon the folly of Las-Casas, what would be the excuses of thy treason?

Elv. The folly of Las-Casas! Such, doubtless, his mild precepts seem to thy hard-hearted wisdom! Oh, would I might have lived as I will die, a sharer in the follies of Las-Casas!

Alon. To him I should not need to urge the foul barbarities which drove me from your side; but I would gently lead him by the hand through all the lovely fields of Quito; there, in many a spot where late was barrenness and waste, I would show him how now the opening blossom, blade, or perfumed bud, sweet bashful pledges of delicious harvest, wafting their incense to the ripening sun, give cheerful promise to the hope of industry. This, I would say, is my work! Next I should tell how hurtful customs and superstitions, strange and sullen, would often scatter and dismay the credulous minds of these deluded innocents; and then would I point out to him where now, in clustered villages, they live like brethren, social and confiding, while through the burning day Content sits basking on the cheek of Toil, till laughing Pastime leads them to the hour of rest — this too is mine! And prouder yet, at that still pause between exertion and repose, belonging not to pastime, labour, or to rest, but unto Him who sanctions and ordains them all, I would show him many an eye, and many a hand, by gentleness from error won, raised in pure devotion to the true and only God! this too I could tell him is Alonzo's work! Then would Las-Casas clasp me in his aged arms; from his uplifted eyes a tear of gracious thankfulness would fall upon my head, and that one blessed drop would be to me at once this world's best proof, that I had acted rightly here, and surest hope of my Creator's mercy and reward hereafter.

Elv. Happy, virtuous Alonzo! And thou, Pizarro, wouldst appal with fear of death a man who thinks and acts as he does!

Piz. Daring, obstinate enthusiast! But know, the pious blessing of thy preceptor's tears does not await thee here: he has fled like thee — like thee, no doubt, to join the foes of Spain. The perilous trial of the next reward you hope is nearer than perhaps you've thought; for, by my country's wrongs, and by mine own, to-morrow's sun shall see thy death!

Elv. Hold! Pizarro, hear me: if not always justly, at least act always greatly. Name not thy country's wrongs; 'tis plain they have no share in thy resentment. Thy fury 'gainst this youth is private hate, and deadly personal revenge; if this be so, and even now thy detected conscience in that look avows it, profane not the name of justice or thy country's cause, but let him arm, and bid him to the field on equal terms.

Piz. Officious advocate for treason — peace! Bear him hence; he knows his sentence.   [*Retires back.*

Alon. Thy revenge is eager, and I'm thankful for it — to me thy haste is mercy. — [*To* Elvira.] For thee, sweet pleader in misfortune's cause, accept my parting thanks. This camp is not thy proper sphere. Wert thou among yon savages, as they are called, thou'dst find companions more congenial to thy heart.

Piz. Yes; she shall bear the tidings of thy death to Cora.

Alon. Inhuman man! that pang, at least, might have been spared me; but thy malice shall not shake my constancy. I go to death — many shall bless, and none will curse my memory. Thou wilt still live, and still wilt be — Pizarro. [*Exit, guarded.*]

Elv. Now, by the indignant scorn that burns upon my cheek, my soul is shamed and sickened at the meanness of thy vengeance!

Piz. What has thy romantic folly aimed at? He is mine enemy, and in my power.

Elv. He is in your power, and therefore is no more an enemy. Pizarro, I demand not of thee virtue, I ask not from

thee nobleness of mind, I require only just dealing to the
fame thou hast acquired: be not the assassin of thine own renown. How often have you sworn, that the sacrifice which
thy wondrous valour's high report had won you from subdued
Elvira, was the proudest triumph of your fame! Thou knowest I bear a mind not cast in the common mould, not formed
for tame sequestered love, content mid household cares to
prattle to an idle offspring, and wait the dull delight of an
obscure lover's kindness: no! my heart was framed to look up
with awe and homage to the object it adored; my ears to own
no music but the thrilling records of his praise; my lips to
scorn all babbling but the tales of his achievements; my brain
to turn giddy with delight, reading the applauding tributes of
his monarch's and his country's gratitude; my every faculty
to throb with transport, while I heard the shouts of acclamation which announced the coming of my hero; my whole soul
to love him with devotion! with enthusiasm! to see no other
object — to own no other tie — but to make him my world!
Thus to love is at least no common weakness. Pizarro! was
not such my love for thee?

Piz. It was, Elvira!

Elv. Then do not make me hateful to myself, by tearing
off the mask at once, baring the hideous imposture that has
undone me! Do not an act which, howe'er thy present power
may gloss it to the world, will make thee hateful to all future
ages — accursed and scorned by posterity.

Piz. And, should posterity applaud my deeds, thinkest
thou my mouldering bones would rattle then with transport
in my tomb? This is renown for visionary boys to dream of;
I understand it not. The fame I value shall uplift my living
estimation, o'erbear with popular support the envy of my foes,
advance my purposes, and aid my power.

Elv. Each word thou speakest, each moment that I hear
thee, dispels the fatal mist through which I've judged thee.
Thou man of mighty name but little soul, I see thou wert not
born to feel what genuine fame and glory are. Go! prefer
the flattery of thy own fleeting day to the bright circle of a

deathless name — go! prefer to stare upon the grain of sand
on which you trample, to musing on the starred canopy above
thee.   Fame, the sovereign deity of proud ambition, is not to
be worshipped so: who seeks alone for living homage stands
a mean canvasser in her temple's porch, wooing promiscuously,
from the fickle breath of every wretch that passes, the brittle
tribute of his praise.   He dares not approach the sacred altar
— no noble sacrifice of his is placed there, nor ever shall his
worshipped image, fixed above, claim for his memory a glorious immortality.

Piz. Elvira, leave me.

Elv. Pizarro, you no longer love me.

Piz. It is not so, Elvira.   But what might I not suspect
— this wondrous interest for a stranger!   Take back thy reproach.

Elv. No, Pizarro, as yet I am not lost to you; one string
still remains, and binds me to your fate.   Do not, I conjure
you — do not, for mine own sake, tear it asunder — shed
not Alonzo's blood!

Piz. My resolution's fixed.

Elv. Even though that moment lost you Elvira for ever?

Piz. Even so.

Elv. Pizarro, if not to honour, if not to humanity, yet listen to affection; bear some memory of the sacrifices I have
made for thy sake.   Have I not for thee quitted my parents,
my friends, my fame, my native land?   When escaping, did
I not risk, in rushing to thy arms, to bury myself in the
bosom of the deep?   Have I not shared all thy perils — heavy
storms at sea, and frightful 'scapes on shore?   Even on this
dreadful day, amid the rout of battle, who remained firm and
constant at Pizarro's side?   Who presented her bosom as his
shield to the assailing foe?

Piz. 'Tis truly spoken all.   In love thou art thy sex's miracle, in war the soldier's pattern; and therefore my whole heart
and half my acquisitions are thy right.

Elv. Convince me I possess the first; I exchange all title
to the latter for — mercy to Alonzo.

Piz. No more! Had I intended to prolong his doom, each word thou utterest now would hasten on his fate.

Elv. Alonzo then at morn will die?

Piz. Thinkest thou yon sun will set? As surely at his rising shall Alonzo die.

Elv. Then be it done — the string is cracked — sundered for ever. But mark me — thou hast heretofore had cause, 'tis true, to doubt my resolution, howe'er offended; but mark me now — the lips which, cold and jeering, barbing revenge with rancorous mockery, can insult a fallen enemy, shall never more receive the pledge of love: the arm which, unshaken by its bloody purpose, shall assign to needless torture the victim who avows his heart, never more shall press the hand of faith! Pizarro, scorn not my words; beware you slight them not! I feel how noble are the motives which now animate my thoughts. Who could not feel as I do, I condemn: who, feeling so, yet would not act as I shall, I despise!

Piz. I have heard thee, Elvira, and know well the noble motives which inspire thee — fit advocate in virtue's cause! Believe me, I pity thy tender feelings for the youth Alonzo! He dies at sunrise!   [*Exit.*

Elv. 'Tis well! 'tis just I should be humbled — I had forgot myself, and in the cause of innocence assumed the tone of virtue. 'Twas fit I should be rebuked — and by Pizarro. Fall, fall, ye few reluctant drops of weakness — the last these eyes shall ever shed. How a woman can love, Pizarro, thou hast known too well — how she can hate, thou hast yet to learn. Yes, thou undaunted! — thou, whom yet no mortal hazard has appalled — thou, who on Panama's brow didst make alliance with the raging elements that tore the silence of that horrid night, when thou didst follow, as thy pioneer, the crashing thunder's drift; and, stalking o'er the trembling earth, didst plant thy banner by the red volcano's mouth! thou, who when battling on the sea, and thy brave ship was blown to splinters, wast seen, as thou didst bestride a fragment of the smoking wreck, to wave thy glittering sword above thy head, as thou wouldst defy the world in that ex-

tremity! — come, fearless man! now meet the last and fell-
est peril of thy life; meet and survive — an injured woman's
fury, if thou canst.   [*Exit.*

ACT IV.

Scene I. — *A Dungeon.*

ALONZO *is discovered in chains.* A SENTINEL *walking near.*

Alon. For the last time I have beheld the shadowed ocean
close upon the light. For the last time, through my cleft
dungeon's roof, I now behold the quivering lustre of the stars.
For the last time, O sun! (and soon the hour) I shall behold
thy rising, and thy level beams melting the pale mists of morn
to glittering dew-drops. Then comes my death, and in the
morning of my day I fall, which — no, Alonzo, date not the
life which thou hast run by the mean reckoning of the hours
and days which thou hast breathed: a life spent worthily
should be measured by a nobler line — by deeds, not years.
Then wouldst thou murmur not, but bless the Providence which
in so short a span made thee the instrument of wide and spread-
ing blessings to the helpless and oppressed. Though sink-
ing in decrepit age, he prematurely falls, whose memory records no benefit conferred by him on man. They only have
lived long, who have lived virtuously.

Enter a SOLDIER, *shows the* SENTINEL *a passport, who withdraws.*

Alon. What bear you there?

Sold. These refreshments I was ordered to leave in your
dungeon.

Alon. By whom ordered?

Sold. By the Lady Elvira: she will be here herself before
the dawn.

Alon. Bear back to her my humblest thanks; and take
thou the refreshments, friend — I need them not.

Sold. I have served under you, Don Alonzo. Pardon my
saying, that my heart pities you.   [*Exit.*

Alon. In Pizarro's camp, to pity the unfortunate, no doubt

requires forgiveness. — [*Looking out.*] Surely, even now, thin
streaks of glimmering light steal on the darkness of the east.
If so, my life is but one hour more. I will not watch the coming dawn; but in the darkness of my cell, my last prayer to
thee, Power Supreme! shall be for my wife and child! Grant
them to dwell in innocence and peace; grant health and purity
of mind — all else is worthless.   [*Retires into the dungeon.*

Sent. Who's there? answer quickly! who's there?

Rol. [*Without.*] A friar come to visit your prisoner.

Enter ROLLA, *disguised as a* MONK.

Rol. Inform me, friend — is not Alonzo, the Spanish prisoner, confined in this dungeon?

Sent. He is.

Rol. I must speak with him.

Sent. You must not.   [*Stopping him with his spear.*

Rol. He is my friend.

Sent. Not if he were your brother.

Rol. What is to be his fate?

Sent. He dies at sunrise.

Rol. Ha! then I am come in time.

Sent. Just — to witness his death.

Rol. Soldier, I must speak with him.

Sent. Back, back! It is impossible!

Rol. I do entreat thee but for one moment!

Sent. You entreat in vain; my orders are most strict.

Rol. Even now, I saw a messenger go hence.

Sent. He brought a pass, which we are all accustomed to
obey.

Rol. Look on this wedge of massive gold — look on these
precious gems. In thy own land they will be wealth for thee
and thine beyond thy hope or wish. Take them — they are
thine. Let me but pass one minute with Alonzo.

Sent. Away! wouldst thou corrupt me? — me! an old Cas-
tilian! I know my duty better.

Rol. Soldier! hast thou a wife?

Sent. I have.

Rol. Hast thou children?

Sent. Four — honest, lovely boys.

Rol. Where didst thou leave them?

Sent. In my native village — even in the cot where myself was born.

Rol. Dost thou love thy children and thy wife?

Sent. Do I love them! God knows my heart — I do.

Rol. Soldier! — imagine thou wert doomed to die a cruel death in this strange land; what would be thy last request?

Sent. That some of my comrades should carry my dying blessing to my wife and children.

Rol. Oh, but if that comrade was at thy prison gate—and should there be told — thy fellow-soldier dies at sunrise — yet thou shalt not for a moment see him — nor shalt thou bear his dying blessing to his poor children or his wretched wife — what wouldst thou think of him, who thus could drive thy comrade from the door?

Sent. How!'

Rol. Alonzo has a wife and child — I am come but to receive for her and for her babe the last blessing of my friend.

Sent. Go in.   [*Retires.*

Rol. Oh, holy Nature! thou dost never plead in vain. There is not, of our earth, a creature bearing form, and life, human or savage, native of the forest wild or giddy air, around whose parent bosom thou hast not a cord entwined of power to tie them to their offspring's claims, and at thy will to draw them back to thee. On iron pinions borne, the blood-stained vulture cleaves the storm, yet is the plumage closest to her breast soft as the cygnet's down, and o'er her unshelled brood the murmuring ringdove sits not more gently! Yes, now he is beyond the porch, barring the outer gate!—Alonzo! Alonzo! my friend! Ha! in gentle sleep! — Alonzo! rise!

Re-enter ALONZO.

Alon. [*Within.*] How! is my hour elapsed? Well — [*Returning from the recess.*] I am ready.'

Rol. Alonzo, know me!

Alon. What voice is that?

Rol. 'Tis Rolla's.   [*Takes off his disguise.*

Alon. Rolla! — my friend! — [*Embraces him.*] Heavens! how couldst thou pass the guard? Did this habit ——

Rol. There is not a moment to be lost in words. This disguise I tore from the dead body of a friar, as I passed our field of battle; it has gained me entrance to thy dungeon — now take it thou, and fly.

Alon. And Rolla ——

Rol. Will remain here in thy place.

Alon. And die for me! No! rather eternal tortures rack me.

Rol. I shall not die, Alonzo. It is thy life Pizarro seeks, not Rolla's; and from my prison soon will thy arm deliver me. Or, should it be otherwise, I am as a blighted plantain, standing alone amid the sandy desert; nothing seeks or lives beneath my shelter. Thou art a husband, and a father; the being of a lovely wife and helpless infant hangs upon thy life. Go! go! Alonzo! go! to save not thyself, but Cora, and thy child!

Alon. Urge me not thus, my friend! I had prepared to die in peace.

Rol. To die in peace! devoting her thou'st sworn to live for, to madness, misery, and death! For, be assured, the state I left her in forbids all hope but from thy quick return.

Alon. Oh, God!

Rol. If thou art yet irresolute, Alonzo, now heed me well. I think thou hast not known that Rolla ever pledged his word, and shrunk from its fulfilment. And by the heart of truth I swear, if thou art proudly obstinate to deny thy friend the transport of preserving Cora's life, in thee, no power that sways the will of man shall stir me hence; and thou'lt but have the desperate triumph of seeing Rolla perish by thy side, with the assured conviction that Cora and thy child are lost for ever.

Alon. Oh, Rolla! you distract me!

Rol. Begone! A moment's further pause, and all is lost.

The dawn approaches. Fear not for me — I will treat with
Pizarro as for surrender and submission. I shall gain time,
doubt not, while thou, with a chosen band, passing the secret
way, mayst at night return, release thy friend, and bear him
back in triumph. Yes, hasten, dear Alonzo! Even now I
hear the frantic Cora call thee! Haste! haste! haste!

Alon. Rolla, I fear thy friendship drives me from honour,
and from right.

Rol. Did Rolla ever counsel dishonour to his friend?

Alon. Oh! my preserver!   [*Embraces him.*

Rol. I feel thy warm tears dropping on my cheek. Go! I
am rewarded. — [*Throws the* FRIAR's *garment over* ALONZO.]
There! conceal thy face; and, that they may not clank, hold
fast thy chains. Now — God be with thee!

Alon. At night we meet again. Then, so aid me Heaven!
I return to save — or — perish with thee!   [*Exit.*

Rol. [*Looking after him.*] He has passed the outer porch.
He is safe! He will soon embrace his wife and child! — Now,
Cora, didst thou not wrong me? This is the first time throughout my life I ever deceived man. Forgive me, God of truth!
if I am wrong. Alonzo flatters himself that we shall meet
again. Yes — there! — [*Lifting his hands to heaven.*] Assuredly, we shall meet again: there possess in peace the joys
of everlasting love and friendship — on earth, imperfect and
embittered. I will retire, lest the guard return before Alonzo
may have passed their lines.   [*Retires into the dungeon.*

Enter ELVIRA.

Elv. No, not Pizarro's brutal taunts, not the glowing admiration which I feel for this noble youth, shall raise an interest in my harassed bosom which honour would not sanction. If he reject the vengeance my heart has sworn against
the tyrant, whose death alone can save this land, yet shall
the delight be mine to restore him to his Cora's arms, to his
dear child, and to the unoffending people, whom his virtues
guide, and valour guards. — Alonzo, come forth!

Re-enter ROLLA.

Ha! who art thou? where is Alonzo?

Rol. Alonzo's fled.

Elv. Fled!

Rol. Yes — and he must not be pursued. Pardon this roughness, — [*Seizing her hand.*] but a moment's precious to Alonzo's flight.

Elv. What if I call the guard?

Rol. Do so — Alonzo still gains time.

Elv. What if thus I free myself?   [*Shows a dagger.*

Rol. Strike it to my heart — still, with the convulsive grasp of death, I'll hold thee fast.

Elv. Release me — I give my faith, I neither will alarm the guard, nor cause pursuit.

Rol. At once I trust thy word: a feeling boldness in those eyes assures me that thy soul is noble.

Elv. What is thy name? Speak freely: by my order the guard is removed beyond the outer porch.

Rol. My name is Rolla.

Elv. The Peruvian leader?

Rol. I was so yesterday: to-day, the Spaniards' captive.

Elv. And friendship for Alonzo moved thee to this act?

Rol. Alonzo is my friend; I am prepared to die for him. Yet is the cause a motive stronger far than friendship.

Elv. One only passion else could urge such generous rashness.

Rol. And that is ——

Elv. Love?

Rol. True!

Elv. Gallant, ingenuous Rolla! Know that my purpose here was thine; and were I to save thy friend ——

Rol. How! a woman blessed with gentleness and courage, and yet not Cora!

Elv. Does Rolla think so meanly of all female hearts?

Rol. Not so — you are worse and better than we are!

Elv. Were I to save thee, Rolla, from the tyrant's

vengeance, restore thee to thy native land, and thy native land to peace, wouldst thou not rank Elvira with the good?

Rol. To judge the action, I must know the means.

Elv. Take this dagger.

Rol. How to be used?

Elv. I will conduct thee to the tent where fell Pizarro sleeps — the scourge of innocence, the terror of thy race, the fiend that desolates thy afflicted country.

Rol. Have you not been injured by Pizarro?

Elv. Deeply as scorn and insult can infuse their deadly venom.

Rol. And you ask that I shall murder him in his sleep!

Elv. Would he not have murdered Alonzo in his chains? He that sleeps, and he that's bound, are equally defenceless. Hear me, Rolla — so may I prosper in this perilous act, as, searching my full heart, I have put by all rancorous motive of private vengeance there, and feel that I advance to my dread purpose in the cause of human nature and at the call of sacred justice.

Rol. The God of justice sanctifies no evil as a step towards good. Great actions cannot be achieved by wicked means.

Elv. Then, Peruvian! since thou dost feel so coldly for thy country's wrongs, this hand, though it revolt my soul, shall strike the blow.

Rol. Then is thy destruction certain, and for Peru thou perishest! Give me the dagger!

Elv. Now follow me. But first — and dreadful is the hard necessity — thou must strike down the guard.

Rol. The soldier who was on duty here?

Elv. Yes, him — else, seeing thee, the alarm will be instant.

Rol. And I must stab that soldier as I pass? Take back thy dagger.

Elv. Rolla!

Rol. ·That soldier, mark me, is a man. All are not men that bear the human form. He refused my prayers, refused

27*

my gold, denying to admit me, till his own feelings bribed him. For my nation's safety, I would not harm that man!

Elv. Then he must with us — I will answer for his safety.

Rol. Be that plainly understood between us: for, whate'er betide our enterprise, I will not risk a hair of that man's head, to save my heart-strings from consuming fire. [*Exeunt.*

SCENE II. — PIZARRO's *Tent.*

PIZARRO *is discovered on a couch, in disturbed sleep.*

Piz. [*In his sleep.*] No mercy, traitor! Now at his heart! — Stand off there, you!—Let me see him bleed!— Ha! ha! ha! — Let me hear that groan again.

Enter ROLLA *and* ELVIRA.

Elv. There! Now, lose not a moment.

Rol. You must leave me now. This scene of blood fits not a woman's presence.

Elv. But a moment's pause may ——

Rol. Go, retire to your own tent, and return not here — I will come to you. Be thou not known in this business, I implore you!

Elv. I will withdraw the guard that waits.   [*Exit.*

Rol. Now have I in my power the accursed destroyer of my country's peace: yet tranquilly he rests. God! can this man sleep?

Piz. [*In his sleep.*] Away! away! hideous fiends! Tear not my bosom thus!

Rol. No: I was in error — the balm of sweet repose he never more can know. Look here, ambition's fools! ye, by whose inhuman pride the bleeding sacrifice of nations is held as nothing, behold the rest of the guilty! — He is at my mercy — and one blow! —— No! my heart and hand refuse the act: Rolla cannot be an assassin! Yet Elvira must be saved! — [*Approaches the couch.*] Pizarro! awake!

Piz. [*Starts up.*] Who? — Guard! ——

Rol. Speak not — another word is thy death. Call not for aid! this arm will be swifter than thy guard.

Piz. Who art thou? and what is thy will?

Rol. I am thine enemy! Peruvian Rolla! Thy death is not my will, or I could have slain thee sleeping.

Piz. Speak, what else?

Rol. Now thou art at my mercy, answer me! Did a Peruvian ever yet wrong or injure thee, or any of thy nation? Didst thou, or any of thy nation, ever yet show mercy to a Peruvian in thy power? Now shalt thou feel, and if thou hast a heart thou'lt feel it keenly, a Peruvian's vengeance!— [*Drops the dagger at his feet.*] There!

Piz. Is it possible!   [*Walks aside confounded.*

Rol. Can Pizarro be surprised at this? I thought forgiveness of injuries had been the Christian's precept. Thou seest, at least, it is the Peruvian's practice.

Piz. Rolla, thou hast indeed surprised — subdued me.
              [*Walks aside again as in irresolute thought.*

Re-enter ELVIRA, *not seeing* PIZARRO.

Elv. Is it done? Is he dead? — [*Sees* PIZARRO.] How! still living! Then I am lost! And for you, wretched Peruvians! mercy is no more! O Rolla: treacherous, or cowardly?

Piz. How! can it be that ——

Rol. Away! — Elvira speaks she knows not what! — [*To* ELVIRA.] Leave me, I conjure you, with Pizarro.

Elv. How! Rolla, dost thou think I shall retract? or that I meanly will deny, that in thy hand I placed a poniard to be plunged into that tyrant's heart? No: my sole regret is, that I trusted to thy weakness, and did not strike the blow myself. Too soon thou'lt learn that mercy to that man is direct cruelty to all thy race!

Piz. Guard! quick! a guard, to seize this frantic woman.

Elv. Yes, a guard! I call them too! And soon I know they'll lead me to my death. But think not, Pizarro, the fury of thy flashing eyes shall awe me for a moment! Nor think that woman's anger, or the feelings of an injured heart, prompted me to this design. No! had I been only influenced so — thus failing, shame and remorse would weigh me down.

But, though defeated and destroyed, as now I am, such is
the greatness of the cause that urged me, I shall perish,
glorying in the attempt, and my last breath of life shall speak
the proud avowal of my purpose — to have rescued millions
of innocents from the bloodthirsty tyranny of one — by rid-
ding the insulted world of thee.

Rol. Had the act been noble as the motive, Rolla would
not have shrunk from its performance.

Enter GUARDS.

Piz. Seize this discovered fiend, who sought to kill your
leader.

Elv. Touch me not, at the peril of your souls; I am your
prisoner, and will follow you. But thou, their triumphant
leader, first shalt hear me. Yet, first — for thee, Rolla, accept my forgiveness; even had I been the victim of thy nobleness of heart, I should have admired thee for it. But 'twas
myself provoked my doom — thou wouldst have shielded me.
Let not thy contempt follow me to the grave. Didst thou
but know the fiend-like arts by which this hypocrite first
undermined the virtue of a guileless heart! how, even in the
pious sanctuary wherein I dwelt, by corruption and by fraud
he practised upon those in whom I most confided — till my
distempered fancy led me, step by step, into the abyss of
guilt ——   .

Piz. Why am I not obeyed? Tear her hence!

Elv. 'Tis past — but didst thou know my story, Rolla,
thou wouldst pity me.

Rol. From my soul I do pity thee.

Piz. Villains! drag her to the dungeon! — prepare the
torture instantly.

Elv. Soldiers, but a moment more — 'tis to applaud your
general. It is to tell the astonished world that, for once,
Pizarro's sentence is an act of justice: yes, rack me with the
sharpest tortures that ever agonised the human frame, it will
be justice. Yes, bid the minions of thy fury wrench forth the
sinews of those arms that have caressed — and even have de-

fended thee! Bid them pour burning metal into the bleeding cases of these eyes, that so oft — oh, God! — have hung with love and homage on thy looks — then approach me bound on the abhorred wheel—there glut thy savage eyes with the convulsive spasms of that dishonoured bosom which was once thy pillow! — yet will I bear it all; for it will be justice, all! and when thou shalt bid them tear me to my death, hoping that thy unshrinking ears may at last be feasted with the music of my cries, I will not utter one shriek or groan; but to the last gasp my body's patience shall deride thy vengeance, as my soul defies thy power.

Piz. Hearest thou the wretch whose hands were even now prepared for murder?

Rol. Yes! and, if her accusation's false, thou wilt not shrink from hearing her; if true, thy barbarity cannot make her suffer the pangs thy conscience will inflict on thee.

Elv. And now, farewell, world! — Rolla, farewell! — farewell, thou condemned of Heaven! [*To* PIZARRO] for repentance and remorse, I know, will never touch thy heart. — We shall meet again. — Ha! be it thy horror here to know that we shall meet hereafter! And when thy parting hour approaches — hark to the knell, whose dreadful beat will strike to thy despairing soul. Then will vibrate on thy ear the curses of the cloistered saint from whom thou stolest me. Then the last shrieks which burst from my mother's breaking heart, as she died, appealing to her God against the seducer of her child! Then the blood-stifled groan of my murdered brother — murdered by thee, fell monster! — seeking atonement for his sister's ruined honour. I hear them now! To me the recollection's madness! At such an hour — what will it be to thee?

Piz. A moment's more delay, and at the peril of your lives ——

Elv. I have spoken — and the last mortal frailty of my heart is passed. And now, with an undaunted spirit and unshaken firmness, I go to meet my destiny. That I could not live nobly, has been Pizarro's act; that I will die nobly, shall be my own.   [*Exit guarded.*

Piz. Rolla, I would not thou, a warrior, valiant and renowned, shouldst credit the vile tales of this frantic woman. The cause of all this fury — oh! a wanton passion for the rebel youth Alonzo, now my prisoner.

Rol. Alonzo is not now thy prisoner.

Piz. How!

Rol. I came to rescue him — to deceive his guard. I have succeeded; I remain thy prisoner.

Piz. Alonzo fled! Is then the vengeance dearest to my heart never to be gratified?

Rol. Dismiss such passions from thy heart, then thou'lt consult its peace.

Piz. I can face all enemies that dare confront me — I cannot war against my nature.

Rol. Then, Pizarro, ask not to be deemed a hero: to triumph o'er ourselves is the only conquest where fortune makes no claim. In battle, chance may snatch the laurel from thee, or chance may place it on thy brow; but, in a contest with thyself, be resolute, and the virtuous impulse must be the victor.

Piz. Peruvian! thou shalt not find me to thee ungrateful or ungenerous. Return to your countrymen — you are at liberty.

Rol. Thou dost act in this as honour and as duty bid thee.

Piz. I cannot but admire thee, Rolla: I would we might be friends.

Rol. Farewell! pity Elvira! become the friend of virtue — and thou wilt be mine.   [*Exit.*

Piz. Ambition! tell me what is the phantom I have followed? where is the one delight which it has made my own? My fame is the mark of envy, my love the dupe of treachery, my glory eclipsed by the boy I taught, my revenge defeated and rebuked by the rude honour of a savage foe, before whose native dignity of soul I have sunk confounded and subdued! I would I could retrace my steps! — I cannot.

Would I could evade my own reflections! No! thought and
memory are my hell!   [*Exit.*

ACT V.

SCENE I. — *A Forest.   In the background a Hut.*

CORA *is discovered leaning over her* CHILD, *who is laid on a bed
of leaves and moss. — A Storm, with thunder and lightning.*

Cora. O Nature! thou hast not the strength of love. My
anxious spirit is untired in its march; my wearied shivering
frame sinks under it. And for thee, my boy, when faint beneath thy lovely burden, could I refuse to give thy slumbers
that poor bed of rest! O my child! were I assured thy father
breathes no more, how quickly would I lay me down by thy
dear side! — but down — down for ever! — [*Thunder and
lightning.*] I ask thee not, unpitying storm! to abate thy rage
in mercy to poor Cora's misery; nor while thy thunders spare
his slumbers will I disturb my sleeping cherub; though
Heaven knows I wish to hear the voice of life, and feel that
life is near me. But I will endure all while what I have of
reason holds.   [*Sings.*

> Yes, yes, be merciless, thou tempest dire;
>   Unaw'd, unshelter'd, I thy fury brave:
> I'll bare my bosom to thy forked fire,
>   Let it but guide me to Alonzo's grave!
>
> O'er his pale corse then, while thy lightnings glare,
> I'll press his clay-cold lips, and perish there.
>
> But thou wilt wake again, my boy,
> Again thou'lt rise to life and joy —
>   Thy father never! —
> Thy laughing eyes will meet the light,
> Unconscious that eternal night
>   Veils his for ever.
>
> On yon green bed of moss there lies my child,
>   Oh! safer lies from these chill'd arms apart;
> He sleeps, sweet lamb! nor heeds the tempest wild,
>   Oh! sweeter sleeps, than near this breaking heart.
>
> Alas! my babe, if thou wouldst peaceful rest,
> Thy cradle must not be thy mother's breast.

Yet thou wilt wake again, my boy,
Again thou'lt rise to life and joy —
    Thy father never! —
Thy laughing eyes will meet the light,
Unconscious that eternal night
    Veils his for ever.   [*Thunder and lightning.*

Still, still implacable! unfeeling elements! yet still dost thou
sleep, my smiling innocent! O Death! when wilt thou grant
to this babe's mother such repose? Sure I may shield thee
better from the storm; my veil may ——
    [*While she is wrapping her mantle and her veil over him,*
    ALONZO's *voice is heard in the distance.*

Alon. Cora!

Cora. Ha!   [*Rises.*

Alon. Cora!

Cora. Oh, my heart! Sweet Heaven, deceive me not! Is
it not Alonzo's voice?

Alon. [*Nearer.*] Cora!

Cora. It is — it is Alonzo!

Alon. [*Nearer still.*] Cora! my beloved!

Cora. Alonzo! — Here! here! — Alonzo!   [*Runs out.*

Enter two SPANISH SOLDIERS.

1st Sold. I tell you we are near our out-posts, and the
word we heard just now was the countersign.

2nd Sold. Well, in our escape from the enemy, to have
discovered their secret passage through the rocks, will prove
a lucky chance to us. Pizarro will reward us.

1st Sold. This way: the sun, though clouded, is on our
left. — [*Perceives the* CHILD.] What have we here? — A child,
as I'm a soldier!

2nd Sold. 'Tis a sweet little babe! Now would it be a
great charity to take this infant from its pagan mother's
power.

1st Sold. It would so: I have one at home shall play with
it. — Come along.   [*Exeunt with the* CHILD.

Cora. [*Without.*] This way, dear Alonzo!

Re-enter CORA, *with* ALONZO.

Now am I right — there — there — under that tree. Was it possible the instinct of a mother's heart could mistake the spot? Now wilt thou look at him as he sleeps, or shall I bring him waking, with his full, blue, laughing eyes, to welcome you at once? Yes, yes! Stand thou there; I'll snatch him from his rosy slumber, blushing like the perfumed morn.

[*She runs up to the spot, and finding only the mantle and veil, which she tears from the ground, and the* CHILD *gone, shrieks.*

Alon. [*Running to her.*] Cora! my heart's beloved!

Cora. He is gone!

Alon. Eternal God!

Cora. He is gone! — my child! my child!

Alon. Where didst thou leave him?

Cora. [*Dashing herself on the spot.*] Here!

Alon. Be calm, beloved Cora; he has waked and crept to a little distance; we shall find him. Are you assured this was the spot you left him in?

Cora. Did not these hands make that bed and shelter for him? and is not this the veil that covered him?

Alon. Here is a hut yet unobserved.

Cora. Ha! yes, yes! there lives the savage that has robbed me of my child. — [*Beats at the door.*] Give me back my child! restore to me my boy!

Enter LAS-CASAS *from the hut.*

Las-Cas. Who calls me from my wretched solitude?

Cora. Give me back my child! — [*Goes into the hut and calls.*] Fernando!

Alon. Almighty powers! do my eyes deceive me? Las-Casas!

Las-Cas. Alonzo, my beloved young friend!

Alon. My revered instructor!   [*Embracing.*

Re-enter CORA.

Cora. Will you embrace this man before he restores my boy?

Alon. Alas, my friend! in what a moment of misery do
we meet!

Cora. Yet his look is goodness and humanity. Good old
man, have compassion on a wretched mother, and I will be
your servant while I live. But do not — for pity's sake, do
not say you have him not; do not say you have not seen him.
                                        [*Runs into the wood.*

Las-Cas. What can this mean?

Alon. She is my wife. Just rescued from the Spaniards'
prison, I learned she had fled to this wild forest. Hearing
my voice, she left the child, and flew to meet me: he was left
sleeping under yonder tree.

Re-enter CORA.

Las-Cas. How! did you leave him?

Cora. Oh, you are right! right! unnatural mother that I
was! I left my child, I forsook my innocent! But I will fly
to the earth's brink, but I will find him.   [*Runs out.*

Alon. Forgive me, Las-Casas, I must follow her; for at
night I attempt brave Rolla's rescue.

Las-Cas. I will not leave thee, Alonzo. You must try to
lead her to the right: that way lies your camp. Wait not my
infirm steps: I follow thee, my friend.   [*Exeunt.*

SCENE II. — *The Outpost of the Spanish Camp. In the back-
ground a torrent, over which a bridge is formed by a felled tree.
Trumpets sound without.*

Enter ALMAGRO, *followed by* SOLDIERS, *leading* ROLLA *in chains.*

Alm. Bear him along; his story must be false.

Rol. False! Rolla utter falsehood! I would I had thee in
a desert with thy troop around thee, and I but with my sword
in this unshackled hand!   [*Trumpets without.*

Alm. Is it to be credited, that Rolla, the renowned Peruvian
hero, should be detected, like a spy, skulking through our camp!

Rol. Skulking!

Alm. But answer to the general; he is here.

Enter PIZARRO.

Piz. What do I see? Rolla!

Rol. Oh, to thy surprise, no doubt!

Piz. And bound too!

Rol. So fast, thou needest not fear approaching me.

Alm. The guards surprised him passing our outpost.

Piz. Release him instantly! Believe me, I regret this insult.

Rol. You feel then as you ought.

Piz. Nor can I brook to see a warrior of Rolla's fame disarmed. Accept this, though it has been thy enemy's. — [*Gives a sword.*] The Spaniards know the courtesy that's due to valour.

Rol. And the Peruvians how to forget offence.

Piz. May not Rolla and Pizarro cease to be foes?

Rol. When the sea divides us; yes! May I now depart?

Piz. Freely.

Rol. And shall I not again be intercepted?

Piz. No! Let the word be given that Rolla passes freely.

Enter DAVILLA *and* SOLDIERS, *with* ALONZO's CHILD.

Dav. Here are two soldiers, captured yesterday, who have escaped from the Peruvian hold — and by the secret way we have so long endeavoured to discover.

Piz. Silence, imprudent! Seest thou not ——

[*Pointing to* ROLLA.

Dav. In their way, they found a Peruvian child, who seems ——

Piz. What is the imp to me? Bid them toss it into the sea.

Rol. Gracious Heavens! it is Alonzo's child! Give it to me.

Piz. Ha! Alonzo's child! — [*Takes the* CHILD.] Welcome, thou pretty hostage. Now Alonzo is again my prisoner!

Rol. Thou wilt not keep the infant from its mother?

Piz. Will I not! What, when I shall meet Alonzo in the heat of the victorious fight, thinkest thou I shall not have a check upon the valour of his heart, when he is reminded that a word of mine is this child's death?

Rol. I do not understand thee.

Piz. My vengeance has a long arrear of hate to settle with Alonzo! and this pledge may help to settle the account.

[*Gives the* CHILD *to a* SOLDIER.]

Rol. Man! Man! Art thou a man? Couldst thou hurt that innocent? — By Heaven! it's smiling in thy face.

Piz. Tell me, does it resemble Cora?

Rol. Pizarro! thou hast set my heart on fire. If thou dost harm that child, think not his blood will sink into the barren sand. No! faithful to the eager hope that now trembles in this indignant heart, 'twill rise to the common God of nature and humanity, and cry aloud for vengeance on his accursed destroyer's head.

Piz. Be that peril mine.

Rol. [*Throwing himself at his feet.*] Behold me at thy feet — me, Rolla! — me, the preserver of thy life! — me, that have never yet bent or bowed before created man! In humble agony I sue to thee — prostrate I implore thee — but spare that child, and I will be thy slave.

Piz. Rolla! still art thou free to go — this boy remains with me.

Rol. Then was this sword Heaven's gift, not thine! — [*Seizes the* CHILD.] Who moves one step to follow me, dies upon the spot. [*Exit with the* CHILD.

Piz. Pursue him instantly — but spare his life. — [*Exeunt* DAVILLA *and* ALMAGRO *with* SOLDIERS.] With what fury he defends himself! Ha! he fells them to the ground — and now ——

Re-enter ALMAGRO.

Alm. Three of your brave soldiers are already victims to your command to spare this madman's life; and if he once gain the thicket ——

Piz. Spare him no longer. — [*Exit* ALMAGRO.] Their guns must reach him — he'll yet escape — holloa to those horse — the Peruvian sees them — and now he turns among the rocks — then is his retreat cut off. — [ROLLA *crosses the wooden bridge over the cataract, pursued by the* SOLDIERS — *they fire at him — a shot strikes him.*] Now! — quick! quick! seize the child!

[ROLLA *tears from the rock the tree which supports the bridge, and retreats by the background, bearing off the* CHILD.

Re-enter ALMAGRO *and* DAVILLA.

Alm. By hell! he has escaped! — and with the child unhurt.

Dav. No — he bears his death with him. Believe me, I saw him struck upon the side.

Piz. But the child is saved — Alonzo's child! Oh! the furies of disappointed vengeance!

Alm. Away with the revenge of words — let us to deeds! Forget not we have acquired the knowledge of the secret pass, which through the rocky cavern's gloom brings you at once to the stronghold, where are lodged their women and their treasures.

Piz. Right, Almagro! Swift as thy thought, draw forth a daring and a chosen band — I will not wait for numbers. Stay, Almagro! Valverde is informed Elvira dies to-day?

Alm. He is — and one request alone she ——

Piz. I'll hear of none.

Alm. The boon is small — 'tis but for the noviciate habit which you first beheld her in — she wishes not to suffer in the gaudy trappings which remind her of her shame.

Piz. Well, do as thou wilt — but tell Valverde, at our return, as his life shall answer it, to let me hear that she is dead.

[*Exeunt severally.*

SCENE III. — ATALIBA'S *Tent.*

Enter ATALIBA, *followed by* CORA *and* ALONZO.

Cora. Oh! avoid me not, Ataliba! To whom, but to her king, is the wretched mother to address her griefs? The gods refuse to hear my prayers! Did not my Alonzo fight for thee? and will not my sweet boy, if thou'lt but restore him to me, one day fight thy battles too?

Alon. Oh! my suffering love — my poor heart-broken Cora!

To scare reflection, which, in absent dreams,
Still lingers musing on the recent themes;
Attention, ere with contemplation tired,
To turn from all that pleased, from all that fired;
To weaken lessons strongly now impress'd,
And chill the interest glowing in the breast —
Mine is the task; and be it mine to spare
The souls that pant, the griefs they see, to share;
Let me with no unhallow'd jest deride
The sigh, that sweet compassion owns with pride —
The sigh of comfort, to affliction dear,
That kindness heaves, and virtue loves to hear.
E'en gay Thalia will not now refuse
This gentle homage to her sister-muse.

  O ye, who listen to the plaintive strain,
With strange enjoyment, and with rapturous pain,
Who erst have felt the Stranger's lone despair,
And Haller's settled, sad, remorseful care,
Does Rolla's pure affection less excite
The inexpressive anguish of delight?
Do Cora's fears, which beat without control,
With loss solicitude engross the soul?
Ah, no! your minds with kindred zeal approve
Maternal feeling, and heroic love.
You must approve: where man exists below,
In temperate climes, or midst drear wastes of snow,
Or where the solar fires incessant flame,
Thy laws, all-powerful Nature, are the same:
Vainly the sophist boasts he can explain
The causes of thy universal reign —
More vainly would his cold presumptuous art
Disprove thy general empire o'er the heart: ·
A voice proclaims thee, that we must believe —
A voice, that surely speaks not to deceive;
That voice poor Cora heard, and closely press'd
Her darling infant to her fearful breast;
Distracted dared the bloody field to tread,
And sought Alonzo through the heaps of dead,
Eager to catch the music of his breath,
Though faltering in the agonies of death,
To touch his lips, though pale and cold, once more,
And clasp his bosom, though it stream'd with gore;
That voice too Rolla heard, and, greatly brave,
His Cora's dearest treasure died to save;
Gave to the hopeless parent's arms her child,
Beheld her transports, and, expiring, smiled.

Piz. Thou knowest the advantage of thy numbers. Thou darest not singly face Pizarro.

Alon. Peruvians, stir not a man! Be this contest only ours.

Piz. Spaniards! observe ye the same. — [*Charge. They fight.* ALONZO's *shield is broken, and he is beat down.*] Now, traitor, to thy heart!

[*At this moment* ELVIRA *enters, habited as when* PIZARRO *first beheld her.* PIZARRO, *appalled, staggers back.* ALONZO *renews the fight, and slays him. Loud shouts from the* PERUVIANS.

Enter ATALIBA.

Ata. My brave Alonzo!   [*Embraces* ALONZO.

Alm. Alonzo, we submit. Spare us! we will embark, and leave the coast.

Val. Elvira will confess I saved her life; she has saved thine.

Alon. Fear not. You are safe.
                              [SPANIARDS *lay down their arms.*

Elv. Valverde speaks the truth; nor could he think to meet me here. An awful impulse, which my soul could not resist, impelled me hither.

Alon. Noble Elvira! my preserver! How can I speak what I, Ataliba, and his rescued country, owe to thee! If amid this grateful nation thou wouldst remain ——

Elv. Alonzo, no! the destination of my future life is fixed. Humbled in penitence, I will endeavour to atone the guilty errors, which, however masked by shallow cheerfulness, have long consumed my secret heart. When, by my sufferings purified and penitence sincere, my soul shall dare address the Throne of Mercy in behalf of others, for thee, Alonzo, for thy Cora, and thy child, for thee, thou virtuous monarch, and the innocent race thou reignest over, shall Elvira's prayers address the God of Nature. — Valverde, you have preserved my life. Cherish humanity, avoid the foul examples thou

Sheridan.   28

The pride of glory — pity's sigh sincere —
Youth's earliest blush — and beauty's virgin tear.
  Such is their meed — their honours thus secure,
Whose arts yield objects, and whose works endure.
The Actor, only, shrinks from Time's award;
Feeble tradition is his memory's guard;
By whose faint breath his merits must abide,
Unvouch'd by proof — to substance unallied!
E'en matchless Garrick's art, to heav'n resign'd,
No fix'd effect, no model leaves behind!
  The grace of action — the adapted mien,
Faithful as nature to the varied scene;
Th' expressive glance — whose subtle comment draws
Entranced attention, and a mute applause;
Gesture that marks, with force and feeling fraught,
A sense in silence, and a will in thought;
Harmonious speech, whose pure and liquid tone
Gives verse a music, scarce confess'd its own;
As light from gems assumes a brighter ray,
And clothed with orient hues, transcends the day!
Passion's wild break — and frown that awes the sense,
And every charm of gentler eloquence —
All perishable! like th' electric fire,
But strike the frame — and as they strike expire;
Incense too pure a bodied flame to bear,
Its fragrance charms the sense, and blends with air.
  Where then — while sunk in cold decay he lies,
And pale eclipse for ever veils those eyes —
Where is the blest memorial that ensures
Our Garrick's fame? — whose is the trust? — 'Tis yours.
  And O! by every charm his art essay'd
To sooth your cares! — by every grief allay'd!
By the hush'd wonder which his accents drew!
By his last parting tear, repaid by you!
By all those thoughts, which many a distant night
Shall mark his memory with a sad delight!

Still in your hearts' dear record bear his name;
Cherish the keen regret that lifts his fame;
To you it is bequeath'd, — assert the trust,
And to his worth — 'tis all you can — be just.
  What more is due from sanctifying Time,
To cheerful wit, and many a favour'd rhyme,
O'er his graced urn shall bloom, a deathless wreath,
Whose blossom'd sweets shall deck the mask beneath
For these, — when Sculpture's votive toil shall rear
The due memorial of a loss so dear —
O loveliest mourner, gentle Muse! be thine
The pleasing woe to guard the laurell'd shrine.
As Fancy, oft by Superstition led
To roam the mansions of the sainted dead,
Has view'd, by shadowy eve's unfaithful gloom
A weeping cherub on a martyr's tomb —
So thou, sweet Muse, hang o'er his sculptured bier,
With patient woe, that loves the lingering tear;
With thoughts that mourn — nor yet desire relief;
With meek regret, and fond enduring grief;
With looks that speak — He never shall return!
Chilling thy tender bosom, clasp his urn;   •
And with soft sighs disperse th' irreverend dust
Which Time may strew upon his sacred bust.

THE END.

VERSES

TO THE

MEMORY OF GARRICK.

SPOKEN AS A MONODY, AT THE THEATRE ROYAL IN DRURY LANE.

To the right honourable COUNTESS SPENCER, whose approbation and esteem were justly considered by MR. GARRICK as the highest panegyric his talents or conduct could acquire, this imperfect tribute to his memory is, with great deference, inscribed by her ladyship's most obedient humble servant,

March 25th, 1779. RICHARD BRINSLEY SHERIDAN.

If dying excellence deserves a tear,
If fond remembrance still is cherish'd here,
Can we persist to bid your sorrows flow
For fabled suff'rers and delusive woe?
Or with quaint smiles dismiss the plaintive strain,
Point the quick jest — indulge the comic vein —
Ere yet to buried Roscius we assign
One kind regret — one tributary line!
  His fame requires we act a tenderer part:
His memory claims the tear you gave his art!
  The general voice, the meed of mournful verse,
The splendid sorrows that adorn'd his hearse,
The throng that mourn'd as their dead favourite passed,
The graced respect that claim'd him to the last,
While Shakespere's image from its hallow'd base
Seem'd to prescribe the grave, and point the place, —

Nor these,—nor all the sad regrets that flow
From fond fidelity's domestic woe,—
So much are Garrick's praise—so much his due—
As on this spot—one tear bestow'd by you.
   Amid the hearts which seek ingenuous fame,
Our toil attempts the most precarious claim!
To him whose mimic pencil wins the prize,
Obedient Fame immortal wreaths supplies:
Whate'er of wonder Reynolds now may raise,
Raphael still boasts contemporary praise:
Each dazzling light and gaudier bloom subdued,
With undiminish'd awe his works are view'd:
E'en Beauty's portrait wears a softer prime,
Touch'd by the tender hand of mellowing Time.
   The patient Sculptor owns an humbler part,
A ruder toil, and more mechanic art;
Content with slow and timorous stroke to trace
The lingering line, and mould the tardy grace:
But once achieved — though barbarous wreck o'erthrow
The sacred fane, and lay its glories low,
Yet shall the sculptured ruin rise to day,
Graced by defect, and worshipp'd in decay;
Th' enduring record bears the artist's name,
Demands his honours, and asserts his fame.
   Superior hopes the Poet's bosom fire;
O proud distinction of the sacred lyre!
Wide as th' inspiring Phœbus darts his ray,
Diffusive splendour gilds his votary's lay.
Whether the song heroic woes rehearse,
With epic grandeur, and the pomp of verse;
Or, fondly gay, with unambitious guile,
Attempt no prize but favouring beauty's smile;
Or bear dejected to the lonely grove
The soft despair of unprevailing love, —
Whate'er the theme — through every age and clime ·
Congenial passions meet th' according rhyme;

www.ingramcontent.com/pod-product-compliance
Lightning Source LLC
Chambersburg PA
CBHW030954110726
47900CB00004B/1272